# Taken

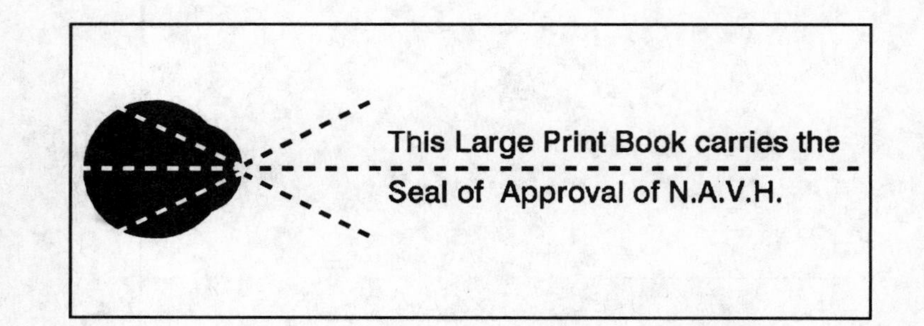
This Large Print Book carries the
Seal of Approval of N.A.V.H.

# TAKEN

## DEE HENDERSON

**THORNDIKE PRESS**
*A part of Gale, Cengage Learning*

Farmington Hills, Mich • San Francisco • New York • Waterville, Maine
Meriden, Conn • Mason, Ohio • Chicago

Thorndike Press, a part of Gale, Cengage Learning.


Thorndike Press® Large Print Christian Fiction.
The text of this Large Print edition is unabridged.
Other aspects of the book may vary from the original edition.
Set in 16 pt. Plantin.

**LIBRARY OF CONGRESS CATALOGING-IN-PUBLICATION DATA**

Henderson, Dee.
Taken / Dee Henderson. — Large print edition.
pages cm. — (Thorndike Press large print Christian fiction)
ISBN 978-1-4104-7772-9 (hardcover) — ISBN 1-4104-7772-X (hardcover)
1. Large type books. I. Title.
PS3558.E4829T35 2015b
813'.54—dc23 2015002705

Published in 2015 by arrangement with Bethany House Publishers, a division of Baker Publishing Group

Printed in the United States of America
1 2 3 4 5 6 7 19 18 17 16 15

# TAKEN

# 1

Matthew Dane collected change from his pocket as the elevator settled into place on the sixth floor of the Bismarck Hotel in Atlanta, Georgia. The doors slid open to a quiet hallway. Most attendees at the conference were still in sessions on the main level. He stopped in the vending area and bought a cold soda.

He felt satisfied with how his presentation — *Best Practices in the Dialog Between the Police and Victim Families* — had gone. He thought his opening section had been too long, as most at this national law-enforcement symposium had heard him speak before and didn't need the background, but the overhead slides designed to lighten the tone had gotten spontaneous laughter from the audience. He'd made his points without beating anyone over the head with his advice. Now that his part was over, he could relax and enjoy the last two days as an attendee.

Married friends had invited him to join them for a late dinner. Inevitably, they would also invite a woman to make up the numbers. His friends were predictable that way. He'd need to spend part of the evening putting whoever she was at ease. He'd deal with the situation with some grace — he just hoped she already knew his life story so he didn't have to tell it again over a meal. His wife, Jessica, had died young. He'd get married again — he knew Jessica would want him to — and he thought about it occasionally. But he'd be forty-two this year, and his life already had enough open chapters.

A young woman was sitting on the floor in the hallway outside his hotel room. She didn't rise when he drew near, just looked up at him. She looked . . . tired. And mildly curious. Her white shorts showed off long tanned legs, and the sandals revealed dainty feet with painted toenails. The contrasting pink top was remarkably sedate, blousy, and pretty. The look suited her and reminded him of his daughter. For that reason more than any other he simply offered a casual, "Looking for me?"

She opened an envelope, pulled out a

newspaper clipping, and held it up. "Is this you?"

He accepted what she offered. The newspaper article with accompanying photo was old, well-worn, and crumbling at the fold. From the *Boston Globe,* he thought, recognizing the photo and knowing the date it had been taken. He was holding his daughter, her head lowered under the hood of a police sweatshirt, walking with her down the police station's steps. She had just turned sixteen — shy, scared, gangly, and thin. The photo had been snapped late on the day of her rescue as he was taking her home. It'd been the best day of his life since her disappearance when she was eight years old. "My daughter and I," he confirmed.

That image had captured the start for the two of them of a journey that had pushed them together into a father-daughter relationship that was to this day still hard to explain. Becky had been, in alternating waves, suicidal and angry, terrified and manic, overjoyed with freedom, so determined to rebuild her life and push away what had happened in those missing eight years. He'd been there for his daughter, getting her through those years and beyond to something now remarkably healthy, happy, and if not whole, at least wise and wonderful and able to deal with the past in a sane way when others brought it up.

"She's finishing her first year in college," he mentioned, smiling as he said it, remembering Becky as she had been this last weekend, straddling a stool in the kitchen of their Boston home on a flying visit home from college to grab more clothes and different posters, munching on a carrot and arguing the fact he just *had* to get a haircut and please, please, *please* could he remember to lose the old leather jacket before he came to meet her new roommate's family? They already thought he was a Spenser-type tough guy with credentials as a licensed private investigator. Introducing himself as a retired cop would be okay, but a PI implied he liked to snoop.

He'd laughed at her request and fed her clam chowder that night, promising to be on his best behavior when he met the roommate's family, pleased that his daughter was moving from a single room to a double and acquiring a roommate. He had in fact done a bit of snooping. He knew more about her new roommate than the girl's parents probably did, and concluded his daughter would be safe with her. The roommate loved to party and be out and about town, but she refused to drink or do drugs and was exclusive in her relationship with her boyfriend. She was the extrovert to his daughter's more reserved nature and, Matthew thought, a very nice girl. One of the reasons he'd agreed to come speak at this Atlanta conference as a last-minute replacement was because his daughter had truly now settled at college, with plans to stay on campus to take summer classes.

Matthew took a final look at the article and photo, then refolded it. He wondered why this woman would have such an old clipping. He offered it back to her.

"Can I show you something else?"

"Sure."

She pulled another clipping from the envelope. Tired of towering over her, he hunkered down beside her, one arm resting casually on his knee, drink in hand. He took the second clipping. A missing-person case out of Chicago, picked up by the Associated Press, this also from the *Boston Globe.* Shannon Bliss, age sixteen, missing along with her car; she had not arrived home after visiting friends over the three-day Memorial Day weekend. A reward of twenty-five thousand was offered for information. The photo looked like it'd come from a high school yearbook. A pretty girl, he thought. He looked at the date on the clipping . . .

this had happened eleven years ago. He studied the woman who had offered it. He could see a good resemblance.

He didn't work many missing-person cases anymore. Becky had asked him to give those up for a few years, to consider going back to being a cop working robberies, or teaching at the police academy — and let his company, Dane Investigations, be run by his staff, at least the day-to-day. A missing sister could explain why this woman had sought him out, and he did know some people in Chicago who might be able to help her. A few of them were at this conference, and he could make some calls and introductions on her behalf. "Your sister?" he asked.

"That's me." Silence lingered after her quiet words. "I'd like to go home," she whispered.

He watched her knuckles turn white where she gripped the envelope, her other hand flexed against the carpet. Her eyes averted from his to stare down the empty hall. A stillness settled into his muscles. "Did you run away?"

She was quiet for so long he wasn't sure she would answer.

"No." More a breath than a word, but he heard it.

He felt his heart begin to crack on her behalf. The nuances mattered now, seeing them, hearing them, and he didn't have history with this woman to fall back on to help him understand her. "What name do you go by now?"

"Shannon White."

"Have you spoken with the police?"

She shook her head swiftly. He didn't let himself show a reaction to that news, just absorbed it. There were things his job had taught him, experiences with his daughter, an awareness that came from so many he had talked with over the last decade, and it all coalesced and settled in his mind. He couldn't afford to project or assume the wrong thing here. The odds she was in fact Shannon Bliss were small, but they were real enough to pursue. She looked as though she was telling him the truth as she knew it. *God, help me.* The quiet prayer went straight to his Father, and he took a deep breath, let it flow out. A hallway wasn't the place for this conversation, but a pause would give her time to change her mind about talking with him, so he stayed where he was. There were things he had to know simply not to hurt her further, and he chose his next words with extreme care. "Eleven years is a long time. When did . . . ?"

Her hand settled very lightly, very carefully, on his arm as she shook her head. "Please don't ask."

Her gaze shifted back to hold his. He could literally see an enforced poise reasserting itself, see the strength of will it took on her part to slide that calm back in place. It would make his job particularly hard, having her choose silence rather than spill out the details of what had occurred in an emotional wave — he needed that story. But she was coping, and she was giving him the first parameters that defined how she was coping. He had to respect that.

*She's learned to hide.* The thought settled deep into his consciousness with such a profound certainty that he suspected it had actually been God's comment to him. It rang true. What he was seeing was the image she wanted him to see, all of it deliberate, down to the painted toenails and the cute sandals. Something eased inside him as he realized that about her. He was seeing her internal strength. She'd need that, however this ultimately unfolded. "Come inside," he said, standing, "and let me make a few calls, push off a dinner meeting I was supposed to be at tonight. Or would you prefer to meet me at the restaurant downstairs? We can ask for a private table —"

"I'd rather not go downstairs."

His eyes narrowed at her quick response. Someone in the hotel she was worried about? He used his card to open the room door behind her, then stepped back from her in the hall. He didn't offer a hand to help her rise. His daughter had taught him a few things. She rose gracefully.

Probably five-foot-seven or -eight, he guessed. She looked healthy — her eyes were clear, her skin evenly tanned, the bones in her arms and legs not overtly visible as a sign she was too thin. If anything, the muscle tone in her arms and legs suggested she was a pretty good athlete. There were small scars under that tan — on the side of her leg, her knee, on her forearm, the back of her wrist, mirroring some of his own from years of activity on the water fishing, boating, hauling ropes, running on the beach, and climbing over piles of boulders that dotted the Massachusetts shoreline between stretches of open sand. The fact there were not more visible scars, especially around her wrists and ankles, was a small sliver of good news.

She glanced around his hotel room. It was a pleasant if impersonal room divided into two parts: a seating area with a two-person couch, barrel chair, and small desk with a straight-back chair set across from a television, which could angle any direction in the room. His suitcase lay open on the second bed. Revised drafts of the conference talk were spread across the desk.

"Do you have a pocketknife with you?" she asked.

There was one on his key chain. He dug out his keys and slipped the knife free, offered it. She used a clean napkin from the beverage tray to wipe the knife blade, then pricked her finger and used another napkin to pressure the bleeding to stop. She folded that napkin over, offered it to him along with the pocketknife. "A DNA test will be necessary to prove who I am. Fingerprints. What should I use for those?"

He picked up two sheets of paper from the desk and the mug on the table, moved into the bathroom. He dumped the cold coffee he hadn't finished that morning across a piece of paper held over the sink and shook off most of the liquid. He put the page on the counter, along with the other blank piece of paper. "Spread out your hands and press down on the wet page, then lift them and press down again on the clean sheet."

She did as he said and then afterward rinsed her hands in the sink and took the hand towel he held out to her. Fingerprints showed on both pages and began to air-dry. Between the two sheets, there were enough ridge details present to generate a set of solid prints. They stepped back into the room.

"May I take a photo?" he asked.

She glanced toward the mirror over the dresser, and he could almost see her mental debate with herself over how her hair looked and what about no makeup. He couldn't help but smile. "The software actually makes the age-progression match easier without makeup."

"Take your photo."

He made it fast and painless for her, pulling the phone out of his pocket and snapping off a series of photos in the next seconds. He showed her the images. "Which do you prefer?"

"The third."

He deleted the others. "You came to find me because of my daughter."

"Yes."

"Any particular reason other than that I've been down this road before?"

"What do you mean?"

"Were you in Boston?"

She gave a small smile and simply dodged the question. "No comment."

"That article makes you twenty-seven. When's your birthday?"

"May the eighth."

"Yeah? Mine's the tenth. Happy belated birthday." He picked up the pages, the one doused in coffee now beginning to curl as it dried, slid them into a folder, and carefully folded the napkin and slid it into his pocket. "I'm going to go down and use the business center to fax your prints to a friend, who can access the missing-persons registry database. Find the room service menu and order us something to eat — steak and potato for me, anything you like for yourself. Find something you'd like to watch on TV. I may be half an hour or more. I'll make calls and cancel evening plans while they're working on this."

"You're going to leave me here with your laptop, your belongings?"

"Shannon . . . you and I are going to have to start trusting each other sometime. It might as well be now."

"Ann." Matthew caught the woman he hoped to find coming out of a session with the title *FBI Joint Jurisdiction Investigations* printed on a placard by the door. He knew her husband had been part of the panel answering questions.

"Hi, Matthew." She stepped out of the flow of departing conferees so they could have a conversation.

"Can you pull a cold case for me from Chicago and give me a good summary look at it tonight?" She had retired as a cop when she married, but her contacts in Chicago and across the Midwest still went deeper than most.

His tone caught her attention as much as the request had, and her gaze sharpened with interest. "What case?"

"Shannon Bliss, age sixteen, who went missing over a Memorial Day weekend." He gave her the date of the disappearance.

"Theo should have it; he catches most cold missing-person cases. I'll make some calls."

He wrote a direct number on the back of a business card. "I'm up late on this one."

She tucked away the card. "Give me three hours. I'll call when I've got details for you."

And with that answer, that smile, he was reminded of a lot of good evenings shared with her. "Remind me sometime why I let Paul snag you first."

She laughed. "Only Paul has the temperament to put up with me."

"You two staying through the weekend?"

"We're heading back to Chicago after the

first session tomorrow."

"I may need a conversation with Paul also."

"I'll give him a heads-up." She still didn't ask what this was about. The woman knew how to keep a secret and respect when details were not being shared. But she did tilt her head to ask, "Is this going to be interesting enough that I won't regret skipping dinner to turn around your request in just a few hours?"

He knew the odds that the woman upstairs was Shannon Bliss were small, but he went with what his gut said. "You won't regret it." They were in the way of people coming in and out of the room, and he stepped away with a catch-you-later smile, only to have her reach out a hand. He paused.

Her curiosity had turned to sharp focus. "Matthew . . . you do recognize the surname, don't you? The brother, Jeffery Bliss, is running for governor."

"I'm not one to follow Illinois elections. A one-percent-of-the-vote kind of candidate, or is he likely to win?"

"I'm voting for him," she answered mildly.

He buried a wince. "I almost wish you hadn't told me that. Tear apart as much of the case as you can tonight. Call me. I'll come to you."

"You'll hear from me in a couple of hours."

"Thanks, Ann."

Matthew headed back to the lobby. She'd get him the case info he needed. He had an idea of who could help move the next boulder he had to shift. Now, if he could just locate the man in this crowd . . . He thought a moment and turned toward the hotel bar.

"Tom." Matthew slid onto the stool next to the sheriff hosting the conference. His friend looked to be sipping a carbonated soft drink and hoping it would taste different than it did. "Who owes you a favor at the lab?" Matthew asked.

"I've got a few names tucked away. Whaddya need?"

Matthew unfolded the napkin. "A DNA panel on this. Tonight."

"This personal or professional?"

"Professional, but unofficial until it's worth saying it's official. No use stirring the pot without good reason." The two went back more than a decade, and his answer was sufficient given the kind of work he often did.

Tom nodded. "As it so happens, the local FBI lab owes me a sizable favor." He pulled a small notepad out of his shirt pocket, wrote something, tore off the sheet and folded it. He snapped his fingers and motioned to a deputy over by the door. "This is Collins," the sheriff said as the man hurried over. "He's good at moving bureaucracies." He handed over his note and the napkin. "I want you to deliver that to Elizabeth Perkins at the FBI lab," he told the deputy. "Then wait a few hours for her to hand you back a memory stick with the results."

"Yes, sir."

Matthew wrote a phone number on the back of a business card. "Please call me when you have that, Deputy, and I'll send Elizabeth a DNA file for comparison. Ask her to then destroy the sample and the results. The memory stick itself needs to go into a safe with the sheriff's name on it."

The deputy accepted his business card and left.

"Anything else I can do for you?" Tom asked dryly.

Matthew slapped the sheriff on the shoulder as he slid off the stool. "Get in touch before you leave the conference. I may have something for you to do in a couple of days."

"An interesting something?"

"Have I ever laid something boring on

you?" Matthew countered and got a laugh in reply. "Thanks, Tom."

"Anytime. Elizabeth is good. You'll have your data in about three hours."

"I'll let you know how it turns out." Matthew headed back to the lobby to get directions to the hotel business center, two of his three pressing needs now in play.

The hotel business center was crowded with cops dealing with emergencies in their home jurisdictions. Matthew squeezed in access to the fax machine as his call to Gregory at the missing-persons registry was answered by a gruff hello. "I thought I'd catch you still at your desk."

"You know me, Matthew. Friday night is when the mayhem happens. You're in Atlanta, I see. What's on your plate tonight?"

"I'm faxing you fingerprints."

"Ah, I see the pages arriving now. Hold on." The voice on the line disappeared for a moment. "What is this, coffee smears? Tea?"

"The moment required some creativity."

"So I see. They're . . . not bad. Decent enough to work with. I'll have to remember that technique."

Matthew stepped out of the busy business center, found a quiet alcove, flipped through the images on his phone. "I'm also sending you a photo." He sent it to Gregory's direct email account.

"Okay . . . got it. Who's our pretty lady?"

"Why don't you tell me if it's Shannon Bliss, an old case out of Chicago."

"Are you kidding?" Gregory's voice rose in surprise. "You're not kidding. The press gets in touch occasionally on this one because of the election. Okay, hold on. I can tell you something on the prints in a matter of minutes. The photo is going to take some time as it's an old case."

"Don't let the photo and prints get logged into the database. This inquiry needs to stay unofficial and on your desk only, for now."

"No problem. They're doing a software upgrade right now, and I couldn't get anything into the system even if I wanted to. I see this photo has a time stamp of less than an hour ago. She's in Atlanta with you?"

"No comment."

"One of those . . . All right, let's see, prints are scanned and are being ridge-defined now. And the comparison matches tell us . . . I'm hoping you know how to get ahold of her again, because the woman is definitely Shannon Bliss. I've got a solid match for the entire ten-print card."

Matthew felt the muscles in his back

tighten with the stress of that affirmative answer. It was good news, but it also presented an acute sequence of next steps that had the risk of turning chaotic on him. "There's no question on the prints?"

"None," Gregory assured. "Give me two hours on the photo. What is it, eleven years? That's a lot of aging cycles to complete. I'm looking in the file now . . . There are three comparison photos — one looks like a school yearbook photo, and two others like casual photos with friends. So I've got a good base to work from. Visually, I think it's right, but she's changed rather significantly in those eleven years."

"Text me when you have the results. What's the registry file look like?"

"Pages deep. I'll text you the inquiry code so you can log on and read through the details. The *call on news* list has fourteen names. Chicago police, Midwest region FBI, family, what looks like two private investigators, and three cops inquiring because they're working similar cases. You want a text with the call-list details?"

"Please."

"I'm sending it now. Her current photo . . . she looks in good health. Was this a runaway situation?"

"I can't comment yet. I'll update you

tomorrow and let you know if we're ready to make this an official submission. It will likely stay *need to know* for a time."

"My lips are sealed until you tell me otherwise."

"Can you source me a DNA comparison file?"

"I just sent you the FTP code. We've got protocols in place with about every DNA testing facility in the country, so you can transfer a copy of the file straight to the lab of your choice."

"Thanks. Listen . . . if this gets away from me, if the press gives you a call, or someone with the family or the cops —"

"I do a nice 'what are you talking about?' non-comment. If I get cornered on the data, I'll say it came anonymously on the tip line, again until you tell me otherwise. I can see the public firestorm this will become. I'll stay out of it, thank you. I like my quiet Friday nights working the desk."

"Appreciate it, Gregory."

"What are friends for if not this? I'm glad for you, Matthew. You needed a win."

"Not one of my cases — it rather dropped in my lap."

"Work them however they come. Take care of her."

"I'm going to try."

Matthew clicked off. Fingerprints were a match. The rest of the confirmation data was a necessary formality. She was Shannon Bliss. And his coming weekend had just ramped up several notches.

He rubbed the back of his neck and wished he had gotten more sleep last night rather than working on further revisions to his presentation. Shannon had seemed pretty collected when she had approached him, but that was likely a carefully constructed mirage. As her story became known, he'd see the layers under that calm. He couldn't afford to lose focus because fatigue crept in. He knew, in many ways, he was going to be the one holding her together as this played out.

Matthew placed calls to his friends and canceled dinner plans, said only that a case needed his attention. He'd have to get Shannon through the coming days with some space to breathe or this experience was going to be as damaging to her as when she'd originally been abducted. Protecting her privacy as long as he could was critical. He couldn't pull that off alone. He was going to need some carefully selected help. Ann and Paul Falcon — they'd have the Chicago connections and clout to buffer matters related to her family. The Falcons were returning to Chicago tomorrow and likely would be taking a private plane, since Ann was an experienced pilot — she'd paid for college by ferrying planes around. Maybe he could talk Shannon into traveling to Chicago with them.

He looked at the time. He had been away from the room for forty-seven minutes. That was too long. Get DNA results to confirm the fingerprints, then get the last pieces of this in motion. He headed to the elevator.

Shannon was going to remember this night for the next twenty years. It was on him to see it turned out as something that helped rather than hurt her. The thought crossed his mind that when God promised to use all things for good, even the tragedies of life, he was now living in one of those moments. He was seeing God pick up and use the tragedy of what had happened to his daughter Becky as the reason, the open door, for why Shannon had sought him out. Shannon would have the benefit of what he'd learned with Becky, and would have an easier time of this return to her life because of that experience. *Okay, game on.* He'd get this done right.

# 2

Matthew cleared any emotion other than polite calm from his face as he unlocked the hotel room door, stepped inside, and found himself deeply relieved to see his guest was still present. He tossed his room key on the dresser and out of habit slid the suit jacket off along with his shoes. The day had been long already, and it was about to get significantly longer. He hung up the jacket in the closet. "What did you choose for dinner?"

"Mexican. They do a nice chicken enchilada and rice."

His room service tray was on the desk. She was curled up in the barrel chair and had a baseball game on TV — an unusual enough selection for a woman that he noted the teams were Chicago and St. Louis. Hometown nostalgia? he wondered. He took a seat at the desk and lifted the cover from his plate, found the meal still hot enough to be tolerable. The steak looked excellent, and the potato was piled with melting butter and sour cream. She'd ordered him an apple cobbler, and he appreciated her thoughtfulness. There were several finger-soft dinner rolls in a basket.

"The napkin with the blood sample is on its way to an FBI lab here in town where they can turn it around in about three hours. Your prints are a match. The photo is crunching now to age-progress a comparison."

She simply nodded.

"How did you know I'd be at this hotel?"

"Your daughter posted online that you were speaking at this conference. She's proud of you."

"As I'm proud of her."

He took his time on the steak, aware that Shannon was watching him as much as the baseball game. She wasn't nervous, but she did look very tired, and mostly she was . . . *wary.* How well he understood that emotion, having lived with it during the years after his daughter returned home.

"Who did you call?"

He knew she wasn't asking about the friends he'd called to excuse himself from dinner. "I've told three people. A friend at the missing-persons registry who knows I'm looking at you in particular. He's accessing records for me, but will keep this work on his desk only, until I clear him to officially file the prints and discuss the matter with others. Another friend here in Atlanta has arranged for the FBI to expedite a DNA panel and make a comparison. I didn't give them your name."

He cut into his steak. "The third person I've told is Ann Falcon, a retired cop from Chicago. I trust Ann. She's pulling the case file so I can get up to speed on what it has looked like in Chicago since you disappeared. Ann's husband, Paul, happens to head the Chicago FBI office, and if this has crossed state lines, he'll be involved in the case soon as a matter of course. Ann's got a lot of history with high-profile cases. She can keep a secret. You'll like her, Shannon. You're going to need someone like her helping you."

"Are you going with me to Chicago?"

"Yes."

Her eyes briefly closed, and she visibly relaxed. "Thanks." She half smiled. "I don't have a valid driver's license and I hate to fly. So I hope you like to make long road trips."

Her words scotched his tentative plans for them to fly back to Chicago with Ann and Paul Falcon in the morning. "You sound like my daughter," he commented lightly. "Give her an unabridged audiobook and ten hours of me driving so she can listen to the story from beginning to end, and she's in heaven."

"That sounds very nice. I'll even let you choose which audiobook." She shifted in the chair. "When we get to Chicago, I want to see only my brother at first. I don't want him calling people and my parents showing up, other friends and relatives. I don't want cops showing up."

He buttered a dinner roll and just absorbed that request. "I'd like to hear the details behind that decision about your family when you are comfortable talking about it," he said as idly as he could manage, "but I'll do my best to arrange that for you. Do you want to stay in the Chicago area after you meet your brother?"

"I haven't decided yet. I may prefer to come back here to Atlanta and let the dust settle, give them time to regroup around the fact I'm alive, before I make contact again — see my brother another time or meet with others in the family."

"Keep in mind there are smaller options if you wish to start some kind of dialog with your family and friends in Chicago. I'm guessing Ann would be more than willing to forward mail on if you would like her to do that for you. That might be better than simply vanishing again. It's going to be quite an emotional time for your family."

"Everyone is going to want to know what happened."

The understatement in those words was titanic. "Yes."

"I'm not ignoring that . . . I'm just postponing it."

"I'll help however you would like me to, Shannon. If you want to come back here after you see your brother, I will see you safely back here. Or if you would like to see some of the country, I can recommend Boston as a nice place to visit for the summer. Finding you an apartment in a safe area of town is something I could arrange without much trouble. You could take some time just to settle in someplace as you decide how and when you want to engage with your family."

"You've suddenly found yourself with another lost duckling."

He looked over. "What?" he said, startled.

"You're arranging life to take care of me."

"Habit," he admitted with a rueful smile. "If I step on your toes, just say so."

"I'm not like your daughter, Matthew. I'm not being rescued at sixteen, finding myself uncertain about how to handle the world. I was that age when this began. I'm twenty-seven, and I probably rival a lot of cops for how acutely I see reality. You really don't need to worry about me. I chose you because it made sense to do so, to have some help, not because I couldn't navigate this on my own. I'm just tired enough I don't want to have to try."

"When I treat you like my daughter — she's my reference point, after all — just correct me and tell me what you need instead," he said. Shannon could navigate matters on her own, but had determined she would rather have help — an adult decision, one well-reasoned. He locked on to the one piece of news he needed to better understand the significance of right now. "How bad is the fatigue? What's going on with that?"

"I feel like I just ran a couple of back-to-back marathons. I've got no stamina. I want a book to read, a baseball game to watch, occasionally I can catch a decent nap. I'm not sleepy. I'm just deeply tired."

"Dreaming much?"

She shrugged rather than answered that query.

"Seriously, it would help me a lot if you would answer this question: how long has this been over for you?"

She reached over to the end table, picked up an envelope, tossed it to him. He opened it and pulled out a single sheet of hotel stationery. Her handwriting was a very neat print.

I arrived in Atlanta two days ago.
This is day sixteen of freedom.
I like donuts and chili cheese dogs and most fast food.
I like lists.
I don't like crowds.
I prefer quiet places.
I'm very tired.
I don't want to talk about it.

The third time he read the statements his tension uncoiled enough to note with some humor that they both liked donuts and lists. "Thank you for this," he said softly. He folded the page and carefully slipped it into his pocket. And for her sake, he changed the subject. "I asked at the front desk, and the room across the hall is available. Would you like me to reserve it for you?"

"I'll decide that after you have the DNA results."

As he'd rather not lose sight of her until he had that answer, he was fine with that.

"Did you join the audience and listen to my presentation?"

"I planned to, but I accidentally slept through it."

He laughed. "I was concerned a few in the audience might as well." He finished another dinner roll, wondering how far she would let him take the conversation tonight. "Are you traveling with anyone?"

"No."

"Is there anyone you're worried about who will be looking for you here or in Chicago?"

"There's no concern tonight, but there will be an acute concern once it's known I'm alive." She offered nothing else.

"A conversation for tomorrow?"

"Possibly."

He pulled out a business card and wrote a number on the back, rose from the desk and walked over, handed it to her and then picked up her glass. "I'll always answer that number," he said as he refilled her soda. The number was one that until tonight only his daughter knew.

She fingered the card. "Okay."

"I'd like to ask one thing from you, Shannon."

"What's that?"

"Don't run. When the pressure hits, when

this becomes unbearable — and there will be that moment — use that number and call me. Don't disappear."

"I can't promise that."

"Then at least memorize my number."

"That I can do." She took the glass he brought back to her. "I'll understand, Matthew, if you change your mind after thinking about this overnight and decide not to get further involved. My brother is running for governor of Illinois. When it's known I'm alive, the publicity is going to be intense. You've already spent more than your share of life in the public spotlight, and you and Becky deserve your privacy."

"I'm going to stick, but thank you for the open door to step away without hard feelings." His phone chimed, and he glanced at the brief text. "Your current photo is an 88.4 percent match to your age-sixteen-progressed photograph. In this kind of analysis, that's a high-confidence match. DNA results will be back in the next few hours. Fingerprints, photograph, DNA — you'll be able to prove in a court of law you're Shannon Bliss by morning."

"And then the fun will begin." She shifted in the chair. "Can we not talk for a while? I want to finish watching this game."

"Sure."

He sent a response text to Gregory, thanking him for the news and asking that her current photo and the age renderings be erased. Entering her fingerprints in the database when they decided to make this official would be enough. The longer they could go without a current photo of her in the public domain, the better this would go.

Shannon fell asleep in the eighth inning. He'd seen her struggling to keep her eyes open, and finally they simply closed and didn't flutter again. He watched her sleep and wondered what it was going to be like in the first few minutes after she awoke. His physical distance and stillness would probably be about the only thing he could do for her that might help. After his daughter was rescued, for nearly two years she hadn't been able to handle waking up in a room with someone else present without feeling a sense of panic.

He stayed seated at the desk and worked on his list of what had to be done in the days ahead. DNA test results. Arrange a private reunion with her brother. Get her medical care. She would need to talk to the cops, both the Chicago police and FBI, given that this appeared to have crossed state lines. They needed to catch and arrest the one or ones responsible. Hopefully she would give him something to work with soon, as it was going to be a time-sensitive situation before the people behind this thing scattered. As the case unfolded, he needed to do what he could to protect her privacy. She would need safe people in her life outside of her family to help her with the emotions involved. Did she have a best friend she wanted him to contact on her behalf? Documentation in her life had to be sorted out and reissued in her proper name and social security number — driver's license, bank accounts, health insurance. Had she graduated from high school? If so, where and under what name? Where had she been for the last eleven years? His list continued until he had filled two pages. Practical matters pounding at him demanded answers as much as the questions surrounding her disappearance.

She stirred in the chair, and he went still. She opened her eyes, studied the ball-game score, listened to the postgame commentary, then looked around the room until finally her gaze settled on him. "No word yet?"

"Not yet."

She found the television remote and changed over to a late-night talk show. He wasn't sure if the calm she showed was a carefully constructed image she wanted him to see, or if she truly wasn't bothered by his company. Within twenty minutes she had dozed off again. She looked beat-up tired, that impression coming through in the color of the skin around her eyes and mouth, and the fact she was able to sleep in his presence curled up like that. He set the ring tone on his phone to vibrate, got up, retrieved the extra blanket in the closet, draped it over her. He picked up the sandals she had kicked off and glanced at the size. They'd need to do some clothes shopping before they hit Chicago, depending on what she had with her. Where had she spent last night? She'd been staying somewhere if she arrived in Atlanta two days ago. She wasn't carrying a purse. She'd arrived in Atlanta from where?

It was going to be a very long process building trust with this woman. Trust was an elusive thing, hard to win, easy to lose, and very sensitive to small nuances when it was forming. He wanted her to end up like his daughter — healthy, happy, and if not whole again, able to handle the past, to have a good life of her own choosing. He couldn't afford the possible price impatience would cost him right now. He returned to his seat at the desk and started listing what had to be done so he could walk out of his own life for an extended period of time and head to Chicago with her. He had no idea how long this was going to take, but he'd learned with his daughter not to make assumptions that depended on predicting someone else's reaction to events. This might be a trip to Chicago, followed by another immediate trip back here to Atlanta. Or he might be in Chicago with her for an extended period of time. Or . . .

Call his daughter in the morning. Tell her the truth about what was going on. He tried not to keep the details of his movements or the reasons for them from Becky. He knew she'd respect the privacy of this news and not share it. His business would be in good hands if he delegated the day-to-day to his Number Two. A call to his neighbor would take care of the house. He could have his assistant sort and forward his mail. A stop at a shopping mall to fill out his wardrobe would deal with the fact he hadn't planned to be gone more than a few days. The page filled up with practical items ahead of him.

The other list of events coming soon — where the only preparations he could make involved buying Kleenex — didn't need writing down. There were necessary conversations that would be tough on Shannon, some she'd have with doctors, others with cops, but inevitably some she'd have with him that he knew would wring his heart out. He'd been outwardly strong for his daughter, had listened with close attention, found ways to draw out the dark corners in her memories, to lance the pain of them . . . all the while feeling torn up inside. He honestly didn't know if he had it in him to go through that again. He looked up from his notes and watched Shannon for a long moment.

*I'm surprised you let her choose me, God. I'm back to feeling . . . inadequate for this. Mainly because I know some of what it's going to be. At least with Becky I was walking blind into what was coming. I didn't know better. This time . . . God, give me wisdom. Patience. The ability to listen. Help me hear what is really being said. I can't afford to miss the nuances, not with someone whose way of coping is to hide.*

He looked down at the lists he had written and numbered the items he had to tackle first, aware he was simply killing time, waiting for the phone to ring, waiting for DNA to confirm what he already knew. Shannon Bliss had reappeared and had chosen him. Even if he didn't want this, he wouldn't turn her away.

Life had been a lot simpler when he had

been worried about such mundane problems as friends setting him up to meet a woman over dinner. He half smiled and put down his pen. Somehow he'd rise to the occasion. He glanced at his phone. But patience had never been his strong suit.

His phone began to vibrate. Matthew glanced at the caller ID and answered it immediately, keeping his voice low. "Ann, that was fast."

"Theo likes me. And it helps that the Bliss case file has been digitized. Do you want to do this on the phone or do you want to come up to the suite?"

He glanced over at Shannon. She hadn't stirred in the last twenty minutes. "Give me the highlights — I'll decide from there."

"It's tough reading. Shannon disappeared over a Memorial Day weekend while driving home after staying with friends. Her car was never found. Cops looked hard at the family, at people around the family — her school, their church, the family's business — but nothing popped as a solid motive or lead. Three similar cases in the Midwest over the prior seven years were pursued for any crossovers but didn't generate much to work with. A ransom was paid after the disappearance went public, but there was no proof of life offered in advance, nor any contact after the money was paid. Three years after she disappeared, the parents divorced in a bitter fight that about bankrupted the family business. A year after that, the uncle committed suicide to avoid being arrested for having embezzled company money. During the contested divorce, the company books were audited by both sides — they were arguing over the valuation of the business — and it turned up the theft of company funds. There's a suspicion that the uncle may have stolen some of the ransom money and handed over blank paper, used the money to try to cover up his fraud."

Matthew had been making notes as she spoke, but that last comment made him pause with a wince. "How certain is that?"

"Ask me again tomorrow after I talk to Theo. I'm reading an eye-opening sixty-page summary of the case he wrote a few years ago. I'll print you a copy."

"I'm coming up. What's your suite number?" He picked up his room key and his wallet, pushed his feet into his shoes.

"Ten ninety-six."

He wrote a quick note for Shannon and left it on the desk in case she woke up. "Tell me about her brother," he asked Ann, shifting his phone to the other hand as the room's door closed behind him. He headed toward the elevator.

"Our next governor, if the tracking polls are to be believed. He's been leading the search to find his sister almost from day one, and from what I can see here, he's done a good job of keeping her photo out there, as well as information about the reward. He paid Chicago-based companies to include her missing-person flyer in every customer mailing they put out — there have been millions of them distributed in the last eleven years. This has been an intense, sustained, and expensive search. He sold his interest in the family business in order to fund that effort."

"So he's serious about finding his sister and may be open to taking some advice on how to proceed," Matthew speculated.

"I'd think so. He makes a point of mentioning her, asking for information from the public, at every event where he speaks."

The elevator doors opened on the tenth floor, and Matthew walked down to suite 1096, showed his credentials to the officer providing security in the hall. The head of the Chicago FBI office wouldn't have a choice about the security; it went with the job.

"Why the interest in this case?" Ann was

asking in his ear. "You have something?"

Matthew ignored the question for the moment. "I'm at the door." He knocked lightly as he spoke and waited for Ann to answer, silencing and pocketing his phone when the door opened. She'd changed into jeans and a Chicago Bulls T-shirt. Her husband was on the hotel phone. Matthew lifted a hand to acknowledge Paul's silent hello, then turned his attention back to Ann and her question. "I may have met Shannon. DNA is running now."

# 3

"So if the woman in your room really is Shannon Bliss, what's the plan?" Paul Falcon asked, settling on the couch next to his wife in their hotel suite.

"She would like to go home," Matthew began, choosing a soda and dumping it over ice. He needed the caffeine to give himself a second burst of energy. "That's the starting premise. What steps get taken in the next forty-eight hours depends in part on that case file and what the situation looks like in Chicago."

"Has she told you anything about what happened? Is there a case to peel back at this point? A name? Location? Time period involved?" Paul asked.

"She's shared a few facts I can tell you once DNA confirms her identity," Matthew replied. He settled into a chair across from the couch, feeling the fatigue of the long day setting in. Paul would be the right person to see that Shannon got justice for what had happened to her. The sooner Matthew could introduce the two of them, the stronger the likelihood this situation would unfold to the good. But that wasn't going to happen in the next twenty-four hours.

His phone chimed. He looked at the screen. The initial DNA panel was ready. He used the FTP code and sent the comparison panel stripped of any name reference on to the lab to have the comparison done. He slipped the phone back into his pocket. Ten minutes, fifteen, he was going to know. He looked back at Paul. "Shannon wants to meet only with her brother initially, not the rest of her family or friends. What do you think? Can the brother meet her and sit on the news he knows she's alive?"

Paul shared a look with Ann, who finally shook her head and replied, "Maybe. Anything is possible. But the practical answer is he can't. We're less than five months away from the vote. He can't talk about her as missing once he knows she's alive; it would be political suicide for him to lie. He can't avoid questions about her when he's made a point of talking about his sister's case, appealing for information in most every public speech he's made. If he suddenly stops talking about her, the press will know something is up and start aggressively pushing. He's in a no-win situation. If she's revealed to be alive before the vote, he'll be accused of unfairly taking advantage of the public attention surrounding her return for his own political benefit. If her story has dark corners to it and the news of her return is held until after the vote, they'll say it was hidden to avoid discussing his dysfunctional family history."

"Best case for the brother, she doesn't make contact with him until after the vote," Matthew realized.

"Which creates its own complications for why she didn't get in contact with her family once she came forward," Ann said, "and why you or I didn't say anything once her identity was confirmed. Today has already become day one in the articles that are going to be written about her reappearance. And this case has got book material written all over it, even before I hear what happened to her over the last eleven years."

Ann had written enough books to know what she was talking about on that score. "The timing of events will get scrutinized," Matthew concurred. *"Day one* — she shows up, and we confirm she's in fact Shannon Bliss. *Day two . . ."*

"That's the question. We can keep under

wraps for a few days the fact she's alive and has returned. Beyond that, this is not so simple. You could admit her to a private hospital, tell her brother she's alive, let him announce it and where she's at, but say he'll make no further comment until after law enforcement concludes the investigation and medical personnel give their okay . . . hopefully stretch that out to get past the vote before she appears. That's probably the cleanest way to keep the public onslaught of interest away from her."

Matthew liked it even as he realized it wouldn't be possible. "I suspect Shannon's not going to voluntarily admit herself to a private hospital that has good enough security to keep the press out — she's not going to willingly go back inside a secured environment, even a comfortable one. Maybe we can arrange a meeting with her brother, and then she disappears and stays out of the state until after the election. He can announce her safe return, that she's recovering in a private location, and he'll have nothing further to say on the matter until after the election."

Ann thought for a moment but shook her head. "Anything that vague, the press will crush him for more information, and anyone else they can hammer on, so the number who know anything at all about Shannon Bliss and her whereabouts needs to remain a very small group. And it had better be a good hiding place — they'll be looking for her with great intensity. The press will reach from Theo to me because I pulled the case file, but I'm good at saying no comment. Your friend at the missing-persons registry will get identified because he accessed her records, but if he can hold the line, maybe the press can't reach through him to you. If we can keep the press away from you, there's a chance we can keep them away from her. You become the buffer."

Matthew hesitated. "That's good in theory, but the problem with wanting to stay beneath the radar — you start realizing how impossible it is to actually do that for any length of time. Tucking her somewhere no one finds her for five months when the press has a reason to be looking for her — it's not going to be simple."

"Whatever you decide, Paul and I can help you with the Chicago logistics," Ann offered. "John Key can arrange a secure place for you to stay. I'll put a call in to him to put that in motion. You won't want to be in a hotel if the press somehow gets wind of this. And as far as a location for that family reunion, why don't you consider using our home? It has good security, it's neutral ground, it's a comfortable place to have a conversation. A candidate for governor making a social call on the head of the Chicago FBI office at his home would not signal anything out of the ordinary to the press. Paul and I can slip away and go see friends for the evening."

"It might be best if I made that first call to her brother," Paul suggested, "and arrange the meeting. It will keep your name out of this until you've been able to meet the brother face-to-face and reach an understanding with him."

"That's a gracious offer and perfect for what we will need." Matthew thought about the coming week and went straight to his top concern. "The situation I'd like to avoid at all costs is my daughter getting badgered by the press for information about where I am and if Shannon is with me. If the press gets to me, I may need to step away from this just to keep Becky out of the public limelight. Can you give me some options for Shannon if she and I need to split up?"

"We can plan some contingencies," Ann agreed. "There are safe places Shannon could go, safe people outside of her family who could help her. Rachel and Cole would be ideal. Bryce and Charlotte. We've got friends who have some experience that would be relevant to her situation."

"I'd appreciate it if you could lay some groundwork with them in case it's needed."

"I'll put together several options you can run by Shannon."

Matthew's phone chimed again. He tugged it out of his pocket. The DNA comparison results were in. He read the text message, sent a thanks, looked across at Ann, then put his focus on Paul. "The FBI lab results are back. DNA confirms she's Shannon Bliss. And from what she's told me so far, this ended for her sixteen days ago."

Paul winced. "Have you ever heard of someone walking free after eleven years?"

"No. Someone helped her. She's not yet talking about *who.*" Matthew pulled Shannon's list from his pocket, scanned it to see what else he would be comfortable sharing. "She arrived in Atlanta two days ago. This is day sixteen of freedom. She doesn't want to talk about it. The rest of what she wrote is more directed to me." He slid the list back in his pocket. "She goes by the name Shannon White. I think she's got a room in this hotel or one nearby, probably some luggage or at least some things she's picked up — her clothes looked new, as did the sandals.

She's probably got a room key and cash in her pocket. She's not carrying a handbag. You'll be able to find her on hotel security if you backtrack the sixth-floor video when she was waiting for me. She says she's traveling alone, that no one is a concern here in Atlanta or Chicago, but that will change once it's known she's alive. She seems physically to be in pretty good shape, outside of being acutely tired."

"It says a lot about how she got free of this that they think she's dead," Paul remarked. "What she can tell us will put one or more people in jail for life. Even those who helped would be looking at a decade or two of jail time. That's reason to cause her harm, to keep her from talking with us, to not let her testify." Paul sat forward. "It's interesting she chose this law-enforcement conference, this hotel, to make her first contact. Did she say why she chose you?"

"Becky. She had an old newspaper clipping from the *Boston Globe* from the day my daughter was rescued."

"Shannon's been in Boston," Paul said, interested.

"That's my guess. She dodged the question rather than say yes or no." Matthew passed over his phone with her photo. "What else?" Matthew asked, more for himself than them. "She said she didn't have a valid driver's license, which might imply she has a false one, but I've no idea what state you would look in. I'd say run her current photo through the entire system and see what shows up, but I don't want that photo out there yet."

"She's what . . . twenty-seven now?" Paul asked.

"Yes. She appears to have a good hold on her emotions for now — either that or she can show you what she wants you to see. I think she has a mental checklist for the chronology she wants everything to proceed on, and she's simply going to balk if pushed to take another course."

Paul handed the phone to Ann, who studied the image long enough to memorize it, then handed back the phone.

"One immediate suggestion," Paul offered, "is to build a photo array of people she can trust with names and contact numbers. Start with us. Take a photo. Show it to her. Give her our contact information. Go track down your friends at this conference and put the word out if Shannon calls, she gets helped, no questions asked."

Matthew saw immediately why he needed Paul and Ann's help. He should have thought of that step himself. "That's a solid idea. I'll get it done tonight."

"I've got a phone you can give her," Ann offered, getting to her feet. "Give me a second. I think it's in my briefcase." She looked at her husband. "That birthday gift for your nephew?"

"If it's not in your briefcase, it's in mine."

Ann found it and returned. "A basic phone, as he likes to hike and keeps losing them. There's a thousand minutes prepaid on it. You might as well have her unwrap it. Blue wrapping paper is probably not her color, but I doubt she's had a lot of gifts recently."

Matthew accepted it with a smile. "She'll appreciate it."

Ann took a seat beside her husband. "Do you think she might be willing to have breakfast with us here in the suite?"

"I can offer, but I'm not prepared to pressure her." He looked over to Paul. "I don't mind you backtracking hotel security video on her, learning what you can, but I'd like your word you won't follow her if she leaves this hotel."

"I'm comfortable with that, at least for the first few days," Paul assured him. "We spook her, our chance of arresting who did it drops below fifty percent. She's chosen to trust you. That's where this has to start. I'd simply ask that you let information flow both directions without much delay when you know something."

Matthew nodded his thanks. "That's not a problem."

"The cold-case detective who currently has the case is Theodore Lincoln," Ann told him. "You'll like Theo. He's thorough and careful and the right mix of patient cop and calm detective. He's the one you want Shannon to talk with when she finally agrees to have a conversation with law enforcement."

"I'm thinking I'll give her that case summary report you printed out and then ask her if she'd like to speak with the guy who wrote it."

"That might work," Ann said. "Just for my own curiosity — how are you feeling tonight, Matthew, about all of this? Her sudden appearance, her choosing you?"

He grinned. "Notes for a book?"

"Humor me."

"I'm deeply aware there is no margin for error right now. Shannon's in the initial euphoria, the joy and relief of freedom stage, showing the first signs of the fatigue that comes on the downslope of those emotions. She's like a fine-blown glass vase that has a hairline crack running through it, and someone just picked it up. The die is already cast. Set the vase down too hard and it's going to shatter. Ease it down and apply some glue, it holds together. If she doesn't shatter in the next six months, I'll have been a help to her. But I can't predict how this is going to go. I'm concerned I'm too much in the dark about what happened that I could make matters worse, because I'm working blind about what she's been through."

"She doesn't know how fragile she is," Ann stated quietly.

"I don't think she has a clue. After the fatigue will come the nerves that rip apart on sounds, smells, motions . . . all the memories and the nightmares are going to hit. Freedom lets the past have room to reappear in full Technicolor, no suppression allowed, and she's not going to be able to avoid it."

"You'll get her through. She needs to trust someone. She chose you."

"Let's hope she made the right choice. I'll call you in a few hours with an update on her plans. She may want to stay in Atlanta for a few days; she may ask that we head toward Chicago. Besides her request that we drive rather than fly, that situation is still evolving."

"Ann and I will get up to speed on the

details of the case file," Paul told him. "Whatever you need, Matthew, just ask. You'll find mountains can be moved with a case that's going to turn high profile once the public knows she's alive. We'll clear what we can for you."

"I appreciate that more than I can say," Matthew replied. "I'll ask one thing tonight. Since Shannon wants to drive, and you two are scheduled to fly back, could you pull Theodore Lincoln into a room, tell him she's alive, and work out who's going to handle the investigation that's coming? I'm thinking four people — you two, Theo, and myself — is plenty to be in the loop while we're still gathering the details. Make that five, as Gregory at the missing-persons registry knows."

Paul nodded. "We'll probably call Theo at his home from the plane. Since Shannon showed up in Atlanta, the FBI can already claim jurisdiction if necessary. But it won't be. Theo has the Chicago police resources, we've got the national ones, and we know how to collaborate when it's in both our interests. Something this high profile — and still a black hole for what will be uncovered — neither department is going to want sole ownership. We'll work out a shared investigation and have it formalized before Shannon arrives in Chicago."

"You make that sound easy when I can guess the politics that will be involved," Matthew commented. "I'd also like to preempt whatever information she might need about her friends and family. Could I ask you to do a background update — who's been married, divorced, had children, passed away, and so forth — among her family and friends, so she has a sense of the current world before she arrives?"

"I'll be glad to do that," Ann said.

Matthew glanced at his watch. "I need to get back. I'm relieved you two came to the conference so I didn't have to try and explain over the phone what's going on."

"We weren't planning to come," Paul mentioned, "as our schedules have been hectic, but we both felt a last-minute nudge that we should fit this trip in. Probably a God-arranged decision."

"Given how many things are falling in place to deal with this situation, I'm certain God is orchestrating much of this," Matthew agreed. He lived his life depending on God to influence how events unfolded. "Ann, was there anything in that case file that mentioned Shannon's religious background? She's going to need someone to talk with, preferably from her home church."

"I'll pull the file and get you the name of the church she attended. I remember she was a regular attendee with the youth group, because the cops looked for some kind of problem with an adult that might have originated there."

Matthew found it helpful to know Shannon had a faith background. "How this has affected what Shannon thinks about God and what she believes will lead to some difficult conversations. I'll need to find someone who can help her work through those issues who is more skilled at it than I am."

Paul glanced over at Ann. "We know someone who might be able to help with those questions," he replied.

Matthew took out his phone and snapped the photo Paul had suggested of the couple, Paul's arm casually draped across Ann's shoulders. Not much explanation would be needed when he showed it to Shannon, Matthew thought, glancing at the image before pocketing his phone. The photo practically shouted that these two people were comfortably married.

Ann retrieved for him the case summary report she'd printed out and walked with him to the door. "Try to get some sleep at some point tonight. This is going to be a marathon, not a sprint."

Matthew smiled. Ann knew him well. He'd run nine Boston Marathons since his daughter went missing. The first ones to gather national media attention — *Cop runs for missing daughter* — the later ones as celebrations of her return. "I'll work on that. I'll call you tomorrow."

"We'll be up for a few hours. If there's news, don't worry about the time."

"Thanks, Ann." Matthew headed back down to rejoin Shannon.

Shannon woke just after one a.m. Matthew was stretched out on top of the first bed, reading the report Theodore Lincoln had written. He let himself glance over, make a single sweeping assessment, before turning back to the report. He spoke quietly. "The room key for across the hall is on the desk if you'd like to use that room. DNA is back and confirms what you already know. You can now prove in a court of law that you are Shannon Bliss."

She set aside the blanket he'd draped over her, pushed to her feet. She walked into the bathroom, turned on the tap, came back with a glass of water. "Have some aspirin with you?"

"The shaving kit on the dresser."

She found the bottle, popped off the top,

dumped a couple into her hand. She leaned against the desk. "What are you reading?"

"A summary of the police investigation on your disappearance. Have you read the old newspaper accounts, looked up online information about the search to find you?"

"No."

"Not curious?"

She shrugged. "If they had figured out what had happened, they would have found me. So whatever is out there is only speculation and a description of what did *not* happen."

"Your family paid a ransom to get you back."

The drink in her hand stilled, then deliberately lifted so she could finish drinking the water. "I gather it was a convincingly done con job."

He shifted his head on the pillow as he studied her, trying to read the subtle expressions on her face. He could hear several layers of emotion in her voice, almost a flat factual curiosity. He would have liked to sit up, but he risked her retreating from the conversation if he moved. "Probably. They didn't catch who made the call or received the money."

"It was a con. I was on the West Coast forty-eight hours after I was taken, in

Washington State."

"Who with?"

She shook her head. She picked up the room key he had arranged, then retrieved her sandals, carrying them with her rather than slipping them on. "I'll call you when I wake up. Maybe we can have a late breakfast and then get on the road?"

"If you like. We need to talk some about ways to avoid the press interest, given your brother's running for governor. Once he knows you're alive, this will get complicated for him."

She half smiled. "Jeff likes complicated. I'll let you two figure it out. I'm going to like any situation that involves as few people as possible knowing where I am. Don't expect my call to be early. I'm not setting an alarm."

"Sleep as long as you can." He picked up the box with the phone and sat up on the edge of the bed. He'd unwrapped Ann's gift and configured it. "Before you go — this is for you. Sorry for the poor re-wrap job."

She unwrapped the box and took out the phone, genuine surprise highlighting her face.

"There are photos in it, names, contact numbers — all of them good friends of mine and people you can trust," he explained. "If you call and say it's Shannon, you'll get helped, no questions asked. They'll do whatever needs done and take good care of you because you're my friend. You can trust them not to pry."

She turned over the phone. "I didn't expect this."

Matthew offered a relaxed smile. "The first of several useful gifts I intend to pass along. Don't hesitate to use it if you're in a situation where it would help."

Her hand tightened around the phone. "Thank you, Matthew," she whispered.

"I hope you have calm and pleasant dreams tonight, Shannon."

"That's a nice hope." She nodded and disappeared from the room.

He closed the report and set it aside. *Washington State.* He'd read nothing in the case summary that indicated any focus there. He picked up his phone, ignored the time, called Ann to have her scan the first weeks in the case file for anything that pointed to the West Coast or Washington State. Had Shannon been out West this entire time? Had she gotten to freedom and instinctively headed as far away as possible, only stopping when she reached the East Coast?

Shannon seemed confident the ransom

demand had been a con job, someone taking advantage of her disappearance. That implied only a limited number of people — possibly two or three — were involved with her abduction, and they had all been with her on the West Coast, leaving no one behind who could have made that ransom demand and pickup. If it had not been a demand from her actual abductors, had her uncle not only taken some of the ransom money but been behind the ransom call itself?

Matthew finished the call with Ann, got ready to turn in for the night, shut off the room light. As the still of the night settled around him, he found himself replaying some of the early days with his daughter. "God, a question," he said softly into the darkness. He focused on one memory in particular. He and Becky were playing a game of Scrabble so they would have something else to do while they talked, could use it as a reason not to say anything when either needed time to just think. Becky had been just beginning to give him facts about what had happened on the day she was taken.

"What's happening inside Shannon right now?" he asked God. "Is she wanting to talk, but hesitant to do so because she's seeking to avoid having a wave of questions come at her when she offers those first facts? Or is she reluctant to say anything and trying to find ways to accommodate me? Like with the list she handed me — I think she put it in writing so she would not have to say one word beyond what she had decided to say. She just now mentioned Washington State. Did she want to do so, or is Shannon's true preference right now to say nothing and she's trying to stay in my good graces by offering a few details?

"It worries me, Lord, if the information is coming because she feels like it's currency she can use to keep me from being annoyed with her silence. I can accept the details if she wants to talk — I do need them — but I can also accept the silence if she needs that for a time. Whatever she needs is how this has to unfold. That was a turning point in Becky's recovery, her freedom to share or not share as she wished. I wonder if I'm on the wrong footing with Shannon already. It's a dreadful feeling."

Just putting it into words was enough to bring some clarity. Matthew turned on the light, got up and crossed over to the desk, pulled over a blank sheet of paper, and wrote a note.

Shannon —

I like lists too.

I like glazed donuts and cream-filled chocolate-topped ones.

I like clams and scallops and Boston clam chowder.

My daughter is my best friend.

I want to hear your story when you are ready to share it.

I will listen to whatever you want to say, whenever you want to say it.

I'm in no hurry.

I can handle your silence.

I don't mind tears.

Only when you are ready to talk about something should we do so.

I want to see arrested those who did this to you.

I have room for another friend.

If you choose me as a friend, you'll find you can trust me.

He found an envelope and folded his page, slipped it inside, wrote her name on the top, dressed, walked across the hall, and slipped the envelope under her door. God had this figured out. What Matthew didn't know about how to handle matters with Shannon would fill an ocean right now, but God understood her and what was going on. He wasn't going to have to navigate this alone. Matthew returned to his hotel room, went back to bed, shut off the light, and this time sleep came.

# 4

Interstate traffic on this Saturday in June alternated between heavy and fast and sparse and fast. Matthew set the cruise control at the speed limit and let other motorists pass him, years as a cop making speeding a personal irritation. Shannon, curled up in the passenger seat beside him, slept through the first three hours of the audiobook by Nancy Rue. She began to stir just before two p.m. Matthew glanced over as she stretched. "Getting hungry? I'm ready for a break."

"Sure. A steak sounds good."

"Just what I was thinking."

Shannon set aside the pillow and pushed her sock feet back into tennis shoes. She had appeared this morning carrying a box of donuts, two black gym bags, and the day's newspaper. She had apparently acquired or accessed some of her own belongings in the last sixteen days. Her attire for traveling was casual — jeans, beat-up blue tennis shoes, a T-shirt advertising the *Mexican Festival Feast* at the Tex-Mex Diner. It was such a specific old T-shirt that Matthew had sent a text to Ann to see if she could track down the restaurant location. It sounded like a New Mexico or Texas interstate kind of place, where T-shirts were sold at cost for free advertising. Her choice of purse was an oversized tan canvas bag.

Her smile, relaxed posture, and calm "Good morning" had given the impression of an unhurried tourist. He'd stayed deliberately light and casual in his own approach, glad to see she appeared to have slept well and that her mood was good. They had shared the donuts, had a brief conversation about the map and the route to take north, debated four audiobook selections, and once the drive began, Shannon had settled in for a nap. Matthew was relieved at her apparent steadiness. He'd been worried that a fine edge of anxious nerves would appear now that events were moving forward, but if anything, she seemed calmer.

A phone rang. Matthew reached for his pocket an instant before he realized it wasn't his. Shannon dug deep into the canvas bag and came up with a phone he didn't recognize, as it had a blue cover. She looked at the screen and held it out to him. "I don't want to talk with him."

Matthew took the prepaid phone, still with store stickers on its back, and answered on the fourth ring, "A woman I know as Shannon just handed this phone to me."

"Tell her the two girls are safe."

Startled, he looked at Shannon and relayed the message. She gave a jerky nod. "Who is this?" Matthew asked.

"Adam York with the FBI, Virginia office."

"Matthew Dane, retired cop out of Boston."

"You're with Shannon. Where are you?"

"No comment at the moment. I don't know you well enough yet."

"She's sent me nine packages over the last six years — photos, addresses, all abducted kids one to four months gone, all entangled in child custody disputes. Eighteen kids in total, from all over the nation. The recent package had this phone number and a note: *Call me once you've got them.*"

Matthew glanced at Shannon, at the oversized envelope she was holding up for him to see. "Apparently we're sending you another one. She's got a manila envelope with your name on it. We're in Tennessee. I'll find somewhere to overnight it to you." He put the phone on speaker.

"Let me come to you instead. I can be on a plane and be with you in a few hours."

At Shannon's nod, he thought for a moment and said, "There's a restaurant in Lexington, Kentucky, the Blue Rose, just off Interstate 75. We'll be there around seven p.m. I'll meet you with the package; no promises Shannon will be with me."

"I'll take whatever I can get."

He glanced over again and saw Shannon wipe at her eyes. "Let me offer some advice. Don't push too hard. She's Shannon Bliss. DNA confirmed it a few hours ago. I'm taking her home. And now that you know that fact, forget you heard it. It's not . . . productive to have that news released just yet."

There was a long silence. "I remember that case. What kind of shape is she in?"

Not as good as she'd be in a few weeks, Matthew thought. "She'll be fine. Look me up under Dane Investigations, Boston. I'll tell my staff to forward your calls. I'm shutting off this phone when I hang up."

"I'll see you at the restaurant at seven."

He clicked off. "Expecting anyone other than Adam to call you at this number?"

She shook her head. He powered it off, handed it back to her, and she dropped it into the bag.

The extraordinary thing right now was

that he didn't find himself surprised to realize what she'd managed to do. He looked at the manila envelope in her hand. "Would that happen to be helpful information on the people who have been doing this?"

"Yes. There's no hurry. They're dead." She shifted the envelope in her hands, added in a husky voice, "They'd have a photo of who to grab, a location, sometimes even a time, plus an address of where to make the delivery, often a few states away. They seemed to all be child custody disputes. By the time the child was dropped off, they would be terrified. They would warn the child, 'If you ever talk about us, talk about where you were living before, give this relative any problems at all, we'll come take you again and *keep* you with us this time.' I doubt any of the kids ever talked about what happened with anyone."

"You're talking about people smugglers."

"Yes. I never figured out who was hiring them."

"Is that what happened to you?"

The silence lasted to the point he didn't think she would answer. Then she sighed and said, "A cop car was in the driveway of the address where I was to be dropped off, so they kept driving. They had a fishing trawler in the Seattle area and put out to sea. They tossed me in the ocean to drown — only I swam longer than they expected. Flynn talked them into hauling me back into the boat."

The pain that swept through his chest felt like a vise. He glanced over, saw that calm mask slip back in place as she simply buried the emotions of that memory. He instinctively reached over and laid his hand on hers. She didn't look at him, but she didn't pull away. When he finally spoke, his own control was running deep, for there was only mild curiosity in his voice. "Your parents were having a custody dispute over you?"

"Not that I was aware of before I was grabbed."

"Did you recognize the address where you were to be dropped off?"

"No. I'd never been to that town before."

"Want to tell me where that was?"

She shook her head. Having this conversation while driving was getting risky, given how he was trying to focus on her and the road at the same time. "Your parents are divorced now," he mentioned, "about three years after you were abducted."

"I'm aware."

"Would you tell me about Flynn?"

"No. I won't talk about him. And for now, I'm done talking about this."

He stopped his questions, let the silence return, grateful she'd given him as much as she had. She'd opened with one of the hardest points of her story. He briefly tightened his hand on hers, then moved his back to the wheel. "Thanks for what you did say."

"Be cautious where you repeat it."

He nodded and waited a long moment. "You don't know what really happened in your family back then, do you?"

"No. So for now I only want to talk with my brother. He's . . . safe."

"The person behind this — it may not have been someone in your family. It may have been someone using you to bring pressure on your parents. It may be totally unrelated."

"Maybe."

And that one word summed up his problem. Without knowing what she was facing, without answers for how this had begun, he would be trying to help her, protect her, while navigating in the dark as to the source of the most acute concerns. "Just to be on the safe side, it would be useful to have someone who's aware of the history watch what your parents, and those around them, do in the days after they learn you're alive."

She looked his direction now. "Someone in my family or around them may have paid to have me grabbed. Would you really want to know that about your own family?"

The thought made him sick. He finally said quietly, "Whoever arranged it will have reason to fear your return, that you know who did this to you."

"When the time's right I'm going to bluff that I do know what happened, that I'll be talking about it, and hopefully they'll tip their hand. But it's not going to happen in this first round of conversations. I've got too much on my list that has to be dealt with first. I'll get to who did this to me in good time. But first things first."

"Are there more kids to recover?"

Her hand flexed against her jeans. "None that can be rescued. Just graves to give their parents closure."

"How many?"

"Enough, Matthew. I'm done talking for now."

He drove another forty minutes, letting the silence have room to settle between them, giving her space to get her composure back. He found a Longhorn Steak House and hoped the person working the grill was turning a perfect steak today. They both needed good food to distract from the pain caused by the details she'd offered, even if the last thing he felt like doing right now was making light conversation over a meal.

He parked, and as they both stepped out of the car, he paused to look across the roof of the vehicle. "Do you trust Adam York?"

She hesitated before shutting her door. "No."

"Why not?"

"He's politically wired and ambitious to move up in the FBI hierarchy."

Matthew waited for her at the sidewalk curb, pushing aside the instinct of habit to reach out a hand as he would have for most women entering a restaurant with him. "Did you choose him for the packages because of that ambition?"

"Adam was the most aggressive field agent in the region, where the first photos and kids were located. He got them out. I sent him the next envelope. He got them out too. I don't have to like him to make use of his skills."

Matthew was puzzled by her opinion and curious as to how it had formed. "What if you've entirely misread him?" He held the first of the restaurant entrance doors for her.

She glanced over at him. "You mean what if he's really a nice guy and will do right by me, even if that comes into conflict with what is best for his career?"

"Yes."

She paused between the two sets of doors, the mostly empty restaurant and hostess waiting to seat them on the other side. "Matthew, you have reason to be altruistic. Your career is dead in terms of advancement, because you stepped away for a decade because of your daughter. You would be welcome back at the Boston PD and given back your rank as a detective, and you could spend the next twenty years working robbery if that was your wish. But you'll never shift to the political track and work your way up to become the top cop for the city. You don't need that ambition to reach your life goal. A guy like Adam York still has the hope to rise to the top, and it's that ambition that causes him to use cases such as this as stepping-stones. He'll care, but only to a point, because he knows the next case is following behind this one. I'm useful to him, and he'll be good to me and helpful right up to the point it might complicate his goal."

"You would handle someone like Adam York as an ally but not as a friend," Matthew said.

"Yes."

"I don't know whether to admire your blunt assessment and decision or feel sorry you've had to make it. Have you ever met Adam York?"

"No."

He held the interior door for her. "Maybe it's best if I meet Adam without you tonight."

She gave him a glimmer of a smile. "That might be best."

Interstate driving was a lesson in monotony. Matthew was thankful Shannon wasn't napping, if only because she gave him something to focus on. "Hey, would you try to relax? Your brother is going to be overjoyed to see you," he said, trying to dislodge the frown he could see forming. Shannon had been making notes on a pad of paper headlined with JEFFERY for the last hour back on the road, and Matthew could literally feel her building tension.

"He remembers someone who looks sixteen," Shannon muttered. "I'm going to need something better than jeans and a T-shirt."

She ignored the real reasons she was tense and had given him the *I have nothing to wear* answer. He nearly laughed because he'd heard that line of retreat so many times from Becky that he could finish the sentence. At least here was something with

Shannon he could understand. "The next town we pass, we'll stop at a mall and you can shop for something else. You'll look just right," he reassured, "because you're the sister he loves and has hoped and longed to see. Just stay with low heels in case we have to hurry down some stairs to avoid the press."

"Contingency planning?"

"We won't need it, but it never hurts to be prepared. It's why you have me helping you out." Matthew spotted an exit sign ahead that looked promising and changed lanes, glad for a reason to take another break from the drive. "Would you not get insulted if I ask you how you're set for cash?"

"I'll need access to a gym bag in the trunk. I have more than enough for a dress, shoes, and accessories."

Matthew nodded. He followed signs and found a reasonably sized mall just off the Interstate. "Which store?"

"Let me start with Macy's."

He found a parking place near the mall entrance. "I'm going to stretch my legs, make a call and talk to Paul. Call me when you want to meet back at the car, otherwise I'll be here in, say, an hour and a half?"

"That works for me."

He didn't look over her shoulder when she opened the gym bag in the trunk. His need for information was smacking up against his desire to give her as much privacy as he could until she chose to tell him facts. She put the phone he had given her in one pocket, cash in another, and didn't take her bag with her.

"If you had to suggest a color for me, what would you go with?" she asked.

"Pink."

She glanced over, surprised.

"Trust me. It's a good color for you."

"It makes me look like that sixteen again."

"There's nothing wrong with looking cute."

She laughed. "I'll see you later." She headed toward the mall.

Matthew waited until she had disappeared inside Macy's, then his smile faded as he dialed Paul's number. What she had told him so far during the drive was going to make for a grim conversation. And he could use Paul's take on Adam York.

Matthew appreciated Paul's ability to listen and not respond until the information had been fully briefed.

"They threw her overboard," Paul repeated, his voice neutral, but each word separated from the next as the image of that hung between them.

Matthew wasn't surprised where Paul chose to make his first comment. "I wish you could have heard her voice when she said it. I don't know how to help her, Paul. It's different than calm. It's almost . . . what? Acceptance? She's icing over the panic she felt, flat-toning the facts."

"I'll put Rachel on the phone and get you some professional advice here. But I'd stay with the basic three rules — listen, try not to react, and keep your reply at the same emotional tone she sets."

"That's instinctive from having dealt with Becky. But Shannon needs something else I can't define. She's looking for a reaction, I think. *Horror* seems to fit, that this is what happened to her."

"An easy emotion to feel, given what she described," Paul said. "There will be the appropriate moment to express that, but it's not on the first day, not to her first remarks about what occurred. If this turns emotional, she won't be able to survive the telling, not if it's the opening card she's laying down. That deck is going to have some brutally hard info still to come. You have to stay even keel enough to let her play them."

Matthew ran his hand through his hair. "I

hear you." He needed to get professional help involved, someone Shannon would trust. He was going to screw this up and do some unintentional damage if he had to fly solo for much longer. He shifted the phone to his other hand. "What can you tell me about Adam York?"

"I know him by reputation," Paul replied. "He's not running a regional office yet, but he's on the short list to get there. He's a case guy, with his fingers in a lot of investigations, rather than moving up the policy side of the shop. He's not strayed too far into organized crime, inter-state trafficking, violent serial crimes. He's aggressive on white-collar crimes — pension fraud, charities that fund someone's personal account, real-estate schemes, political kickbacks, bribery. Insurance fraud is a favorite. He arrests a lot of lawyers."

"That's not what I expected to hear."

"I've been scrolling through his personnel file while we talk. Shannon's envelopes to him on the child abductions seem out of place in his portfolio, but it looks like he's done an excellent job with the information she provided. He's exploited every bit of intelligence those mailings have produced. As far as the rest of his career — the people tapping him when something goes across regions are the top guys in the get-it-done side of the bureau. Simply from the ones who are using his time, I can tell you Adam is in the category of being a very good, very solid, agent."

"That's useful to know. Is he the kind of guy willing to share? I'm trying to sort out how to make sure this next package lands on your desk too. There's a high probability one or more of these people were involved in Shannon's abduction. You and Theo both need to see the contents as soon as possible."

"I'm guessing Shannon put Adam's name on the package for a reason. Let him open it. Tell him to reach out to me concerning the implications regarding Shannon and Chicago. He'll take that advice. If he doesn't . . . well, I'll just move around whatever is necessary and shift him over to work for me. One way or the other, I'll have the package details on my desk. Keep your priority with him on keeping the news Shannon is alive under wraps. Imply her further cooperation depends on how he handles what she's now giving him."

"I can play that tune without a problem." Matthew saw Shannon heading back to the car, carrying a garment bag and two other bags. "I need to go. I'll call you later tonight, Paul."

He put the phone in his pocket and leaned against the side of the car. When Shannon was near enough for him to use his normal voice, he offered a smile and remarked, "Trying to impress me with your shopping speed?"

"You said pink. I think I look like a bit of cotton-candy fluff, but I admit it's a nice dress, and I love the shoes."

He laughed and opened the back door of the car so she could use the garment hook. "Then I'm grateful you took my advice." He opened the trunk and deposited her other bags. "Like to do some more shopping, have a longer break, or do we head north a few more hours, choose a hotel to stay at for the night?"

"Let's drive. What's nearby this restaurant you mentioned to Adam York — shopping malls, movie theaters?"

"I remember a few."

"I'm thinking I'll see a movie tonight while you go chat with Adam. Either that or just crash at the hotel with room service and take another nap."

Matthew waited until Shannon was settled and he had the car out of the mall parking lot before he mentioned, "One of the things

Becky did that first year was watch every chick-flick movie she had missed seeing. Have you started your list yet — things you want to do to fill in the gaps from the missing years?"

"I've got a list, but not that kind. I may start one of those. Not that many movie holes will need filling in. I wasn't isolated, Matthew. Captive, yes, but not as you would assume. I watched most of even the B-grade movies as they came out."

She didn't explain further, and Matthew just tucked the information away. The day-to-day of what her life had been like would be a string of land mines, and it was best to let her share comments when and where she chose. The details would fill in over time, and then he'd ask some careful questions to complete the picture.

"Do we continue with the audiobook?" Shannon asked.

"Sure. Start chapter four." He smiled. "I'll give you the Cliff's Notes version of what you slept through."

Shannon laughed, tugged around the pillow to get comfortable, ready to continue that nap should she drift off listening to the book again. Matthew reached the Interstate ramp and once more headed north.

# 5

Ann Falcon rang the doorbell at the Bishop home in Chicago shortly after four p.m. on Saturday, aware that security would have called the house to announce her arrival when she pulled into the driveway. Bryce Bishop opened the door with a smile before the chimes had finished. "Ann, welcome back from Atlanta. I'd ask how the trip went, but first tell me — did you get to see anything other than the airport and the inside of the hotel?"

She laughed. "Not much. Does Charlotte have a minute?"

"For you? You don't have to even ask. She's in the studio. Head on back."

Ann set her bag on the kitchen table and walked through to the sunroom that Charlotte used as her art studio. She was sitting at the drawing board, her attention focused on a large piece, working in colored pencil.

"Am I interrupting?"

Charlotte glanced over her shoulder, and a smile lit her face. "Never. Hi. Welcome back from the conference."

Ann crossed the room to see the work in progress. The kindergarten-classroom scene had added definition since she'd last seen the work. The teacher was now fully in place, as were most of the children. "I like it. A lot."

"Not too cute?"

"That age, you want the innocence of childhood still showing through," Ann replied, moving to the couch.

Charlotte began slotting pencils back to their places in the trays around her, which spanned all shades of the color spectrum. "What brings you by? I figured you would be curled up with a book with the phone shut off, trying to catch up on some rest."

"The perfect description of where I'm headed after this. Paul needed a couple hours at the office to move some voicemails and paperwork, so we went our separate ways until dinner. Something came up that I need to talk with you about."

"Sure thing. And a nice break for me." Charlotte went to one of the comfortable chairs facing the couch.

Where to begin, how to approach this, wasn't a simple matter. The weight of having worked homicide for years that Ann carried with her, the dark past Charlotte dealt with, were both deliberately left to the side so their friendship could be forward-looking. They made a point of keeping things lighthearted and positive, a safe zone where they could both flourish. This coming conversation would be pushing against that unspoken agreement.

Ann knew who Charlotte Bishop really was — Ruth Bazoni — and knew her history. They didn't talk about it often because it didn't need to be said. Charlotte had been at the center of the most famous kidnapping in Chicago history — four years and three ransom demands before cops had shot the two men and rescued her. Buried inside that crime lay another even deeper tragedy and the death of a child. And that past was why Ann was here this afternoon. She hoped, though, their friendship could handle what she was going to ask. "I need to tell you about something that happened at the conference."

"All right," Charlotte said, looking both curious and a little guarded.

"Do you remember my mentioning Matthew Dane?"

"The guy from Boston you dated for a few months, back when his daughter was still missing?"

"That's the one. Matthew was at the conference. I was able to introduce him to Paul. My husband has decided he likes the guy anyway."

Charlotte laughed. "From those I've met whom you dated, you had good tastes. They all seem to share a streak of honor and . . . I guess chivalry, for want of a better word."

"That probably describes Matthew better than most."

"I hear a story coming. Let me get us something to drink," Charlotte offered, getting to her feet.

"Ahead of you, honey," Bryce said, stepping into the room carrying two glasses. "Ann, I wasn't sure what you might like on a day like this, so I made it lemonade."

"That's perfect, Bryce," Ann said. "My voice is still hoarse from trying to carry on conversations in crowded convention hallways."

He handed her a glass and napkin, the other to his wife. "I'll leave you two ladies to chat. Swing by my office before you leave so I can hand off some nonprofit information for Paul."

"Actually, Bryce . . . would you mind staying for a few minutes? What I need to speak with Charlotte about she'll want to run by you later. It might be easier if you both heard it now."

Bryce's gaze narrowed a bit at the careful but casual way she said it. He changed directions to take the chair beside Charlotte. "Of course." If it affected Charlotte and referenced the past, Ann knew he was going to do everything he could to be the wall between his wife and that news. He ran his hand down Charlotte's hair as he sat down, an affectionate gesture Ann had seen many times. "What's the topic?"

"Matthew Dane's from the Boston area — I've mentioned him to Charlotte in the past. He moved over from cop to private investigator when his daughter went missing at age eight so he'd have more time and resources for the search. Becky was recovered at age sixteen. She's doing well, is in college this year. Anyway, he was one of the speakers at the conference this week, talking about best practices in the dialog between the police and victims' families."

Charlotte leaned over against her husband's shoulder. "Ann used to date him, for a few months during the years his daughter was missing."

"I see."

Ann felt a faint blush. "You'd like him, Bryce. Paul does. You're all of the same type. Men of integrity, for want of a better definition."

He grinned. "Compliment appreciated."

Ann pulled out a copy of the newspaper article Shannon had shown Matthew; she'd found the same AP story in the *Chicago Tribune* archives. "A woman is on her way back to Chicago today. She tracked down Matthew at the hotel in Atlanta last night. This lady." She handed across the article for Charlotte and Bryce to read.

Charlotte's smile faded, and her hand trembled a bit as she read. Then she wordlessly handed the clipping on to her husband. "Tell me the rest of it."

"She's asked Matthew to bring her home. She hasn't said much about what happened yet."

"How long has she been free?" Bryce asked.

"Seventeen days."

Bryce flinched. Charlotte closed her eyes.

"Have you met her?" Bryce asked, his voice husky.

"Not yet. The timing worked better for Paul and me to return to Chicago on schedule and put some things in motion here in preparation for her arrival."

"The last name Bliss," Charlotte said, looking back at the article, "her brother is running for governor. He's spoken often about his missing sister."

"That's the family. She'll have some unique challenges simply returning home."

Charlotte reread the article before folding it carefully and offering it back. Ann looked at her friend, and took a big risk. "Would you be willing to meet with her?" she asked carefully.

Bryce shifted, leaned forward, clearly not liking the question. Ann kept her focus on Charlotte.

Her friend took a long breath, gave an obviously forced shrug. "I'm not a counselor, Ann. There must be others —"

"I think it might help her to know you've now got a worthwhile profession you love, that you're married to a good man, that you have friends around you who you can trust. She needs to see *hope* — to see what her future can be once the pieces get fit back together. It's going to be a rough couple of months coming up for her. I think it might help her to meet you, to speak with you."

"Ann —" Bryce tried to intervene.

She shook her head, not disagreeing with his concern but wanting to make her case as best she could. She kept her focus on Charlotte. "I'm not asking you to tell Shannon details of what you went through, but of your life now, and how it's going with you and Bryce. You love him. He loves you. That's what you can show her. She needs a friend, someone who can understand her and what she's been through. That's all."

"Your *all* is a pretty big word in this context," Bryce put in.

"Ann . . ." Charlotte struggled to find words.

"I will understand if you want to say no, Charlotte. This is going to be raw pain for her for quite some time, and it likely would push memories of your own back to the surface."

"It's not that." Charlotte slid her fingers through her hair. "She's going to need . . . a lot of time. A good doctor. A best friend."

"Matthew will find the right doctor to help her. I don't know if there's a best friend in the picture or if she will have to identify a new one. Eleven years is a long span to bridge."

Charlotte bit her lip and turned toward her husband. "Tell me what you're thinking, Bryce."

"I agree she's going to need a lot of help. I think you and I are both more than ready to help her get that help, be it financially or through influence with medical doctors and psychologists we know. But I'm not sure if you're the right person to be involved in personally providing that help."

Charlotte looked curious. "Because?"

"You're at present in a fight with your own memories. I can see the progress you're making, but we both know every step since our wedding day has been a hard-won fight. You'd be adding her memories on to your own, even if it's simply listening sympathetically to a few comments she might let slip in an otherwise light conversation. They would reverberate through you in a way they would not with Ann or me. They would feel alive and real and devastating to you because they would echo your own memories. I don't think you're ready for something that could possibly be very intense."

Charlotte considered him and his words for a long moment. "Maybe it would help me to put my own memories in perspective. You know, try to help someone going through the early stages . . . a way to see for myself how far I *have* come in this journey," she said thoughtfully. "I feel the stress of wondering if I'll ever get better because progress is so slow, maybe all I see is how much there is still yet to recover, and I miss seeing how far I have come. It might be good to have that perspective."

"I'm not opposed to you helping, Charlotte," Bryce responded, laying his hand on hers. "The opposite. I think you've got something to offer Shannon that no one else could bring to the table. But when and how that happens — there's virtue in moving slowly. Six months from now, a year from now, there's firmer ground. The woman made contact —" Bryce looked quickly over at Ann — "Friday night? Late yesterday?" After her confirming nod, he continued, "There's been no time for Shannon to process what is happening in her life, for cops to begin a debriefing. This is too early, Charlotte. She needs time to get her bearings."

"Bryce." Charlotte reached over and put her other hand over his, offered a small smile. "Ask me tonight about my first days. Those very first days in the hospital before my sister hired John to be my bodyguard. I am remembering what it's like to figure out how to 'get your bearings' when freedom is abruptly there, when you doubted it would ever come — it's because of that I'm inclined to say yes to meeting Shannon this early." Charlotte tightened her hand on his. "You'll have my back. You won't let this get to be too much for me. And for that I'm very grateful. I can count on it."

Charlotte looked over at Ann. "Two casual

meetings, maybe three, over a couple of months," she offered, "if she wants to meet me. But I'd ask that you first give Shannon a copy of the book Gage wrote. The one thing I don't want to have to do is tell her my story. It's enough to be willing to say I'm Ruth Bazoni. I'd like to be able to leave it at that."

"I can do that."

"And I'd need you to show that article to Ellie before then. Talk with her so that she's aware of the same details I am."

"I can do that too," Ann agreed. It was with Ellie Dance, her closest friend as well as business partner, that Charlotte had shared the most difficult memories of what those years had been like, far more than she had shared with her husband. Ellie had her own dark history, and it was one of the reasons Charlotte and Ellie were so close — it had formed a bond that those who hadn't been in that place couldn't share.

Ann looked at Bryce. She knew how hard he was trying to help his wife get back to full health — body, soul, and spirit. She didn't want to undercut him. "Are you okay with this, Bryce?"

"I'm comfortable with opening the door and assessing how it's going as things progress, if that's what Charlotte wants to try. How do you propose we do this, and when?"

"I was thinking a casual meal to introduce Shannon to some people she needs to know, that I would intentionally make it a small gathering of people who know each other so she doesn't feel like she has to do a lot of interacting if she isn't ready for that yet. Matthew and Shannon. Paul and myself. You and Charlotte. John and Ellie. Theodore Lincoln, one of the cops on the case, and his date if he's currently seeing anyone. Rachel and Cole, because I'm hoping Rachel might be able to step into that best-friend role and fill that void if it's necessary. All safe people, unrelated to her family, ones Shannon can turn to in Chicago when she needs something and not worry about how they'll react. The evening itself should be casual fun, good food, friends catching up with each other."

Bryce considered the suggestion, then nodded. "It's a good approach. I propose we have that meal here — a cookout on the back patio. Charlotte can show Shannon this studio, and I'll try to have a couple of conversations with her over the course of the evening. She has to be comfortable with both of us if this is going to play out as you hope."

"If she wants to spend some time here as the summer unfolds, I won't mind the company in the studio," Charlotte offered. "Security is good, the press won't be a problem here once that begins to be a factor. What I can offer might simply be a quiet, non-stressful place to read a book, but sometimes that's enough. Knowing there's a place where you can disappear for a while can be a lifesaver."

Ann looked at their clasped hands. They had a common concern in meeting Shannon, facing the memories it would stir up. It might be just what Charlotte and Bryce could use themselves without even realizing it. Ann raised her gaze to meet theirs, offered a smile. "Thank you, both of you. I'll give you a call when I've spoken with Matthew, keep you updated as I learn more. I'll see what date might work for them."

"Is there anything we can do to help in a practical way to smooth her return to Chicago?" Bryce asked.

"I've already asked John to arrange a secure place for Matthew and Shannon to stay when they reach town. Paul's going to make arrangements for Shannon and her brother to meet at our home — neutral territory, so to speak. A lot of what unfolds after that is going to depend on what Shannon is able to reveal. I'm hoping we can have this gathering maybe Tuesday or Wednesday evening."

Bryce looked at Charlotte, then back at Ann. "Our schedule is free this week," he confirmed. "We'll leave it open and wait to hear from you."

"What about this one?" Ellie Dance asked, stepping out of the dressing room in an elegant short-sleeve, knee-length blue dress.

John Key thought his fiancée had never looked more beautiful. "The dress is stunning. If you don't get it to wear on our honeymoon, I'll be buying it for you shortly thereafter."

"It is lovely, isn't it?" Ellie spun around to show him the full effect. "You're going to have to take me to some very fancy places to take advantage of all these items you're talking me into buying."

"I'll just add days to the length of the honeymoon," John replied, perfectly content to do just that. It had taken years for Ellie to reach the point she would say yes to marrying him. He didn't mind their yearlong engagement while she planned the wedding she wanted. It gave him time to have days like this one with her, hanging out together, doing some shopping, letting her enjoy being beautiful and loved. He truly enjoyed romancing his future wife. A long honeymoon would be a nice beginning to their marriage.

He waited in the chair provided while she slipped back into the dressing room and returned in her street clothes. "I've decided I'd like to tell Bryce about Marie before the wedding," she said, the blue dress hanging over her arm. "I think it's time he knows."

Her comment surprised him. They had discussed Marie a few times, but they'd made no decisions. "There's no urgency, Ellie, but yes, it would be good if he had the details. You're comfortable with him knowing?"

"Charlotte knows. Bryce needs to know too. If there's a concern after the wedding, you're going to need a friend. I'd prefer to be the one to tell Bryce rather than leave it for you in what could be difficult circumstances. But I was wondering if you would talk with him first, sort of prepare the way?"

"I'll do that for you — and be with you when you tell him, if you like."

"I was thinking maybe a conversation at the gallery would be appropriate."

John held out his hand, and she slid hers into it. "He's going to be fine with what you tell him," he reassured her, standing. "It's going to be interesting to see what question he asks first, if he even asks one. I suspect he's simply going to offer one of those all-encompassing okays of his and give you a hug."

John's phone interrupted them with the emergency tone. They both tensed. His primary security clients were Charlotte and Bryce Bishop, and no one was closer to Ellie than Charlotte. The caller ID was blocked. "John Key."

"Sorry! Sorry, it's not an emergency. I'm just . . . sorry, John."

"Relax, Ann." He gave Ellie a reassuring smile. "It's no problem. You've still got this number in your speed dial."

"Which I realized *after* I hit the call button. Though I guess this is sort of an emergency in order to pass on a message. I just told Charlotte and Bryce about Shannon Bliss. Ellie needs to be in the loop on this for Charlotte's sake."

"Ah. Yeah. I figured that was coming. Can I deliver the news? It's been awkward sitting on it for the last few hours."

"Please. I'll send you the link to the newspaper article."

"I've still got it on my phone. How did Charlotte react?"

"She got very quiet, but she's open to the

idea of meeting Shannon. Ellie should give her a call, do a better debrief than I could."

"I'll make sure that happens."

"Any problem on finding a secure place for Matthew and Shannon to stay?"

John pulled out his wallet to retrieve a credit card, offered it to Ellie, nodded toward a clerk waiting nearby — taking advantage of the fact he faced less argument over who was buying this addition to her honeymoon wardrobe when he was on the phone. "None. It's been arranged. Our favorite diplomat is in Eastern Europe trying to put volatile tempers back on simmer; he said he'll be out of the country another six weeks and we're welcome to use his place. The unit across the hall is being renovated, and I'm taking that as well. I've got a couple of guys a phone call away if it's necessary to add security when they are out of the place. We're set. They'll be secure while they're in Chicago."

"I'm guessing they'll arrive Monday, mid-afternoon."

"I'll make sure food is laid in for them. Have you heard anything else?" he asked, watching Ellie as she stood at checkout with the dress.

"Shannon was passing photos and locations of abducted kids to an FBI guy in

Virginia — eighteen kids over the last six years."

He felt pleasant surprise at the news. "Good for her."

"She's a survivor. Another item she mentioned: when this started and her kidnapping went bad, they put out to sea, tossed her in the ocean, and waited for her to drown."

John felt a stillness slow his heart rate, the trained response to wanting to take on an opponent. His hand clenched around the phone. "We're going to make the next few weeks calm and peaceful for her, or we don't know how to do our jobs. And we're going to put people in cuffs."

"Paul's sentiment too. What's on your schedule?"

"Nothing I can't delegate," John assured Ann.

"I'm going to put something together so she can meet you and Ellie, Charlotte and Bryce, a few others. She needs safe names and faces outside of her family in Chicago, people she can trust."

"Just let me know when and where. Ann, is her brother, this Jeffery Bliss, is he a good guy?"

"I'm hoping he is."

"Same here. Call me if you need me."

"Thanks, John."

He ended the call.

"What's going on?" Ellie asked, returning with a garment bag holding the dress.

He scrolled back to the article link, brought it up, and handed her the phone. "Shannon Bliss is coming home."

Paul Falcon heard the elevator security faintly chime as a key was used to stop it on the fourth floor. They were owners of the entire floor, and the elevator opened into the entryway of their home, where the first sight to greet their guests was a large sculpture of a horse and rider beloved by his grandfather. Paul tugged a clean shirt off a hanger as the dog lying at the foot of the bed startled upright to race away and greet Ann. Paul smiled as he finished changing his shirt. It felt good to be home.

He heard the rumble of a low growl come from the living room as Black found his favorite toy, then the unmistakable sound of the dog's feet skidding on the polished floor of the entryway. "Yes, I'm delighted to see you too, Black," his wife crooned to her dog. "And I'm glad to see poor bear is still in one piece."

Paul listened to the familiar interactions, relaxed just hearing them. There had been years in this home where the only sound had been the music he put on to break the silence. Having a wife and her dog around suited him just fine. His phone buzzed. He paused, picked it up, scrolled through the text message. Shannon Bliss and her situation was only one of four hot items on his plate right now. He'd moved on the most urgent items during a few hours at the office, then packed up a briefcase of work to bring home with him. He sent a reply. He had good people working the problems, and nothing was in particular crisis. This could wait an hour. He went to find his wife.

He found Ann in the kitchen, looking in the refrigerator. She'd fed the dog. Black had his paws on either side of his bowl, holding it in place while he practically inhaled the contents. Paul paused to ruffle the dog's ears, then joined his wife.

"Need some help?" He slid his arm around her waist, leaned over to offer a lingering kiss. "Glad you're home."

"I never want to leave it again."

He smiled, understanding the sentiment. "What have you decided?"

"Hamburgers."

She handed him a new jar of dill pickle slices to open. He did so and set it on the counter. "I'll handle dinner. Sit. Keep me company." He turned her toward a stool. Ann gave it her best effort, but she wasn't much of a cook, and he rather enjoyed fixing meals for them.

She took a tapioca cup with her and sat on the stool while he pulled out hamburger and cheese, found wax paper to help make the burgers ultrathin. He got the meat sizzling in a large hot skillet, put on the lid to cut down spatter, found the last of the German potato salad his sister had sent home with them from her restaurant. It was better warm, so he put the bowl in the microwave, turned the hamburgers and adjusted the heat to low, took the potatoes out of the microwave, then slid onto a stool next to his wife, carefully sampled the potatoes. Not so hot they would burn the tongue. He held out the fork with a bite to share with his wife. "How did Charlotte take the request?"

Ann borrowed the fork to take another bite of the potatoes, gave it back. "She's open to meeting Shannon. Bryce has some reservations, but he offered to host the casual get-together. Unsaid is that he knows Charlotte will find it easier if it's a first meeting on her own turf. It would be good if you scheduled a run with him, sound out what he didn't tell me."

"Already on my short list for the next few

days," Paul agreed.

"Did you hear anything more from Matthew?"

He summarized the latest call.

"Shannon made a good choice approaching him," Ann said.

"She did."

Paul liked this guy Ann had once dated years before she had met him, liked how he briefed details on the phone, liked how he handled a very important victim without appearing to be managing her. The information she was sharing wouldn't be coming if Matthew hadn't established that elusive, subtle line of trust with Shannon. "I think she wanted to talk and knew she could only handle telling the story one-on-one, so she deliberately selected who it would be. A smart move on her part, and one that helps us. She's not shutting down like many victims in her place would do. She's simply being deliberate. A week, I think, and this will be a case with some rapid, unfolding movement. It's going to feel good to make arrests on Shannon's behalf. Theo echoes that sentiment. We've put together space to work this on the director's floor to keep it quiet for now."

"Good. Theo needs a case like this, something that turns out positive. He spends a lot of time on situations that end up with only recovered remains."

"I know." Paul slid off the stool to check the hamburgers, found them almost done. He split the buns and put them on top of the hamburgers in the pan to warm, took another close look at his wife as he worked. She looked content. Relieved to be home. She also looked drained. She'd enjoyed herself at the conference, but was paying a price. Even before Matthew had tapped her shoulder with Shannon's situation, the trip had been taking a toll. "How are you feeling, Ann?"

She hesitated before she answered. "I'm just tired."

He set down the towel, stopped beside her, put his hands on either side of her face and tipped it up to study. She'd hide it all with most people, but she was learning not to do so with him. "I think *exhausted* is the word you're looking for," he said gently. "Bad enough the nausea is setting in, given what you chose to eat first."

"Too many people. Too much noise."

Three days at a conference, travel on either side of it, was her physical limit now. She was an introvert, and time with a lot of people drained her. She'd had more reserves when she was single, when most of her time was spent alone. Marriage had changed what she could manage now. Moved things in closer. Solitude was a precious commodity when part of a couple, and she wasn't getting enough of it. He had known before he married her that solitude would be nearly as critical to her well-being as sleep, and the two years since the wedding had only reinforced that.

He rested his hands on her shoulders to rub his thumbs against her collarbone. "I think you should disappear and go paint for the next week," he suggested. She had a studio attached to their apartment with its own private bedroom suite — his wedding gift to her, a place to hibernate and get a big dose of time alone.

"I'll be fine —"

She started to tell him it wasn't so bad, and he shook his head, stopping her words. The timing for it wasn't ideal with Shannon arriving in town, with Matthew needing help, but it was necessary. "That was our deal, Ann. I want my wife, not a shell of who you are. You can't be what you need — what I need — when you're exhausted. You can disappoint other people for the next week to please me. We'll host Shannon's meeting with her brother here. You can come to the cookout when that gets arranged. Talk with Matthew when he calls. Otherwise, silence the phone, get some solitude and some rest. Do some painting. I'll step in and handle matters regarding Shannon." He tipped up her chin to kiss her. "If I'd been thinking, I would have gone to see Charlotte and Bryce today on your behalf."

"I needed to do it. She's my friend, and it was a lot to ask."

"Charlotte's been a good friend to you and you to her," Paul agreed. "You're brutally tired, Ann. You can't ignore that, wish it away."

She conceded the point. "I'll go paint — five days, starting tomorrow after we get back from church. What about Black?"

He smiled. "Black and I could use some guy time to reconnect. No one fussing when I share my breakfast with him or wondering why we pause on a walk to watch a nice poodle stroll by."

She laughed, rested her hands on his arms. "Thank you. More than you can know — most guys wouldn't get me, but you do. It's no wonder I love you. But could I make one change to that plan?"

"What are you thinking?"

"Let me go talk to Theo, look at the case board, and pose some questions. I've spent since Friday night pushing case-file information into my brain, and I can be useful to him for a few hours. You know I can."

He leaned in to softly kiss her again. "I'm not questioning your usefulness, only the timing. Spend Monday afternoon with him. Sort out whether things are going the right direction. Then leave it to Theo and me for a few days, all right?"

"All right."

"Good," Paul replied with a nod of his head. "Now, what do you want on your cheeseburger? The works?"

"No onions."

He smiled. "For either of us," he decided. He finished the meal prep and set their plates on the counter where they often ate.

He knew others wondered at the way he guarded his life with Ann, the privacy they maintained, the quiet schedule they kept most of the year. He knew something they did not. In her element, Ann was one of the best thinkers he had ever met, able to make intuitive leaps and see connections that even seasoned investigators missed. She'd been an excellent homicide cop, she was a good writer, and had a relationship with God he envied. Those facets of who she was had developed because of the time she'd been able to spend thinking. He'd married her wanting to share that life, not push her into being a different person after adding the title *wife.* It mattered to him that he cared for her well, that the woman he'd met and fallen in love with would still be found in his wife. The trade-off of some solitude for her was a rich marriage for himself — he knew how to protect what mattered.

The cheeseburgers tasted delicious. Still, Ann passed over half of hers and got herself another tapioca.

"Did you ever meet Adam York?" he asked her, curious.

"The one who's been catching those missing-kid packages from Shannon?"

"Yes."

"I've been trying to place where I've heard his name. I don't think I've met him, but a case out of Ohio crossed with one of his, I think. The cop thought the FBI was being pushy, so I tucked away the name."

"Ideally, Shannon has only one contact with the FBI other than me, and it doesn't sound like York is the right agent. I'd go with Rita as my first choice, but she's involved elsewhere. While Sam would be able to set the right tone, I think we need a woman."

"Shannon's better off if it's Matthew Dane and only one cop," Ann suggested.

"I'd choose Theodore Lincoln for the conversations. He knows her case, he has history with her family, he's thorough and careful and the right mix of patient cop and calm detective — he'll work the case and stay out of the press limelight until his boss sends him to a podium. I predict Shannon is going to meet Theo and be very comfortable with him. Let the FBI sit back in the information flow. You want Shannon to give you details, you need to keep her initial world small — under five people if possible. Matthew Dane, Theodore Lincoln, a good woman doctor, her brother, and maybe Charlotte. Make that the inner circle she deals with for the next several weeks."

Paul thought Ann's read of the situation was solid, and he had no problem with the FBI drafting behind Theo for the details. "I'll keep the case on my desk for now, haul in Dave and Sam as the next additions. They get along well with Theo. Once we get the information suggesting the geography this case is going to cover, I'll reassess who we need."

The dog was pushing his bowl around the kitchen in a not-so-subtle reference to the fact it was empty. Paul got up to take plates over to the dishwasher. "Would a walk help, Black?"

The dog's head came up, and he abandoned the bowl to dart into the entryway. His leash was draped over the saddle of the sculpture, and they heard it hit the floor. Black trotted back into the kitchen, trailing the leash behind him. Ann was laughing as she leaned down for it. "Thank you, Black. One long walk coming up." She glanced over at Paul. "We need to send him up to the ranch with Quinn for a couple of weeks so he can stretch his legs and chase things, burn off some energy."

"You know he slept the entire time we were gone," Paul pointed out, as Black fidgeted impatiently while Ann clipped his leash on. "I'll take him." Paul took the leash, and the three of them headed out. Black didn't love the elevator, but he'd learned to tolerate it. The animal was the first one on. Paul was glad the dog had transitioned to the concrete of living in downtown Chicago as well as he had. Ann and her dog had walked a lot of miles together before he'd met her, and Paul was beginning to appreciate the joy this animal brought to their lives. Black never failed to entertain. "Two miles tonight?" he asked as the elevator opened. And with Ann's agreement, he turned them south so they'd pass by one decent-sized park during the walk.

# 6

"Matthew Dane?" The man had his hand already extended. "Adam York. Pleased to meet you."

Matthew rose from the corner table in the Blue Rose restaurant to shake the agent's hand. He could already tell they were heading toward a collision if he didn't let York take the lead in this conversation. But given it would be to his advantage to have Adam do most of the talking, Matthew smiled and planned to give the man as much space as he wanted. "Please, have a seat," Matthew said, gesturing to the chair across from his. "I figured this might be a long conversation, so I've already ordered appetizers to keep our waitress happy. We'll be monopolizing a table in her section."

Adam York drew out the chair. "The meal on the plane comprised a found bag of stale pretzels, so I'm already in your debt." The waitress came over, and Adam requested both water and a soft drink. The man didn't deliberately scan the restaurant, but Matthew could see his curiosity as he glanced around. "Is she here?"

"If I said no, would you believe me?" Matthew answered mildly.

"I've seen her photo from when she was sixteen. I might recognize her, but figure it would be just a guess after this many years. What can you tell me about her?"

"Beyond the fact she's alive, in reasonably good health, and beginning to share what happened, I'm not planning to say much."

The appetizer sampler arrived, along with their drinks. They both placed main-course orders, choosing the day's special.

The manila envelope with *Adam York* written on it lay on the table between them, but Adam didn't reach for it. He ate one of the stuffed mushrooms. "I've got eighteen kids who would like to tell Shannon thank you," he mentioned around a bite.

Matthew relaxed. Maybe a touch too aggressive, like the proverbial bull in a china shop, but also a guy with a clear sense of the important to go with that direct approach. He thought he might come to like this FBI agent.

"Your Shannon was getting very early photos of the kids in their new locations,"

Adam said, reaching for a napkin. "By the time we received the package and were on scene at the various addresses, the kids' hair would be dyed a different color, it would be shorter, they'd have papers giving them a different age, different birthday, a few had new names, but it was them. None of the abducted children ever told us who had moved them to their new location. None ever mentioned Shannon or gave a description that might be her.

"The most surprising thing," Adam continued, "was that we'd get them returned home to their rightful parent, only to realize the kids were terrified to be there. They were convinced someone was going to come grab them again. In every case we ended up advising the parent to move, change their names, give their kid a sense of a new, safe start in order to find balance again. The abductions and how they were done put a deep scar in these kids' lives."

Matthew absorbed that information while he ate his share of the fried zucchini. "What were you able to tug loose about how the abductions were arranged?"

"As a group, the parent arrested illegally holding the child all had a variation on the same story. When the case looked like it would go against him or her, the lawyer suggested someone might be able to help. They could circumvent the courts and get their child — that was guaranteed. But it would be expensive and criminal. If they paid the fee, they were told to walk away from their present life, set up in a new place with a new name, then wait for the child to be delivered. The parent didn't know the person who dropped the child off, and none were willing to give a full description. A white guy, maybe in his forties, a white panel van with muddy license plates — that was pretty much it for what we could get them to say."

Their dinner orders arrived, and the conversation paused until the waitress had moved away. The seafood looked good. Matthew considered ordering the same as a carryout for Shannon when this meeting was over. "Did pursuing the lawyers get you anywhere?"

"All the abductions were different lawyers, some in Northern states, some in the South. The four lawyers who finally ended up cooperating with us said they'd received a business card at a family-law conference. They had a phone number, a description offering 'special assistance for special circumstances.' They got paid a cut of the fee to provide information and a photo of the child. The distance between where a child was grabbed and where they were dropped off, along with the timing involved, suggests two or three drivers trading off to get the kid delivered as soon as it could be done. One of the kids confirmed that, in a roundabout way."

Adam picked up an onion ring, split it in two, and ate half. "There was one rather odd thing we realized early on. Put the location where the child was abducted on the map, where each ended up, and it was always east to west across the Northern states, or west to east across the Southern states. A regular circuit. Also, the abductions in the North happened in the summer, while abductions in the South in the winter."

"So they weren't accepting every job they were offered, only those that fit their travel plans?" Matthew guessed.

Adam reached for his drink. "Had to be. I'd receive a package by first-class mail from Shannon in the spring, another in the fall, addressed to my attention. The return address would be real but taken at random from ads in the Yellow Pages in the town where it was mailed. She managed to get the packages put together without leaving any useable prints inside or out. She had to be with the group doing the abductions. Either that or in direct contact with someone in the group."

The implications of that were worrying, but Matthew merely nodded. He pushed the manila envelope on the table over to Adam. "The people doing the abductions are dead," he said. "Shannon doesn't know who was hiring them. I think there was one more layer between the business card and these people. They'd have a photo of who to grab, a location, an address of where to make the delivery. Terror did the job. If the young child told anyone, gave the other parent any trouble, they would come take them again, keep them this time — implying a threat to kill the parents."

Adam winced. "That would indeed terrify a child into keeping quiet." He opened the envelope. Five photos spilled out. Four men, one woman. On the back of each was a name, the letters *DOD* followed by a date. A note with neat printing read: *The children abducted over the years should be able to pick these people out of a photo display with ease. It will help them to learn these people are gone and cannot hurt them or their families again. Gravesite locations are coming.* Adam picked up some of the photos, turned them over. "The date of death is the same for these three. Right at a year ago."

Matthew checked the other two. "These are also identical — four months ago."

"I'd hoped for something interesting when you told me there was another envelope, but I wasn't expecting this," Adam said, studying the photos with a frown. "We can run these names and photos through the databases, see what aliases and locations pop up. You don't turn into people smugglers without getting caught for lesser crimes along the way."

"May I suggest that you take it slow with this information? I think Shannon has more that will be useful to you before you start knocking on doors."

"One or more of these people abducted her?"

"That's my guess," Matthew said.

"Maybe the names and locations for these five, set alongside the lawyers' information, will yield a common denominator — someone was putting these players in motion. At least it will give us beginning and end points for the money that had to move hands. Maybe the guy that's the key will show up in the money trail."

Matthew was still focused on the implications of what Shannon had told him. "We need to know if someone in Shannon's family set her up to be abducted, or if someone arranged it to pressure her family," he told Adam quietly.

"The kids she's given me — the oldest was ten. Shannon was sixteen when she was taken. That's old for a custody dispute."

"Maybe they shifted to only custody disputes and younger children after what turned out to be a debacle with her. Shannon said she was grabbed, taken by these people to a specific address where she was to be delivered, there was a problem at that location, and she was forced to stay with them. So someone paid them to take her, gave directions on where to take her. We need to identify that person."

"Who's working this in Chicago?"

"Paul Falcon and his wife, Ann, are involved. Paul's going to need a look at this envelope's contents."

"He'll have it tonight." Adam gathered up the photos. "If someone paid to have Shannon grabbed, if they are still around, they're going to react badly to the fact Shannon turns up. I'd be careful about the ones you trust."

"That's what we're trying to sort out now. The fact that her brother's running for governor of Illinois isn't going to help matters."

"Politics and crime make for very interesting press," Adam agreed. "I need to talk with Shannon, and sooner rather than later," he insisted.

"That's not going to happen in the near term," Matthew replied flatly. "Neither of us can afford to cut off the flow of information. If you push, she's going to stop talking."

"Are there more kids to rescue?"

"She says no."

Adam pulled out a business card, wrote a number on the back. "I looked you up. I'm sorry about your daughter."

"Appreciate that."

"Becky's the reason Shannon found you?"

"Yes."

Adam pushed the card across the table. "I'll keep that in mind when we butt heads on the timing of things."

Matthew smiled and offered a card of his own. "I might come to like you, but don't take it for granted."

"Ditto. I'll call when I've got something useful on these five. Tell Shannon thanks."

"I will."

Matthew waited until Adam had left the restaurant before he paid the bill and exited with a carryout order for Shannon. He drove south for ten minutes, watching to see if he was being followed, then turned north and headed back to the hotel. Rooms had been booked for them by Ann under names she'd selected at random from the phone book.

Matthew wasn't surprised to find Shannon still up. They had adjoining rooms at the hotel, and the connecting door between them stood open. Shannon was curled up on his couch, watching television. She didn't ask how the meeting had gone, but he offered something anyway. "I like Adam York."

"I figured you might."

Matthew set down the bag he carried in. "I brought you a meal if you want to add something further to that room-service tray."

She uncoiled from the couch. "Yeah, thanks, I am hungry again."

"Becky taught me early on that food started to taste really good to her again in the first months she was home."

Shannon lifted the lid on the container, and her pleasure was obvious. "This is great." Matthew pulled out a chair for her at the table, then stepped out to retrieve beverages from the vending machine. He settled in across from her at the table while she ate, working on a package of M&M's as his dessert.

"Did you enjoy being a cop?"

He was surprised at the unexpected question. "Yes. I was good at it. I liked solving robberies."

"You didn't aspire to something else . . . maybe like homicides?"

"No. I liked property crimes. All too often it was someone poor stealing from someone equally poor. It mattered that the theft be solved."

"You quit because of your daughter's case?"

He nodded. "I needed more income than my salary could provide in order to hire people to stay on the case full time. Starting my own private firm let me keep working my daughter's case as I wanted to have it run."

"I like that about you — that you kept a full press on to solve your daughter's case. A dad's instinct, I know, but it says something that you persevered through all those years." She gestured with her fork. "Will you ever go back to being a cop?"

He shrugged. "Probably. It's what I enjoyed for the first eight years of my daughter's life. They've asked me back. I've got staff who can run the day-to-day of Dane

Investigations without me."

He waited for something else, but she didn't offer anything further. "What prompted the questions?" he asked.

"I know where something is that was stolen. I might have us stop and pick it up tomorrow."

He lifted his root beer, considered her over the rim. This was getting even more interesting. He wondered what had been stolen. "People smugglers. Also thieves?"

"Think of it as a family of smugglers. Half the family liked the money that came from dealing with people. The other half preferred dealing only in objects. They smuggled art goods mostly, some jewelry. They'd let things sit for five years or more, then deliver them to a trusted broker in another part of the country."

"Which side of the family did you spend most of the eleven years with?"

She shook her head.

He tried another query. "Were they good smugglers?"

"They liked boats. They moved a lot of goods up and down both the East and West Coast. The people side of the business was a strictly pickup and drop-off affair. But the objects — sometimes they'd wait a few years and have someone in the circle claim the reward for the item's return. Most of the time they would sell it. They didn't actually steal the items; they acquired them from those who were fencing the goods or from brokers who had a deal fall through."

"How many from the family can you identify for the police?"

"Identifying is easy. Locating is hard. They travel the country in a way that's somewhat predictable by season, but they never stay within a hundred miles of a place they've been before. And they have trip wires all over the nation — people they do business with, places they stop, names that change, even check-in calls. Have a cop ask the wrong question, mention the wrong name, raid the wrong place, detain the wrong person, and the entire family folds up shop and disappears like ghosts."

He thought about that and realized her dilemma. "You're aiming to get them all."

Shannon nodded. "I chose my time when I could run with enough information to tear the group apart. Some of the information I needed was on the West Coast, some on the East Coast. It took a while to get enough."

*And the danger in that decision she'd made was breathtaking.* He forced himself not to follow up on her comment, kept his voice casual. "It sounds to me like a conversation with Paul is in order."

She shook her head. "The children side of this is first, if there's someone who hired them that can be traced. The five are dead, but I don't know who was hiring them."

"How did they die?"

"A family dispute settled with guns. The two sides of the family are like the Hatfields and McCoys right now. What was left of the kidnapping side of the family shut down and disbanded a year ago. These last two girls taken were an outlier — it's what got the last two people in those photos killed. The rest of the family has gone quiet, sort of hibernating, shaking off the internal implosion."

"Could you have gotten out earlier?"

"When Flynn was around, I could . . . *maneuver* is probably the right word. It's how I got the packages mailed. But getting out would have meant someone left behind got killed. They were good at controlling people, making you responsible for someone else's well-being. If you exhibited no concern over what happened to your assigned person, they assumed you were uncontrollable and put a bullet in your head."

She glanced up, caught the expression of horror on his face, wiped hers clean of any emotion. "Sorry."

He simply shook his head. "How big is this family?"

"Eighteen deserve to be in jail. Another six are . . . 'mercy cases' is how I think of them. They knew, but couldn't do anything about it without such a price being paid that staying silent was all they reasonably could do." She pushed back from the table.

Matthew reached over and rested his hand on hers before she could rise. "Shannon, did someone die because you ran?" He asked it as gently as he could, but he had to ask, had to know. Nothing would destroy her faster than carrying around that kind of crushing guilt.

She blew out a breath. "No. They think I'm dead. I was one of the names on the cleanup list after the family implosion. Flynn was assigned to do it, but he didn't use a bullet. He simply said 'good luck' and let me try to swim back to land." She faintly smiled, remembering. "I'm pretty sure he was hoping I would make it, because he tucked a locker key to one of his private stashes in my hand before he pushed me overboard."

"Where was this? How far did you swim?"

He caught a very brief change in her expression before she gained control again. Whatever the answer, at some point she'd thought she wouldn't make it, that she'd drown. She shook her head.

"Is Flynn someone who deserves mercy?"

"Flynn is . . . nearly as dangerous to the family as I am."

# 7

"Matthew, you've got to convince her to have a conversation with us," Paul said early the next morning after he heard the update on what Shannon had shared.

"I'll see once we arrive. She's dumping the story at such a pace I think I'm going to have most of it by the time we reach Chicago. That may in fact have been her intention all along."

He had his phone on speaker, making notes as they talked. He reached for his coffee and stilled as he saw movement. He lifted a hand in greeting to Shannon and motioned her to come on in. He'd pushed open the connecting door a foot when he heard her moving around. He pointed to the box of donuts he'd gone out early to buy, and the quart of orange juice he had opened. She smiled her thanks.

"If we knew the address where she was to be dropped off, we could very likely solve the reason for her abduction and who paid to have it done," Paul pointed out, his voice sounding slightly hollow on the speaker-phone.

"I know." Matthew looked over at Shannon, who shook her head. "Whatever her reason is for holding it back, I think it's deliberate. I'll ask her on the names, see if she recognizes anyone. Anything else you have on your short list?" He turned the pad of paper toward Shannon as he offered the comment so she could read the list. She looked over the nine names, shook her head no.

"John Key has arrangements made for a safe place to stay in Chicago. You'll need two security codes for the entrances, but not a key. I'll direct you once you hit town, as its location is a bit tucked away."

"Tell him thanks. Once we've arrived, give us a day to shake off the travel fatigue, then call her brother and set up a meeting."

"That works for me," Paul agreed.

Matthew took back the pad of paper. "Shannon's looked at the names and drawn a blank."

"Well, that's . . . disappointing," Paul finally said. "We'll keep digging."

"Appreciate it. I'll call you again this evening once we've settled for the night."

"It's a plan. Talk to you later."

Matthew clicked off the phone.

"Who are they?" Shannon asked, tipping her glass of orange juice toward the list of names.

"Lawyers connected either directly or tangentially to your parents and extended family eleven years ago."

"You think someone on that list helped put in motion what happened to me?"

"If the pattern holds, it's probable. It's also possible what happened back then is why they started doing only child custody disputes from then on. You might have been the last of some other kind of general business."

"I was definitely the first case where they couldn't make a delivery as planned. They were furious I was still with them. And the custody disputes were lucrative enough they might have decided to specialize after that."

Matthew got up to pour himself more coffee from the small coffee maker in the room. "Paul's right, you know. The address where you were to be dropped off is a very big deal. With that address we can get a name of who was there eleven years ago, develop a bio, find out who we're dealing with. That can be done quietly. They won't even know we're looking. The person who was expecting you to arrive that day is the one person who can answer the most questions about what happened to you and why."

"I'm not prepared to give you that address. Not yet."

"Would you tell me the reason?"

She shook her head. "I can be ready to be on the road in about an hour if that suits you."

"That will be fine. No one is expecting us in Chicago on a particular day. If you'd find it helpful just to stay put, take some extra time to rest, we can do that."

"I'm kind of enjoying sleeping in the car."

Matthew laughed. "I don't mind the quiet company."

Matthew thought about that "quiet company" remark more than once over the next few hours. Shannon was asleep in the front passenger seat, turned slightly toward him, one hand slid under the shoulder strap of the seat belt, the other resting in her lap. She didn't always sleep easily — he noticed the frequent dreams — but she did sleep, and that was something he was pleased to see. There would be a point where depression would trigger her to sleep too much, but this looked more like a body too long under stress trying to heal.

She eventually began to stir, and he mentally reviewed upcoming towns and where to stop for lunch. Rest, food, conversation when she wanted to talk — the basic equation he'd figured out with his daughter that had to undergird everything else he hoped might occur. He glanced over as she stretched, caught her yawn, shared a smile. "You look better for the sleep."

"Feeling a bit better too."

"How are the dreams?"

"Why do you ask?"

"Becky didn't want to deal with the details of what happened, so her mind suppressed most of them. But they came back first in her dreams, then in random clips of memory, then as something which wouldn't fade from her thoughts until she talked about it. Eleven years is a long time. Are you dealing with something similar?"

"Yes and no. And no, I don't want to explain that answer just yet."

He nodded acceptance of the closed door.

She studied exit signs and noted, "There's a town south of Columbus called Seymour. If you can find it, there's a stop we should make."

She'd mentioned she knew where a stolen item was. If they were going to pick it up, that raised all kinds of interesting questions about who should search the place — Indiana State Police, FBI, cops in the town of Seymour? And how did he explain matters to the appropriate agency without complicating this further? Matthew found an Indiana State map in the driver's side pocket, handed it to her. "Search out Seymour."

She unfolded the map and studied the area. "It looks to be only about twenty minutes off our route," she said. She put her finger on the map, and he glanced over at it a couple of times, nodded that he had it. She folded the map to center Seymour on the page. "Can you not wonder too much about what it is until I first see if it's even still there?"

She had a point. "I'll try," he said. "Tell me about the place we're going, if not the item we're hoping to find."

"It's an old apple orchard and roadside fruit stand. Nothing much to look at now, other than the apples being still pretty good on the trees that haven't gone wild or died. The property probably was no longer a well-maintained business a few years after I was taken."

"You've been here?"

"I've been through this area several times, stopped at this particular place just once.

But it was memorable enough I should be able to find it again."

They found the apple orchard forty minutes later. Matthew pulled off and parked beside a lean-to structure that, from its faded sign, once served as the roadside store. The roof was still attached, but one wall had collapsed and was simply waiting for the next good windstorm to flatten the last of it.

They got out of the car and looked around. Not a soul was in sight. Birds were singing, the sun was hot, and some of the trees looked like they could give some good apples. Shannon walked back into the center of the roadway and lifted her hand to shade her vision as she scanned the area. "I think we go that way." She pointed toward the orchard.

Matthew picked up the bottles of cold drinks from their last stop and handed her one, locked the car. "What are we looking to find?" He fell in step beside her as they set out.

"A tree."

"In a sea of trees," he quipped.

"It's not an apple tree."

"That will help."

They walked ten minutes through the orchard and reached its northern boundary.

A plowed and planted field to the right, a fairly steep ravine on the left going down to a trickle of a stream that likely gushed after a big rain. More trees, oaks and elms and a few hickories, he thought, unsure about his leaf identifications.

"That one." Shannon pointed out an oak tree at the point where the orchard met the field. An old building with stacked packing crates around it and what might have once been a tree sprayer and a conveyor belt, its engine now rusted, rested forlornly nearby.

"You're sure?"

She walked over to the tree and looked up. "It's grown."

He laughed. "Was it not supposed to?"

"Give me a boost."

"You mean to climb that tree."

"Not very far, but yeah. I'd rather trust you than that wooden ladder that's probably sun-rotted years ago."

"How are you going to get down?"

"Matthew — I climb trees. It's an odd hobby, but I'll be fine. Now give me a boost."

He put his hands together, and she put her foot in the cradle. He helped her reach the lowest limb of the oak tree, its circumference as big as a good-sized tree itself. She hoisted herself up to straddle it, then moved back to the trunk and stood up. She reached the next branch above her, picked her toeholds, and climbed up one more level. She looked into a hollow in the trunk where an owl might sit and nest. "It's still here," she called down. "What's it worth to you?"

"What are you asking?"

"An ice-cream cone."

"Deal."

She reached into the hole and pulled out a small box covered with leaves and twigs. She shook it clean. "Catch!"

He moved swiftly and caught it. It was a bit fatter and stockier than a cigar box, carefully wrapped in white butcher paper. He placed it on the ground and moved to where he could watch as she came down a level and straddled the lowest limb.

"I'm not jumping for you to catch me. Move out of the way. I'm going to drop and roll."

"You'll break an ankle."

"Trust me, this isn't even high enough to be a challenge. I break a bone, you can say 'I told you so,' and I'll even answer twenty questions without saying 'no comment.' "

It was a confident wager. "Just be careful," he insisted. "You break something, I'll never live it down with my daughter."

She laughed, and a moment later hit the ground and rolled. She rose to her feet and dusted herself off. "Down, safe and sound."

He walked over and picked up what she had risked life and limb to retrieve. "What's in the box you just rescued?"

"Someone's dowry, I think. A woman named Ashimera Tai. It's engraved on the top of the jewelry box. From what I overheard, you're holding three hundred thousand in jewelry. They wanted it to cool off for a very long time before they did anything with it, hence the tree."

"I would have expected a safe-deposit box."

"Depends who was in charge of the hiding. Some of them didn't like banks and guards and cameras and having to get permission to claim their stuff."

"How did they find this place and decide to put it here?"

"Flynn and I used to do a lot of geocaching — you know, that game using GPS where you locate metal tins or plastic containers holding a logbook to record you were there, and sometimes small trinkets to exchange. It's how we would kill time on a cross-country trip. There was a find box near the roadside fruit stand. Flynn thought this place was interesting, so we walked around, and he found this tree. I watched Flynn put the package up there." She looked at the wrapped package. "So . . . do you call the cops and report you found a box, or do we get to take it with us to Chicago to deal with there?"

"Is there anything else hidden around here?"

"Not that I know of."

He made a decision that getting to Chicago rather than explaining matters to local authorities was the better part of wisdom. "Put it in one of your gym bags, and I'll ask Paul what he wants me to do with it."

"You're killing me here, Matthew. You're a robbery cop. You don't want to open it, search the database of stolen goods, find the owner, learn how it was originally taken, talk with the insurance company that probably paid out on the claim, be the one to return the stolen property to its rightful owner, see her face light up when you return her jewelry?"

He would enjoy every bit of doing just that, but his shrug belied it. "Retired cop."

"Un-retire. You're dying to get back on the job with something interesting, and you're holding interesting."

He was more intrigued by what this item told him about her. "How many more stolen items are stashed somewhere you might be able to find?"

"Okay, fine. A few. But I'm not climbing any more trees for you if you're going to be a stick-in-the-mud about it," she muttered as she headed back to the road.

He laughed, jogged after her, dropped his arm casually around her shoulders, and was pleased when she didn't flinch or shift away. "I haven't heard that phrase in decades."

"Can we talk some about Chicago?" Matthew asked after they had eaten in Seymour and were back on the road. She was quiet but not brooding, and they shared a comfortable silence listening to music on the radio. He took a calculated risk that he could push a little.

"Depends on what you ask me."

"You need to see a doctor, Shannon, and it's a time-sensitive concern. I'd like to arrange for you to see a woman doctor who can give you a complete medical checkup, and for you also to meet with a woman counselor — someone who can give you some pointers regarding what kind of help would be useful to you over the next year."

"No."

He wasn't as surprised by the answer as he was by the speed of it. "It's in your own best interest to have these people in your life. It's strictly private. No one has a conversation with either of them without your permission. I'll even promise never to speak with them outside your presence if that would help."

"Matthew —"

"It's not a stigma to seek help, Shannon, and Becky proved to me the value of these early appointments. It's useful to have help from professionals who don't have the emotional ties of family and friends. At least let me arrange the medical work-up."

"It's not that. I know why you're asking. I'm not discussing my medical situation with you, but I've had that medical review. I went to someone I trusted. The blood work was extensive. I know every bone that broke and how it healed, every injury that's going to give me problems as I age. At some point I'll see a counselor to help me process what happened, but it's not an immediate concern. I'm processing it on my own terms in a way that is working for me right now. I don't need another voice in my head directing what to work on next."

Questions circled in his mind — who it was she had seen and where, how many bones had broken, what physical injuries were going to linger — but he didn't ask them. He pushed the questions to the side and forced himself to simply nod. "That was smart, going to someone early on. Did she recommend follow-up with another physician?"

"I asked for the facts and she provided those. She then offered her advice. I'm taking most of it."

"Good."

Shannon smiled. "Shift your thinking just a bit, Matthew. I'm an adult, able to make unpleasant decisions and do what needs done. I hate having to see a doctor; I thought that when I was ten and I still think that. I did so anyway. I don't mind you asking if something is on my list, questioning its priority compared to another item on the list, but I have a pretty good sense of what needs to happen."

He felt intensely wrong-footed and finally said, "Let me apologize for my assumptions behind the question, that you would be inclined to avoid medical care and wouldn't have done anything about it on your own. It's not that I thought you were immature — like my daughter, and needing direction . . . well, maybe I was feeling that at the edges. I'm not used to a victim handling her own needs, not when it's this close to the trauma's end. You're responding in ways

I would expect in six months, Shannon, not in the first weeks after freedom. I clearly haven't adapted yet to where you are — physically, mentally, emotionally — and for that too, I apologize."

"Apologies accepted." She reached over and briefly touched his arm. "I didn't know the day freedom would come, Matthew, but I've been preparing for this for a few years, and I've a working to-do list. I tried to anticipate what I could. I knew once I reappeared, matters were going to unfold quickly with a lot of pieces moving around. That's why I sought out your help, not because I couldn't handle this, but because I didn't want to deal with all these different events on my own. But the details themselves — most of them I've thought through."

"That's helpful to me, Shannon." He would figure out how to get on the same page with her. "Very helpful." Her reply told him she thought she was ready for this. That actually gave him a good clue for where the first emotional crack would appear. She was braced and ready for what she had anticipated, but she had little margin right now for the blindside surprise. Protecting her from one, buffering her against such a thing when he couldn't prevent it — that would be a good outcome if he could pull it off. "I like that about you. The fact you planned this, are facing head-on the difficult items like finding a doctor. I don't know how best to say this . . . but I'd like to be your backup when you have more of those hard things on your list to do, if you'll allow me to do so."

"I'd appreciate that."

"Good. Now, let me ask a different question."

"Sure."

"You meet with your brother. Then you meet family members as you choose to do so after that. Talk to me about the broader picture. Do you want to see a particular friend from high school? A best friend? Would it be helpful for you to have a conversation with someone from your church?"

"Friends from high school will have gone on with their lives. Catching up with them can wait until the news has died down. There are some I'd like to call in the first day or two after this goes public, say hi in person. But friendships have a natural lifespan, and a best friend will have to reappear to fit my present situation."

She shifted in the seat to face him. "I'll enjoy being back at church, but which congregation I settle in with depends on where I'm living, and I doubt I decide that question for some months. While I'm still unknown, I wouldn't mind going to services to sit in the balcony with you if we can avoid the church my family attends. Jeffery is a known face right now, and I'm not interested in calling attention to myself. But that wasn't the substance of the second question you asked. You want to know if I would find it helpful to have a conversation with someone from my home church — have someone to talk with about the tough questions my experience has raised."

"Yes."

"Your daughter struggled with her faith because of what happened."

He hesitated. "I'll let my daughter talk to you about that one day. I won't try to characterize her concerns. But it was a topic which did prompt a lot of conversations."

"Thank you for that — for respecting Becky's confidences. You gave an interview when your daughter was still missing. You were asked the question: 'What has this done to your faith?' You answered along the lines of, 'God is good, and I love Him. Right now, God is permitting a very hard thing. Why, I don't know, but I still trust Him. God will help me find my daughter.' That interview and statement stuck with me. That's one of the reasons I tracked you down. Do you still think that way, now that Becky is home and you know her story?"

"I do. I struggled with trusting God in the first years after she was home, knowing what Becky had gone through. But I still believe God is good and I do love Him. It came back to what I knew to be true. My faith today is firm in that."

"I'm glad. To your question, no, I don't require a conversation with someone from my church, someone to help me with what this did — or did not do — to my faith."

He looked over. "Your faith survived what happened?"

"Yes. You seem surprised."

"I think I am. Puzzled at least."

"My relationship with God is fine."

"Seriously?"

"I'm a cactus, Matthew. Not an orchid. They're beautiful, but they can't handle heat or a tough environment. The circumstances throughout my life have made me who I am. I can plan. Strategize. Think across long periods of time. Put me in a room with those who hate God, and I can still thrive. God has made me into a tough, battle-hardened believer. I am very grateful to have those eleven years behind me. But I used them. I chose to survive with my faith intact. I chose to come out strong and together. I endured, and now I'm going to thrive. I don't expect life to be easy. I do expect God to be there with me. He was during the last eleven years."

Matthew hesitated. "I'm not sure what to say."

She smiled. "I'm my own person, Matthew, with my own strengths and weaknesses. You just bumped into one of my strengths. I can think for myself. Hold on to decisions I've made. I believe certain things about God. I *know* certain things about God. A family of smugglers didn't stand a chance of changing my mind about that, no matter how . . . horrifying my circumstances became." Shannon briefly went quiet, then added, "I can tell the difference between the acts of a man and the acts of God. That's why I still believe. I could always tell the difference."

"You were hurt. Bones broken . . . and other violence," he said, alluding to what he suspected had happened. She didn't flinch from the comment. Her gaze held his when he glanced over. But it was the controlled gaze he'd seen in Atlanta, the enforced calm.

"It was men who hurt me, not God."

"God allowed it," Matthew said quietly,

going to the heart of his daughter's struggle with God.

"He did. And I wondered for a time if God still loved me." Shannon was silent for a long moment, then smiled. "I used to wonder how I'd answer this question once freedom came and someone asked me about God. It's not a conversation I think I want to have very often. But would you listen to my long answer, let me see if it makes sense to you?"

"I'd like to listen to whatever you want to say," Matthew replied, surprised she was willing to further open this particular door with him.

"I realized something, probably about year two," Shannon said, "that changed how I thought about God and what was going on. I'd like a featherbed world where falling out of a tree didn't break a bone, where a guy couldn't land a blow on someone smaller than himself, where no one ever got to touch me without my consent. That's the world I would have created. But God decided to create a world where free will was more important than no one ever getting hurt. There must be something stunningly beautiful and remarkable about free will that only God can truly grasp, because God hates, literally abhors, evil, yet He created a world where evil could happen if people chose it. God sees something in free will and choice that's worth tolerating the horrifying blackness that would appear if evil was chosen rather than good. I find that utterly remarkable."

Matthew nodded slowly as he considered her answer. "From the very beginning, all the way back to the Garden of Eden, human beings have had a choice," he agreed, beginning to sense how she'd settled this matter for herself.

"Can you imagine how marvelous Eden must have been? God walking with Adam and Eve in the evenings where they could talk face-to-face. God gave Adam and Eve that free will and a choice. He gave them one warning: eat of any tree that is here, including the wonderful tree of life, but don't eat from the tree of the knowledge of good and evil." Shannon paused. "I wish Adam and Eve had thought more about what *knowledge* meant. Eve saw it as a good thing, to know more. But how do you really *know* something? You experience it."

Matthew looked at her, realized how pale she had become, and reached over to cover her hand with his. He felt her suddenly shiver. "I got a nasty taste of what evil is like these last few years," Shannon went on.

"The sad thing about evil . . . we did this to ourselves. It wasn't God's plan. God expected, fully intended, for Adam and Eve to obey what He had said, to leave the tree of good and evil alone."

Shannon turned her hand under his, gripped it, seemed to seek and find comfort from that contact. "We're Adam and Eve's children, reaping their decision. We chose the knowledge — the *experience* of good and evil — and we found out just how bitter and dark evil really is. We experience it now. That's our reality. There's probably not a person alive who wouldn't want to go back and see that decision changed, now that we have tasted how bad it turned out to be. My faith survived because I realized God didn't *want* this for us, He never had. I'm passionately looking forward to a new Heaven and Earth where only good exists once more."

Matthew drove for three miles after Shannon finished her answer before he said, "I'm stunned at your reply."

"Why?"

He quoted a couple of her statements back to her, about Adam and Eve choosing knowledge, which brought about the experience of good and evil. "That's pretty deep theology, Shannon."

"Time was heavy on my hands; I had some time to think."

"It's wisdom." Matthew hesitated. "But it's also abstract."

"Then let's not be abstract. God didn't stop men from hurting me. Does that fact make God *not good*? I concluded that God was suffering as I was, but He didn't want to end free will or bring the world to judgment yet, so He permitted what happened. People hurt me, not God. He didn't divinely rescue me from the world I live in, even though that was within His power. He simply walked each hour and day of it with me, and promised me that justice was coming. And as hard as it was to accept, I reached the point I could accept it. God is *Immanuel* — 'God is with us.' It's enough truth to rest on. God has been acting honorably throughout history regarding what He wants. We're the ones at fault. God is good. And I still really, truly like Him. My relationship with God is fine."

Matthew drove in further silence, thinking about what she'd said. At last he offered, "Thank you, Shannon."

"For what?"

"For convincing me better than anyone ever has that there is such a thing as a tough, God-fearing, bring-it-on woman left in the world."

She burst out laughing.

He smiled. "I hope my daughter turns out a bit like you one day."

"God help you if she does," Shannon replied with good humor.

The conversation felt mostly finished, and Matthew accepted that. "I'm glad it's okay with you and God."

"So am I. I'm not saying there weren't some very dark stretches between myself and God. We certainly had our moments. But we worked through them as time passed — that had to happen early on, Matthew, or I wouldn't have survived. The strength to survive, the planning, the long-term game theory, the strategies — that was God and I getting inside the dynamics of this group. I did it with God. So you can mark off your list wondering about my relationship with Him."

He smiled faintly. "I'm like you, I appreciate lists. They keep life orderly."

"You're going to love my list then, because the next item on my agenda is to take another nap."

He chuckled. "At least you don't snore."

She looked distinctly embarrassed. "I hadn't even thought of that."

"You look . . ." he began, then stopped

and shook his head. *Adorable, cute, lovely* — all of them fit what he could say about how she looked when she slept, yet they weren't appropriate to the conversation. "I'm glad you feel like you can rest when we travel. Chicago is going to take a lot out of you quickly. I'd rather you arrive as refreshed as possible." He offered a reassuring smile. "Get some more sleep while you can, Shannon. It's the best use of your time right now."

She shifted around the pillow and settled back in the seat. "Thanks for listening to my long answer."

"I'm blessed by it," he said quietly. She'd understood God at a deep level. She was right. Her relationship with God was fine.

"What did I miss?" Shannon asked sleepily.

Matthew glanced over. "Not much. Some cows. Small towns. We're still in the state of Indiana."

She straightened in the seat, stretched her arms out, looked around at the dark countryside, broken only by the occasional dusk-to-dawn farmhouse light.

"I bought you a hot chocolate." Matthew nodded to the covered cup he had picked up for her at the last truck stop. She hadn't stirred when he pulled in and shut the car off.

She slipped off the plastic lid. "I thought we were going to stop around nine tonight."

"We were. Nine came and went, you were sleeping heavy, traffic was running light, so I decided to keep driving. I'm thinking we'll stop near Valparaiso, find a hotel for twelve hours, let you get a good meal or two, and me a comfortable bed."

"Maybe find a place with a pool?"

She asked it casually, but he shot her a look, thinking it had been asked almost too casually. "Sure. Got a swimsuit tucked in one of those gym bags?"

"Yep. I like to swim."

He was surprised she still liked the water, given how close she'd been to drowning at least twice in her life. "I'm glad to hear it. Swimming doesn't beat up your knees the way running does."

"Do you like running marathons?"

"I was wondering if you were ever going to mention my *Boston Marathon #9* shirt," he replied to encourage the conversation.

She smiled. "I noticed the shirt. And your pride wearing it."

"Becky's gift. I like the accomplishment of finishing a marathon. I like the running. But do I like mile seventeen when my body says 'stop'? I can't say I run races for the enjoyment of that moment. I run because it's time to think, and I prefer being outdoors rather than lifting weights in some room. Besides, running the Boston Marathon is a rite of passage. You live in Boston, you try to qualify and run that race."

"That makes sense."

She fell back into silence. He let it linger for a long while, glanced over to see a faintly pensive expression on her face. "Something on your mind?"

"Not particularly."

"You've said quite a bit over the last day. I'm grateful for that trust, Shannon. I don't take it lightly."

"You're surprisingly easy to talk to."

"What's got you most worried?" he asked, keeping his tone light. "Sorting out what happened in the past that led to your abduction? Talking with your family? Dealing with the cops to locate the people who now need apprehending? Coping with the press?"

"Yes."

He laughed softly. "Yeah, I suppose I asked for that."

Silence returned, and this time Matthew didn't try to break it. It was a nice night for a drive. Clear skies. Bright stars. Brighter moon. Peaceful. He found a radio station playing mostly jazz, let the music fill the quiet.

Soon Shannon drifted back to sleep.

The hotel's pool room smelled heavily of chlorine, the water calm under the overhead lights. The place was empty at just after midnight. On the table just inside the door, Matthew put down a carryout container from the restaurant around the corner. Roast beef on rye, French fries — comfort food for when stress was high. His was increasing as they got closer to Chicago.

Shannon came into the pool area ten minutes later, a towel draped around her shoulders, wearing a black one-piece swimsuit and matching jacket. "Eat first, then sleep. I like your priorities. But you don't need to watch out for me, Matthew."

"I like to unwind for a bit before I turn in, and I'd rather do that here than with the TV."

She nodded, put her towel and wrap on a nearby lounge chair, and walked over to the poolside to sweep a foot in the water. "Not bad." She stepped off the side into the water, going under the surface, reappeared, pushed wet hair away from her face, then rolled onto her back for a lazy kick toward the deep end. "The water's warm," she told him as she started swimming laps.

He ate the sandwich and fries, not particularly hungry but not interested in the food going cold. She looked comfortable swimming that crawl stroke, but flipping for a turn seemed awkward for her — it kept breaking her rhythm. She'd reach the wall before she was ready for it, strike her hand on the edge, or flip for a turn and be early so her feet gave only a small push off the wall. Shannon obviously wasn't accustomed to a pool.

She seemed determined to sort out the turn problem. She kept swimming laps, and he soon lost count of them. He finished his meal and moved to a lounge chair to lie back and close his eyes for a while, opening them occasionally to watch her swim. He checked his watch and finally got up and moved to the poolside, hunkered down to watch as she made another awkward turn. "You okay, Shannon?"

His question startled her and she stopped to tread water. "Sorry, what did you say?"

"Are you chasing away bad memories or just getting some exercise? You've been swimming laps for almost an hour."

"I wasn't really thinking about anything in particular. I just like to swim. Actually, this is how I zone out and stop thinking."

"Where do you normally swim?"

"I'm sorry?"

"You obviously like to swim, but this pool length seems awkward for you. Where do you normally swim?"

"The beach. I'm definitely not used to chlorine this strong. It's burning my eyes."

*An ocean swimmer? The coasts? Gulf of Mexico?*

"I'll get out if you're heading back to your room," she offered.

"No, it's okay. Swim as long as you like. You know where to find me if you need something." They had adjoining rooms again, the reservations called in by Ann to keep their names off the records. "We'll do lunch, maybe hit the road around noon, if that seems good to you."

"Sure."

"Enjoy the pool while you have it to yourself." He wasn't enamored with the idea of leaving her here alone, but he didn't want to appear like he was hovering. If she wasn't in her room after another hour, he'd wander back to the pool on some casual pretext.

Even traveling at a leisurely pace, they would be in Chicago tomorrow, and with that would come the next chapter in this story. Matthew glanced back at the pool as he opened the door. Shannon was already swimming laps again. He wondered about the memories she was trying to avoid. He thought he might be seeing her first real case of nerves — and her attempt to avoid them. She wasn't as calm about what was coming as she would hope to appear.

# 8

On Monday afternoon, Matthew used the security code Paul had given him to open the door to a brick residential building. Located in the center of an otherwise downtown block of office buildings hosting architects, product designers, and marketing firms, nothing from the street indicated it was residential property, adding a layer of anonymity to the place that he appreciated. "We're on the seventh floor," he said over his shoulder as Shannon followed him to the elevator, carrying one of her gym bags and the dress she had bought. Private parking for the building was good for Chicago, accessible through the lower level of the adjoining building.

The seventh floor hallway had four doors, though only three had numbers on them. He walked across to 714 and used the panel beside the door to enter a second security code. As he stepped inside, room lights automatically came on. He found the inside control panel and reentered both security codes in reverse order and watched the security system turn green. He relaxed.

Shannon had wandered past him into the apartment. "Your friends found us a nice place."

He looked around for the first time. It was the home of a diplomat who presently was working in Eastern Europe. The distinctly male tone of the interior suggested that the man lived alone, but it was an elegant home just the same, with artwork, sculptures, framed photographs, leather couch and comfortable chairs, a multitude of books, and a recessed television. The most personal possession in view was a guitar braced against a stand. "Very nice."

"I'm going to check out the bedrooms."

"I'm told there are three. Take your pick." He'd be across the hall in the unnumbered apartment under renovation, the work stalled now for some reason. John had said there was a bedroom and bath still untouched, while the rest consisted of freshly plastered walls and sparse furnishings. For giving them both some privacy and providing a place he could meet with cops to discuss the case without bothering Shannon, the arrangement was ideal.

Matthew went to check out the kitchen here, see if he needed to bring in groceries. John must have shopped for them. He set out fixings for grilled cheese sandwiches. Shannon eventually wandered in and took a seat on a stool. Matthew passed over a can of peaches he'd already opened. "We will stay right here for twenty-four hours, just vegetate and be slothful."

She grinned. "Do you even know how to be slothful?"

"It's time I learned."

She ate a peach slice. "I like the plan."

"Do I tell Paul to call your brother, or do you want more than a day?"

"Tell Paul to call him before I talk myself out of it."

"Watch the sandwiches so they don't burn," he instructed and handed her the spatula. He pulled out his phone and walked into the living room. She was setting the sandwiches off onto paper plates when he returned. "Looks good." He helped himself to the bag of potato chips she'd found, lifted the lid off the dip.

She searched the refrigerator. "You're going to steamroll me on matters where I show the slightest sign of any hesitation, aren't you?" She turned, two soft drinks in hand.

"When it's for your own good," he decided. "You want to do this. If in twenty-four hours you've changed your mind, Paul and Jeffery can simply have a conversation about your case, and Jeffery will be none the wiser about what was really behind Paul's invitation."

Shannon conceded his point with a nod. She finished her sandwich. "I'm staying up late to watch the lamest old movie I can find."

Matthew grinned. He couldn't have prescribed a better choice. "I'll leave you to it. I'm going to do some reading. Does our host have an office in this place?"

"Second door on the left. The chair looks comfortable, the desk intimidating — it's the size of a battleship."

Matthew finished his own sandwich. "I'll head downstairs, bring up my luggage and laptop and the rest of your things, see if there's a current newspaper left in the rack. Do you want the security codes in case you have to get out of here for some reason?"

"You won't be gone that long, and I'm tired of knowing facts like that."

He found himself oddly pleased with her remark, the first sign her guard was coming down. "Go find your movie. Think of this as your first day of vacation."

She laughed. "You know, I think it is." She

took the bag of chips with her and went to check out the entertainment system.

Matthew set up his laptop on the oversized desk, gathered his notes out of his briefcase, scanned his working lists. He called Ann. "Do I dare admit we're now in Chicago?"

She chuckled. "We've got a conference room set up for Paul and Theo, with Adam York conferencing in. The case board is looking interesting. You're welcome to come over. We only want to inundate you with questions."

"I'll let you four do the heavy lifting, thank you, and hang out here with Shannon. It's a very nice place."

"I can imagine. I haven't seen the man's home, but I know him. He's a diplomat's diplomat, meaning he comes in to smooth the feathers of ruffled bureaucracies. His patience is legendary. He's tranquil while built like a Sherman tank. I can imagine his place has a feel of elegance and comfort. He lived among the Brits for quite a while, and their idea of proper protocol rubbed off on him."

Matthew smiled. "Buried in that was actually a pretty decent description of his home. When he's here, it looks like he's in relaxation mode."

"He's a good man," Ann added, then said, "I sent over an update for Shannon on her family and friends. Marriages, divorces, births, deaths — a lot has happened in eleven years."

Matthew checked his email. "I've got it. I'll print a copy for her. Thanks, Ann."

"She'll find it helpful, I think."

"What else do you have for me?" Matthew asked as he found more paper for the printer and searched the desk drawers for a stapler.

"Paul heard back from her brother. Does tomorrow night, seven p.m. our place work for you?"

He would have liked to give Shannon another twenty-four hours before the meeting, but it would work. "We'll be there around six thirty."

"What Paul told Jeffery was that the FBI is determined to take advantage of the election press attention to generate more leads and would like to coordinate when FBI experts might speak at one of his press events. Paul basically laid out a reason Jeffery would want to make a priority of having this conversation. Not that Jeffery needed the nudge. He seemed pleased and eager to follow up on the offer. He's speaking at a hotel near the airport tomorrow, gives a speech at five, and will come by here from there. He's off to St. Louis later this week, so the timing worked out."

"I like the approach. He'll be in the right frame of mind when he shows up, thinking about Shannon and in a hopeful mood. Maybe that can help with the shock that's going to land. I don't like the idea of him getting on a plane so soon after he sees Shannon, though. I'd like to have a conversation with him the next morning if possible."

"I checked his campaign schedule," Ann said, "and he's not slated to appear at any public events until Friday morning. It won't be hard to convince him to stay in Chicago an extra day or two."

Matthew could see the last pieces settling into place. "In forty-eight hours, what we're dealing with is going to be a lot more complex. But at least all the important items will be in motion. Tell me about the case board."

"Sure. We're still drawing a blank on who arranged to have Shannon abducted," Ann replied. "The cities where she mailed the packages to Adam tell us a few things about her travels, but they don't give us much to work with on her whereabouts during the last eleven years. The good news is those five names and photos are generating a lot of aliases and places. We're trying to sort out if we have any legal names in that list of aliases, see if we can get a handle on the larger family of smugglers."

"Has Adam begun showing those photographs to the rescued kids?"

"He's shown them to six of the eighteen children. All six had no problem picking out the five photos from a stack of images. Adam said the fact they are dead seemed to generate intense relief in the kids."

"I'll let Shannon know. At least part of this is ending well."

"Shannon mentioned a fishing trawler in the Seattle area. I've been searching to find old mooring records, Coast Guard inspection logs. If she can remember the name of that boat, I think I can do something significant with that information."

Matthew made a note. "I'll ask. What else?"

"If Shannon sees her brother and decides to stay in town rather than immediately head back to Atlanta, I'd like her to come to a cookout. Paul and I will be there. Theo. She needs to meet us, and it's the simplest icebreaker I can come up with. I'll invite some others so it feels casual. Maybe Rachel and Cole, John Key and his fiancée,

Ellie Dance. We'll have it at Bryce and Charlotte's place. One meal, she'll put names and faces together for people she can trust in Chicago if she needs help. No pressure beyond a 'Hi, nice to meet you. Do you want a hamburger or a brat?' After that, we'll see if she's ready for a sit-down conversation."

"When I think the time might be appropriate, I'll ask her."

"Ask me what?"

He looked over to see Shannon in the office doorway, putting a piece of candy in her mouth. "It's Chicago," he told her. "It's soon to be summer. Friends are thinking about having a cookout."

"Can I bring the potato salad? I'm good at making that."

Matthew smiled. "Ann, put us down as good with the idea. Shannon's bringing the potato salad. I'll get one of those cheesecakes you like so much for dessert — the one that comes in that red-and-white-striped box."

"Perfect. The day after she meets her brother. Say five p.m. I gather she's joined you?"

"Yes."

"Then I'll let you go for now. Ask her about the fishing trawler name. And tell her thanks on behalf of eighteen kids. What she did over the years was extraordinary."

"Will do. I'll call you back." Matthew hung up the phone. "Planning to share those?"

Shannon held out her hand. "Depends if you're into cherry-flavored sugar."

He took three of the candies. "I'm ridiculously addicted to all things sweet. It's arranged for you to see your brother tomorrow at seven p.m."

She suddenly looked sick.

"Wear your pink dress. Don't feel a need to say much."

"Okay." Her voice had fallen to a whisper. Even though she was facing him, he didn't think she was seeing him. Her thoughts had taken her somewhere else.

He reached over to the printer and picked up the pages, stapled them. "Shannon." He waited until her gaze focused back on him. "Ann gathered some info for you about what's happened with your friends and family over the last eleven years. When you don't know what else to say to your brother, simply ask him something about one of these people, let him talk."

She took the pages. Took a deep breath. "I can do that."

He circled the desk. "You're going to be

fine," he said gently.

"He'll want to know."

Matthew would give anything to be able to crawl inside the coming meeting and make sure her brother reacted properly, said the right things, that Shannon had the courage to be in the moment and not retreat behind her protective wall. "You don't have to tell him anything about what happened."

"I can't. Not yet."

"Then why don't you tell him the cops are looking at things first and would rather you not talk about the details with him. Tell him it's better if he can say 'I don't know' when the press asks him a question about you. Tell him there will be a time to talk, but you're not ready to do so yet — however you need to word it. Redirect the moment back to a question about someone on that list and stay with the present rather than the past."

"And if he asks why I don't want to meet the rest of my family, my friends?"

He leaned back against the front of the desk. "You can say fatigue, the emotions of it all, are too much to deal with a larger reunion right now. That you're in Chicago only briefly and didn't want to stun the entire family with your return until you could spend more time with them. You need to spend a few days helping the police, and that will require some travel —"

"Will I be?" she put in.

Matthew smiled. "Whatever you need as an explanation, we'll make that our plan for what we do next. Shannon, it's not the end of the world if the meeting tomorrow lasts only twenty minutes before you feel like you need to leave. Seeing Jeffery is a step, that's all. If it gets too stressful, all you have to do is say to me 'It's time,' and we'll step back, regroup, have another conversation with your brother in a few days, maybe by phone instead of in person. We'll deal with this transition. There's no list of things you have to accomplish when you see him. I think your meeting with Jeffery is going to unfold smoothly and be a joy for you both. I don't think you need to be nervous, but I understand why you are."

"It's scary."

"What is?"

"Losing my privacy. Being seen again. Knowing the questions are going to come at me in waves."

He reached over and squeezed her hand. "I imagine it's terrifying. But the thing about your brother is that he can keep this quiet — though that might not be easy since he's a politician."

She half laughed.

"But he can stay in the boundaries of what you want to have happen. Do you want him to tell others in your family you're alive?"

"If he says anything to anyone, the news takes on a life of its own, and within hours it's going to spill out to the public."

"Probably."

"What do you think I should do?"

He gestured toward the door. "Come on, let's go to the living room and get comfortable. We'll talk about it."

Shannon curled up in the corner of the living room couch. Matthew delayed the start of the conversation long enough to find a can of cashews in the kitchen cabinet, retrieve the vegetable tray she'd been munching from earlier, place them on the coffee table. He brought in drinks. He knew that having something in hand to eat and drink could be helpful — could buy a few moments of time to get past hard topics when otherwise the conversation might end rather abruptly. Matthew took the other end of the couch rather than a chair.

"I see two security concerns," he began matter-of-factly, "that arise from the news you're alive, plus a more general one from the magnitude of the press and public interest your case will generate. The two specific concerns: someone paid to have you abducted. That person is a threat if they believe you have information which will point the cops in their direction. Second, those in the smuggling group have a vested interest in your not being able to testify against them. If they could do you harm, see you dead, they would do so. Do you see the same concerns?"

"Yes."

Matthew rested his arm on the back of the couch, his body turned toward her, tried to read her rather closed expression. "Shannon, both these threats can be neutralized. You could give us the address where you were to be dropped off, and we could use it to identify who was behind your abduction. You could give us the names and identify photos of those in the smuggling family, so that we can locate them, bring law enforcement resources to bear, know who to watch out for in a crowd. The more information you hold back, the more likely it is that the individuals responsible for what happened to you will make trouble . . . or burrow into the shadows and become ghosts."

"I have my reasons for why I haven't shared that information yet."

"Can you talk about those reasons?"

"I'd prefer not to."

"How much time do you need before you think you might be comfortable sharing the information?"

She shook her head.

"Those security concerns come into play when it's known you're alive," he said after a while. "If we ask your brother to tell no one you're alive, not even your parents, we can buy another week or two. Is that enough to make this easier on you? There is security in silence."

"That delay will cause Jeffery problems."

"He's a big boy. He can deal with it."

Shannon pulled at a loose thread in the hem of her shirt. "A week or two may not change my dilemma. I know for a fact the people who held me are on the move and won't be easy to find. Only a few times a year do they assemble as a group, typically in November and again around March. There are two places, one within half a day's drive of here, and one on the East Coast where they often gather. Home bases, for want of a better description. They'd be deserted right now."

"So if we want to arrest the majority of the group, if we don't want them to realize what's coming and scatter, we should wait until they reassemble."

"That would be ideal. Yet it's really not practical to wait that long. That internal family dispute and shooting last year started something that won't be tamped down. Regardless of what I do, they're coming apart at the seams. They might not hold together another year. And I suspect long before November, Flynn will be causing some chaos for his own reasons."

"You said there are gravesites."

"Besides the five members of the family, I know of seven. They're . . . dispersed. Some are kids."

It hurt to take a breath. "I'm very sorry to hear that, Shannon."

She gave a jerky nod. "Before my time, but I heard the stories." She looked over and caught his gaze, shook her head, and changed the subject. "There are stolen items that can be recovered stashed all around the country. There's a long list of people the group dealt with that law enforcement should know about. But it's not . . . helpful to turn law enforcement loose on what I know about this group yet."

He thought she might have already told him why in what she hadn't directly said. "You're waiting on someone else to get clear of the group."

"I wasn't the only name on that cleanup

list. I'm hoping someone else was also able to get out."

"Is there anything I can do for you, somewhere I can check for information, a description or name I can follow up on?"

"I'll get a call. I've been expecting it for a couple of weeks. They're . . . late."

"Can you tell me about that person?"

She shook her head.

"If you can't talk more about the group yet, what about the address where you were to be dropped off?"

She lifted her chin and looked him in the eyes. "What if I give you that address, and cops end up doing something unthinkable like arrest my mother?"

He felt as if his heart were being squeezed. "You're truly afraid the abduction originated within your family," he breathed. "Did you overhear something?"

"I know someone paid to have me abducted. I know this group was dealing with child custody disputes in the years after I was snatched. I know they were to drop me off at a house I didn't recognize, in a town I'd never been to before. And I know my parents later divorced. I have no idea what happened to set things in motion. I'm not sure I want to know." She picked up the can of cashews and moodily shook it, took a handful. "When they couldn't drop me off and were angry about what to do, I heard them arguing, and some things didn't make sense at the time. But later, as I watched kids being dropped off in custody disputes, I pieced together some of what it meant. Worst case, this did start somewhere in my family, possibly with my mother. And that's —" she paused, shook her head — "inconceivable. But what if it's true? What I would want for justice and what the evidence might cause to happen may not be . . . equitable in my eyes. I give you the address, this moves forward in unpredictable ways. I don't know that I can take that risk."

"You're afraid of what the truth is going to reveal."

"I can deal with the truth. What I can't deal with is what might happen because of that truth. I don't want to plunge my brother, myself, other innocent parties in the Bliss family into twenty years of further pain while we visit someone we love in prison."

Matthew rested his head against the back of the couch, feeling the weight of that impossible box she found herself in. "You tell law enforcement the address, they learn who lived there eleven years ago, from that learn why you were taken and who paid for you to be abducted. You get answers. Those responsible get punished. Only you fear the punishment might land on someone you care about and be more than you want to have happen."

"Maybe my mother had an affair, and it's my natural father who lives in that house. Maybe someone paid, not to take me but to make me go away. Maybe someone thought they were protecting me by getting me out of Chicago. Maybe my parents were about to split in a nasty, bitter divorce and Dad was going to throw Mom and me out. I don't know. But I won't cause my family more harm by blindly giving law enforcement that address and hoping for the best. I can't live with the possible outcome.

"There's mercy and forgiveness and justice," she continued, reaching for the drink he had brought her, "and I want — I think I deserve — to have some control over what that all looks like related to the person who put this abduction into motion. I paid for that right with eleven years of my life. If it's a stranger, throw the book at them. But if it was from within my family . . . I simply can't put blind justice into motion. I'm the one likely to be hurt the most by that outcome. It hurts me and it hurts Jeffery.

"I can just see it, Matthew. My brother is

running for governor, spending a private fortune out of his own pocket trying to find me, enjoying time with the parents he loves who are good grandparents to his daughter, and the next week I'm back, our mom is on trial looking at twenty years, and his political career is over. That's not justice."

Matthew decided, given the unthinkable options she was already considering, his own conclusions about what had happened might not be the shock he had feared. He reached over and patted her knee in a small gesture of sympathy. "Shannon, I think it was a true abduction for ransom. But the person who did it wanted some deniability. So they hired this group to be the ones to grab you and transport you to somewhere out of the way. Then they made their ransom demand, got paid a lot more than it cost them to have you taken. You were supposed to be gone only a few days. Only the group dropping you off ran into complications, and they couldn't drop you off as planned. What happened to you was the unintended tragedy of a failed abduction-for-ransom scheme."

She stopped swirling the can of cashews to stare across at him, stunned. "You think my uncle was behind the whole thing."

"Actually, I do. He embezzled company

money and committed suicide before he could be arrested. But he was taking money out of the family business long before you disappeared. I think eleven years ago he was on the verge of being caught and needed a lot of cash quickly to cover up what he had done. Someone desperate for money would see a ransom amount as an attractive solution. We know your uncle delivered the ransom money. There's a suspicion he turned over some of it as blank paper, that he used some of the ransom money to cover his original theft from the company. It's assumed that he took advantage of the opportunity your disappearance presented, that he acted on the spur of the moment to cash in on what had happened, to get some money to hide his theft. But it's not a big stretch from that option to the possibility your uncle may have been behind your abduction from the very beginning."

Matthew tried to read what she was feeling and couldn't. "He set it in motion, thinking it was going to be a few days' disappearance, a ransom demand, and you're back home. Instead you went missing, the family business was driven into near bankruptcy by your parents' divorce, those proceedings triggering audits of the company's books, which revealed his embezzlement of company funds and led to his decision to commit suicide before he could be arrested." Matthew settled a comforting hand on hers. He so wished he could take some of this pain away. "It's ugly, but it's a lot more acceptable than the possibility your mother had an affair, that the person at that address is your real father, that someone paid to 'make you go away,' as you put it."

"I agree it's less . . . painful. My uncle is dead. It would be nice to have an ugly truth be historical." She shook her head. "I can't take more tragedy in my life, Matthew. I'd rather not return than spend the next decades living in more pain because of what justice now brings down on my family. Which is why I thought seriously about simply not coming back." She let out a long breath. "I can't take the chance."

"Shannon . . . give me the address. Let me help you find out answers and at least make it possible for you to think about this rationally. You *have* to know. You don't have a choice. What is done with the information . . . I understand the dilemma. But you need to let me look and put your mind at rest if I can. I won't tell anyone what I find. I won't give the address to anyone else. But you'll know."

She was crying, silently, but the dam in

her control had cracked and wasn't going to close. His heart ached for her grief.

"Forty-seven Kline Street, East Brisbane, Colorado."

He closed his eyes briefly. "Thank you."

"Don't tell me what you find. Not until I say I'm ready to hear it."

"Whatever it is, I promise, I will help you deal with the truth."

She struggled against the tears, wiped at them with her palms. "So much for the start of my first day of vacation."

It was too much for him, that attempt at humor while her heart was shattering. He shifted on the couch to turn her into his shoulder, very carefully rested his arm around her back, and felt his own eyes grow wet. "Eventually, it's going to be okay." He knew better than to promise it would be okay anytime soon. She needed to cry, and he said nothing else, just stayed bearing witness as her tears fell with a small layer of the pain washing away. Healing could come after the emotions surfaced, and he was relieved to see this first wave arrive.

He had an address. He'd know. At least he could protect from one of the two threats he could foresee. He very carefully slid a hand down her hair. Her tears were easing. When she shifted back, he let her go.

"Thanks," she whispered.

He offered her another tissue, and she disappeared toward the restroom. He leaned forward, his head in his hands. He'd ask God if he was being an idiot right now, the way he was letting her into his heart. He knew he should put up a wall to safeguard his own emotions, but he wasn't sure he wanted to hear that, so he left the question unasked.

He had an address. He got up from the couch and went to find some answers.

# 9

Forty-seven Kline Street, East Brisbane, Colorado turned out to be a three-bedroom, two-bath ranch house in a quiet neighborhood about two miles from a high school and four miles from a hospital. Matthew made notes as he read the results of the search. It had sold three times in the last twenty years. The owner eleven years ago was Sanford Bliss.

Matthew read that last piece of information with a looming sense of dread. He'd been hoping for a stranger's name, maybe someone with a record known to law enforcement. Instead it was Bliss, and that put him from the father's side of the family.

He needed to see a family tree to know where Sanford Bliss fit. He pulled up the case index, searched for the name, and came up with a blank. The cops working Shannon's disappearance had never spoken with a Sanford Bliss. Which made Shannon's comment about a cop car being in the driveway of the home where she was to be delivered stand out as even more unusual. It hadn't been an officer following up with her family members stopping by to ask questions. So why had a cop been there on the day they arrived to drop her off?

Did East Brisbane have its own police department or was it patrolled by officers from an adjacent town?

Was Sanford Bliss himself a cop?

Maybe the man went by his middle name. Sanford was an unusual enough first name that Matthew would have remembered it had he seen it in any of the files.

Okay, Shannon's family tree on the father's side. He picked up the phone and called his friend at the missing-persons registry. "Gregory, how good are your genealogy resources?"

"Decent. A significant percentage of missing-kid cases turn out to be family situations, so we try to know the matrix of relatives."

"I need a family tree for Shannon Bliss, as wide and deep as your system can build it."

"Give me an hour."

"Thanks."

Next, Matthew went online to the Colorado Newspaper Association, found the local paper for the East Brisbane area. He accessed their archives and ran into a wall — they went back only eight years. If the police had filed a report with this address, the only way to find out would be a paper search. He saw a link to request one, twenty dollars for an hour of a researcher's time. Given he knew exactly what dates to check, he would have an answer within a fraction of that hour. But when Shannon Bliss became part of the national news, the one handling the search for this name and this date was going to remember *Sanford Bliss* and might wonder what that search was about. Matthew saved the web page and took a different tack.

He called the East Brisbane Police Department and got a night-duty officer, a sergeant, and after a little tap dance of East Coast and mountain pleasantries, he got the answer he needed. Yes, there would be electronic records back that far should the proper agency request a search be made. Matthew added the number to his private notes. Paul could determine what a cop car was doing at that address during those first forty-eight hours. Which was a nonstarter until Shannon let him reveal the address to Paul. He needed some time to think about this.

He could hear Shannon in the kitchen fixing popcorn in the microwave. Popcorn sounded good right now and smelled even better. Matthew finished writing his notes, flagged the next questions to pursue, then left the desk and went to see if she was inclined to share the popcorn.

She had returned to the living room and was watching a Godzilla movie.

He caught up with the story line within half a minute, unexpectedly captivated by the now-amateurish level of special effects. "I thought they would have burned these movies a decade ago."

She held out her bowl of popcorn to share. "He's a national treasure of Japan."

"You're making that up."

She smiled. "Probably."

Her eyes were slightly swollen, and the smile was an effort, but she was making a best attempt to force aside the sadness. He moved to the couch to watch some of the movie with her. Scary monster movies had been the fun theme of his childhood, and he'd watched scores of them, but he couldn't remember this one. She shifted on the couch and found a pillow to put under her feet on the coffee table. When she sat back, her shoulder rested against his. Unintentional as the contact was, he noted it as significant because she didn't move away. He was glad, yet puzzled too. Some of the problems Becky had dealt with, ones he'd anticipated would be Shannon's experience, were not there, and he wasn't sure how to read their absence. He was grateful, though, that she was growing comfortable around him.

"If I see one more pizza commercial," he murmured after three-quarters of an hour, "we'll have to order one and have it delivered." He took a final handful of popcorn. "I'm going back to my reading."

"You just don't like feeling scared when people scream."

He chuckled. "Something like that."

His phone chimed as he walked back to the office. Gregory had sent the Bliss family tree. He acknowledged with a thanks and then checked his email, found the document. Matthew pulled it up and scrolled around on the visual tree, tracing the father's side.

Sanford Bliss was a cousin of Shannon's father. He was deceased. Matthew stared at the square and the listed years of births and deaths and whispered, "Huh." Nine years ago. There would be an obituary somewhere with more details. It meant when the house had sold eight years ago, it wasn't because the owner had moved. It was because Sanford Bliss had died. Matthew wondered who had packed up his personal papers, if anything was still around, like old bank account records or letters . . . or if any backup files from his computer might still exist on a CD tucked away somewhere.

He went back to the newspaper archives and widened the search to all of Colorado, looking for the name Sanford Bliss. The obit led the list, and he opened the link. No photograph, just a single paragraph. Complications from cancer. He had been sixty-eight. *And wasn't this a mess?*

Someone had paid to have Shannon taken to the home of her cousin on her father's side. The person he needed to ask about that was now dead. What had been going on in her family? Did Shannon know Sanford Bliss? Was this person a stranger to her? Matthew wondered if he dared ask her. Maybe if he printed out the family tree and asked her to talk about her family, worked his way over to the name as part of a list of names, she'd mention whether she knew him. He shook his head. She was smart enough to see through what he was doing, given she'd just told him this man's address. Probably not worth pursuing with her until he knew more.

Someone had paid to abduct her and have her taken to a relative. Why? To get her out of the way, as Shannon believed? To protect her? Or because it was a ransom and Sanford Bliss had been involved in that plan? Who else might have been involved, or had it only been Sanford Bliss? That was a new thought. Maybe this man had set the entire thing up. He'd hired the group to take her, bring her to him, have someone else working for him in Chicago who was to pick up the ransom, and he'd look like the hero for being the one to get the girl safely home. Only two things had gone wrong: her uncle took advantage of the opportunity and stole some of the ransom money, delivered blank paper, and the cops had been at Sanford's home on another matter, complicating the arrival of Shannon.

Matthew blew out a long breath as he pondered that possibility. It remained a kidnapping-for-ransom plot gone wrong with tragic results, but originating in an entirely different direction. What better deniability than to kidnap a girl who lived states away? It actually began to feel likely that Sanford Bliss had been the one behind the entire kidnapping plot rather than the uncle. If he could prove there was bad blood between Sanford Bliss and Shannon's father, it got even more plausible.

Did he dare tell Shannon any of this? Hopefully put her mind at rest about the idea of her mom having an affair and her natural father living at this address? Or would it only leave her with the larger unknown of what it all meant? It would just complicate matters for her if he gave her half the picture.

Matthew raked his hand through his hair. He didn't do well when shoved into a corner. He printed out the family tree, took the six pages and taped the edges to make one large square, and laid it out on the desk. He found Shannon's name and put a big red circle around it, capturing other individuals closely related to her. He picked up the phone. "Paul, I need a favor, and I don't want a lot of questions about why."

"Try me."

"I'm sending you a list of twenty names in Shannon's family — some are individuals already looked at pretty thoroughly, but others not so much. I need one of your best researchers on that list to tell me about these people — finances, business troubles, relationships, rivalries within the family, job details and travel, personal vices like gambling, alcohol, having an affair — anything you can learn about their lives, particularly back eleven years."

"You know how this got started."

"I know . . . something. I'm going to shake the family tree and see what might fall out. These twenty were either in the Chicago area, were in touch with the parents, or are in the right age bracket for something like this. I'd like to know details about who they are. I'll send over the family tree and the list of names. Theo might want to add another name or two. There's some urgency to this request."

"I've got a researcher. Send me the names."

"Thanks, Paul."

"How is Shannon tonight?" Paul asked.

"Talking. Crying. Currently watching a Godzilla movie. I'd say she's going to be fine with time."

"Godzilla, huh?" Paul said, sounding amused. "I'd say it's time to go rent a stack of movies. Need a break from being the only one with her?"

"I'm doing okay. Becky thinks what I'm doing is admirable, so I've got my own support network."

"Theo and I put together the draft of a plan to deal with the press once it becomes public. When you want to walk through it, I'll come your way, add your ideas."

"One thing — I think John gave us a secure place to tuck her away while she's in Chicago, but I'm not familiar enough with Chicago streets to be the one driving if we're either followed or the press is staking out locations."

"John's got a couple of people in mind to handle just that concern."

"Good to know. We'll be at your place tomorrow around six thirty. You're going to debrief the brother after he meets Shannon?"

"John and I are going to make sure he doesn't get near a phone until he's processed matters enough not to say the wrong thing to the wrong person. How he handles his wife is going to be my biggest concern. His parents he can simply avoid calling or talking with them for forty-eight hours. But however the situation begins to break once her brother knows she's alive, we'll handle it. Just keep your focus on Shannon."

Matthew appreciated that plan. "I'll have my hands full just with her," he concurred. He hesitated. "Paul . . . this is just a heads-up, no specifics. There was someone else Shannon thought might have been able to get free of the family. She's been expecting a call that hasn't come. And she mentioned there's a place within half a day's drive of here that was a home base of sorts for the group. Some of the graves she mentioned might be there."

"Did she give you anything else on the person she's hoping to hear from? Gender? East or West Coast . . . ?"

"No. But it's why she isn't saying more than she has. When she starts talking, I get the impression there will be a lot of names."

"I'll put out some quiet feelers, see if there's someone else, like Shannon, who they're trying to keep out of the news while they sort out what the whole story is. I'll get back to you with whatever I learn."

"Thanks, Paul." Matthew emailed the family tree and list of names, closed down his laptop, stored his notes, and cleared the desk. He'd done as much as he could deal with for now.

Shannon had already turned in for the night. Matthew debated a moment, decided to take the second guest room in the apartment — he wasn't comfortable being across the hall the first night she was in this new place.

His mind was even more tired than his body. It felt like a month had passed, rather than simply three days since the Friday evening she had appeared. He drifted to sleep wondering about Sanford Bliss and what might be discovered when detectives began digging into his life.

Matthew got up six hours later, ran a weary hand through his hair, thinking in equal urgency about hot coffee and a hot shower. He was facing a tough thirty-six hours. He knew the day was going to end with a very stressful event, and tomorrow could be just as stressful if the meeting with Shannon's brother didn't go well tonight.

He was aware she hadn't slept much — had heard her up in the night, another movie on low volume, heard her officially begin her day just after five a.m. He'd chosen to give her space rather than check on her. Just after seven o'clock he wandered into the kitchen to get himself coffee. She'd made a batch of oatmeal cookies; they were cooling on the kitchen counter. He had one with his coffee and hoped baking was one of her preferred ways to deal with stress. The woman made excellent cookies.

There was a piece of paper on the kitchen counter, and her neat printing read:

PRESS RELEASE

Jeffery Bliss, along with the entire Bliss family, is pleased to announce the safe return of Shannon Bliss.

My sister made contact with a retired member of law enforcement and returned to Chicago on the night of June the fourteenth. She is in good health and good spirits. I am grateful to all those who have helped in the search to bring her home over the last eleven years.

She is working with the FBI and Chicago police to bring those responsible for her abduction to justice. Due to the complexity and size of the organization that abducted Shannon and several other individuals, it will likely be several months before further information is made public on this matter. The authorities will release information regarding her case when it is appropriate.

Shannon is now recovering at a secure out-of-state location. She has chosen not to speak with the public until after the election, and I will respect her wishes. All inquiries to me and to the Bliss family will be directed back to this press statement. Thank you.

Matthew found Shannon curled up on the couch in the living room, watching one of the morning newscasts. He paused to catch the weather forecast before he mentioned, "It's a good press release."

Shannon leaned her head back to see him.

"Thanks. When the news gets into the public domain, I'd like Jeffery to release that, or something like it. I've decided I want my brother to stay quiet while some of this is being worked out. He can tell my parents, his wife, but leave it at that, insist they tell no one else. Two weeks from now, maybe three, he can make the news public if it hasn't leaked before then."

Matthew perched on the arm of the couch, drank his coffee, considered the plan. "That will be helpful to all concerned. Jeffery will have time to get his own thoughts in order, your parents will be past the shock, cops will have made more progress with what you've provided to them, and it will give you further time to settle. Have you heard from your friend? I heard a phone ring while I was shaving."

"The call was an automated callback activating a very accurate GPS app on the phone you gave me. We're going to need it."

Her list must now include recovering more stolen items from hard-to-find locations, and he was more than willing to help her out in that endeavor. "I told Ann we'd be at their place around six thirty, so we'll leave here at quarter after. John will drive us so we don't have to sort out parking."

"Tell me when it's five o'clock. I'm going

to try and ignore 'The Meeting' until then." She made air quotes as she said it, offered a smile.

Matthew smiled back. "I can do that for you."

"John's the one who arranged for us to stay here?"

"John Key. He's a friend of Ann's. I put his contact information in your phone. He does private security work in the Chicago area, is a silent partner with Chapel Security. I'll introduce you to John tonight, and at the cookout tomorrow you'll meet John's fiancée, Ellie Dance. If you choose to stay in Chicago, they are people you'll find helpful to know."

He got to his feet. "Would you like to spend the day being a tourist and wander around some of Chicago? A baseball hat, sunglasses, there would be little risk of your being recognized."

"I was thinking more a good book, and I'd make lasagna for a late lunch."

"Works for me." He hesitated. "There's a book Ann sent over, written by a reporter about a kidnapping case here in Chicago years ago. The woman at the center of it, Ruth Bazoni, is going to be at the cookout tomorrow. You'll have to start collecting new friends by some criteria, and I can pretty much guarantee she's not going to be asking you questions or be unduly curious about what happened. But she will understand a bit of the history. Hers lasted four years and three ransoms, and it got . . . bad. You're going to have a lot in common without having to say a word. She's married now, according to Ann. She'd be the kind of comfortable friend you might enjoy having."

"Let me have the book."

Matthew nodded. "I've got more reading to do of my own. And I'm thinking maybe a nap. Short night."

She smiled. "I wondered when you would begin to wilt under the weight of being my sole watchdog — for want of a better description."

"I'd prefer *friend,*" he said carefully with a little shrug and smile.

"You're becoming that, Matthew, or I wouldn't still be here."

"Good." He got her the book, then settled in the office to spend more time reading the case file. In twenty-four hours this was going to be a different reality. Her brother's reaction, her parents', would have significant impact on how Shannon coped going forward, and there was very little he could do to influence that except be there for her afterwards.

While reviewing his notes, Matthew came across a list he had begun on a page halfway into his yellow legal pad. He started to pass it by but forced himself to stop. Maybe it would be out of place and wouldn't do what he had hoped, but there was nothing wrong with the list itself. He added another item to it, then pulled the page free, folded it, slid it into an envelope and wrote Shannon's name on it. He dropped it on the bed in her guest room. He felt a bit like an idiot, but he didn't go back for the list. Over time Shannon was going to come to associate him with hard topics, emotionally draining events, difficult discussions. He needed to put something on the other side of the ledger, something light in this relationship. And the list was the only idea he'd come up with that might add that other tone.

I like to play Scrabble. Just saying.
I like it when Becky calls me to talk rather than just sending me a text.
I'm glad you still like God.
I see a strength in you I admire.
I'm also glad you are willing to cry; please don't hide the tears.
We agree on monster movies.
I like the fact you still swim.

You make good oatmeal cookies. How's your chocolate chip?

# 10

The clock by the door indicated ten minutes after six. Matthew checked to make sure he had enough cash for an emergency, that his phone didn't need a fully charged battery swapped in, located the notes he'd made about Jeffery, and slid the page into his pocket.

"I'm ready to go."

He turned as Shannon joined him. She looked lovely in pink. Young and beautiful . . . innocent, as though tragedy had never touched her. Matthew smiled in appreciation. He leaned over to a side table and retrieved a gift he'd bought that afternoon and hidden in the refrigerator across the hall. He offered her the sheaf of pink roses wrapped in cellophane. "I thought these might color-coordinate."

She buried her face in the blooms. "They're . . . very nice." She had choked up and was having a hard time speaking.

He'd hoped they would be balm to a wounded heart and didn't mind the tears she was blinking back. She was lovely, and if it wasn't a date, it was still a night for dressing up. He was determined to fill in the good experiences she had missed out on over the years in any ways he could.

He reached out and lightly brushed her arm. "Bring your roses along — Ann will have a vase. Let's go surprise and dazzle your brother with your smile, and that dress with its matching shoes."

She peeked over her roses. "I didn't find low heels."

"I'm noticing," he replied dryly. Vanity over practicality, he thought, and couldn't disapprove. He'd just have to make sure they didn't have to slip away from some sharp reporter tagging behind her brother — she sure wouldn't be hurrying anyplace fast in those shoes. The woman was all legs and athletic form, and the too-high heels only accentuated her attractiveness.

He wisely said nothing more as he held the door for her. Even the nail polish at the end of the open-toe shoes matched. In about five years, some guy was going to ask her on a date and get himself bowled over when Shannon appeared. Matthew was feeling just the edge of that power tonight. She did make an impact on a man, he thought. It was something he was actually grateful to see — she wasn't downplaying her looks.

She had come through what happened with a natural self-confidence still intact. That poise would matter in the year ahead. People would make a first impression and think either *survivor* or *victim.* Shannon needed to feel comfortable with being beautiful. She appeared to be tonight. And he was truly enjoying the image.

Matthew thought the Falcon home conveyed a nice mix of style and comfort. The fourth floor of an old brick warehouse from the turn of the century had been custom-remodeled, and it was spacious and quiet — perfect for the meeting this evening. He handed Shannon a glass of iced tea. "John will call ahead. You'll have some warning before Jeffery appears. Try to relax." He could see the nerves shimmering in her.

"I'm trying." She wandered around the living room, paused briefly to look at a painting. Arrangements had been made for John to drive her brother over from the hotel where he was speaking. On the return drive to Jeffery's home, Paul would join Jeffery to debrief this meeting.

"Try harder," he said mildly. "Your

brother is going to be happy to see you."

"I'm just . . . I'm ready to have this over." She settled on the couch and picked up a magazine.

Ann and Paul had left to visit friends shortly after their arrival. Ann had told Shannon with a laugh that their friend's young daughter was in love with Black and hoped for a dog of her own soon, so he was going with them. That remark had broken the ice, for it was clear watching Shannon meet Black that she was comfortable with dogs. Matthew thought Shannon would benefit from a pet as soon as she was settled somewhere — there was comfort in having a dog's company to enjoy. Shannon had been reserved with Ann and Paul but not particularly wary. She'd offered a cautious smile, as well as a genuine thanks for allowing the use of their home. Matthew thought if the first moments with her brother went as smoothly, this evening would be fine.

His phone rang five minutes later. Shannon was turning pages in another magazine and her hand stilled on the page as he answered. "Yes, John." She set aside the magazine. "We're ready." He pocketed the phone, offered her a reassuring smile. "You're going to be fine. They're in the lobby."

"Stay with me, please," she asked as the elevator came up. "I need you to remember the details of what he says, so I can clarify what I heard with you later."

"Sure."

They heard the two men arrive. Shannon stood and nervously clasped her hands behind her. Matthew stopped beside her, touched a hand lightly to her back. "Breathe," he teased in a whisper and got a smile from her.

"This way, sir." John preceded her brother into the room and then simply moved to one side.

Matthew had seen photos of Jeffery Bliss, had watched him on video at press conferences talking about his sister, knew he was thirty-seven, a confident man who had weathered a great deal in the years Shannon had been missing. But he watched the man pale and nearly slip into shock before a joy so intense it filled the room appeared on his face. "Shannon?"

"Hello, Jeffery."

He didn't ask her a single thing. He just crossed the room, wrapped her tightly in his arms, and held on like he'd never let go. "Shannon, I can't believe it. Welcome home," he finally managed, his voice breaking.

Matthew saw Shannon's eyes close as they filled with tears, and he stepped over and joined John to give them a moment of privacy.

Matthew leaned against the east wall in the living room, watching Shannon and Jeffery on the couch. They were half turned to face each other, not sitting close but still near enough to converse easily and reach out a hand. Matthew listened to the conversation, but mostly read the body language. Both looked more comfortable as time passed. Shannon's tension had eased considerably, and her hands were open now and in motion. He'd just heard her first laugh. Jeffery was past the disbelief and had moved solidly into joy, his attention so focused on his sister that Matthew doubted he was even aware of his surroundings. The evening was going both as Matthew had hoped and expected . . . and oddly not.

"I married Cindy Mae. Remember her? I met her in high school, brought her home when we started dating."

"I remember she paid attention to me, even though I was so much younger. I really liked her."

Jeffery grinned. "So do I. You're an aunt now. We have a daughter. She's two years old. We named her Ashley Heather after both our grandmothers."

He was pulling out pictures from his wallet, and Shannon looked at each of them, delighted. "She's beautiful."

"She's got a sweet personality, along with this gracious, almost regal smile. Keep those photos. There's more where they came from. Here's one of Cindy Mae from our wedding." He held it out.

"I'm sorry I missed that day. She looks . . . in love."

Jeffery laughed. "She has to be to put up with me." He slid the photo back in his wallet, and his expression turned more serious. "Mom and Dad are divorced now. I'll tell you more about that another time. They're still involved with the family business. Dad's an advisor to the board, and Mom with the charity fund. They love their granddaughter. Their health is still pretty good, though Mom's getting forgetful. Dad's still wishing he was the boss and had the energy to run the world."

"That's good to know," Shannon said, and Matthew noted she didn't follow that topic further. "You're liking being a dad."

Jeffery smiled. "I love it. I travel the state, so I don't always get to read the bedtime story or be there for breakfast as often as

I'd like, but I do have daddy duties — she especially loves riding on my shoulders when we walk the neighborhood. Cindy and I bought a big house that we've been fixing up, slowly but surely. We want a large family, and it's been nice to put down some roots in a neighborhood where we hope to live for the next thirty years. I'd love for you to come and stay for a while, move in with us if you like. There's a wing of the house already prepared for family who come to visit. You could claim baby-sitting privileges if you want an excuse to have Ashley to yourself for an evening."

Shannon laughed, yet she slid past his offer with a noncommittal "I'm comfortable where I am for now. How did you end up in politics, now running for governor? I hear you're likely to win. Good for you!"

"I got accustomed to dealing with groups of people during the search to find you," Jeffery explained, "and over time I became very aware of how difficult it can be to solve problems without good leadership. It's been an unexpected career, being in public service in a range of elected positions. Governor is a big step up for me, but the right next one."

Matthew suddenly realized what was off-kilter about this reunion. Jeffery wasn't asking her any questions. Matthew didn't know if her brother was simply being extra sensitive, if he didn't know what to safely ask, or was so overwhelmed he couldn't get his thoughts together. Shannon had been braced for Jeffery's questions, and they weren't coming. Matthew listened as Shannon asked about some of her friends, relatives in their family, and he finally stepped in. "Why no questions, Jeffery?"

Her brother looked over at him, then back at Shannon. "I don't care what the answers are," he replied. "Shannon is here. The rest is details."

"You really mean that," Shannon whispered.

"I've had only one prayer, that God would bring you back to your family, that I would have a sister again. I just got my prayer answered."

Shannon wiped her eyes. "I've missed you so much, Jeffery."

"I've missed you just as much," he said, his voice husky. "The details matter to me, Shannon, and the lack of questions isn't a lack of interest. But it's a matter of perspective. I have what I longed for — you back in my life."

"I don't think I can stay in Chicago. I'm not ready for that yet."

Jeffery simply nodded. "What can I do for you? What do you need from me? I'll gladly provide whatever you desire."

"For now, I just wanted to see you." Shannon leaned back against the cushions of the couch, studying her brother. "I expected . . . I don't know. For you to want to be calling families and friends, for you to be asking me questions about what happened. . . ."

He shook his head. "You arranged to meet with only me, and to do so in a place neutral to both of us. It's not that hard for me to figure out why that might be. I don't mind at all that you want to unfold what happens next based on what you need, Shannon. Many years from now you'll have told me most of the things I'm wondering about at the moment. I don't need the answers tonight. And based on the two I've met here, asking if you need practical help, a place to stay, security, would be pointless. I think you have two good men willing to help you in any way you're willing to let them. I'm in that same camp. Whatever you need me to do, want me to do, the answer will be yes."

"It's going to mess with your campaign . . . my return."

He shrugged. "Let it."

"The details aren't going to be pretty."

"Given we're meeting at the Falcons' home, I assume Paul Falcon is in the circle of people you're talking with about those details."

"I tell Matthew, he tells Paul. The information gets where it's needed."

He nodded and reached out a hand to her. "I'm your brother, Shannon. The one who has loved you since you were in diapers. If you want me standing between you and law enforcement, I make a great brick wall. If you want me to be the guy you come hang out with for hamburgers on the grill and some teasing about how smartly dressed you look — you look lovely tonight, by the way — I'm that guy too. You can pretty much expect I'd like to talk to you every day for the rest of your life. What you want our relationship to be beyond that, what role you want me to play in your life, is up to you. I want everything you're comfortable with, and I can be patient as that sorts itself out."

"I'd like your phone numbers and email," she said. "Dates of birthdays for your wife and daughter. Things like that for now."

He dug out a business card and wrote the info on the back, offered it. "I know the press follows me — will even more as the campaign gets close to the vote, but I can slide free of it. Whenever you want to spend some time together, let me know the time and place and I'll be there. If you're not in this state, I'll fly to you, no questions asked. I'll bring the family with me as soon as you like, friends of yours, whoever you want to see."

"Thank you, Jeffery. I'd like you to tell your wife and our parents about tonight, but work it out so they don't say anything to anyone else for the time being. There are some sensitive items still being played out. You can make the news public in two weeks, maybe three, if the news hasn't leaked before then. When this becomes public, there's a press release I'd like you to consider putting out that might help me."

"You have text for that press release in mind?"

Matthew had a copy with him and handed it over.

Jeffery scanned it and nodded. "Shannon, you talk with Matthew . . ." Jeffery looked over to Matthew. "Matthew *Dane*?"

"Yes."

"I remember now . . . Boston, you have a daughter. Becky, is it? I was relieved when she returned home. I couldn't help but have new hope for Shannon's return."

"That's right, and thanks."

Jeffery looked back to Shannon. "You talk with Matthew . . . Paul knows, John Key. Who else is on the safe list?"

"Paul's wife, Ann. A Chicago detective, Theodore Lincoln."

"That small circle is good. It helps to contain the information."

She shrugged. "I chose Matthew. The rest are his decisions."

"You found him because of Becky?"

"Yes."

Jeffery looked over to Matthew again, then back at Shannon. "Still glad you made that choice?"

She offered a small smile. "He's been just what I needed. He even brought me roses tonight. Those roses." She nodded toward the vase on the side table.

Jeffery blinked, then laughed. "And that probably does sum up things best." He folded the press release and slid it into his pocket. "You look . . . really tired, Shannon. So I am going to suggest we call it an evening, even though I'd like to stay and talk with you until the sun comes up."

He reached for her hand again and got to his feet. She rose with him. He gave her a hug goodbye, a long one that Shannon returned. She stepped back, wiping her eyes. "Good night, Jeffery."

"I like those words, *good night.* Call me in the morning and say 'good morning' — and then I'll have a matching pair."

She smiled. "I can do that."

Jeffery turned to Matthew. "You'll take good care of her."

"I will." Matthew handed him a business card as he walked him out to the hall, where John was waiting. "Paul's sharing the ride back to your home," Matthew said quietly. Jeffery nodded and stepped onto the elevator with John.

Matthew returned to the living room. One major step in the process was over, and he felt that weight slide off his shoulders. Shannon was sitting on the couch again, head back, eyes closed, a hand lifted to the bridge of her nose, either fighting not to cry or a headache — likely both. Matthew took a seat beside her, reached over for her free hand and simply sat with her. He'd spent hours with Becky over the years, holding her hand after doctors' appointments, crying jags, and days she was especially sad. Shannon needed someone to hold her hand tonight.

"I felt like a prized rose under glass being inspected by an overloving rose enthusiast."

It was such an unexpected reaction and odd description, Matthew squeezed her hand. "It's the pink." He was glad to hear her laugh. "You looked and sounded poised and sure of yourself. He's had an image in his mind of you at sixteen, and he just got walloped with the fact his little sister is alive, grown up, confident, and beautiful. I think you wowed him. He was observing you closely for any clues he could get — spent most of the night trying to read your mind, I think." He waited, and the silence stretched. He didn't know Shannon well enough to judge the fleeting emotions he could see. "You okay?" he asked softly.

"I will be. Just replaying the evening. The lack of questions from him really bothered me."

"It bothered me as well until I shared a long look with your brother. He's not a politician because he's bad at the craft, Shannon. He made a quick and immediate choice that *you* he was simply going to love. But he's going to hit Paul tonight and probably me tomorrow with all those hard questions and want straight answers. The man is being honest with you — he takes seriously his role as your brother and wants that relationship restored as swiftly as possible. He'll go to others for the answers to his questions, for the tactics and decisions and how this is going to unfold from here."

"He's handling me," Shannon said.

Matthew thought that summed matters up beautifully. "Yes."

She half smiled. "I'm going to let him. I don't want a conversation with him about the details. Let him go through Paul, bug you."

"We'll manage it for you, Shannon."

"I'm exhausted. Let's go . . . well, *home* isn't the right word, but I don't know what else to call where we're staying."

" 'Home' will do for now." He rose and held out his hand, drew her to her feet. "I do love those shoes." He circled them in a dance step. "One day when you're not so tired, we'll go out for the evening so you can properly show off the dress and high heels on a dance floor."

She laughed as he had hoped, and he shared a smile with her. "Let me get a wet paper towel to wrap around your rose stems, and then we'll go. John arranged a ride for us since he'll be a while with your brother."

"I'm ready to call it a night," Shannon agreed.

# 11

Matthew loosened his tie as he stood in front of the refrigerator and considered food options. Shannon had only pushed food around her plate before they left to see Jeffery. He pulled out the lasagna she had made. She had gone to change, but he wouldn't be surprised if she turned in without saying good-night. He was still running on an edge of adrenaline, and it needed to wear off before he crossed the hall to the other apartment and turned in himself. His phone rang. "Yes, John."

"He would like to meet with you."

"I expected he would. When and where?"

"His home, eight a.m. If it needs to be a phone call instead, he'll accept that."

"It's okay — that works for me. How did he seem to you?"

"He'd been expecting to hear one day that she was confirmed dead. He lost it for a few minutes on the way back to the hotel, quietly cried, mostly relief. Paul filled him in on everything Shannon has said so far. It didn't make sense to hold back the information. The details shook him hard, but he came back with questions by the time we reached his home. He struck me as . . . a good guy. For what it's worth, he took Paul's advice to heart on how matters should best play out for law enforcement's needs. There won't be comments from Jeffery about the case once that press release goes out, so I think it'll be safe to keep him informed on further details. He was asking good questions about Shannon, what doctors she might need, how best to handle family and friends."

"Any concerns?"

"Jeffery wants to put a lawyer in the loop, someone Shannon can call when she has questions — not necessarily to step in as a buffer. Paul gently pushed back on that, suggested Jeffery talk with her about what questions she has and then hand matters on to a lawyer when appropriate. Paul explained that the plan for the first few weeks was to keep Shannon's immediate circle to no more than five people. Jeffery accepted the point so long as he and Shannon are having regular conversations."

"I was expecting something of the kind. If

he can't be in on everything to protect her interests, he'll want someone he knows in that loop. I'll make sure he's hearing whatever concerns Shannon voices. Thanks for this evening, John."

"Call if you need me."

Matthew put his phone away and heated up a plate of the lasagna. He took his meal into the living room to find an old movie — Shannon had the right idea there. He found *Chariots of Fire* and settled in to be distracted. He was too tired to process tonight yet. At least his initial impression of her brother was good. Shannon had the first brick in place toward rebuilding a solid foundation for her future.

Matthew left a note for Shannon on the kitchen counter, hoping she would sleep in late enough that he'd be back from the meeting with her brother soon after she saw it. The cookout was tonight, which would cover the evening, and maybe this afternoon he could get her out shopping. It would be best to keep her busy. She had his number should she need anything while he was gone, and he noted down again John's number as a backup. He checked to make sure he had his phone turned on and headed out to meet Jeffery Bliss.

The directions John had provided led north out of Chicago to a sprawling early-era home in a neighborhood where trees decades old shaded the roadway, the lots had large front yards, and *Children Crossing* signs warned motorists to drive with care. Matthew pulled into the drive and parked behind a minivan. That his arrival had been anticipated wasn't a surprise. The front door opened before he reached the steps.

"Thanks for coming, Mr. Dane." Jeffery Bliss's tone was expansive in its welcome as he invited Matthew in, the oversized coffee mug in his hand and the still slightly damp hair suggesting it had been a rushed morning.

"Please, make it Matthew. I'm certain you've had an interesting night."

"I haven't slept much," Shannon's brother agreed with a smile, "hence the mega cup of coffee I've already refilled. I don't mind. I haven't felt so good since the day my daughter was born."

"That I can understand," Matthew said, remembering well the day after Becky was first home.

"Can I get you coffee, a Danish?" Jeffery asked.

"Sounds good."

Jeffery led the way back to the kitchen.

"My wife will join us in about twenty minutes. Our daughter has found that kittens are the new joy in life, and our backyard neighbor has four. She has to go say hello to them as soon as her shoes are on."

Matthew smiled. "Been there with Becky. Her love was ducks." He accepted the coffee. "I wanted to give you this before our conversation got started." He offered the documents he had copied for Jeffery. "The DNA test confirming her identity. The fingerprint analysis and photograph comparison. There will come a point in some press conference or interview when you'll need to confirm those steps were taken in the first hours after she identified herself."

"Thanks." Jeffery accepted the papers, walked over to a desk and put them in its center drawer. He came back with an envelope, held it out. "While we're dealing with practical matters, an ATM debit card and a prepaid credit card for Shannon. The statements will come to me. There's enough money in the account to provide Shannon some security and options. I'll keep the account topped off at that amount as she begins to spend it. Tell her it's eleven years' worth of Christmas and birthday presents, and she'll be doing me a favor if she would accept the gift."

Matthew pocketed the envelope. "She needs to hear the message behind the gift as much as she does the funds. She's traveling with some cash of her own — I have no idea how much. That will probably become clear over the next few days. I'm in the role of listening, providing some advice, handling logistics, dealing with law enforcement while trying to stay light on asking questions. I'm getting answers, but I'm in the mode of easing through doors as she opens them."

"Sounds like a real tightrope," Jeffery replied.

"My job is to help keep her together as this unfolds and get her to a good outcome," Matthew explained. He took a Danish and then pulled out a chair at the kitchen table. "It's a job mostly of patience. There are a lot of pieces she needs to turn over, and if I'm careful I can make that process less stressful on her as well as fruitful for the investigators."

"I'm glad Shannon found you," Jeffery said, pulling out a chair angled toward his. "Paul filled me in on more of your history with the Boston PD and Dane Investigations, Matthew. I'm not sure what my sister is facing right now, but I'm very relieved a man of your caliber and experience is there to help her figure out those next steps. She hasn't had even a month of freedom yet. I'm stunned by the implications of that. I'm aware that I'm walking on a lot of fragile ice right now, that it's best if my role in this stays that of her brother, that I let the questions that need asking remain with the authorities. But that's not easy, given how compelling the need is to see justice come swiftly on her behalf. There's a fierce anger in me that's simmering just below the surface."

"Having been in that role as a father, I know where you're coming from," Matthew replied with sympathy for what the man was feeling. "I've felt both that overwhelming joy . . . and the overwhelming anger. She needs you as her brother. You're the only one who can fill that role in her life. There are good people working to unravel what occurred during the last eleven years. Trust them to do their job. Paul will keep you informed on where the investigation is progressing. I can answer any questions regarding how Shannon is doing."

"I accept that. Paul's got a good reputation," Jeffery said.

Matthew decided staying direct was probably the best way to handle this conversation. "What you and Shannon need from each other over the next few days is what I'm here to work out with you. But one thing I've learned from my daughter's experience is that expectations may need to slow way, way down. Your sister is running on adrenaline right now, and her body will only let her do that for so long. Her recovery is going to depend on having a lot of days where nothing happens. The sooner we get to that point, the better off Shannon will be."

"That's what I want most from you, Matthew — advice. You've been here with your daughter. What can I do to make this transition for Shannon easier? What needs to be on my list?"

"She's got some very difficult things to tell the cops. If she's emotionally flat with you, not engaged, don't let it throw you off in your interactions with her. I don't know what is coming as she unpacks the last eleven years, but it's going to be intensely difficult for her, I know that much. You've got to be the calm in the storm, the normal in her life."

"My present world is rarely normal or particularly calm, but I'll work on it," Jeffery offered.

Matthew smiled. "You'll learn. Give her time, Jeffery. Shannon asked for your phone number last night, but she didn't give you hers. I noted that as significant. When she calls this morning, and she will, keep it casual — a 'Hi. It's good to hear your voice. What's in your day?' kind of call. Suggest you'd love to hear from her for a couple minutes every morning when she wakes up. Or that you'd love to always talk to her at noon every day. Whatever you suggest, make very sure you can always answer in person if she calls. Tell her what your daughter did the day before. Tell her about something you and your wife did on vacation. Talk about hobbies you've had, a book you've read. If you can't think of something better, tell her what you're doing that day on the campaign. Give her touch points so she feels like she knows you again."

"I'm filling in the blanks for her."

"Exactly. Think of her life right now as a pitcher of muddy water. She's got to dump out what she's had in her life, and she's got to refill it with something clean and good. You'll be the refill. Paul, Theo, myself, we're the ones helping her pour out the bad stuff. She'll be giving us a lot more of her energy and emotions — more than she will be giving you over the next few days and weeks — because she has to do that, but what you're building into her during those same days and weeks is what's going to be there after we're done helping her get the past dumped out."

"I'm the normal life — a wife, daughter, house, job, family — a life that doesn't have cops and painful facts to deal with," Jeffery realized out loud.

Matthew nodded. "Shannon needs to get to a normal life. She doesn't even know what that looks like yet. You're part of her answer. When she paints a picture of what she wants, do everything you can to assist her. Help, but don't push. Give her time to paint that picture — where she wants to live, what she would like to be doing. It will come. She's just had years where she hasn't been able to make decisions for herself, whether large or small, and it's going to take time. That's your role as a brother. You walk beside her. You *be there* through the process. But you give her space to define what she wants those steps to be and where they will take her."

"The one thing I can guarantee, Matthew, is that I'll be there for her."

Matthew was glad for that intensity and certainty. He offered a caution. "Shannon may not engage much with you initially. You'll know she's gaining capacity to deal with people when she offers you her phone number. She's overwhelmed right now, and she's exerting control as best she can over her world and how much comes at her. She loves you — this holding back has nothing to do with your place in her life. It has to do with capacity. She may need to curl up in a ball now and then, limit how much comes at her. Good stress, bad — it doesn't matter to her body, it's just stress. The best thing you can provide is to be emotionally the same when she calls you. The same calm, normal, interested, reassuring voice of her brother. You'll find over time she starts to lean against that and depend on it. Her calls may not get more frequent, but she'll become more engaged with you."

Jeffery's wife came through the back door with their daughter, and the conversation paused as introductions were made and Matthew heard about the kittens. When the conversation resumed, their daughter watching her favorite movie upstairs in her room, Jeffery's wife, Cindy, joined them at the kitchen table.

"How are your parents handling the news?" Matthew asked Jeffery.

Jeffery looked over at his wife, the kind of shared look that was a conversation without words. He glanced at Matthew. "I find myself in a bit of a quandary about how to answer that."

"I'm known for my discretion. If it's something that's going to affect Shannon, it's probably best I hear it before she does."

"Let me first tell you about last night," Cindy said, reaching to rest her hand over her husband's. "He came home and told me, then called his parents. To say there was a significant celebration last night would be to understate their reactions. They came over, and we talked for a couple of hours.

"You don't have to worry about this news leaking beyond family before you're ready to have it be public, Matthew. If we can't duck a question about Shannon, we agreed to simply say, 'The authorities occasionally receive leads which are promising, and we remain hopeful there will be a good outcome in her case,' then try to move the conversation to another subject. We can duck and weave around questions for a week or two.

"There was a great deal of joy in this house last night," Cindy continued. "It was the first time I've seen Jeffery's parents being anything more than politely civil with each other since the divorce. They both showed enormous relief that Shannon has come home alive rather than receiving the dreaded news that she had died and they needed to plan a funeral. So it was a good evening." She looked over at her husband.

Matthew studied the two of them, asked quietly, "What's the problem?"

"There's a problem, primarily with Dad," Jeffery replied, then hesitated. "Shannon is not his daughter."

Matthew went still. He didn't let himself show a reaction to that news but simply took it in.

"That fact came out during the divorce," Jeffery continued, "though it never became publicly known. Dad's not sure he's . . . able to see Shannon just yet, so her approaching me first was an enormous relief to him. Mom . . . she's shaken. She knows the truth is going to come out, and she's scared over how Shannon is going to treat her when she knows.

"I'm *certain* Shannon doesn't need this shock right now," Jeffery added. He pushed back from the table, got to his feet, paced as far as the kitchen allowed. "She and Dad were close. Have always been very close."

He shoved his hands into his pockets, studied Matthew. "I love my sister," he said abruptly. "Next to my wife and daughter, I love her more than anyone else in the world. So I'm willing to do anything we can figure out to help her. Maybe we can try to keep her return out of the press until she's had a few more weeks to recover, can be told this news and given a chance to absorb it herself. . . ."

Matthew knew doing so risked Jeffery's campaign once the press got a sense something was going on and learned Jeffery had stalled the news for weeks. He wasn't opposed to letting that fallout hit if it was necessary to protect Shannon, but the news was going to be devastating enough that a long delay might only make matters worse for her. "I'm not sure if that's possible."

Jeffery stopped pacing to lean against the counter. "There's no way to hide the truth from her," he said heavily, "which is what the big brother in me longs to do. I've spent the night worrying this problem in circles. Listen for a minute, Matthew, as I run through some thoughts, and maybe it will give you something to work from."

"Sure," Matthew said.

"My parents managed to keep it quiet and out of the official divorce record — the cops don't have it or the press. But my own people discovered the details when I was being vetted in anticipation of a run for governor. My father had arranged for a DNA test to be run on himself so he could check paternity with Shannon. The cops had done Shannon's DNA panel with hair taken from her hairbrush so they could put the record in the missing-persons registry. My opponent is likely to also find what my father did and may use it at the last minute in the campaign, especially if he's losing, to take a cheap shot at my family. Someone would eventually dig up the information because of the campaign, even without my sister's return. But it's guaranteed to be found out and made public once she reappears alive and people start digging into the entire story of my family."

"It's out there to be found. So someone finds it," Matthew agreed. Something like this didn't stay hidden.

Jeffery shared a long look with his wife, then turned back to Matthew. "We've talked about my stepping out of the campaign, but it wouldn't stop this information from coming out. The only thing I can think of that buys some time and helps buffer this would be if you take Shannon back to Boston with you, tell her the press here is too engaged given the political race, that she's better off staying far away from Illinois for a few weeks. Let me fly out there to see her and be the one to tell her. If she's not in Chicago when she hears the news, it means there can't be an immediate drive over to Mom to confront the matter, and possibly a family explosion. There's no question it's going to be a crisis, but I'd like Shannon to survive it as well as she can."

"It's an option," Matthew said, unsure what he thought about it, though the idea of getting Shannon out of Chicago before this erupted appealed.

"Two things that need to stay at the center," Jeffery continued. "Mom loves Shannon. And Dad loves Shannon. She's always been Daddy's girl. He just doesn't have the words yet to deal with the fact she's someone else's daughter too. That Shannon was thought to have died was his protective wall against the pain of having to figure out how to have a relationship with her when she's no longer his own flesh-and-blood child."

Jeffery turned his chair around and sat back down, folding his arms across the back of it. "Dad needs a few days, maybe a week. I think that will be long enough. He'll find his footing and come around. What I don't want is for there to be lunch tomorrow with my parents, where Shannon finds her father unexpectedly stiff with her. Or worse, after she knows the truth, Shannon and Dad see each other and they can't find a way through this. She doesn't need to be put in the situation of also having to grieve the loss of being Daddy's girl. He needs some time so he can adjust and be able to embrace her as still being his Shannon. We put the two of them together before that's possible and they're both going to get seriously hurt."

Matthew heard Jeffery out, then made sure he kept his voice level as he asked the question that had to be asked. "Do you know who her birth father is? Did he ever come forward?"

Jeffery shook his head. "Mom wouldn't say. He may not even know he has a daughter. I would have thought her disappearance could have led him to come forward if he'd known about her."

"Give me a minute," Matthew said. "You've given me a lot to weigh, and we need a course of action sorted out." He walked out to the hall where he could pace while he thought through the implications of such news. He ran his hand across the back of his neck. Getting Shannon past this land mine had to be his number one priority. How could that unfold with the highest safety margin — and when? He was recalling everything Shannon had told him about her family, about her mother, her suspicions, and felt sick as he put the pieces together. He didn't like the answer he came up with, but it was the only one that seemed to best protect Shannon.

He returned to the kitchen and leaned against the doorjamb. "It's going to have to be you who tells her, Jeffery, and it's got to be done before she learns about it from anyone else. I'm not able to share information Shannon has told me in confidence, but there are crosscurrents going on related to this news. How this all is going to impact her is . . . worrisome to me."

"It's going to be hard for her to hear," Cindy said, her own concern apparent.

"Very hard," Matthew agreed. "And I'm thinking she must be told sooner rather than later. Tomorrow evening is what I'm thinking. I'll bring her by around nine, she can look in on her sleeping, beautiful niece, and then, Jeffery, you need to tell her. From there I'll take her on a long drive and help her deal with it. If you can show me what was said in the divorce proceedings, if there was an admission or copy of this DNA test, or just an allusion to this fact . . . however it unfolded, that would be useful to have."

Her brother had risen to his feet. "Matthew —"

"I can't explain, Jeffery. Trust me when I say it's an incredibly serious set of circumstances or I wouldn't be jumping time like this. My only priority here is Shannon. I believe I can get her through it, but you'll have to let me orchestrate how things go. Time isn't going to help matters. This absolutely can't be something she learns anywhere else. And if the news is delayed, the broken trust may never be repaired. Worst-case scenario, Shannon disappears. I've got to finesse this to avoid that outcome."

"I feel like I just got my sister back, and I'm going to lose her again," Jeffery said, a catch in his voice.

"You tell her you love her, you tell her the news, you tell her again you love her, and then you let her go deal with what just hit her. She's a survivor, Jeffery. What I'm afraid could happen is that she looks at you with blanked emotions, says 'okay,' then comments that she likes what you've done with the house, that it feels like a nice home, and never mentions the matter to you again. That's what I'm trying to avoid."

His wife was pale, but she rose to stand with Jeffery. "Tomorrow night, nine o'clock," she said. "We'll welcome Shannon into our home and make sure she knows she has a forever kind of welcoming place here. She's loved, Matthew. We'll make sure that gets through before any of this has to be said."

"Good. That's what she needs to hear."

Jeffery's phone rang.

They all watched as he picked it up and looked at the screen. "It's Shannon."

Because Jeffery was way too churned up to keep the rough emotion out of his voice, Matthew stepped in and said, "Remember — calm, normal, emotionally level."

Jeffery took the direction, drew a deep breath, and firmed up with a nod. He strode toward the living room as he answered the call. "Hey, Shannon. Good morning. Had breakfast yet or are you being lazy and sleeping in?" he asked, his smile projecting in his voice. "Ashley told me over breakfast that just one kitten isn't going to do because she's got too much love for just one. The neighbor has four. I think our little lawyer is angling for at least two. Want the other two? I think at least one is a ginger tom like that cat we used to have when we lived over on Court Circle. Do you remember his name?" He paused to listen. "Peanuts, yes! I figured you would know it. I'm getting old, Shannon. I'm about to become a cat owner." He laughed. "No, you don't get to help my daughter make her case. She's already got me wrapped around her little finger."

Matthew glanced over as Jeffery's wife

stopped beside him, rested her hand on his arm. "He's a born politician. He can be boiling mad over some news, then slide on a genuine smile to greet someone the next moment. Both emotions are true. I didn't understand that for the first few years I knew him. I thought most of the kindness and smiles were just him being polite. But he lives in the moment that is in front of him, and unlike most people he can switch from minute to minute."

"It's impressive to watch."

"He loves his sister. He's devoted his life to getting her back. Shannon will be safe with him. Whatever is necessary, Jeffery will do it. He's already got a clear hierarchy in his head — his wife, his daughter, his sister, then his parents."

"What he's offering Shannon right now — that's how she gets through this," Matthew pointed out. "There's nothing as simple as kittens in her life right now. She needs to borrow that from him while all the painful pieces shake out into the light."

"He'll give it," Cindy replied. "Head on back, Matthew, be there as she gets her day started. I'll tell Jeffery you'll be in touch tomorrow morning."

It was good advice and probably best. "Thanks." He silently took his leave of Jeffery with a raised hand and headed out to rejoin Shannon.

# 12

Matthew entered the security code at the apartment door, opened it, out of habit dropped his keys on the side table, and stepped out of his shoes. He knew Shannon was up. He made a point of thumbing through the newspaper as he went to find her. Casual body language could hopefully cover some of the stress. Shannon was seated at the kitchen table, eating a bowl of Cheerios. Peeled and chunked potatoes were boiling on the stove. It looked like she was serious about making potato salad for the cookout tonight.

"How was my brother this morning?"

Matthew spread out the sports section on the table and pulled out a chair. "He said that next to the day his daughter was born, seeing you was the happiest day in his life."

She smiled. "Nice." She got up to take her bowl to the sink, stabbed a fork into a potato, turned off the heat. "We need to make a road trip today. We'll be back before the cookout at five, but we should get on the road soon. I'm sorry, I can't tell you why in advance."

Anything that diverted the conversation from her brother was fine with him. "I can take you wherever you'd like to go. But I'd be more comfortable if I could touch base with Paul occasionally, let him know our location."

"That's fine."

She put together the potato salad, slid it into the refrigerator to chill, then went to find her tennis shoes. Matthew swallowed two aspirins and hoped the day did not come with any more hard surprises.

It was a quiet trip heading north away from Chicago. Shannon gave him directions occasionally, but otherwise sat quiet, lost in thought. It bothered him, but he chose not to interrupt the silence. Not quite two hours after their trip began, they entered the small town of Leesburg, Illinois, population twelve thousand. They passed nice subdivisions with new construction, a bank, grocery store, pharmacy, crossed a railroad track, and entered what looked like an older, less prosperous side of town.

"Take a left at the stop sign," Shannon directed.

The homes were mostly two-story with porches, weathered white paint in need of touching up. Blocks passed. The homes became one-story with a detached garage in the back. "At the next stop sign, take a left, and we'll be heading out of town."

They were soon surrounded by more cornfields than houses. He had to ask, "Where are we going?"

"It's about three more miles on this road."

He checked the odometer and began to mark off the miles.

Shannon touched his arm. "Up ahead, on the left."

"The cemetery?"

"Yes."

He found a place to pull off the road. Shannon got out of the car. He joined her.

"We're looking for a woman named Eddie Malleton." Shannon began walking lines of gravestones. It was an old cemetery in the country, mostly full, set between two sizable fields of corn and beans. Matthew noted some of the gravesites went back a hundred years or more, and some monuments were several feet high, ornate with figures and spires and angels with spread wings. It would be an interesting place to visit if it weren't for the fact Shannon was searching for a marker relevant to her past.

"Here it is," Shannon called. He walked over to stand beside her. Eddie Malleton's resting place lay beneath a monument resembling a square tower topped with a brass dome. Shannon leaned against the headstone, and when it rocked back on its base, she nodded to the other side. "Hold this for me, this angle, like I'm doing."

Matthew grasped the stone, pushed against it, and held the angle steady. She reached under the exposed lip and pulled out a white butcher-paper-wrapped package about four by six inches in size. He should have been expecting something like this, but he was still startled. "What is that?"

"One of Flynn's private hideaways."

He carefully let the stone drop back in place. Shannon unwrapped the paper, then multiple layers of plastic wrap, to reveal a thick stack of the old-version twenty-dollar bills and a sealed, standard-size white envelope with a bulge at one end. Shannon opened the envelope and pulled out a deposit slip and a key for a safe-deposit box. "The bank in town we passed by," she said, reading the name.

"I wonder where we're going next?" Matthew asked dryly.

She handed him the deposit slip with the number 917 written on it.

"We can't access the box without a warrant," he said.

"I'll be on the signature card."

"You've been here before?"

"Not in the bank. Flynn had his own way of getting things finessed. I signed a lot of signature cards that he'd bring to me and deliver back. It wasn't uncommon for him to set up five deposit boxes in an area when he would slip away to conduct his own business. What name I'm under is the more critical question."

"We should make a call, Shannon. At least talk to the bank manager before we show up."

"And have what I need to recover be pulled into evidence by the local cops? I'm not opposed to turning things we recover over to law enforcement, but you need to give me some leeway here or I'm going to walk away and recover these things without you. Some of what I'm looking for is personal enough I would ditch you if I had to."

"Please don't do that, Shannon, not over this. We'll work out any issues that come up."

"After I open the box and we see what's inside, you can make the decision on what to do next. I promise, if you insist I stop, I'll do so and let you make some calls."

"What do you think is in the box?"

"That depends on whether Flynn has been here in the last few years."

"Let's go find out."

The bank was on Main Street. He parked at the curb next to a bench and flagpole. The breeze fluttered the flag above them as they walked up the sidewalk to the bank entrance. "Let me do the talking, please," Shannon requested.

It was a small bank: a counter with three teller windows, two employees with desks just off the lobby, and three private offices opposite the entrance. Two tellers were working the counter at the moment. A sign indicated their vault and safe-deposit boxes were located to the left.

Shannon moved to the first free teller. She set a key on the counter and smiled. "I'd like to access a safe-deposit box, please. Number 917."

"Could I see some ID?"

"Sure." Shannon pulled out a change purse from her canvas bag and offered a driver's license.

"Thank you, Ms. White. I'll meet you back at the vault. Will you require a privacy booth today?"

"Yes."

The teller nodded. "One moment while I

get the keys."

Signing the check-in card, handing over the key, getting the box retrieved and brought to one of the two privacy booths took five minutes. Shannon turned the check-in card so Matthew could see that the name above hers was dated three years ago and was illegible. "You want to open the box?" Shannon offered when they were alone.

Matthew nodded toward it. "Go ahead."

She lifted the lid. The box held a slightly bulky nine-by-twelve-inch manila envelope. "Good, it's still here. Flynn's emptied this box, I think, as I would have expected to find something of his, if only a few cigars. That envelope is mine, my handwriting, my real name — can I have it? I know what it contains."

"Yes."

She pulled out the envelope, unwrapped the thread tie, slid out the contents. A well-worn small book, covered in blue fabric, with a date embossed on the corner in gold script. It was eleven years old.

"My diary, from the month I was taken. I had it in my backpack in the car. They let me keep it." She was quiet for a long moment, then glanced over, met his gaze, and held the volume out to him. "You should probably read this."

He accepted it, but she didn't release her hold. "I have two conditions: I don't want to talk about it, and I don't want you to give it to the cops unless I make the decision to do so."

He knew the implications of what she was offering. "Agreed."

She closed the safe-deposit box. "This was a casual drop site. Flynn would use it for his personal business matters. He'd occasionally store things for me — a diary, small objects that had some sentimental value."

They left the bank together. She said, "You can have someone find out who paid the safe-deposit box storage fees and pull the signature cards, but I can tell you right now the inquiries will lead to a dead end. And just looking may trip an alert he has set up. Don't pursue this location just yet. You'll have numerous other storage locations to unwrap soon enough."

"I trust your judgment, Shannon." Rather than head to the car, he pointed to a corner store to get a fountain drink to take along. "Is there anything else around this area we should investigate today?"

"No. Let's get back to town for the cookout. Unless you'll let me back out."

"They're friendly people," he assured her. "I think you'll be glad you went tonight, but I'm not going to insist."

"We can leave when I want?"

"No questions asked, we leave whenever you wish," he said. "Becky and I had this deal. I could choose the place, the event, and she could choose the amount of time. She didn't have to explain to me why she wanted to go home. Over time I started figuring out patterns I could predict. Sometimes it would be the dark corners in a restaurant, or smells could be a trigger, but most of the time it was a nervous stomach bothering her. She was hypervigilant for a long while to the feeling of being watched."

"I'm sorry that was her experience, Matthew."

"It'll be helpful for you to meet these people or I wouldn't be suggesting we go. But you're the one sorting out the impact of what's happening. I'm not going to feel let down or disappointed if you want to change how this is unfolding. I'll work with your decisions, Shannon. You're going to get through the next few weeks intact if it's the only thing I can promise you."

She had begun to smile. "I like that about you. That I'm in that circle you're going to care about and protect, like some knight of old in a definition of chivalry."

"Are you surprised?"

"No. I'm pretty good at reading people. You've got 'Becky II' written over my name. It's why you're in Chicago with me, disrupting your own life, rather than in Boston. It's . . . helpful to me to know that this is personal to you, not just business, that it matters to you that this unfolds in a safe way. I'm frankly taking advantage of that. I should be excusing you to get back to your life, but I'm selfish enough that for now I want you to stay."

Matthew put his arm around her shoulders and gave her a friendly hug. "You couldn't budge me if you tried." He opened the door to the store. "Find us drinks, make mine something orange or cherry. I'll get some snacks."

"No more pretzels. I've eaten so many of them I'm becoming twisted too. Cheese puffs. Cheese curls. Something cheese."

Matthew laughed. "I'll find something."

He went to review the snack options, his smile fading when he was alone. He thought about what she'd handed him: the diary from the month she'd been taken. The implications . . . he understood the trust she was placing in him. He had now been hit with two fastballs in a matter of hours

— the confirmation she wasn't her father's daughter, and the existence of a diary from the first month of her abduction. The contents of which were likely to hit him like a third fastball. He'd be reading that diary tonight after they were back from the cookout. He needed this evening among friends, if only to give him a chance to break up the stress landing on him. Shannon needed it even more — a taste of something normal, a chance to meet in a casual setting those she would be dealing with from law enforcement.

He found cheese puffs. The last time he'd eaten junk food like this had been in the days after his daughter was recovered. Cheese puffs, old movies, ice cream, Scrabble, all familiar favorites to fill in the hours he was spending with her while those shattered nerves began to heal. Shannon wasn't in nearly as bad a shape as his daughter had been, which was something that continued to surprise him. *Or she was in her own way, and she was doing a good job of hiding it.* He looked across the store to where she was filling drinks at the fountain, watched her expression when she didn't think she was being observed. *Hiding,* he realized. But also exerting a tough strength to get things done like recover that diary, then trust him enough to hand it to him.

Shannon would get herself through this, and he'd help her where she let him. And when the inevitable hard days arrived, when she wasn't managing as well as she was today, he wouldn't be surprised. He'd be as ready for them as possible. He walked over to meet her at the checkout counter. "Cheese puffs. And I might share one of my Twinkies."

She grinned. "I'm enjoying this break from eating healthy."

He put cash on the counter, accepted the change. "It's going to turn me into an early fossil. I already did a round of this with Becky."

She laughed, and he decided the rest of the day was going to flow by as she needed it to — nothing else particularly stressful in it unless she raised a particular subject. He had enough on his plate to mull over without asking her anything else right now.

# 13

Matthew stopped Shannon with a light hand on her arm before she picked up the bowl of potato salad from the back seat. "You've met Ann and Paul, along with John," he reminded her. "They'll handle introductions to the others. And, as we agreed, whenever you'd like to leave, we'll do so."

She nodded and smoothed the red-and-white-striped cotton shirt she was wearing with jeans. "Get past the weather, asking about any kids, what they do for a living, I'm out of conversation topics."

"I'll step in if it starts to get awkward. You can depend on that," he reassured her.

They were met by John Key before they reached the front door. "Welcome to the Bishops' place. Anything else I can carry for you?"

"We're good," Matthew replied. "Should I move my car or are we okay where it is?"

John considered the array of vehicles. "You're fine where you are. I want you to be able to leave first just as a precaution." He pushed open the front door for them and gave a quick tour. "Living room to your right, kitchen to the left, guest bath down the hall. We're congregating in the backyard."

John led the way into the kitchen. "Rachel, two more arrivals." The woman cutting a pan of brownies looked up with a smile.

"This is Shannon, and this is Matthew," John said, pointing to each with an easy smile as if she wouldn't know.

"Welcome to you both. I recognize that box, Matthew. Put it in the fridge for now. I think you can find space. Potato salad, Shannon?" At her nod, the woman beamed. "Excellent. A good picnic needs potato salad, and it's a project to make. My time today was limited to calling my husband and asking him to put brownies in the oven."

John filled a celery stick with Cheez Whiz, said to Shannon, "Rachel's the one with the pager going off tonight — she's working the aftermath of a bus accident that injured some high school students from a summer baseball league. She's good with kids. Her husband, Cole, is around here someplace

— he's the arson investigator on call this shift. We're taking wagers on who gets called away first."

"There speaks the man who happens to at the moment be on the job," Rachel replied, amused. She reached over to the array of drinks and tossed John a bottled water. "Find Ann's dog. He's around here somewhere and panting in the heat."

"Will do. I'll tell Bryce it's safe to put meat on the grill. Everyone's here but Theo. He's a punctual man, which tells me his date is not."

"I'm sure she's got other good qualities," Rachel suggested with a soft laugh. "Help yourself to a drink, Shannon. We've got everything from tea and sodas to lemonade. It's always a bit of chaos when this group gets a chance to catch up. You already know Ann and Paul. Come on through to the backyard and I'll introduce you to the rest. We like to eat and laugh and forget work for a while."

Matthew took the glass Shannon handed him, found she'd poured him iced tea, and they both followed Rachel through a sunroom set up as an artist's studio and out to a spacious patio and backyard. There were several conversations among small groups around the yard, a sweeping glance confirming to Matthew the casual, relaxed postures of friends.

"Shannon, Matthew, I'd like you to meet Bryce and Charlotte Bishop. They're hosting tonight's gathering."

Bryce stood in front of an impressive grill, his apron announcing his place as Grill Master. His wife was seated nearby in one of the cushioned patio chairs. "Glad you could join us this evening," Bryce said, then offered his hand to Matthew and a smile to Shannon. Charlotte stayed seated but smiled her own welcome.

"You have a beautiful home," Shannon told them, "and a fabulous backyard."

"Thanks," Bryce said with a nod. "We both work from home, so we keep tweaking this place to make it even more comfortable. This grill is a recent addition, hence a nice excuse for a cookout."

"It's your studio, Charlotte?" Shannon asked, gesturing with her glass to the sunroom.

"It is. I've been sketching life for a lot of years. Ellie Dance, John's fiancée, is around here somewhere. She manages my art, co-owns the gallery where my work is displayed. Want to come wander around, see what I've done recently? The guys are likely to take another half hour setting up the grill the way they're fussing."

Her husband just grinned. "Only way to have a respectable cookout, I say."

Ann's dog rolled to his feet from under the table. "Have you two met Black?" Bryce asked.

Matthew knelt to greet the animal. "We have."

"Don't let his lazy nature at the moment fool you. He knows these events mean good food with some errors coming his way. This is a guy who knows the word *steak.*"

The dog's ears perked up as his attention slapped to Bryce. The group laughed. "Don't tease him, Bryce, unless you plan to deliver," Charlotte chided, rubbing Black's head.

"Top shelf of the fridge, brats and hamburgers for us, a small steak for the dog. I know how to treat my guests."

Ann joined them. "And you wonder why Black wants to hang out over here. Speaking of which, where are your dogs, Bryce?"

"We've got two golden Irish Setters," Bryce explained to Shannon. "They'll be home in an hour," he told Ann. "They're out on loan to a neighbor who's starting a dog-grooming business. They're going to be the stars of his marketing materials."

"Nice work if you can get it," Shannon offered with a small smile. "Get pampered and brushed and immortalized, all in one sitting."

Charlotte laughed. "How true. Come on, Shannon, let's go find out what kind of art you like. Maybe I'll do a sketch of Matthew before the evening's done, if you want something to tease him about. Ann, bring Ellie. We'll leave the guys to their grilling."

Matthew shared a brief look with Shannon and thought she'd found her role for the night — amused listener to other people's stories. She'd be okay. It was an evening she desperately needed, among people who were friends.

"I'm partial to nature images, Charlotte," Shannon mentioned as they moved inside. "The seashell sketch in the kitchen already caught my eye."

Matthew glanced over as Paul stopped beside him. "Well, she didn't bolt in the first two minutes," Matthew offered.

Paul smiled. "It's the women. Put a group of them together, kick out the guys, and they can work through any stress lingering around like it was melted butter. Want to play a game of croquet? We're debating the possibilities of setting up a truly difficult course."

Matthew scanned the yard. The guy who

would be, by process of elimination, Rachel's husband, Cole, was getting out the equipment. "You could put a hook shot around those railroad ties and bank one along the woodpile," Matthew suggested. "I'm in." Paul nodded. Before Paul could step away, Matthew paused and said in a low voice, "We need a word in private."

"Sure." Paul stepped over toward the garage. "What's the recent news?" he asked.

"Shannon handed me a diary this afternoon, covering the month of her abduction," Matthew began. "She had the diary with her when she was taken, and they let her keep it. I haven't read it yet, and it's not coming to you until she agrees, but whatever I can give you on names, locations, I'll have for you by morning."

Paul glanced toward the house. "No matter the hour, call. I'll let Theo know. The news she isn't her father's daughter was its own earthquake this morning. Theo's been looking, but he hasn't seen anything in the financials that looks like someone was blackmailing the mom. It's going to take several more days to figure out if that information and the fact of her abduction are in any way connected."

"I don't know which will be worse for Shannon — to have her mother's affair and the news she's not her father's child be related to the abduction, or have it be an independent sorrow."

"I hear you. Anything else significant?"

"She's getting a lot more reserved. The call she's waiting on would be my guess as to why."

"My national inquiries have drawn a blank so far. If there's a second person who slipped free of this, there should be something to find. I've got people checking local reports and hospitals around Atlanta, Boston, and Seattle, given we don't have much else to go on for locations until she tells us more."

A new guest stepped out onto the patio. "We'll talk more later," Paul said quietly. "Theo, about time you made it," he called, walking back into the yard. "Grab a mallet and join us for some croquet. Where's your date?"

"That didn't work out as planned, so I brought along Nancy Beach. She just disappeared somewhere with a lot of laughter and hugs when she and Rachel spotted each other."

"Nice compromise. I didn't know she was in town. Bryce, what's the official clock?"

"A few more minutes and the meat goes on."

"Let's get gates in the ground and balls in play. Dogs interfering count as your bad luck — you play wherever it stops."

Theo laughed. "I can see where this is going."

Matthew helped finish setting up the wire gates, then selected blue as his ball and mallet. It was mild fun made competitive because it was guys playing the game. He tapped the mallet against the side of his shoe, glad for the evening. He'd needed exactly this kind of break.

Food came off the grill, plates got filled, and people sat around the back patio and inside at the kitchen table, enjoying the meal, laughing at stories, showing good humor as events from the past few months were recounted. Matthew tracked down Shannon every twenty minutes or so, found her relaxed, settled back in listening mode and simply being in the moment. That was the best news of the evening — Shannon staying engaged among a group. She liked Nancy Beach, with the two women getting deep into a conversation about favorite travel destinations. And Shannon loved Charlotte's artwork. She pointed out several to him she particularly appreciated among the sketches on display. On more than one occasion Matthew spotted Shannon reaching down to pet the dog. Black certainly approved, planting himself near her and leaning in.

Matthew eventually brought Shannon a piece of cheesecake and hunkered down beside her. "One hour plus. Doing okay?" he murmured.

"Another hour is fine," she replied, offering him a bite of the cheesecake. He wasn't turning it down and nipped it neatly off her fork. "Which one is Ruth Bazoni?" she asked.

He raised an eyebrow. "You haven't figured that out yet? Charlotte."

She looked surprised, then thoughtful. "Okay."

"I'm going to be out back. Come hit a ball around later. It's surprisingly fun."

She grinned. "I might do that."

Matthew walked outside, content with the way the evening was working out. He rejoined Cole, an interesting man with a good eye for how the yard played. It wasn't golf, but the tall grass and the occasional past rabbit nest with its bald spot of earth meant some tactics were required to make it through the eight gates in only a few shots.

They had worked it down to fifteen shots as par when the Bishops' two dogs arrived home and the backyard game of croquet turned into a melee of great shots and dog interference. The comedy was worth the evening, and the women wandered out to watch. Black was determined to chase down any ball Paul hit, and the two Irish Setters were paws down on the earth, waiting for a ball to come their direction. Matthew spotted Shannon talking with Bryce between shots and delayed walking over to join them until the conversation looked like it was coming to a close. Shannon seemed more relaxed than she had in all the time Matthew had known her.

In the end, Bryce laughingly declared the dogs the winners of the croquet match. The group began to break up, calling out their good-nights. Matthew added his thanks for the evening and chose to steer Shannon out as one of the first to depart.

"Are you glad you went?" Matthew asked as they drove back to the apartment.

Shannon stirred to glance over at him. "Mmm. They're nice people. Nancy travels a lot with her job. We were comparing favorite parts of the country, great scenery, tucked away places to find really good food — we've overlapped quite a bit. Rachel bubbles, I really liked her. And Bryce and Charlotte seem . . . like a close couple, nicely in tune with each other."

"They've put together a good marriage."

"It looked like it."

Shannon went quiet. Matthew decided it was as peaceful a time as he would get to tell her about the next evening. "We're going to stop by your brother's home tomorrow night around nine so you can meet his wife. Their daughter will already be asleep, but you'll be able to look in on her. Jeffery heads south for three days of campaign-related events, and this makes sense for the timing."

"I would like to meet his wife again, so I can update my memories of her."

"The rest of the day is wide open. I'd even be okay with shopping as the plan for the afternoon."

She offered a tired smile. "I'll think about it."

Shannon broke the silence a few minutes later. "Matthew, earlier today I know you accepted my conditions, but before you start reading that diary I need to repeat one of them. I don't want to talk about it."

"I'll respect that, Shannon." He'd be reading it tonight, and he was already bracing for what it would say.

"Thank you. For the cookout too. It was . . . nice. Really nice."

"Did you put more numbers in your phone?"

"A few more."

"I'd encourage you to call them, if only for a few minutes of casual conversation. 'It was nice to meet you last night,' that kind of thing."

"I'm not accustomed to calling people just to chat."

"Think of it as practice. I should give you Becky's number. She loves to chat."

"Do that, please. I think I'd like to meet your daughter by phone and at least apologize for you being in Chicago when she expected you back in Boston."

"Becky thinks you're good for me."

"How so?"

"You're the perfect age — old enough I won't treat you like I do my daughter, but young enough I may try to shed a few of my years and appear more youthful, energetic, and up on current trends."

Shannon's laughter pealed through the car. "Oh, I love her already."

# 14

Matthew didn't pick up the diary until Shannon had turned in. He knew it was going to be tough to read. He took it across the hall and settled into the chair in the bedroom, propped his feet up on the corner of the bed, and opened the fabric-covered book to the first and the last pages. He started by looking for dates, noting how the blue ink had faded but was still legible. The diary began a week before the Memorial Day abduction and ended on a Saturday, three weeks after she was taken.

He started reading page one. Diaries were particularly powerful things, he found. She'd been so young. He could hear it in the words on the page. High school. Sixteen. He felt like an intruder into Shannon's private thoughts.

The first several entries were comments about a boy she liked at school, the girl he was interested in instead of her — Matthew heard just a bit of the woman he knew today in the younger version's comments. She shifted to talking about two girlfriends who both wanted the same part in the school play, and the price playing honest broker was having on her friendships. She worried about her math exam since she'd run out of time to finish it. Jeffery was being a pain again — not inviting a girlfriend over to the house to meet Mom until he thought she was "the one," which meant every boy Shannon brought home was being looked at by her family as "the one." She'd never be able to have a life so long as her brother insisted on letting all Mom's curiosity fall on her. But at least Jeffery was being generous. She had her license and loved being able to drive the car Jeffery had passed on to her when he upgraded to a used truck.

Matthew had to smile at the all-so-common trials of being a teenager ringing through the pages. Memorial Day weekend was a single paragraph in the diary.

Jenny is hosting four of us for the long weekend, which promises to be painting her room, talking boys, getting some sun by the pool, and hopefully saying hi to her brother Stephen. He's nice for a college guy. Annabel has the repaired guitar ready for me to pick up. I promised Mom I'd be home by seven Monday night. She's encouraged me to go for all three days. I think she wants a private weekend with Dad since Jeffery will also be out of town.

The normal entries ceased. Matthew found pages of the diary ripped out with a jagged, hurried tear, the remaining edge only blank. The next scrawled entry began on a crumpled page that had folded over. The entry went on for several pages. He smoothed out the paper.

I can't hear him anymore. I'm writing fast. I love you, Mom. I love you, Dad. Jeffery — I wouldn't be mad if you beat them up for me.

There are six of them I've come to realize, traveling in two cars. Mostly just voices. My ears are still ringing from the blow when I talked, so silence is the order of the day. If I sleep they ignore me, so even when I'm awake I'm trying to be motionless. Though the younger man beside me in the back seat isn't fooled. My face hurts so bad. He got in a fight with the woman for handing me an ice pack, but must have won because they let me keep it. He's the most rational of the six.

Do what he says and he's businesslike with me. It's the middle of the night. I'm mostly traveling in the back seat, now wearing over my T-shirt an oversized sweatshirt with a hood. The hood is an effective blindfold the way he can drop it and tug it down at a moment's notice. I'm beginning to think that's as much for my security as theirs. He's being careful I don't see many faces, and none clearly. A light in my eyes, the hood, I might be in the middle of Kansas for all I can figure out. I'm sure we're heading west, but that's all I'm sure about.

He handed me my backpack I had tossed in my car with a toothbrush and change of clothes and pointed toward this bathroom. I figure I have ten minutes max. He didn't remove this diary or the pen, though I know he searched the bag earlier and wouldn't have missed them. He took the phone but left me the music player and the cash. He knocks, I have to leave this small place of safety. I've left a note stuffed inside the toilet paper roll and hope it falls out when someone puts in a new roll. They search where I've been and they find anything obvious and it's more than a slap then. My body aches, and worse, I'm sure no note has gotten through. I'm an idiot to try again the way I'm hurting, but hope is eternal. I think he left the diary in the backpack, because he knows it's going into a fire somewhere, and for now it's a way to pacify me with an illusion I can keep some of my own things.

What has it been . . . thirty hours now? A few more days of this and I'll be a total mess. If I can keep away from the woman, the older man, maybe I can hold it together. It was the older guy beside me for the first ten hours after they yanked me out of my car and shoved me into this one . . . I don't want any of them near me, but please, God, don't let that younger man decide to change cars. Tossing the car door open and tumbling out onto the highway seems like a decent risk to me. I've almost made it twice, but each time his hand flexed across mine, silently stopping me. My hand goes back in my lap and he lets me go, no other response, like he had anticipated the attempt was coming and simply waited to counter it. I don't think I'd still be breathing if I'd pulled that on the older guy. We're close to wherever we're going. I've heard them say enough that I know that. I worry where that is. The third time I try, I'm going to have to get out of that car no matter what happens. This highway is my best chance to be seen by someone who can help me. They get me any more isolated, I'm dead.

The entries stopped again.

Matthew didn't want to turn the page. She hadn't escaped, as he knew she'd spent years with this group — or with a larger group this one was part of — and she'd survived. He should be able to read her words with some distance knowing this was history, but it didn't change the impact her account was having on him.

He forced himself to turn the page. Flinched. There was dried blood staining the edge of the paper.

He read until two a.m. He had to put the diary down several times, get up to pace, give himself a few minutes to get his composure back. It got progressively harder to read, the words of a terrified teenager, followed by the hardened words of someone determined to survive. His heart at times felt like it was pounding so hard it would burst. The entries were sporadic, sometimes several entries for one day, then gaps of several days. Her writing had changed in the span of weeks, from open, flowing cursive to a small print that shook and often became hard to decipher. The private written prayers to God were crushing. When he turned the last page he felt like he wanted to puke, so intense were the emotions the words had triggered.

He forced himself to go back to the beginning and methodically read it again, writing down every name, location, and date he came across. When he was done, he picked up the phone and called Paul. He'd learned the younger man's name was Flynn. She'd latched on to him even in the earliest hours as a possible aid for her survival. Flynn *had* helped her. He just hadn't been able to help her enough.

Matthew crossed the hall shortly after eight a.m., carrying the diary. He entered the security code and let himself into the apartment. Shannon was eating breakfast. A glance showed him her choice this morning was Cheerios with strawberries. He poured himself coffee. He placed the diary on the table beside her. "Thank you for letting me read it," he said quietly, the most emotionally careful words he'd ever said. He'd practiced them repeatedly as he dressed to get the tone right. The thanks had to be said because of what she'd been willing to let him learn, and she needed to know he'd read every word.

She ignored the diary, even as she gave a terse nod to acknowledge his statement.

He put sugar in his coffee, though he normally preferred it black, and found a spoon to stir it. "Did you keep a diary for most of the eleven years?" he asked, keeping his tone even.

Her gaze met his. "Yes."

He refused to lower his eyes or alter his expression. Eleven years of truth was going to be brutal to absorb. "Did the other books survive?" he asked quietly.

"Probably. It depends on where Flynn decided to store them for me."

He pulled out the chair opposite her and sat down. "Would you like me to put that one in a secure location for you, or would you prefer to keep it with you?"

"I don't need to see it again. I wrote it. I know what it says."

"I'll put it somewhere private," he promised.

She nudged a strawberry from atop the cereal with her spoon. "They don't need to be read. There's no reason you need to know more, why anyone needs to know. It's history now."

"But it's your history. Someone should stand as witness."

"God did."

*And wasn't that its own tragedy?* "I'd rather not talk about God today," he admitted.

"I was never as young again as that first diary reads. The others may be hard to read, but I'm tougher-minded in them."

"A fact which makes your story even sadder."

She pushed the container of strawberries over to him. "I accept your horror on my behalf, but let it go. Look at me." She held out her arms. "I'm fine."

"I'll get there, Shannon. But not easily." He drank the sweetened coffee and changed subjects. "What do you want to do today?"

"I was going to ask you the same question," she replied with a brief smile. "I wouldn't mind shopping for shoes. But before the shoes, there's another place near here we might check."

"That works for me. Want to leave soon or wait until after lunch?"

"Let's go after you eat something more substantial for breakfast than a few strawberries."

"We could find a drive-thru someplace and order a fast-food breakfast," he suggested.

She grinned. "Now you're talking."

Matthew didn't know the suburbs of Chicago. The community Shannon directed him to was an older area — smaller homes, not much grass, kids playing ball in the street. "Take a left at the stop sign," she said. They passed a school with a nearly empty parking lot, a corner hardware store, an insurance agency, a small shoe-repair business. "Can you park on the street, just past that car-repair shop?"

He pulled to the curb in front of an old brick building that looked as though it had been a repair shop for the last fifty years. Two men in coveralls were working on a car's engine inside the open bay. "Wait here," Shannon said and pushed open her door. She walked across the parking lot to a collection of cars parked tight in the limited space. She picked up two wooden parts crates and carried them over to the building's side door. She looked up at the round oil-and-gas sign that still had some neon edging it. She stacked the crates, stepped up on them, reached up to the sign and pulled something out from inside the curved mounting bracket. She slid it in her pocket, returned the crates, and walked back to the car. She settled into the passenger seat.

"What is it?" he asked.

She pulled the tape off a folded handkerchief and showed him a red circle tag attached to a key. "Flynn has a preference for deposit boxes. This one is at the wine shop half a mile back — if it's still in business. They have temperature- and humidity-controlled boxes you can lease. The shop probably doesn't open for another hour, but it's worth driving by."

The neon sign OPEN glowed in the window. Matthew parked in the side lot.

Shannon handed him the key. "All you need is this to have access. Why don't you go empty the box? I'd rather not walk in there. You should take the grocery sack. The box might be full."

Matthew wondered if this would identify his summer — Shannon showing him out-of-the-way places, recovering stolen items. Actually, the thought had some appeal. He would be seeing places she'd been these last eleven years, doing something useful, mostly building trust with her as she shared information. She needed that bedrock of trust to form. As put together as she presented herself, he knew most of it was what she wanted him to see. Inside, there had to be a deep slice of raw emotional pain that had yet to surface. She'd need someone she trusted around to help her when that time came, and he thought road trips would be useful when talking about hard things. But first, this leased box. He *was* curious about what it would contain. He left the car running and the air-conditioning on for her. "I'll just be a minute."

He took the key and sack and went inside the store, saw the wall of leased boxes. He used the key to open box thirty-eight. There were four items inside: a stationery box, two square mug-sized boxes, and a manila envelope. The envelope had Shannon's name written on it, but this envelope was smaller and didn't feel like it held a book. He closed and relocked the box, pocketed the key, and took the items back to the car. He passed the sack to Shannon.

"Want me to show you the treasures?" she asked.

"Sure, if only so I can tell Paul what I'm bringing him."

She carefully opened the stationery box. The papers inside were in cellophane sleeves, neatly stacked. "They're very old letters. They're worth something because of the signatures."

"How valuable?"

"Maybe a few thousand? I don't know for sure. Flynn had a romantic streak — he liked to be the one to tuck away things like this."

Shannon used his pocketknife to open the

two square boxes. She grinned. "Interested in old baseballs?" She held one up. "Autographed, and worth something."

He didn't recognize the signatures, but the condition of the ball suggested something from the early era of the sport.

"These two should be easy to trace. They've probably been in that storage box for years," she said.

He pointed to the last item. "The envelope has your name on it. Something else Flynn stored for you?"

"Yes." She picked it up, unwrapped the thread tie, turned it to dump out the contents. A handful of smaller sealed envelopes slid out into her lap.

"What are they?"

"Memory cards for a digital camera. Photos I've taken."

His interest sharpened. "Over the last eleven years? Anything that will be helpful to the cops?"

Shannon sorted out the smaller envelopes, turning them so the initials and dates written on the flaps were visible. "Sorry, not on these. There aren't people in these photos, just landscapes, trees, animals, sunrises, that kind of thing. I can tell because the sealed sleeve is marked with the initials and date of the person who checked the memory card before I was allowed to keep it. These individuals would delete any photo that had a person in it, whether it was one of them or a stranger's baby — if a person, it's gone."

The dates covered a variety of random years, some recent, the oldest eight years ago. "How many photos are here?"

"I'd guess between five hundred and a thousand across these memory cards. I don't know if they can still be read or if they've gone bad."

"A camera shop will have the adaptor needed to read them. If you don't mind me looking at them, I'll see which cards are still good, load the photos onto my laptop, then get them transferred to a flash drive for you."

She dumped the smaller envelopes back into the larger one and handed it to him. "I appreciate the help. Take these other items to Paul, would you?"

"We'll swing by and drop them off on the way to the apartment. Is there anything else we can check in this area?"

"There are a few places I don't want to be the one to disturb. But there is something . . ." She tugged a notepad out of her canvas bag and flipped to a blank page. "Do me a favor and put this note in the box you just emptied. Flynn might convince the shop owner to open the old box for him by saying he lost his key."

He read the note: *Flynn, I needed the baseballs as a gift for my brother and dad. Shannon*

"He should know me well enough to see right through the note. He knows I'm not going to give stolen goods to my family. But if someone else is with him, it's an explanation that would seem plausible for the empty box. If they think it's me, they'll react differently than if they think it's the cops who cleared it."

"You don't mind tipping Flynn to the fact you're alive."

"He would already be acting on the assumption I might be. It won't change his behavior much to have it confirmed. And it might be . . . useful if he thought I was alive and talking to the cops. It might speed up whatever he's doing this summer."

Matthew wanted more details about Flynn, about what might be going on in the family, but didn't think probing would get his questions answered just yet. "Give me a minute." He walked back into the store and put the note in the box.

Matthew tabbed through the pictures Shannon had taken. Driftwood. Beaches. Sand crabs. Ocean waves. "Do you remember where you took these photos?"

Shannon came over to the kitchen table and looked over his shoulder at the laptop screen as he moved through the images. "Yes."

"Would you tell me something about that place?"

"One day I might," she replied lightly. "It's not that far from Boston. I'll show it to you."

He turned to look at her. It was the first time she'd hinted at coming east. "I'd like that."

"I'm not going to want to be in Chicago once this becomes public. The East Coast is not the most pleasant place to drive with all the traffic congestion, but there are some nice places I wouldn't mind revisiting as a tourist."

He nodded and turned back to the laptop. She'd offered something he'd be able to come back to at another time. He looked at more of the images. "They really are good photographs. Nice compositions, interesting subjects. These" — he pointed out two — "are visually stunning."

"Thanks."

He'd been loading the memory cards without a problem. Even the oldest ones had been readable. "Is this all your photos, these cards?"

"No . . . there are more."

He caught something in her voice. "Shannon?"

She slid into the seat across from him with a small shrug. "It was how I survived, staying out of people's way and spending my time with a camera when I wasn't expected to be doing something else. They photographed and indexed every item they were going to store and later sell, and it was tedious work. A good photograph meant a better sale price could be negotiated before they actually risked transporting the item to the buyer. I volunteered to do it because it kept me out of the way of what else was going on. Since they could check my work with what I had on the memory card, they let me take the photos.

"I convinced them the better I handled a camera, the better the photos I could take for them. I could carry around one of the older cameras so long as they saw the thumbprints showing every photo on the card and deleted what they didn't like. And I could keep the old memory cards of photos so long as I bought a new memory card to replace the old one. I'd send these memory cards of photos away to storage;

otherwise they had a habit of disappearing. Flynn would do that for me — drop off the memory cards at one of his private boxes. There are more cards I might be able to locate, depending on where Flynn put them."

"These photos mean a lot to you."

"They were the only things that were mine."

He now understood why they mattered so much to her. Taking photos was the only thing in the eleven years where she'd been able to be herself. "Would you mind if I had the camera shop print these images for you onto decent photo paper?"

"That would get expensive."

"Consider it a gift. I'll take a copy of a couple photos I like as payment, hang them on the wall in my office one day."

She hesitated, then nodded. "I would like to see them printed."

There were 417 photos, and Matthew had the camera shop owner print the first 50 while he waited for the Chinese restaurant next door to prepare his to-go order.

The shop owner handed him a sturdy box holding the prints. "Yours?"

"A friend's."

"There are some stunning photos here. A

few would look really sharp enlarged, maybe up to twenty by thirty. Keep that in mind when you look through them. I'll offer a good price on the printing, even make it a trade if she'd share a few of the images. They'd make for good advertising in my window."

"Yeah? That's nice of you. I'll let her know."

Matthew told Shannon the shop owner's remark after they'd finished dinner and she was opening the box of prints. "It's been several years since you saw these photos if the memory cards have been stored for years. What do you think of your own work?" The photos spread across the tabletop made an impressive panorama.

"I think I liked nature," she said with a smile, sorting through the images.

He picked up one. "You had to be high in a tree to get this perspective."

"I'm sure I was. I enjoyed climbing trees and looking down at the world."

He studied a few of them, appreciating how they'd turned out in print. "I told your brother we would be over around nine this evening. You could take a couple of these prints to them if you like."

She considered the suggestion. "Not tonight, but I might enlarge and frame a couple of the better ones for him."

Matthew thought that was a good idea. It would be a visual record of her missing years, but one of the few nice memories she'd been able to make for herself. "He'd like that, I'm sure."

Jeffery welcomed Shannon to his home with a hug, introduced Cindy, and made a point of letting the women set off on a tour of the house without him. Matthew appreciated the move. He followed Jeffery into the living room, accepted with a thanks the soda already poured.

"She's looking more rested," Jeffery remarked.

"She had a good day."

"Now, you . . . you're looking worse."

"There's a diary from the first month," Matthew replied, and he proceeded to heavily edit what he chose to say about its contents. This journey with Shannon was going to require bearing up under very difficult information, and Jeffery seemed prepared to deal with that reality. Matthew gave Jeffery points for simply nodding when he finished.

Matthew made sure Shannon was upstairs with Cindy before he turned the conversation to what was coming this evening. The good parts of the evening were coming to an end. A root canal without Novocain was how he would describe what was ahead. Matthew took a deep swallow of the drink he'd been handed. "Are you ready?"

Jeffery paced. "Are you sure about this — doing it tonight?"

"It has to be done. Make it as simple and as direct as you can. Don't bury the lead or try to downplay it. Just level emotion. 'I love you, we're family, Mom made a mistake a long time ago, and I wanted you to hear about it from me rather than from some reporter.' "

Jeffery shook his head. "I'm about to hurt the innocent person in this family who has already taken enough hurts for a lifetime. It would be easier to take a bullet."

Matthew understood the sentiment. "You're feeling what she's about to. At least you'll be able to truly empathize. You've warned your parents?"

"Yes."

"Can either one of them handle a conversation with her tonight?"

"I wouldn't recommend it. Mom's already sobbing her heart out, and Dad's basically the opposite — emotionally numb. Mom would give Shannon a variation of 'I'm so sorry. You must hate me. I never wanted you to find out this way. Your father was so focused on the business I never saw him,' and turn self-absorbed throughout the conversation. Dad wants to apologize and say the marriage was having some problems, he's deeply upset she had to learn about her past this way, that the divorce wasn't about her but about the affair and that he couldn't rebuild trust with her mom. He won't be able to get through it to say a clean 'I love you, Shannon,' even though he gets there by the time he's done. Neither one are going to be helpful to Shannon. She needs a hug, an 'I love you, and it's going to be okay,' and neither will be able to give her that tonight. They'll be piling their own history of marriage troubles onto Shannon's shoulders while breaking her heart."

Matthew accepted Jeffery's read of the situation. Given what he said, Matthew worked out what best could be done. "We'll have Shannon talk with you, we give it a few hours, and then I'll suggest she call you later tonight, mention that again in the morning, again tomorrow night. I'll keep pushing that she should call you until we make sure she's going to keep the lines of communication open. As I said, stay emotionally level: 'I love you. This is our parents' problem, not ours. I'm still your same brother. Cindy wants you to come over and see the wedding photos.' You'll know what will work in the moment."

Jeffery nodded. "Get her to call me and I can deliver on that." He paced the room again. "In forty-eight hours this has gone from one of the best moments of my life to one of the worst. We need to be past this, Matthew."

They heard the women coming down the stairs. Matthew moved to a nearby chair while Jeffery took a seat toward the opposite end of the couch, ensuring Shannon would sit between them.

Shannon came with Cindy into the living room. "Your daughter's beautiful, Jeffery. And her room is a child's delight." She glanced over at Cindy with a smile. "I love what you're doing with the house."

"It's been a joy. I can't wait to have your help on paint samples and fabric choices. I'm trying to figure out how to finish the upstairs. Jeffery's no help, I'm afraid."

Shannon laughed.

"Sit and chat for a while," Cindy suggested. "I'm going to go and freshen our drinks." She took Shannon's glass to add with her own. "I'll be right back."

Jeffery patted the couch beside him, and Shannon went to join him.

"I'm glad you came over tonight," Jeffery said. "I so wanted you to get to see our Ashley. Cindy's been busy getting an envelope full of pictures to send back with you, from the hospital on through first steps and first birthday cake." He handed it to her.

Shannon thumbed through the envelope of photographs. She looked over and smiled as Cindy brought back their sodas. "Thanks, Cindy," she said, holding up the envelope. "This is really nice."

"I love pictures."

"Me too."

Shannon hadn't brought in her canvas bag, so Matthew held out his hand. "I've got room in my pocket for those."

Shannon handed him the envelope.

"I'm glad you came over tonight for a lot of reasons, Shannon," Jeffery said, and Matthew heard in his tone of voice a shift in the conversation. "You can't believe how nice it is to have you in this house. It's a joy that you're here. But a more serious reason I'm glad you're here is that it gives me a chance to tell you a piece of news you'll need to hear at some point — something I wish I didn't have to say. Would you mind if I just got it over with tonight? It's nothing to do with our relationship, but I've got something you need to know."

His distress was obvious, and she reached out her hand to his, offered a tentative smile. "Okay. Just tell me."

"Shannon . . . Mom made a mistake, a long time ago. I wanted to tell you about it before you heard it from someone else. Dad . . . he isn't your biological father."

She blinked, and Jeffery wisely didn't say anything more.

Matthew saw that control he'd seen in Atlanta smooth the emotion from her face, until calm became the only thing that showed through.

"Jeffery . . . you're his son? You've checked?"

"I've checked."

"Dad —" she stumbled on the word — "your father, I mean . . . he doesn't want to see me?" she asked, her words both a statement and a question, and it made them all fight against tears.

"He will, Shannon. He needs some time to get his words together. Mom is trying to figure out how to ask your forgiveness, also for your having to find out this way." Jeffery's hand tightened around hers. "You're my sister. I love you. They're still Mom and Dad to the two of us. They are both so glad and relieved you're back. They just need some time. They weren't prepared . . .

weren't ready to explain this to you, to tell you what happened. Given the campaign, and the risk that some reporter makes this news into a story, telling you couldn't wait. I didn't want you to hear it from anyone other than family. I love you. Nothing has changed. We're still family. They'll figure out how to answer your questions. They just need some time."

She slowly nodded. "Okay." She looked over at Matthew. "We need to go."

"Shannon . . ." Jeffery began.

Matthew stepped in and cut him off with a murmured, "Later, Jeffery," then offered Shannon his hand.

To his credit, Jeffery didn't try to intervene further, nor did Cindy. With softly said goodbyes and brief hugs, they walked them to the front door and let them leave.

Shannon's vision would be blurry with the tears she wasn't letting fall. Matthew put his arm around her waist as they left to make sure she didn't trip going down the steps. He guided her into the car and helped her with the seat belt, ran a comforting hand down her arm that she didn't appear to notice, walked around to the driver's side, then silently held up his hand in the shape of a phone to let Jeffery know he'd call.

Matthew started the car, backed out of the driveway.

"I don't want to go back to the apartment," Shannon whispered.

"Choose a direction."

"West."

Matthew took any road heading west, set the radio to music. He reached over and put his hand over hers. She didn't turn her hand to link with his, nor did she move it away. Instead she disappeared into her thoughts and tuned the world out.

# 15

"Did this have anything to do with my abduction?"

Matthew knew it was coming and had been dreading the question. Shannon was sitting with her hands neatly resting in her lap, her body still, subdued, her eyes on the passing roadway. "The early answer is no, but we don't know. We're looking." He wasn't sure what she needed from him right now, and he took a careful step onto thin ice, trying to get a feel for where her thoughts had taken her. "I can tell you something about the house where you were to have been taken, if you would find that helpful."

"Tell me."

The information she had previously insisted she didn't want to know now barely stirred her flat and hollow tone.

"Eleven years ago the house was owned by Sanford Bliss. He died eight years ago from cancer. He's a cousin of your father's."

She was quiet for a long time. "I vaguely recognize the name, but I don't know him."

"He may have been an innocent third party to this. Maybe your being dropped off on his doorstep was supposed to happen after the ransom had been paid, after this was over, because he could be trusted to get you back to your family."

She looked over at him. "An interesting possibility."

"They grab you, a ransom gets paid, they drop you off with a family member, and keep driving. There's elegance in its simplicity, if I can describe a horrific act in those terms."

"Or it could be something entirely different."

Matthew hesitated. "Yes. At the other extreme, Sanford may have been solely responsible for arranging your abduction. Maybe he had a problem with your father, and abducting you for ransom would be a fast way to make his point and cost your father dearly while at the same time he'll play the hero and bring you home. The middle ground answer, Sanford and your uncle were working some scheme together. We just don't have the answers yet."

"Thank you for finding out about the

house," Shannon finally said. "But there's an option you haven't mentioned." She sighed and continued, "My mother knew her affair was going to come out, was facing her marriage ending in a divorce, and to save her marriage she arranged to have me taken to Sanford in the hopes that my few-days'-long abduction would so shake my father —" she faltered — "her husband, that he'd accept me even if I wasn't his child. If that didn't work, and he still threw us out, she'd use the ransom money as a nest egg for both of us."

That answer was just as plausible as his own theories — more even, because it summed up all the moving pieces. And yet it presented a devastating reality for her, and he desperately wanted something different to be the truth. "Don't run that direction, Shannon. It will eat you alive. Suspend judgment for now. Let us figure this out so you'll know, and then you can deal with the actual truth, not guesses."

"Who's my real father?"

Matthew would have closed his eyes if he were not driving. "Jeffery doesn't know," he replied. He glanced over to her. "Do you want to know?"

"Yes."

"You can ask your mother."

"No," she whispered.

Matthew pondered the options, but none were particularly good. "My firm can find out," he finally said. "Twenty-eight years ago, who was in your mother's life? Work out the possibilities from there, figure out how to get a DNA sample from the most likely possibilities — a tossed-out coffee cup or water bottle, for starters — then run discreet DNA tests to confirm a suspicion until there's a yes."

"I need to know."

"I'll make a call."

She was crying and trying to do so quietly. And she was breaking his heart. He retrieved the box of Kleenex he'd put in the car. "Your tears aren't going to bother me . . . well, not too much," he said with an attempt to lighten the mood. "Go ahead and let them come. You'll feel better afterwards. I have that on good authority from Becky — tears are helpful."

Shannon wiped her eyes. "Quit being nice, okay?" she whispered.

It was a good thing he was driving or he'd wrap her in a hug and not let go . . . and wasn't that a tough twist to deal with? He settled for reaching over, lightly brushing a hand down her arm. "It will eventually be okay, Shannon. That I can promise you.

Even this eventually gets better."

"Yeah." She found another tissue. "Don't look my way when my face gets all splotchy with crying."

The ache in his heart eased a bit. Vanity he could deal with. He offered her a small smile. "I'll think kind thoughts even if you look like you've cried a river."

She attempted a smile in return. "And what an image that gives. I'm probably going to do so tonight." She swiped the back of her hand across her eyes again. "I'd like to bawl, and won't that be a pleasant thing." She blew her nose and rested her head back against the seat.

He saw her eyes were closed but she was still crying. He didn't say anything. She needed to cry, needed the pain to wash out tonight so that tomorrow she could begin picking up the pieces. She'd taken the worst hit he could imagine and was going to get through it. He'd figure out a way to help her do that. She's shown him repeatedly that she was a survivor. She'd make it past even this.

The sun was coming up. Matthew stopped and bought her a pair of sunglasses as they looped east, back into Chicago. She'd cried her heart out over the course of the night's drive — her eyes had to be burning.

She'd finished a sport drink and ate some of the oatmeal cookies he'd tucked in a zip-lock bag in anticipation of a long drive. He'd get some real food in her when he could. They would be back to the apartment within the hour.

"Matthew?"

He'd hoped she was dozing, as she'd been silent the last half hour. He looked over at her. "Hmm?"

"My friend should have called by now. I think she's dead. Tell Paul I'll give him what I have tomorrow."

There was no emotion left in her voice, but he could read the body language: drooped shoulders and folded arms, the break in her voice. Her sadness was overwhelming.

"I'll tell him, Shannon," he said gently. "You can take another day if you need it before you talk with him."

She shook her head. "It's time."

He reached over for her hand, squeezed it. "I'm sorry."

She gave a jerky nod.

There was nothing he could say that would help. She'd been holding on to hope for so many days. To give up had to feel like a betrayal, of accepting a reality she so wished to change. He wondered how many prayers God had just let pass by with the continued silence from her friend. He'd like to know her name, details about how Shannon knew her. But those questions would only make this moment worse, so he put them aside.

"One thing, Matthew — I'm still not prepared to tell Paul the address where I was to be taken. All that answer does right now is open up more questions."

"I promised to keep that address between you and me, and it will stay that way until you tell me otherwise," he reassured.

They reached the parking garage just after six a.m. He pulled into a space and turned off the ignition, but neither of them moved.

"Thanks for just . . . driving me around. That was nice of you."

"I wish I could have done more. This will get better, you know that, Shannon. Give yourself time."

"Sure." She sighed and pushed open the car door. As they walked through the connecting tunnel to the elevator, he put his arm around her shoulders, offered a hug. She was staggering from the lack of sleep, from the bitter knowledge of her parentage. And further, he was well aware that his heart was entwining with this woman in ways he wasn't prepared to deal with.

Once they were back in the apartment, he gave her a smile, stepped aside. "Head to bed. Text or call me when you wake up. I'm going to crash across the hall."

She nodded and disappeared down the hall.

He rubbed his own burning eyes, then walked across the hall, debating the value of a hot shower to ease the aches in his body. The night had gone about as bad as he'd feared, but it was over. He pulled out his phone and called Jeffery.

Matthew was working on his laptop at the kitchen table when Shannon appeared a little after four p.m. Her tears had ended, and it looked like she'd slept. "Hungry?" he asked, trying to assess her mood. It was hours after an emotional explosion, and for his daughter this had always been the most fragile time.

"A bit." She pulled out a chair at the table.

He lifted his mug of coffee. "I've had breakfast in place of an early dinner and saved some for you, if that suits."

"Sure."

He walked over to the stove, plated bacon and scrambled eggs, added fried potatoes he'd kept warm. "It tastes better than it looks," he told her as he put the plate in front of her.

She half smiled. "I'm always good with fried potatoes." She ate in silence, and he didn't try to introduce a topic.

He wasn't sure how Shannon regrouped — whether it was pushing aside the issue and moving forward with other activities while she processed it, or if she needed the opposite — to circle back around and talk it through before she could move on. He had a feeling, though, that explosions in her world during the last eleven years hadn't been followed with conversations. Just to survive she would have learned to bury the matter and move on, because she had no choice.

Shannon finished the meal and took the plate to the dishwasher, came back with a refill to her glass of milk. She rested her head on her crossed arms.

He could see she was physically blitzed. Mentally, emotionally . . . it was still hard to read her, though. The thing he most feared was that she had made the decision to walk away from Chicago, from all the pain and tragedy she was facing. That she'd possibly cracked in a way he couldn't help repair. "Do you regret returning home?" he asked quietly.

She raised her head to look at him. "No. Jeffery needed to know I was okay."

She sat up, propped an elbow on the table, rested her chin on her palm. "I need paper maps I can mark up, a national one and state maps for the lower forty-eight. Could you arrange that?"

"Yes."

"I'm going to go shower, wash my hair. Maybe later tonight I'll paint my nails."

He smiled. "Want me to find you a bunch of colors so you can rainbow your toenails while you're at it?"

She looked at him with a small smile. "Becky?"

He nodded. "I'm an expert on nail polish now. She needed those bits of fun."

"I'm fine with my present raspberry pink." She pushed back her chair. "Feel free to do whatever you want tonight. You don't need to stay around here. I'm not leaving this place. I've got some work to do to get ready for the conversation with Paul tomorrow."

She hadn't changed her mind about talking with Paul. "Anything I can help with?"

"Just the maps."

"I'll make a call and get them sent over." He nodded to the laptop. "Some of this is business from home, some is follow-up with Theo and Paul. I've got a couple hours of this before I figure out the rest of my evening."

She nodded and stepped away, hesitated, turned back. "I have something else for you."

"Okay."

She disappeared and returned with a book in her hand — another diary, he realized.

"This is from year four. I got it from a box in Atlanta before I met up with you. Sorry they're out of order. I'm not sure where Flynn put most of them. Don't feel you need to read it."

"Shannon . . . I would like to read it, if you're okay with me doing that."

She held it out. "Same conditions. No questions. And it doesn't go to anybody else unless I want it to."

"Agreed." He accepted the diary. "Thank you for trusting me."

She gave an awkward nod and left him. He held it in his hands a moment, then set the diary aside. Maybe tomorrow. He couldn't handle another one quite yet.

Matthew raided the canister for the last of Shannon's cookies, poured himself the final inch of the coffee, and then made the call he was both relieved and stressed to make, given all that was behind Shannon's decision. "Paul, she wants to have a conversation with you tomorrow. She got the news about her dad not being her biological father last night. And her friend still hasn't called. Shannon thinks she's dead. She's going to start giving you what she has."

Paul sighed. "This is very much the wrong way I wanted to reach this point."

"I hear you. Keep it small," Matthew recommended. "You and Theo, maybe Ann. Or maybe just you, depending on how it goes."

"Where's best to have it? What time?"

"I'm thinking we have it at the FBI office so she can walk away from it when it's over. A conversation here or at your home is an easier environment, but that becomes her memory of the place. Let's do it early in the day so she's not spending too much time dreading the meeting."

"Nine thirty here, then. We'll use my office," Paul suggested.

"We'll be there. I'm going to guess you'll hear a list of names for those in the family. Locations they'd been or might be. The gravesites. She's presently marking up state maps." Matthew thought through the coming meeting. "Just let her talk, try to avoid asking questions. She handed me another diary from year four. That may be the only way she's ever able to share the details, via those written diaries. She's going to need a counselor reading them before she needs cops reading them."

"You can relax, Matthew. I know how fragile this moment is and the foundation it needs to set for the future," Paul reassured him. "I'll let Shannon say what she's comfortable sharing, and not push. This is a process I have no desire to rush with her. Hopefully this becomes the first of several smaller conversations. We need names, locations, confirmations on photos. We need to know who to protect her from once this becomes public. If we're any good at our jobs, maybe she'll only be a minor footnote in the trial, the majority of it built on physical evidence we can seize, IDs from abducted children, and confessions we can get from the family."

"Thanks, Paul. The more you can keep her involvement to a minimum, the better for her future. As it is, I'll need to make a break for her for four or five days, get her some breathing space."

"Leave town?"

Matthew rubbed the back of his neck. "I don't know. Maybe. I'd prefer not to travel again. It sets up being too easy for her not to want to return. But we stay in Chicago, it's obvious she's not seeing her parents. She needs to get her mind off those problems."

"Talk to John. He's good at coming up with ideas."

"I'll do that." Matthew checked the time. "One last thing before I let you go. Don't press her for the address where she was to be delivered. She's still not comfortable giving you that detail."

"Any guess why she's holding it back?"

"Maybe."

"I'll read into that that she's expressed reasons she's withholding it that you can't share with me. I won't quibble. Your first priority has to be Shannon's trust. She stops trusting you, or this process, and our ability to unravel the case falls precipitously."

"So far I think we're both walking that line about as well as it can be done. This is moving as fast as it could, given what I see."

"That's useful to know."

"See you in the morning, Paul. I'll keep my role tomorrow to that of interested bystander, unless I see something with her that warrants my stepping in."

"Understood."

# 16

Matthew settled on the living room couch, found an old movie, filling in time while he waited for Shannon to finish marking up the maps. She'd been working at the kitchen table for the last two-plus hours. He had a mild headache, along with a desire to call Becky and hear the world was right in at least one corner of it. But he knew his daughter was out for the evening with friends and he would just be interrupting. He had a craving for something cold and set aside the remote. Maybe ice cream? He got up and fixed himself a bowl, set its twin on the table beside Shannon. She said a quiet thanks as he took a quick scan over her shoulder — dots and red lines now crossed the state of Georgia. He went back to the movie.

Just after ten p.m., Shannon stacked the open maps rather than try to refold each one, rolled them together, used several rubber bands to secure the roll, then placed them beside the canvas bag she had placed by the door.

"Ready for tomorrow?" he asked.

"Mostly."

She leaned against the doorpost into the living room. She didn't know what to do with herself, he thought, didn't particularly look sleepy, even though he could see exhaustion in her overall appearance.

"What are you watching?"

"The first *Star Trek* movie." He hit pause, as the movie was simply a placeholder while he'd been waiting. "Shannon, you're a survivor. Tell me what to do that will help. Would you like to talk? Go for a walk? Want me to find a hotel with a pool?"

She ran her hand through her hair, an oddly vulnerable gesture for her because he rarely saw it. "I'll be okay, Matthew. It is what it is."

"You're not okay right now."

What he didn't want to do was leave her alone, trapped in this sadness. It was one thing to carry the weight of the sorrow, to feel it, to grieve — but it was quite another to be alone during that process.

"Move over," she said.

He did so. She curled up beside him on the couch. He offered the remote. She sorted through options, then came back to the one he'd been watching.

"Tomorrow when I talk to Paul, don't go very far."

"You know I won't," he promised. At the next commercial he returned to the top item on his list and mentioned casually, "Have you called your brother?"

"I don't have much to say yet. I sent a text that I needed more time before I called him."

"You could just dial and say you wanted to say good-night."

She poked a finger in his ribs. "Quit pushing." She sighed. "But, yeah, maybe. When the movie is over."

If he had his hope, she'd fall asleep on the couch before the movie was done. She coiled her feet up and tucked her head in against his shoulder. He stilled, then relaxed, smiled. He didn't know if she actually realized how much simple proximity represented security to her, but he was growing aware of the pattern. He suspected her primary love language was related to touch — to be handled roughly was a strike against her person, to be touched with gentleness a significant statement of her worth. But he knew she was seeking comfort and doing it in the only way she knew how.

For Shannon to be restored to wholeness, someone had to pour in that emotional balm she needed. He figured he was part of that for her. He didn't mind. He was a better man when he was needed. Tomorrow was going to be a very long day for both of them. But it would be over . . . that initial wrenching conversation with law enforcement. For merely a week since he'd met her in the hallway of an Atlanta hotel, it was good progress.

He watched a commercial while he wondered how the next week with Shannon would unfold. He had seen a strength that was bearing up under terrible news. On the other hand, she also seemed extremely fragile. Her dreams were being shattered now — her knowledge about her family, her hope for her friend's safety. Freedom was proving to be not as wonderful as she had imagined.

He realized his own emotions were becoming tangled with her, more than was wise. But having his own heart slightly bruised when she was ready to thrive without him wouldn't be such a high price to pay for this journey. Becky was right. Shannon mattered to him not only because she had sought him out for help, because she reminded him of what had happened to his daughter, but because he simply enjoyed being with her, liked her. Based on that first diary, on what she had described, Shannon had a long road ahead of her. He wanted to walk it with her.

Which meant once she turned in tonight, he was going to be reading her diary from year four. The only way to be able to help her tomorrow was to be as fully aware of her history as he could piece together. His heart already ached, but he'd deal with it. She needed one person besides God who knew it all, knew her, and accepted her as she was. Becky had taught him the significance of that. Shannon's brother would be filling part of that role for her. A doctor and counselor would fill more of it in the future. But she also needed friends who knew, whether in whole or in part, who still unreservedly accepted her. He was determined to be one of those friends.

He watched the movie, idly turned a strand of her hair around his finger, knew she was drifting to sleep. He'd send her to bed shortly and then go turn in himself. The movie went to commercial again.

"Matthew."

He glanced down at her profile, surprised she was awake. "Hmm?"

"I need to tell you something when the

movie's over."

"Want me to turn it off?"

"No. It's about the graves. But it can wait a couple of minutes."

"I'll listen when the movie is over to whatever you want to tell me," he reassured.

She shifted away, got up and went over to her canvas bag to pull out a legal pad, the edges of its pages curled. When she sat down on the couch again, he saw the pages were covered in notes. *Her long list toward cleaning up the last eleven years,* he thought.

She watched the end of the movie with him. The credits began scrolling by. He muted the volume rather than shut it off, not sure if she might need the next movie as a distraction after they were finished with a difficult conversation.

She flipped through the pages to midway in the pad and carefully removed four sheets. "I wrote out what I could remember about the graves." She handed them over. "Would you give those to Paul?"

"Yes."

"I'd like to tell you about the graves so I don't have to tell him. There are . . . too many of them." She was silent for a long time. "I don't think I can do this more than once. I thought I might be able to do it with Paul, but I can't."

He reached over and settled his hand on hers in a gesture that had become habit between them, the one piece of contact they both needed. "Just start somewhere." He could see the sadness and weight of this pressing on her, and he felt it pressing on him too, even though he didn't yet know the details.

"The family itself, that last set of photos I gave Adam York — the ones involved in smuggling kids, who were killed in a family dispute — I was a witness to three of the shootings. I was nearby but didn't see the other two. I helped bury all five at the farm."

"Were you shot during one of those confrontations?" he asked carefully, putting what he suspected on the table. When she wore that swimsuit, there were some scars not fully faded that suggested she had been.

"Shrapnel, I think. Gunfire in a kitchen hits a lot of things." Shannon's gaze turned distant for a while before she blinked and focused back on him.

"There were three other family murders. Year two for me — so it would have been nine years ago — George Jacoby shot his son Robert in the back of the head. They were in an argument about following the rules of the family, and Robert was at that age, probably eighteen, where he wasn't going to do what his father wanted. He'd been pulled over for speeding with several valuable paintings in the car trunk — a close call with law enforcement, and it put the family at risk. Things escalated, and I saw George's face change. The next thing I know, he's pulled the gun and killed his son. He stood over the body and said, 'Let this be an example that I mean what I say.' I don't know where Robert is buried, but I think maybe along Bluff Road near Cedar, Montana, where a bridge crosses a creek."

The harsh violence so early in her eleven years with the family appalled him, but if he showed that emotion it would only make it harder for her to say what she needed to tell him. He forced himself to keep his voice level as he said, "That's enough detail to give the police somewhere to look."

She took a deep breath, let it out, seemed both resigned and relieved to be telling someone. "Year three, Kyle was assigned responsibility for Jason that day. Kyle decided he was going to ditch the route and go see his former girlfriend for a few hours, try to patch it up with her. His plans went awry, and he was gone forty-eight hours. They shot Jason because he was Kyle's responsibility. When Kyle showed up, they shot him for not caring about what happened to Jason. Both are buried outside Plum, Texas. The details on where — as best I can remember them — are on that written list."

"You liked both Kyle and Jason." He could hear it in her voice.

"They were . . . decent-enough guys. Trapped in a family that was what it was. I'd like them to at least get decent burials, markers for their graves."

"Agreed."

"Outside the family deaths, most of what else I have about deaths are things I heard. There was a disagreement in Ohio with another party over the sale of two small statues. They shot the buyer in his home, buried him outside of town in an old cemetery. He's buried between a Maggie Thomas and a Joseph Lindstrom." She worried her thumb in the palm of her opposite hand.

"There was a girlfriend of Thomas Jacoby in Alabama who broke it off with him and was killed. She's buried in a cemetery near the movie theater where they used to meet — laid to rest as an addition to the plot of a recently deceased Lewis Tobias." She gestured to the pages he held.

"I'll flag several locations at the farm. They might all simply be dirt, or some of the stories I heard may be true. I think there's a child laid to rest under a willow tree. Another by an old windmill overlooking a pond. A first name Lacey for the girl, and a surname Prize for the boy. Those were before my time, so they'll need to look longer than eleven years back."

That news suggested this family had been active long before they had taken Shannon, and it left him concerned the investigation was going to span twenty years before it was concluded.

"There was a child — the third year in, so eight years ago — in an abduction that went wrong. She ran from the car at a gas station, drowned in a stream, was buried where it happened. All I have is Emily Lynn and Lazy Jill Creek, Colorado."

He tightened his hand on hers in sympathy. The father in him, along with the cop, took those facts as a heavy blow. He knew what it was like for Emily's parents, not knowing where their daughter was, if she was dead or alive somewhere, and it would be a crushing blow for them to hear the confirmation of her death.

Shannon used her free hand to wipe at tears. "The fourth year, there was a car wreck on the West Coast. They had an abducted child with them, Lindsey Bell. I know she died; I don't know how. They buried her in a pet cemetery outside of Dark, California."

Shannon stopped talking. She looked over at him, the misery on her face clear. These were her facts, her history, and she dealt with them because she had no choice.

"That's a lot of deaths to carry with you," he said softly.

"Yes."

And he worried more deeply than ever before what the years had done to her. "Reliving many of them?"

"I trigger easily when I hear a gunshot," she whispered. "A full-on fight I tend to expect to end in a shooting. But no, the reruns in my mind have calmed down."

He thought she told him the truth about that, and he knew in an odd way she might already be through the worst of it. Her mind would have accepted the facts about the deaths, done its best to shield her from the emotions of those facts. To survive it, she would have fought to keep that distance. The recent deaths would be fresh, but also a relief — the people she feared were no longer able to hurt her, unable to abduct other children. There would be guilt over being glad they were dead rather than sadness. "What do you need from me, Shannon?" he asked.

"To never have to repeat that summary. To not have to be the one to tell the cops. To not have to testify in court."

"I will do everything I can to make sure that is the case. Can you show us the farm? Or give us directions to find it?"

"It's difficult for me to pinpoint on the map. It would be best if Paul and Theo go with us to locate it. I can point out places, then hopefully never have to discuss or see it again."

"We'll arrange that." That trip was one more heavy matter coming in her near future. He was aware of the calendar. This needed to be told, and then she needed space. He desperately wanted to get her away from all this. "Let me talk with them about what might work best, make the arrangements."

She nodded. He waited but she offered nothing else. It was late, pushing past midnight, but he didn't want to end the evening like this. "Want me to make some popcorn so you can watch part of another movie?"

"I'm okay calling it a night. I just didn't want to have to take this list of graves into tomorrow's meeting. It's going to be a long enough conversation without it."

He nodded to her notepad. "That's the list of what you need to do, and of items to tell people?"

She fluttered the pages. "I do like lists. This one puts closure to the last eleven years."

"I'll help you get it finished if you will let me."

"I will. There's also a personal list. I'll probably let you help me with that too."

He smiled, pleased at the trust she was offering him. "Okay."

She got up from the couch, returned the pad to her bag. She turned back to face him, her expression hesitant. "I'm guessing you're going to read that fourth-year diary tonight, or call Paul and talk about what I just said. Please don't feel like you have to fix me. It's enough that you've been here to listen. That's what I need, Matthew. That's all I really need."

"Becky called me her shadow — her white shadow rather than her dark one, since she rather liked me — but she couldn't get rid of me."

Shannon's expression brightened, and she laughed. "I like that." She nodded. "Good night, Matthew." She turned toward her room, and his own smile faded as he shut off the television. He thoughtfully picked up the pages she had given him. She was wisely handing off to him the worst of it, he thought — her conversations on the drive to Chicago, the conversation tonight about the graves. She'd worked out a plan to tell her story one-on-one, and he'd been the lucky one — if that was the right word — selected to hear it.

He took the diary with him, walked across the hall, and called Paul. The retired cop in him was becoming fully engaged with the work that was unfolding. The man dealing with matters and trying to help her through this process was feeling every bit of the weight and the sadness.

# 17

Shannon was on the phone with her brother. Matthew covered the scrambled eggs in the skillet to keep them warm till she was finished. He poured juice, found more strawberries.

Her hand brushed his shoulder as she moved past to get a plate. "Thanks for fixing breakfast again."

He glanced over at her, surprised at the calmness he could both hear and see. "Scrambled eggs and fried potatoes two meals running — I'm not sure I deserve the compliment."

She smiled. "It helps that I like them. You said Paul is expecting us at nine thirty?"

"Yes."

"I'd like to stop for a box of donuts on the way. If I'm going to talk about everything on my list, I'd like to do it with a steady stream of sugar and caffeine. It might dull the edges of a headache I'm certain is going to be part of my memories of this day."

"The sugar and caffeine will likely contribute to a headache, but I can relate to the sentiment. We'll stop for donuts."

Paul was waiting for them in the secure parking lot of the FBI building. Dressed casually in jeans and a pale blue shirt, he walked over with a relaxed smile as they stepped out of the car. "Hello, Shannon. Welcome to the FBI."

"Hello, Paul."

Her words were calm, but Shannon's hand tightened to white knuckles on the canvas bag she carried. Matthew saw it, as did Paul, he noted. Matthew let his hand slide down her arm in a comforting gesture even as he gave Paul a slight shake of the head so he wouldn't pursue it.

"We stopped for donuts on the way in," Matthew mentioned, "had a nice debate over the merits of cream-filled versus Long Johns and glazed, ended up with some of each." He opened the back door to retrieve the donuts and the maps Shannon had marked. He handed Paul the maps, kept the two boxes of donuts. "We brought enough to share."

"A nice way to begin the morning. I've

got fresh coffee to go with the donuts." Paul turned to Shannon. "I appreciate your coming in for a conversation, Shannon. I thought we'd talk in my office if that's okay with you."

"Sure."

Paul coded in their entrance into a back hallway and led the way to a waiting elevator that bypassed the lobby. "Ann's upstairs with Theo. Would you like Ann to join us?"

"Whatever you think is best. Is there a table to spread out the maps, maybe a whiteboard?" Shannon asked.

"Would you prefer we stop by the case room first?"

"That might be easier."

"We'll go there then." He changed their floor destination and, when they stepped off the elevator, led the way to a conference room.

Theodore Lincoln was there, studying a financial printout with Ann. He looked up, gave a welcoming smile, and rose to his feet. "Hello, Shannon. It's a pleasure to have you here."

"Hello, Theo. Hi, Ann."

"Nice to see you again, Shannon," Ann said.

Shannon looked around the room at the information displayed: the photos she had provided of the five people who had died, the children rescued, ignored the boards with her picture and those of her family, the timeline on her own disappearance. She nodded to herself and walked over to the last whiteboard where there was still empty space. "May I?"

"Sure," Paul said.

She placed her canvas bag on the table and pulled out a folder. "Do you have any more of those magnetic clips to hold photos?"

Theo offered her a container of them. She started putting photos up. "I can build you kind of a loose family tree."

Theo and Ann moved around to better see what she was doing. Matthew unrolled the maps on the table, then pulled out a chair and settled back with a donut to watch Shannon work. No preliminaries, just what she had come to say, nerves nearly screaming now they were so visible. Ann leaned over. "What's wrong?" she asked in a whisper barely above a breath.

Matthew shook his head. He had no idea, but something had Shannon fighting nerves to an extent he hadn't seen before. He didn't think she was bothered by public speaking, so it had to be the information she was unpacking. She'd arrived at the FBI prepared to have this conversation, and yet her nerves had abruptly coiled tight. Ann found a bottle of water in the refrigerator, set it by the whiteboard ledge for Shannon. She tucked the folder of photos under her arm, picked it up, nodded her thanks. Matthew didn't like what he was seeing. Shannon was brutally pale.

*Any ideas for me, God, on what is happening?* He hadn't prayed much in the last couple of days since reading that first diary, the simmering anger that God hadn't stopped what had happened still being worked through his system. He'd been in that same place with God after he heard Becky's story, so he knew the emotions would subside over the coming days and he'd have a more level conversation with God again. But this prayer was on point, and one he needed answered.

Paul filled a mug from the coffeepot, walked over to stand beside Shannon. "How were you able to get the photos out?"

She placed another photo on the board, which looked like it had been enlarged from a wedding announcement. "I took advantage of anything that meant the family photos or wedding albums should be boxed or moved to get myself access to the images. Bad storms, roof leaks, broken windows — whenever water threatened to damage items — to more mundane reasons like birthday nostalgia and Christmas gatherings." She took a sip from the water bottle. "I created an extra envelope of miscellaneous negatives and photos that had fallen out of other collections. I managed to get that envelope slipped into a stolen-item package on its way to storage. Once I had gotten away, getting to the envelope meant getting to the right state and remembering where it had been placed. Some of these photos are pretty dated, and others are enlarged from a group picture, but I can recognize the person in the photo."

Paul scanned the images. "No worries. They're good enough for us to work from."

She picked up a marker and began writing names and some birthdays beside the photographs. "I don't know if I have official names or longtime aliases for some of these people. This is the birth date they celebrated. I don't often have the year. If you can find any details in a database that match up, like a more current photo, I can confirm it's the right person. They rarely travel using these names, so I don't think you'll find a driver's license even if I knew the state to check. There's still a New England accent within the family, so I think northeastern states are the places to start."

"Theo?"

"I'm on it."

Shannon drew a square with a question mark for five names, indicating she didn't have a photo, but wrote down gender, age, a description of their build, and identifying features. She sketched in eighteen people, adding the family connections and affiliations, before she finally stepped back. "This is the Jacoby family, or more accurately, the U.S. offshoot of the larger family, as best I could figure it out. The branch of the family in Poland and the Jacobys in Canada appear to be law-abiding and didn't have any involvement in what was going on here in the States."

She added stars beside some of the names. "The photos and names with the star are those who dealt with smuggling people, mostly children. The rest were smuggling objects."

Matthew was relieved when she stepped back from the board, got herself a donut, leaned against the table to study the graph. She was going to drop that water bottle if her hand tremor got any stronger. He leaned forward and reached out to get her attention, could feel the fine tremor in her arm too, and she turned to hold his gaze briefly. Not nerves as much as reaction — she was losing that grip of control she'd had in place since Atlanta.

"You want to go, just say the word," he murmured. Tears shimmered briefly before she blinked them away. She shook her head.

She walked back to the whiteboard and put a roughly drawn anchor beside three photos. "These three are very rarely on dry land, so they're going to be an interesting chase. One prefers a sloop and the East Coast, the other two fishing trawlers and the West. They get a hint you are coming, you won't catch them in U.S. waters."

Theo carried printouts to pin on the adjacent board as he found matching police records for some of the individuals.

Matthew wasn't entirely surprised by the fact Flynn was on the board as a blank square with no photo and no description. "Shannon, nothing on Flynn?"

She hesitated, then shook her head. "If the investigation finds him, you find him. I owe him . . . something. For now, I've decided silence is appropriate."

Paul, watching the exchange, nodded that he'd accept that.

Shannon erased one of her notes and redid it in smaller lettering to make more whiteboard space available. "The boat names change more frequently than you can say 'false papers.' What I have will likely already be dated." She wrote out fourteen of them. "There were probably a few name changes I didn't hear about."

"The first year, the trawler was named *Sea Sprite*?" Ann asked.

"Yes."

"It's showing up in the Coast Guard records." Ann sent the screen of data she was studying to the printer. "Did the captain have a routine, visit the same ports?"

Shannon thought about the question. "More so than the others did. The same refueling points, favorite mooring spots." She came back to the maps Matthew had unfurled, thumbed through them for the states of California and Washington. "I marked the places I remember in red, those I heard mentioned I put in blue."

Ann leaned over the maps with her. "These are the travel routes they took?" Ann asked, referencing the lines that flowed into California.

"Yes, they were professionals at it and would use interstate highways and back roads with equal ease. Their geography is somewhat predictable by season. They travel in pairs or as a group of three, but rarely more than that. They might be in two or three vehicles through the same general area, but they're acting independently of each other. They never stay near where they've stayed in the past. Oddly, that's one thing you can depend on. I've never seen an overlap in eleven years." She referenced the California map. "Hence this spider-web effect when you look at travels through the state over the last decade. They didn't want to be remembered. They used to argue when they approached a favorite restaurant if anyone in the group was unknown there and could go get a carryout order." Matthew heard her voice break and trail off, and for a moment Shannon wasn't in this room but somewhere in the past. He reached for her hand, gripped it hard, brought her back to the present.

She was still disturbingly pale but took a breath and finished her thought. "Everyone I put on that board is on the road most of the year. They aren't gypsies, but they consider their safety best maintained by being in motion. If they picked up something stolen, they would be at least a hundred miles away before stopping for gas, two hundred miles before thinking of stopping for the night. Never in a place they'd stayed previously." She reached for the water bottle and took a long drink of water.

"It never stopped. The top echelon on that board has an incredible thirst for money and things, and it's both an addiction and an adrenaline rush. Could they get away with something, how much profit could they make on deals, when and where should they sell what they had in storage? Those in the family willing to smuggle children were opportunistic — they'd accept work that fit where they planned to go. This time of year most of the people on the board should be in the northern leg of the circuit. If I had to choose the most likely states going into the Fourth of July weekend, I'd be looking at Colorado, Montana, maybe as far south as Iowa."

"What's the earliest they ever travel down the West Coast?" Paul asked.

"August."

"Did they stay at hotels? Private homes?"

"Mostly they traded off driving — one would sleep while another drove. Knocking on the door of an acquaintance late at night, being on the road again at dawn, was fairly common. Two- or three-day stops at a motel were also common. When they would stay put for a period of time — ten days, two weeks — they'd be mostly in out-of-the-way rentals." She finished the water, and Ann brought her another bottle. "They never call ahead for reservations. That you can depend on. They travel mostly on prepaid credit cards rather than cash. Part of their safety is the fact nothing's planned in advance, decisions are made on the fly. Even buying and selling is free-form. Arrive in an area, make a call, make the buy or sale within the hour, and then be traveling again."

Her hand trembled as she tried to set the bottle of water down. Matthew's eyes narrowed with sudden understanding. She was *afraid.* Whether God put the thought in his mind or he finally figured out what he was seeing, the answer settled in his mind with certainty. Shannon was afraid right now. It wouldn't be for her physical safety while in a building full of armed cops. It was the implications of what she was saying that was causing it. She feared how this was going to unfold. Eleven years living with the knowledge that her conduct determined someone else's safety — maybe someone else's life — and she was blowing that wide open. He needed to get her out of here, get her some breathing room. The realization was so intense he was pushing back his chair before what he should do was clear to him. "I'll be outside in the hall for a moment, Shannon," he said. "I need to make a call."

She gave him a surprised look, nodded.

When he returned, she was studying a map of Illinois with Paul. "They reassemble as a group twice a year, typically in March and November. There's a farm about half a day's drive from here. A sort of home base for the group. It's about here." She put her finger down between two towns. "I'll need to show it to you — I can find it once we're there, but I never saw the approach, just worked out over time where it must be. The other place they considered a home base is on the East Coast. Again, easier to show you than to try to put my finger down on a map."

"Will anyone be there this time of year?"

"It's possible one person was left behind on the property as a caretaker, but in the past everyone has traveled. They might lease out the farmland for someone else to plant, but they'd simply winterize the buildings and leave. And if those places weren't abandoned in a rush, they'll be pretty innocuous on the surface. They didn't trust that law enforcement would not stroll through the property when they weren't around."

"That's useful to know." Paul looked over at Ann. "Do you know the sheriff in that county?"

"Sam Dellherd. He'll be cordial to work with."

"When we're ready to make the trip, we'll want to give him an early call. We'll make that drive when you feel up to it, Shannon."

"The next few days, I think, as it's something I want off my list."

Matthew interrupted them by holding out his phone. "Paul, sorry to interrupt. John needs a word."

Paul accepted the phone with a nod and stepped away to have the conversation. Matthew didn't bother to look over — John would now be telling Paul to nod and say yes occasionally, that the only thing real about the call was the diversion it created.

Shannon was sorting through maps of the East Coast. Matthew leaned against the table beside her. "You need a break, Shannon," he said quietly. "Now would be a good time. The gym down the block has a pool. A couple of hours, we'll come back and continue this conversation, or leave the rest of it for another day. They've got a lot on their plate with what you've already given them. Let them work on finding database names and photos you can confirm."

"I have to get this done today."

He laid a hand on her arm. "Then let me

help you. Let's take a break. Catch your breath. Otherwise you may not get to the end."

She closed her eyes, and her hand on the table trembled. "One more thing first." She looked over at Paul, who had lowered the phone and was now refilling his coffee. "How big a favor can I ask of you?"

"Ask. You've earned yourself a great deal of goodwill," Paul replied.

"I know you're going to dig into anyone and everyone with the Jacoby name or a relation, but I'd ask you to trust that after eleven years of learning this family, I understand some of the history. These eighteen are the only ones who were involved or conspired with those who acted in the crimes I saw occur. I'm going to write a second list of names you could consider helpful material witnesses but not pursue on charges. I'm not putting a name on this second list lightly. If I don't know enough about them, I'm leaving their names off both lists. These are the ones I know were *not* involved."

Paul considered what she said. "Write your list. I'll talk with you about the individuals and what we've discovered about them before I do anything."

Shannon nodded and started writing out

names. Three were Jacobys, another six were various surnames that Matthew assumed would turn out to be Jacoby women now married. When she finished, she placed the marker in the tray, stepped back from the board, studied it, nodded to herself.

"Were there others besides this family involved in what was going on?" Paul asked.

"They did business with a lot of people whose names I can give you, but the family trusted only blood, and even then it was 'trust but verify.' They were a law unto themselves. What the head of the family decided would be done was the final word and complied with or you were kicked out of the family, and your freedom didn't last long — you were in jail or dead within months."

"Thanks for all this, Shannon. And it's a good place for a break. Let's have a late lunch around two o'clock, then talk about the other names on your list," Paul suggested. "Possibly call it a day at that point. I'll order in. Chinese sound okay? Or would you prefer Mexican?"

"Chinese is fine."

# 18

Matthew waited until they stepped onto the elevator and the doors closed before he asked what he had to know. "What went through your mind when we reached the FBI? What brought the fear rushing in?"

Shannon leaned her head back against the elevator wall, her face the picture of distress. "The Jacobys will clean house. The guys at the top of that family will simply kill the others. As soon as they realize their world is coming down around them, they will silence those who could speak against them, then disappear."

It was a fear with a solid basis behind it, an all-too-possible outcome. The realization of it was overwhelming her. "I'll take you for a swim so you can turn this off for an hour, Shannon. Ellie has brought over a swimsuit for you. She'll meet us at the gym."

"Should I be doing something different than what I am, Matthew? Not tell Paul any more? Or should I have told him a week ago?"

"Don't revisit your decisions so far. Waiting to hear if someone else had been able to get free was a calculated choice, and your silence gave her the best chance. That's a good decision. Hopefully people are dispersed enough in their travels, can be located quickly enough that it's not possible for what you are fearing to happen. But this ends this summer. That's a good thing."

She physically shivered, lifted her hands to rub her arms. "I should have gotten out years ago, at least risked trying. I didn't because I could name the person who would die if I made the attempt, was able to make it. I just couldn't take that step. Maybe I should have made that sacrifice, one for the many. Maybe the family wouldn't have been as cohesive then, had a few less members."

He took her hand and interlaced their fingers. "Enough," he said huskily. "One thing I learned from Becky — when you're in survival mode you make the best choice given what you know, and move on. Trust those choices and don't look back."

"I feel nauseous."

"It's nerves. We swim. Eat lunch. Spend another couple of hours talking with Paul.

Then I'll get you free of this. Let me handle those future hours, just stay in the moment. Don't think beyond the present."

She gave a jerky nod. "This is why I came and found you, Matthew. I couldn't handle walking alone into an FBI office and telling what I know. I couldn't do it."

"You're stronger than you realize. You're doing it now. And you're doing it with a clear, concise focus that is helpful to Paul. To everyone."

"I've got more names to give. Facts. But don't let Paul get to questions about what happened with me. Not today."

"He won't go there, but if someone does, I'll step in," Matthew promised.

Matthew held the door for Shannon as they returned to the conference room shortly before two p.m., gave a nod of thanks to the escorting agent. He thought the swim had helped. She was quieter now, that calm control she'd shown him before back in place, strong enough to handle the last few hours. Better to be done in a day than to let it stretch out for her to face another day.

Lunch was spread out on the table, open cartons of various Chinese choices. Ann and Theo were eating while they worked. Two more whiteboards had been brought up to the room. Printouts were clipped beside a few of the photos. "You've been busy," Matthew remarked, holding a chair out for Shannon.

"The last name for the family, enough first names to give confirmations, revealed the historical center of the family as the small town of London, New York," Theo replied.

Shannon shook her head. "They never visited there."

"Wise on their part. The men at the top of the family tree went to high school there. We'll be able to dig through layers now that we've got the family group located," Theo said. "Paul's on his way back. When my boss called, I elected to hand Paul the phone and let them sort out the particulars. Bottom line, this case stays in this room for now, as do I."

Matthew nodded, pleased to hear that news. Shannon selected an open carton of white rice, then went to the sweet-and-sour pork and the cashew chicken, not taking much on her plate but enough to be an attempt at lunch.

"Shannon, I have some questions about the road trips," Ann said — a softball topic, Matthew thought, glad to hear that approach.

"Sure."

"Travelers come in different types. Did they stop at the Grand Canyon when they were in the area? Did they regularly visit flea markets or antique shops? Were they food buffs, wanting to try out places in the best-of restaurant category lists? What kind of vehicles did they favor, and how often did they change them? Did they make a habit of speeding? Any particulars along those lines could be helpful."

Shannon half smiled at the list of questions. "I think that's why they separated and traveled in smaller groups. They could all indulge their own styles and interests. There were . . . *assignments,* for want of a better word. *You'll deal with this, you'll handle that,* kinds of decisions. The direction of travel and a time frame for arriving somewhere would be loosely agreed upon. The family liked to arrange itself as a patrol string, so if one group got into trouble there was always someone else in the family within one to two hours available to assist. But within that loose agreement, it was up to the driver. Some groups stopped at every antique store — probably scoping out an overlooked prize that wouldn't have to be stolen — others favored an evening at some local stock-car race, while others drove straight through, getting business done, then spent a few days being tourists while they waited for the rest to reach the area. Flynn and I were more the kind of travelers to take the back roads and enjoy the scenery."

Paul joined them and fixed himself a lunch plate.

"It was a cardinal rule that you didn't speed," Shannon continued. "The cars were traded in when the mileage got to a certain point. Never a new car, nor a particularly old one — something dependable in a color that wouldn't stand out. There was only one van in the mix. Most were midsize sedans."

"That's useful," Ann commented.

Shannon took her plate over to the trash can, stopped to consider the beverage choices, came back with a Cherry Coke. She resumed her place at the table, looked over at Paul, who appeared relaxed in the facing chair.

"Give me a semihard question," she suggested.

He considered for a moment. "The graves. Thank you for what you gave Matthew. There are cops in California looking for Lindsey Bell now. About an hour ago officers in Colorado found Emily Lynn."

She briefly closed her eyes.

"On behalf of the families, thank you," he said.

She slowly nodded. "And the question?"

"Are you dealing okay with the fact there was nothing you could do to stop what happened to them?"

She flinched and rubbed both hands down her face, blew out a breath before placing her hands flat on the table. "Yes. Mostly. Those first years there was no way I could help. They stopped abducting children after the second death, took a break, and I hoped they wouldn't go back to it. They did. The best I could do was figure out how to get packages out about the kids they were abducting. Stopping the family, getting myself out without causing someone else to die, wasn't . . . easy to figure out. In the end, it was still more chance than plan that got me here." She sighed. "I'm resigned, Paul, that I couldn't stop what the kidnapping side of the family was doing over the years. And I'll have to live with the fact that the explosion within the family leading to their deaths was probably in part my doing."

Matthew looked over at her sharply. Paul took that comment without showing a reaction. Then he moved on.

"Let's talk about something easier," Paul said. "They smuggled stolen items. Who did they do business with? How did that work?"

Shannon pushed back from the table, picked up a marker for a new whiteboard. She began writing names. "These are people I know the family dealt with on more than one occasion."

Matthew shared a long look with Paul. *She'd had a role in triggering that internal family explosion, killing the five smuggling children.* Matthew could almost feel the painful edges of that conversation in the future, the dynamics that would have been in play. He hoped she handed him her diary from that time period so he wouldn't have to ask her to elaborate on the statement.

Shannon was listing names along with a city and state, occasionally referring to her notes. "The family didn't steal items. They would buy from a fence or from a broker who had a deal fall apart, put the item in storage, then sell it at a later date to private collectors, brokers, pawn dealers. They would never sell the item in the area it was acquired. Something gotten in the North would be sold in the South and vice versa."

"What kind of records did they keep on the stolen items?" Paul asked.

"Good ones. They would store items for a long period of time. Five years was the norm from when they acquired it to when it was sold. But you're going to have a problem, because as soon as they know you're coming for them, anything they can reach is going to disappear. They don't need access to bank accounts to flee; they just need time. They've got a fortune hidden in places around the nation." She drew a line and began listing private collectors who had bought items from the group.

"There are two ledgers for each year, one for the East and one for the West. They record the location and date they received the item, the purchase price, the place they stored it, a photo reference number of the item, eventually listing the buyer and the sale price. In recent years they started adding GPS locations. Every three months they would photocopy the ledger pages and store that copy somewhere as insurance against the original being lost or seized. They dispersed the photos of items into collections for a region, would store them for safety just as they did the stolen items. I was able to get to one of the photo collections for the Midwest."

She lifted out of the canvas bag a sunglasses case, opened it to show several flash drives. "This is one of the newer collections. The photos are between two and six years old, so most of these articles should still be in storage around the Midwest. Unfortunately I haven't been able to get to any of the ledger copies from those years to tell me *where* these photographed items are stored, but I think I know where a couple of the ledger copies can be found. What I did manage to get ahold of is the full East Coast ledger from four years ago." She tugged it out of her bag and unwrapped the plastic around the book. "It was stored in a box I cleared out in Atlanta. I didn't know it would be there. They may have been in a hurry to get it stored, or they had used the place recently and put it in the most convenient location."

She opened the book and showed Paul a page of entries.

Paul studied it, thumbed through the ledger. "This is priceless, Shannon, for what can be done with it."

"I'm hoping the hideaway sites I can give you will yield more full ledgers or ledger copies so you can have precise lists to work from. I think I have seen probably twenty percent of the locations they used around the country. There are a lot of them that fall into the category of 'I know there's one in this town. I remember it's somewhere around that library building or by the Civil War statue,' where I'm going to have to visit the location to jog my memory unless a particular ledger shows up. So it's probably going to be necessary to cut a few deals with people to locate where the ledgers or the ledger copies have been stored."

Paul was scanning pages and counting entries. "Having one in hand to know what we're looking for is already a big step forward. We'll figure out a way to locate them." He looked up at her. "They've been dealing with a *lot* of merchandise." He must have noted her expression. "What's your concern?"

"Is it five years or ten for dealing in stolen goods?"

Paul closed the ledger and considered her. "Shannon, if I can't put together the sum total of what has happened in the last eleven years, put all eighteen of those people still alive in jail for the rest of their lives, I shouldn't be in this job. We need the evidence gathered, and there's much work to come, but we *will* get it done. You can ask my wife to confirm it when I tell you I'm good at my job. Just sayin'."

Shannon glanced over at Ann.

"He hates to brag," Ann said with a smile. "Trust him, Shannon. Paul won't let anyone the law can reach get free. It won't be a slap-on-the-wrist sentence."

Shannon turned back at Paul. "Can you

do it without me having to tell my story in court?"

"I'll do my best to restrict what depends on you."

"Then I need to ask, could further questions wait for another day? What's on the boards now is most of the facts I can give you."

"You gave us a lot today, Shannon. When you're up for it, we'll take a drive and see that farm. And it would be helpful to have a list of the storage locations you can remember. Let's make those the next steps whenever you're ready."

She nodded and pushed back her chair. Matthew was already picking up her bag and handing it to her, with a grateful nod to Paul that the day was ending here.

# 19

Matthew glanced over at Shannon. She hadn't spoken since they drove away from the FBI building. "We'll stop and get a bite to eat, give you a chance to unwind in an environment that's not the apartment's same four walls."

"Whatever you think," she said absently.

"It went well today, Shannon."

"It got done," she said. "Once it's known I'm alive, they'll be looking to find me, to make sure I can't testify."

"John and I will make sure nobody can get near you. Of everything you might worry about, don't pick that one up."

She nodded. "Thanks for being there today. And that swim really helped."

"I'm glad. You've 'done good' today, Shannon. You did the right thing."

"It helps to hear that."

Matthew found the restaurant he wanted, a place named Cues, parked in the side lot and moved around the car to open Shannon's door. "This is an Italian restaurant Bryce mentioned. He and Charlotte often come here on Saturday nights to have dinner and play some pool. If they're here tonight, they won't be offended if we wave and then do our own thing. But if you want some conversation that's unrelated to any of this, Charlotte's probably the safest person I can suggest."

"I like them, Matthew. If they are here, let's at least stop and say hello."

Bryce and Charlotte had just arrived themselves. The four ended up sharing two medium pizzas, with the conversation moving easily around upcoming Chicago summer events, the campaign for governor, Charlotte's career in art, Ellie and John's impending wedding — absolutely nothing during the meal touching on Shannon's story or her FBI debriefing that day. But Matthew thought Shannon had to make an effort to stay engaged even while she was enjoying the evening.

Charlotte had brought along her own custom pool cue, offered to share it, and the ladies moved to a free table to play a game. Matthew joined Bryce at an open dart board. It had been years since he'd played, but as he hefted a dart it felt right in his hand. "Thanks for mentioning this place, Bryce. Shannon needed the break." He tossed his first dart and was pleased with where it landed.

"I'm glad it worked out — for you and us." Bryce tossed a dart, and Matthew realized his chance of offering a good match was going to be mostly luck. Bryce had the dart board zeroed in. Matthew did his best to offer a competitive game, was halfway pleased when Bryce won the game by only several points rather than dozens.

Matthew was watching the women as Bryce collected the darts. "What do you think they're talking about?"

Bryce studied his wife with a narrowed gaze, smiled. "Shoes."

"You're serious."

"My wife has a thing for them, and she just spotted what Shannon's wearing. They'll be planning a shopping trip soon, I imagine."

"Shoes. Okay. It *is* the one thing Shannon has expressed an interest in shopping for since we reached Chicago."

Bryce laughed. "They'll be fine, those two. Charlotte's good at reading people. She'll nudge the conversation in a direction that'll be helpful to Shannon."

"We've had a long day. Shannon spent

most of it talking with Paul and his team."

"I wondered," Bryce said. "She has that expression like she's gone down a dark memory lane and isn't quite fully back yet."

"How does Charlotte handle the dark memories?"

"She works on her art, though sometimes she decides it would help to talk — mostly with Ellie, I think, but occasionally she'll bring up something to me. She's not looking for much feedback, simply to have someone else know the memory and share it with her."

"I haven't figured out how Shannon deals with a day like this. Shopping, going for a swim, talking — whatever it is, she needs more of it right now, and I don't know what to offer. I'm not sure even she knows that answer. She hasn't had her freedom long enough to have found a pattern."

Bryce squared a dart in his hand, sent it flying to start another match. "Charlotte said the first days after her rescue were like being hit with a tidal wave — the volume of things happening around her, so many people coming and going. Constant change. Nothing ever the same. She longed for things to be the same from one day to the next."

Matthew stopped a dart mid-throw.

"That's utterly profound. How did I miss it?" Shannon's life since Atlanta had been constant change. He could do a lot more to help her find a daily rhythm. "What else did Charlotte say?"

"She wanted to talk about the process going on, not the things in her past. She wanted to know what to expect in the days and weeks ahead. She needed to know the future in order to get comfortable with it before it arrived."

"What was the thing that got her through those weeks?"

"John hired on as her bodyguard and instinctively provided for both needs: a constant she could depend on, and a heads-up for what was going to happen. He didn't allow anything to be a surprise."

The ladies had ended their game and were walking back to the table. Matthew watched them be seated and saw they were settling into a conversation. He turned his attention back to the game. "Tell me something, Bryce. Did you marry Charlotte knowing her past, or was it a long discovery?"

"Both."

Matthew glanced over. "Any regrets?"

"None."

"Mention that to Shannon sometime, would you? It might help her to know your perspective. For that matter, mention it to my daughter should she ever visit Chicago."

Bryce smiled. "My wife is an interesting woman, both despite what happened and because of it. It's her history. With time it becomes our history. A marriage can work with that."

They finished the dart game and walked over to rejoin the ladies. Matthew slid into the booth beside Shannon, picked up the soft drink the waitress had refilled, considered another slice of the pizza.

Shannon leaned into his shoulder as she reached across for the hot pepper. "I'm going shopping with Charlotte tomorrow."

Matthew had to grin. "Okay. Becky tells me that retail therapy is good for the mind, body, and soul."

Shannon poked him with her little finger. "There speaks a skeptic. Charlotte also said we could probably slip into the balcony at their church, come and go unnoticed, if we attend the eight a.m. service tomorrow."

"It's a plan. I'll work out directions with Bryce."

Shannon dropped the pepper stem on the edge of her plate. "Is darts an easy game to learn?" she asked, changing the subject.

"Can you read that sign over the door?" Matthew asked, pointing it out.

"What? Why?"

"If you can, you don't need glasses, and I can probably teach you. If you can't, you need to see an eye doctor first, then we'll be in business."

She looked at the sign and gave an exaggerated squint.

Charlotte laughed. "Come on, Shannon. I'll teach you darts. We can play teams against the guys next week. And you two be prepared to lose . . . badly," she added, looking meaningfully at the men as she shifted her pool cue to Bryce for safekeeping.

Matthew and Bryce chuckled and got to their feet so the women could slide out of the booth. Matthew watched as they chose a board and began divvying up the darts between them, laughing together. "It looks like we're going to be joining you again next week. Sorry about that. I realize this is probably your date night with Charlotte."

"No problem," Bryce said. "We're working on a list — top ten favorite dates. It gives me an excuse to take her out a few times every week. We can afford to share the occasional Saturday night."

"Shannon really needed this evening. It's a good break for her from the hard things of today."

"I'm glad we can be of help. How are you

doing, Matthew?"

He grimaced.

"That bad?"

"She came to find me. I'm not walking away before this is finished. But she's dealt with it over eleven years. I'm hearing the story in about eleven days . . . and it's not an easy thing to absorb."

Bryce picked up his glass and tapped Matthew's. "I know it's not. But it helps her on her journey back. So you do it without flinching."

"I'm doing my best. She'd be able to do it on her own if necessary. There's nothing fragile about her," Matthew admitted.

"She hasn't shown it yet but, yes, there is. That broken part that will wonder, 'Am I still worth loving?' " Bryce replied.

"You married Charlotte."

"A good move on both our parts, done for our own reasons," Bryce said with an easy smile.

"You're in love with her."

"Of that you can be certain." Bryce leaned back, studied him. "And yes, before you have to ask, that question was a large part of Charlotte's struggle with trusting me. Don't worry so much about the timing of things, what people will think, what makes logical sense when it comes to a woman like

Shannon. You've got a good friendship forming there."

"She's between the age of my daughter and myself. That pushes me both ways — she's someone to take care of and someone to care about."

Bryce chuckled. "Both nice sentiments. You're a good friend to her, Matthew. So be that. Shannon's healing is faster with you than without you. So carry what she'll let you carry, do your best to fill in the gaps for her. That's basically my story with Charlotte — a really good friendship that evolved into the trust and depth of a love affair within a very good marriage."

Matthew's eyebrows raised. "Why do I get the feeling you're asking me something?"

"Shannon's simply the . . . interesting woman who's walked across your path," Bryce offered with a smile, defining reality for him. "I look at the two of you and I see . . . the possibility of something that is also interesting. Let's find a pool table. You can take some of the emotion of today out on a game or two."

"You're only trying to tie me up in knots, throw off my concentration for the game," Matthew said as they stood.

"Distracting you," Bryce corrected with a laugh. "Have you thought much about what happened today since you've been here?"

"No," Matthew conceded.

"See? I'm good at this."

Matthew laughed. "Yeah, you are." He tilted his head, curious. "Has Charlotte got your number yet?"

"She had that done long before she finally accepted my marriage proposal."

"How long did she make you wait?"

"After the proposal? Months."

Matthew shot a glance over at Charlotte. *Interesting.* She'd made a good choice and also read Bryce very well, from the look of it.

Matthew hunkered down beside the restaurant booth, picked up the last breadstick in the basket, enjoying the garlic and the melted cheese baked in. "Shannon, we'd better head out." It was coming up on nine o'clock, and he'd lost the last three games of pool to Bryce. And as comfortable as Shannon was right now, sharing a piece of cake with Charlotte, she needed sleep even more than he did.

Shannon nodded and finished her drink, slid out from the booth. Matthew smiled a thanks at Charlotte. "Bryce says John's going to act as chauffeur for the shopping trip tomorrow, so if by chance I don't see you, I want to wish you good luck finding perfect outfits and their matching shoes."

"Our plan is to start with the shoes and work our way up from there," Charlotte said with a chuckle.

They said good-night to Bryce and Charlotte, and Matthew led Shannon out of the restaurant. She covered a yawn before they were halfway to the car. "I am wiped."

"I can imagine. I'm really glad you were able to relax."

"I like Charlotte," Shannon mentioned as she settled in the car. "A lot."

"I can tell you do," Matthew said lightly. He closed her car door and circled around to take the driver's seat. "Bryce impresses me too."

"He's charmed by her, and she feels safe with him. It was kind of interesting to watch their interplay tonight. They're close for being a married couple."

Matthew was amused at her remark. "The way it should be in a good marriage."

"Did you have a good marriage with . . . I'm so sorry, but I don't remember your wife's name."

"Jessica." He smiled. "We had a great marriage. We were young and very much in love. She died way too soon, long before the passion between us mellowed."

"How did she die?"

He wanted to avoid answering at the moment, but it was a relevant question. He tried to give Shannon a word picture as a reply. "It was the kind of accident that was no one's fault. A man had a heart attack while driving. She couldn't avoid the resulting collision. Her loss left a huge hole in my life, in Becky's too. Jessica was the bright light we both revolved around, took our cues from. She made our days flow together as a family. It took a while to find our footing again."

"I'm sorry I asked and made you uncomfortable."

"Don't worry about it, Shannon. It's part of my past. Not as crushing as yours, but my own version of memories and emotions that need some thought before opening them once more. I don't mind talking about Jessica. It's a good history, being married to someone I truly loved, and I've made peace with the loss. It's just . . . big."

"It's like the rock that the rest of your life now rests on."

He liked the analogy. "A big, flat rock, as it underlies most areas of my life. I can build whatever I wish to on that history, but it's there."

"My rock is very jagged. My history hasn't

been worn down by time yet, hasn't been smoothed off."

He thought that image was right on target. She was just beginning to smooth down her past's rough edges, just beginning to figure out what she would build on it in the future.

A couple of minutes passed in silence.

"How long will it be before I'm back together enough that I could get married?" Shannon asked.

He shot her a surprised look, turned thoughtful. He mulled over the two diaries he'd read. "Five years, I think. Seven, if you want to get to a really good outcome. You'll need a doctor in the mix to help you process that whole part of your life."

"That's a problem."

"My assessment?"

"No. You're probably right, which is depressing. But it's way too long."

"You need time to work through the past, Shannon. Wanting to fly through that process will only cause problems and a crash you won't be ready for. Becky tried rushing things and quickly learned that healing is time-consuming work. The best thing you can do now is to accept that truth."

She shifted around to look at him. "If I tell you something that might end up embarrassing you, would you just listen and hear me out? I didn't plan on putting this into words. At least not yet."

"If I get too embarrassed I'll tell you," Matthew said with a grin.

She grinned back. "Fine. Okay. I'm twenty-seven. You know that. I've got a personal list that matters a great deal to me — it's one of the ways I survived. It's my list of five major things I would do when I had my freedom. Item three on that list is to get married. Item four is having kids. I don't want to be watching my son or daughter graduate when I'm sixty. Hopefully I'm having my first child by the time I'm thirty-five, so I've got the family I want before I'm forty."

He pictured Shannon as a mom and nodded, easily able to see little girls who looked like her.

"I know I have a horrible past that some guy is going to have to cope with. And I haven't even graduated from high school yet myself. So the thought of locating and choosing a husband is not a small concern for me. I've spent considerable time deliberating on the problem. It's going to have to be someone who can handle who I am, a Christian, someone who doesn't use violence or anger in his voice or actions. That's the stuff I know for certain. I chose you as the person I contacted for a long list of reasons. One of which is simple. You might already know the guy who's going to be my husband, or a friend of yours knows him."

Her words startled him, and he was glad for the red light so he could turn to look at her. "Shannon —"

"Just listen, okay?" she asked, stopping his comment. "Let me dump the whole thing. I considered the ways you could help me, and it wasn't just that you'd be able to smooth the way back to Chicago and meeting my family, be a buffer with the cops, be helpful in finding the right doctors — though those points were on the list. It was that you would understand my past and how it has impacted me. It's not going to be easy finding a man who wants to be my husband, who's willing to stick with me for a lifetime. I want someone of strong character, someone able to work through whatever is going to arise. The best place to find my husband is very likely going to be a guy who had a family member or friend who went through something like you endured with Becky or who has someone in their life still missing. Those are guys you know, so don't dismiss this hope. Guys like . . . well, Bryce, but he's already taken."

Matthew smiled at the name. "Perfect. But

as you say, taken." He nodded thoughtfully, not really surprised by what she'd said. Shannon thought far ahead, he knew that about her. "I accept your point. It's actually a rather elegant point." The light changed, and he put his attention back on the road. "The man you want as a husband should have all those dynamics."

"And I don't have time to be casual about this, Matthew. I have eight years to go from where I am now to being happily married and having my first child. That is, frankly, a rushed proposition. According to your timeline, it may be nearly impossible, but I'm determined to keep that dream alive. My decision to track you down was deliberate."

He risked a quick glance over at her. "I've figured that out."

"Then in the spirit of being honest, you probably deserve to know I'm using you to answer some questions I have," Shannon admitted. "Here are three: I want to know if I've got a panic reaction around guys. I've figured out I probably don't. Second, I still like being held. I wondered about that for years because I'd come to hate it. Third, it's nice being the center of a guy's attention. I've tried to stay unnoticed for so long, I wasn't sure how it would feel to be the focus of a guy's attention. And just to put an embarrassing point out there — I'd like to know how I react to a kiss, given how bad the memories are of some others I'd rather forget. If that question happens to get checked off with you, I think it would be nice. You're a nice guy."

He didn't dare look at her.

"I'm trying to sort out in my mind how bad the damage is," she summed up, biting her lip. "What do I need to fix in order to have my personal list come true? Husband is on that list. Having a family. I'm not thinking about you that way, mainly because you're too important to my long-term plan for me to risk messing things up. But I decided early on that the better you know me, the better the advice you're going to give me when I ask you who you think I should date." She reached over and rested her hand briefly on his arm. "Now I'm done. What do you think?"

The silence lingered after her startling speech.

"There are only five things on your personal list?"

She nodded. "It's a short list so I can tick them off on my fingers, focus on them, get them accomplished. Five items."

"Tell me all five. I'll help you get them done."

"No reply to what I just told you?"

"I'm thinking about what I want to say. I won't make the mistake again of underestimating how much you strategically think and plan."

"You're insulted?"

"You're reading me wrong. I'm fine, Shannon. Fifteen years my junior and you just . . . impressed me." Parking for the apartment was ahead on the left, and he had never been so relieved to know a conversation was going to go to pause. "Show me your list. We'll have round two of this conversation later."

"Or maybe not?" she said softly, clearly bothered by his neutral response. He shot her a quick glance, could see her retreating, regretting having said what she did.

"It can't be more embarrassing than round one," he mentioned, hoping to lighten the moment. He parked the car, came around to her side as she stepped out. He locked the car, and then he deliberately rested a friendly arm across her shoulders as they walked to the elevator so he could put this conversation into its place in their relationship.

"Shannon, I will help you reach your dreams. Including the important one of finding a husband. And because I'm not an idiot, after I see you back to the apartment, I'm going to head out for a couple hours, go talk to Paul about what they've found since we left this afternoon, and give us some breathing room before I comment on what you told me. You can call if you need me, but otherwise I'll see you in the morning."

"Distance being the better part of valor."

He looked at her quickly, saw her expression, and smiled. "Something like that." They had reached the elevator and stepped inside. "I don't mind a bit of flirting, just to see how it might feel. You are beautiful, and you're finding your balance as a woman. It's enjoyable to watch. I just don't want an eleven p.m. moment with you I'm going to regret in the morning, or for that matter, any situation I wouldn't be comfortable with if my daughter were in the room. We're friends. It's going to remain that way."

"Round two of this conversation should be interesting," she said, sounding like she had regained her footing.

"Not tonight." The elevator opened, and they walked to the apartment. He suddenly realized what was going on. "You needed a distraction, didn't you? This entire last half hour was your way of not having to spend the night thinking about what you said to

Paul today. You figuratively threw a live grenade into the mix so you'd have something else to deal with."

She considered that, half smiled. "Yes. Maybe not consciously planned it, but that sounds about right."

The fact he'd run headlong into one of her coping skills and hadn't seen it coming rather startled him. Her way of coping was to focus on her future. That was what had gotten her through the crushingly hard moments; that was why her personal list of five items was so critical to her, and why talking about those items, thinking about them, planning for them mattered so much to her. He realized the layers he'd just seen her play out, and it actually rather pleased him.

He entered the security code for the apartment, swung open the door, and then he leaned down and lightly kissed her. "Think about this instead." He pushed her gently inside, closed the door, and headed back down to go find Paul.

# 20

Matthew was braced for some awkwardness when he first saw Shannon on Sunday morning. She was sitting at the kitchen table, a bowl of cereal and the comics in front of her. She glanced over, smiled. "Coffee's hot. Do I have half an hour to finish getting ready for church or forty-five minutes?"

He glanced at the time. "You can take forty-five. It's about a half hour drive. I want to slip in after the first song, leave before the final prayer."

Shannon held out her mug. "In that case, pour me another cup of coffee."

He brought the pot over. "No comment, Shannon?"

"On last night?" She gave him an amused look. "No."

He'd like to know what was behind that smile, but thought better of asking. He moved to the stove to fix an omelet.

She left to finish getting ready. He sat down with his breakfast plate, reached for the comics she had been reading, enjoyed a leisurely breakfast. She rejoined him, putting on her earrings as he was finishing his last bite of toast. He folded the newspaper, noticed the worn book she'd set on the table. "You were able to keep a Bible with you?"

"It was in my backpack, along with that first diary. They weren't anti-religion; they just considered it not for them."

"May I?"

He gestured toward the book, and she handed it across. He considered personal Bibles to be interesting statements about people. Hers was well-worn, heavily underlined, slips of paper between various pages. There were no notes that he could see.

"They would have torn out the page had I written anything," she remarked.

He nodded and handed it back. "I'm glad your faith survived, Shannon."

"It was something that was mine, that faith, something they couldn't take away from me. I wasn't going to *let* them take it away. Long before this happened, I used to write out a prayer I found once in a devotional book: 'Give me endurance, Lord, and help me to go the distance for your kingdom.' I liked Paul's analogy of running a race, a soldier serving on duty."

"I like that comparison too," Matthew agreed.

"You don't train warriors by keeping them out of the dirt and out of the fights," she went on, turning thoughtful. "You train warriors by giving them what they can handle, then giving them progressively bigger assignments. You develop the best warriors by training them the hardest. God used what came to answer that prayer I had repeatedly written. He would have found a different way to train me if this terrible evil hadn't intruded, but once it did, God was able to create a useful outcome. A solid faith is one of those outcomes. I'm stubborn, Matthew. I wanted my faith, something I deeply valued, to survive. God was there for me. It did certainly help that process that I was able to keep a Bible with me — this book and I have traveled a lot of miles together."

"Did you do some memorizing?"

She offered a slight smile. "I could probably do okay in one of those Bible trivia games." She set the book aside. "What I could keep was what I could carry in a gym bag. I learned to live comfortably with the basics: a Bible, camera, diary, clothes, and a constantly changing novel."

It was an interesting statement about her life. He chose to shift the subject. "Do you hate traveling now?"

She shrugged. "Not really. I'm good at it. I know how to find something in each day's journey that is enjoyable. Like how to sleep deeply while someone else drives. But I'm seriously looking forward to putting down roots and being in one place for forty years."

"Any more thoughts about where that will be? Here in Chicago near your brother and his wife?"

"Reality is shifting my answer. I think Illinois is going to be too much publicity and media attention should my brother become governor — which I think he will — and he'll probably be in that job for the next eight years. So I'm beginning to consider where else I'd enjoy living. I'll visit Chicago but not live here."

"You've got an entire nation to choose from. Warm and sunny. Mountains. Open plains."

She tipped her head. "I miss the ocean," she finally said. "Not necessarily lying on the beach, but the sound of it, the sight of it, and the pleasure of being able to swim good distances. The ocean is big and free, and I love it."

Matthew liked the way she said it. "Do

you like to sail?"

She shrugged. "I'm a good sailor, but I wouldn't care if I never stepped foot on another boat. I do prefer a sailboat if given a choice. It tends to have more interesting things to do."

It was time to leave for church. Matthew carried his plate to the dishwasher. "If you do come east, I know some very nice beaches that don't get a lot of tourist traffic."

"I'll head that way one day," she replied easily. "I'll enjoy seeing them."

"John's picking me up at one thirty," Shannon mentioned as they reentered the apartment after church. "Charlotte and I are going to try the stores near her home first, then work our way this direction. I figure I'll be back around five. Have you decided on your day?"

"I'm going running with Paul and Bryce this afternoon. They use the track over at the university."

"I like my plan better than yours," she said with a smile.

"Want a sandwich before you go?"

"Sure. Turkey and Swiss, just a touch of mustard." She turned toward her room to get changed. "Give me ten minutes."

Matthew moved to the kitchen to fix them an abbreviated lunch.

Fifteen minutes later, Shannon joined him, having changed from her Sunday dress into slacks and a blouse, working to fit new earrings in place. "That looks like more than just a sandwich."

He was cutting a tomato into slices for his own sandwich and used the knife to gesture to the place he had set for her. "Tapioca pudding. With a side of strawberries to go with the sandwich. You can start with the dessert."

She laughed. "You know my weakness."

"I'm learning," he said with a grin. "Your sandwich is on sourdough bread and has a hint of mustard."

"Perfect."

She dropped a sheet of paper on the counter beside him. "My personal list."

She pulled out a chair at the kitchen table and studied the sandwich he had built for her and how best to pick it up. He paused in his own sandwich preparation to lean over and read her list.

1.) Graduate from high school
2.) Get a career established in photography (start with selling photos I've already taken)

3.) Get married
4.) Have kids (three would be nice)
5.) Every Christmas Eve and New Year's Eve ████████

She'd blacked out the last part of the fifth item. He wiped his hands, picked up the sheet, and held it to the light but couldn't make out the words.

"That's cheating," she told him with a mock frown.

"I'm curious." He put it back on the counter, read the list again, then finished creating his own sandwich. Five items held her personal dreams for her future. Number two intrigued him. "You're interested in pursuing your photography. I like that. *Shannon Bliss, Photographer.* It has a nice ring to it."

"I think I'm a pretty good one. That one rather depends on me figuring out where Flynn stored more of those memory cards. I've got a couple of ideas for where to check."

He carried his plate and her list over to the kitchen table, pulled out a chair across from her. He scanned the list again. He could help her get her GED, he thought — Illinois would have a process in place for an adult with some high school credits already completed. The photography — Ellie would be a place to start. She could help assess the artistic quality and monetary value of the photos, provide feedback on the overall compositions. If the Dance and Covey Gallery itself didn't deal in photography, Ellie would know those who did.

Getting married and having kids . . . enough said for now on that subject. Shannon had calculated correctly that her future husband would best be found among those who had experience with a missing-person case — there would be grace, compassion, and knowledge that would be helpful in making a successful marriage. She'd even correctly reasoned that he would be able to help her meet men who might fit that description. The fact she had planned that carefully before choosing to approach him was . . . illuminating for how her mind worked. Item five where she had scratched out part of it was striking for how interested he was in what she'd listed.

"I'd like to add one thing to my remarks before we have round two of our embarrassing conversation," Shannon mentioned, laying aside her half-eaten sandwich.

Matthew wanted to wince. There went any hope she was going to skip over last night. "All right."

"I find it easy to give my affections." She gave a small shrug, an equally small smile as she picked up her tapioca cup. "I instinctively latch on fast when I find someone I can trust. Because I know that about myself, I was careful in my choice of whom to approach. I had a list of names, and you were at the top of it."

"I'm flattered."

She smiled. "You should be. Which brings us to today. You have my affections, Matthew. I like you. I can accept that the friendship we have now is all it will be, be content not to change your boundaries. But if you want to be part of my life some day in the future, I would welcome your company. I enjoyed that one-off kiss very much. I placed my affections well, I think. I don't know if I can ever love as freely as someone without my history, but I believe I could make you happy. I'm the faithful, loyal, one-guy kind of gal — I do know that."

The generosity in what she opened her heart to say could only be met in kind. "I've toyed with the idea of asking you out on a date in three years."

She laughed, bobbled the glass she'd just picked up, spilling some of the water. "Forgive me, Matthew, but three *years*? I'm trying to be patient with a plan that has me waiting three *weeks.*" She waved away his move to help with the spill with good humor. "I'm fine." She used her napkin to soak up the water. "Oh, I do like you, Matthew. I need some time to get over what happened, and I do accept that. Six months is going to be plenty to know where my personal land mines are, a year after that for whatever therapy can do to have its first effect. Then I'll reassess what life looks like. My plan was to find a guy to date sometime before the third year even starts."

He couldn't help but laugh, and she joined in too. Turning serious, he responded, "You may need a little more time than that. But to be fair, you were right in assuming I could make introductions to good guys you might enjoy getting to know. And I would put myself on that list — you're an interesting, appealing woman, Shannon. You've just rather . . . thrown me off-balance."

"You thought I'd be pretty damaged coming out of what happened."

"Yes."

"I am. I'm also just delighted to be alive. I'm not planning on letting those years be an anchor pulling me down. The interior waters are murky and still slopping around — I get that, but I can swim. I can deal with the problems that have to be faced. But I do want my dreams, and time's a-wastin', as they say. I'm ready to get on with my list."

"You've got a good future ahead of you, Shannon. The past isn't going to stop those dreams of yours. But you need time. And I am keenly aware I'm the first safe guy in your world —"

She lifted her hand and cut him off with a sudden grin. "It's okay, Matthew. Enough said on this awkward conversation. I promise I won't contribute to an eleven p.m. moment to regret. I'm simply going to enjoy the delight in having you around. It's sort of like having a crush on a guy, something I should have been able to enjoy when I was sixteen." She pushed her chair back from the table. "John will be here to pick me up soon. Do you think our host might own a Scrabble game or should I buy one while I'm out shopping?"

He tried to stay with the change in conversation. "There's one on the shelf in the hall closet."

"Want a game later?"

He wanted two aspirins, then to rewind the last half hour of conversation and hit delete. "Sure."

Her phone rang, and she reached for it as she finished the last strawberry on her plate.

"John's on his way up," she confirmed. Matthew pushed back his chair and went to greet John and see Shannon safely off to her afternoon shopping. Then he returned to the kitchen to finish his lunch.

He thoughtfully returned to their conversation. She was in the early days of coming out of a tragedy, fifteen years younger than him, and their friendship was already beyond complex. Friendship was where the line had to rest. Maybe in three years, five, he could let himself consider inviting her on a date. He liked her. A lot. It was good that she liked him, that trust had formed, and true affection had followed. But she needed to live a lot longer in her new freedom before she could even be sure of what she wanted. He would do everything he could to help her spread those wings. So . . . *friends,* with some exquisite care to avoid any steps that caused her emotional turmoil. She was freer with her feelings, despite all that had happened, than he had ever learned to be with his. She'd be an easy woman to love, he realized, as she was at times simply enchanting. But he refused to let himself follow the thought.

He was glad he had a run scheduled for today. Maybe after five miles he'd have his mind wrapped around the conversation they'd just had. *Maybe make it ten miles.* The woman so easily tied him in a knot.

He should buy her a camera. That thought came out of left field as he cleared the table and put away the lunch items. He pondered the idea while he went to change clothes. Those five items deeply mattered to her. It was time he put a good camera in her hands. He'd concentrate on that idea for a bit, as it was a lot more manageable than the discussion they'd just finished. Maybe the camera shop would have a decent used one in a newer model so she wouldn't balk at accepting the gift. He found his keys, confirmed he had his phone, and went to join Paul and Bryce.

# 21

Shannon played a Y, completing the word *yellow.* "Tell Paul I'm ready to take him to see the farm."

Matthew looked up from the Scrabble board. She'd been playing in silence for the last half hour, had said very little over dinner. Tired, quiet, on the edge of subdued — he'd expected as much after an afternoon of shopping, and on the heels of all that had unfolded during the last week. He wasn't unduly worried at the emotions he was picking up from her. "Tomorrow?" he asked.

She nodded.

She'd managed to get the board into a very unwieldy layout. All he could do was play the simple word *fun.* "Do you want to see your parents after that? Jeffery thinks it's time. They both want to see you."

"He told me. They weren't ready for it last week, and it turns out I'm not ready for it now. Maybe something at Jeffery's this

Friday or Saturday evening. If we run out of things to say, we can always talk about my niece."

Her fears for the reunion physically hurt to hear. "The evening will be fine after the first few minutes. Your parents are truly overjoyed to have you back, Shannon."

"I know, and I'm sure it'll be welcoming smiles and hugs, followed by polite conversation with everyone trying to ignore the underlying awkwardness. I just need a few more days. If my mom asks for my forgiveness I'm going to have a difficult time replying. And what do you think, do I call him 'Dad' or use his first name?"

Matthew briefly closed his eyes. "Dad," he counseled softly. "Nothing in this changes the heart of the matter. He's been your father since the day you were born." He placed letters on the board to extend a word to *joyful.* "Give him a chance to show he wants the relationship with you that you've always had. Hold that door open for him," he encouraged.

"And Mom?"

"She's still your mother. You need her, Shannon, no matter how deep the hurt is right now. Show her grace, make it easy on her. She needs her daughter back. She's mourned for you, missed you every day, every hour, for eleven years."

Shannon didn't answer him. She played *time,* then arranged the letters for *throw* on her next turn.

Matthew shifted the subject slightly. "So it's a visit to the farm tomorrow, see your parents Friday or Saturday night, have Jeffery make the news public the following Monday?"

She nodded. "He'll have to by then, if not before. Once cops enter the farm, word will get back to the group, they'll scatter, and the only way Paul will be able to track them down is to make their photos public nationwide."

"Adam York can release the photos in connection with the abducted children who have been returned home, buy us a few more days before the reporters make the connection between the abductions, the farm, and you," Matthew suggested.

She shrugged. "Whatever seems best. It would be good if the next week could end it. The farm, meeting my parents, making the news public, giving Paul what I can remember about the other stash sites. I'll still need to show you their place out East, and there will be some sites I'll have to visit to see what I can remember about the precise locations. But otherwise my initial list will be finished. It would be seriously helpful to me to get this over with."

Matthew considered that an exquisite understatement. He extended a word to play *halftone.* A year from now, her life would likely be depositions and trials. "I've got a few things on my list for you to consider. Choosing a doctor you'd like to help you process everything. You need a valid driver's license. Do you want to be known as Shannon Bliss or switch to another name that might not attract attention? This would be the right time to decide that."

"I hadn't thought about it." She played *falling.* "Charlotte obviously decided changing her name made sense."

"It's something to consider. I don't know that it's realistic to keep you entirely out of the public eye, given your brother may be in the governor's office. You'll just be setting up reporters to watch him until he leads them to you, regardless of the name you're using."

"I'll talk to Jeffery about what makes the most sense. I won't be seen in public until after the election — that much I've decided."

"For the next five months until the vote, that would be wise," Matthew agreed. "Any plans with Charlotte? You were talking with her by phone earlier."

"She has coffee Saturday mornings with Ellie and Rachel, Bryce's mom and sister. She invited me to join them."

"You'll enjoy that."

Shannon half smiled. "I'll have to start a social calendar. Was that your doing?"

He didn't have to ask what she meant. "No. Charlotte's invitation didn't originate with me."

"It's awkward, figuring out who to trust."

"You don't have to decide that right away, Shannon. Simply observe, try out some low-key interactions, and determine whom you're comfortable with. And if you're overly cautious for the next few years, you don't need to apologize. People will understand."

"I've decided I like Charlotte."

"I'm glad." She was in the early stages of making new friends, which was one of his hopes for her. Once she spoke with her parents, finished talking with the FBI, and the news became public, her focus would need to shift to working with a doctor and getting whole again, physically and emotionally. The last big question would then come into play: where did she want to settle down to start her new life? He thought maybe somewhere in Wisconsin or Indiana. A few hours outside of Chicago would be ideal — close enough that John could help her with security matters, where she could still be with family for an evening or a weekend, but still be outside the reach of the Chicago press. The national press interest in her would continue throughout the first year, but after that it would start to settle down. He'd help her look at some towns in the Upper Midwest when she was ready.

The letters left in the Scrabble box lid were down to less than a dozen. He took three more to fill his tray.

"Do you have someone in mind for a counselor?" Shannon asked.

He considered his word options, re-arranged letters on the tray. "Rachel suggested a friend of hers, Sandy Post, and Bryce gave me the same name. She works primarily with women veterans who have seen combat. She sees a few patients in the Chicago area, and could meet you for a walk one morning. Afterward you could both decide if it feels like a good fit. Rachel mentioned she's a bit . . . unorthodox in her style, but that's why she likes her."

"How so?"

"She'll train and run a marathon with one patient, design and landscape a flower garden with another, take a Spanish class with a third. She's not one for appointments in an office if there's another way to accomplish her goal. She wants to get inside your head, your heart. And she's going to stay on mission until she's done that, until she's figured out where your perceptions of yourself and the world are affecting your mental health."

"She's a Christian?"

"Yes. If you aren't comfortable praying aloud with someone, you'll have an interesting time adapting to her help. She's as likely to address a question to God *about* you as she is to ask *you* the question."

The thought seemed to intrigue Shannon. "A nice way to keep a conversation honest. 'God, is she lying to herself or to me with that answer?' " Shannon smiled. "I'd be willing to meet her for a walk, maybe next week, after the conversation with my parents. One thing at a time is about all I want to handle right now."

Matthew nodded. "It's going to help you — having a professional in the mix."

"Do you think I should let her read the diaries?"

He hesitated before he answered. "I don't know. I think it might be better if you talked about matters first, let her see how the memories of events are playing out for you now. But if you can't talk about a subject, then yes, giving her the appropriate diary would be better than her not knowing."

"I'm doing a good job coping right now by simply accepting it happened, and then moving on."

"You are," Matthew agreed. "But you're still in survival mode. Do you realize that? It's useful for me to see it, because the pace you're moving through all the details would be trouble for you otherwise. But there will be a day you're past this initial unpacking of events, and then that survival mode is going to begin to ease. It needs to. You'll be able to grieve about what you lost over the last eleven years, and you'll feel a natural sadness begin to swell."

"I've already grieved, Matthew."

He didn't think she had even begun that process, but he only said, "You'll grieve some more, Shannon. And those days too will pass. A good life is going to form over the next years, and I'm looking forward to seeing how that happens for you."

"You're expecting me to be fragile, like your daughter. I'm not like that, Matthew."

He gave her a searching look. "Becky had a period where she was truly fragile, but that's different than what I see in you. *Fragile* implies being unable to handle something, of cracking when the pressure and stress arrive. I agree you're not fragile right now. You're extraordinarily strong in some ways because it's necessary. But grief isn't fragile. It comes along with strength, facing the losses in life, the reality of what you won't have back, then turning to the future to create what can be built. Grief is part of accepting what was; it's what takes the sharp edges off your history. It's emotion and it's reality. It's mostly not hiding, letting your mind present what needs processing and dealing with all the implications of those memories."

She was listening, toying with the final letter on her tray.

The game was finished, but he didn't move to total the score or put away the pieces, but instead looked at her and carefully selected his words. "You survived by hiding, Shannon. It's still how you cope when events or situations hurt you," he said gently. "I'm glad it's a strong instinct because it's getting you through this. But it's a defense. Grieving is about letting down that shield, not having to keep that defensive wall in place. When you can lower it and not get overwhelmed by the memories, you'll know your healing is mostly complete, you'll have 'rubbed off the jagged edges' of your history, as you described it, and be ready to move on."

She thoughtfully began storing letters in the box. "Not sharing something is not the same as not being aware of it. I'm not hiding from myself."

He thought maybe she was right, and yet . . . not. "You've learned to endure, to live strong in spite of all that's been thrown at you. That's powerful and good. Maybe what I'm trying to express is that I think you've dealt with matters by a sequence that was basically 'It happened, it was horrible, it's over, move on,' and your emotions learned to function that way as well. But that was a learned pattern. Freedom is going to shift your emotions to something that's more . . . *expansive* is maybe the word I want. You'll *feel* things with larger and wider emotional swings again, because now you have the freedom to experience those normal emotions. It's going to be a good thing."

"You don't think I have that now?" she asked, looking curiously at him over a handful of letters.

He realized she didn't see it yet and simply looked at her for a long moment, pondering how to present it. Finally he said, "I think you have a shadow of it, but not the substance, and I'd hate for you to misjudge which you have. I'm hoping, praying, that the wall you've had to put in place around yourself and your emotions will come down. That there will be more of *you* appearing. Wider emotional swings both up and down. More energy. Dreams for your life. Things you want. Desires of the heart. And, yes, also a deeper sadness. Grief. All of it. That's life, and the more of it you are *feeling,* the closer you are to being whole again."

"That's what healing will look like," she said, thoughtful.

He nodded. "Mostly. It will be the ability to see the world around you as it exists, both good and bad. It will be having a life that isn't being steered by the past, where it doesn't feel like the past is a daily anchor weighing on your thoughts, or on your impressions of places and people. Healing will be the capacity and the ability to love family and care about friends. It will be about having dreams for yourself and the confidence to work toward them. Healing in part is being able to *feel* you are free of the past."

Shannon dropped the last letters in and slid the lid onto the Scrabble box. "Was Becky able to make that transition?"

"It took five years before I could look across the breakfast table and see my daughter as she should be, not my daughter with a painful memory or two still lingering there with her."

"It was her concept of herself which got shattered."

"Yes."

"I'm different from Becky in one key respect, I think. When I described myself as a cactus, Matthew, able to handle a tough environment, it was because I made a decision early on. I looked at that group and decided it was possible to get inside their logic and work the angles, and it provided a way to survive. I began proactively living inside that bubble they put me in, not just responding to it. I accomplished something in captivity during those eleven years. That internal 'me' survived. I was never passive about what was going on. If anything, my sense of who I am is stronger today because of what happened. They couldn't get to the core of me. Yes, I have hard things to work through, but I'm not as injured as you might think. I'm like a beat-up old car that's won a few stock-car races. I need some dents hammered out. But the guts are still running fine."

Matthew had to laugh at the imagery. Yet

again Shannon surprised him with her inner strength. "Maybe you're right, Shannon. I do love that visual. I'm going to be pleasantly surprised to find out I haven't understood how far along you are in this process, that it's going to be a shorter journey for you than I expect. I'd love for that to be true. Just give room for some caution about how long it might take."

She nodded as she pushed back her chair. "To repeat something I've said before, your perspective because of Becky is one of the reasons I chose you. If you're right, I'm going to lean hard on your advice for what I should do to get through it. I want what your daughter has, Matthew. A good life back."

"And I'm going to help you get there," he promised.

Matthew placed a call to Paul Sunday night after he had walked across the hall and had some privacy for the conversation. "Shannon just gave me a long, handwritten sheet detailing locations she can remember where stolen items were stored. I'm going to fax it over to you. She said there are a lot more to come, but this is a place to start."

"I've got people in mind that can start

clearing them once we decide to tip our hand."

"Shannon's ready to take you to see the farm. Let's do it tomorrow, if that fits with your schedule."

"Good," Paul said. "It does. She needs to be done with this, and I need cops on the property. I'm figuring five days from the time we raid the farm, put out public word we're searching for these people, distribute the photos with a reward, to Jeffery needing to release the news about Shannon's return. Can she handle that?"

"She knows it's coming. But she needs to have met with her parents before the news is made public. I'm working on those arrangements now. Can you get me more than five days?"

"It may not even hold for five. Day one, the farm; day two, we release the photos of who we're searching for; day three, Adam York briefs on the children recovered and he'll have to reveal it was someone inside providing the information; day four, we have a press conference about the farm and what's being recovered; day five, Jeffery reveals his sister is alive. Can she meet with her parents in the next few days?"

"She's not quite ready yet. They weren't ready for the conversation when she first arrived, and she's not ready for it now that she knows the truth about her father. She needs a few more days before that family reunion."

"Then we go to the farm, Jeffery's announcement comes five days later, seven if we think we can hold it off that long, and you buffer matters between Shannon and her family as best you can. Plan on keeping her out of Illinois once the news breaks. There's a reason she hasn't met with her parents yet, she was helping the FBI, and she's out of state to avoid causing problems with the election. Something like that could work."

"Yeah." Matthew could see next week's calendar compressing. This case had a dynamic of its own now. Even if everyone agreed to slow it down, there would be a limit to the amount of additional time they could get. A day or two was about it. "Call the county sheriff, give him a heads-up we're coming. If we leave before eight in the morning, we should be on the property by early afternoon with enough daylight to be useful."

"I'll get things in motion here. Tell Shannon thanks for me. I know this won't be easy, but it's critical."

"It'll be good to have this behind her," Matthew agreed. "I'll tell her."

# 22

"Take a left at the faded church sign," Shannon directed. Matthew noticed the closer they got to the farm, the quieter she became. Other than instructions, she hadn't offered anything in the last hour. Matthew glanced in his rearview mirror to confirm Paul and Theo were still with them.

"Now a right after we pass over the railroad tracks."

They were deep into the countryside. Cornfields, the occasional bean field, pastureland with cows, and a few solitary farmhouses. The only thing differentiating one gravel road from another was the variation in potholes from heavy farm equipment. The closest town of any size was twenty miles behind them.

"The farm is just up ahead. Tell Paul he should fall back a bit."

Matthew made the call and the trailing car slowed.

Shannon sat forward, the most animated she'd been since beginning the trip. "It's rained on and off in this area the last couple of days," she said, pointing. "Look at the ditches. There will be tire tracks going into the farm if anyone's traveled it recently."

She pointed. "See the fence that runs down to the road? That's the edge of the property. Drop your speed to about twenty-five, and let's drive past the entrance and see what it looks like. It's on your left after this bean field, tucked in between two hedgerows. The driveway in is narrow."

"They bottlenecked traffic into the property."

"Yes. The hedges run about forty yards along the entrance."

She craned her head to the left as they passed. "Not a single tire track in that muddy lane. Slow as you reach the top of this hill so I can look east between the trees."

She turned to see out the back windows. "No cars visible. No trucks. The barn doors are closed." She settled back in her seat. "Up ahead by that grain storage bin, there's a turnaround. Pull over, let's talk to Paul."

Paul and Theo pulled in beside them. Matthew lowered the car windows.

"From the condition of the driveway, the lack of vehicles, I think the property's empty

— what I would expect this time of year," Shannon told them. "Paul, how much trouble would you be in if you fired off a single gunshot over that cornfield?"

"To what purpose?"

"The dogs will bark. If there are no dogs, it's fifty-fifty the property is abandoned, not just empty. Normally they're here year-round, trained to approach vehicles, make it difficult to get a door open unless they're called off."

Paul glanced at Theo.

Theo shrugged. "Worst case, a car or two exits the property at high speed. We've got the sheriff and his deputies in the area waiting to come in when we indicate where precisely we're going and that we're ready for them. They can block the roads if someone makes a run for it."

"Given that hedgerow, the problem of not knowing what we're driving into, finding out if dogs are on the property before we drive in, it seems like common sense," Matthew concurred.

Paul stepped out of the car, walked a good distance away so that the noise wouldn't deafen those in the cars, removed his service revolver, and fired the single shot. The echo sent a flock of blackbirds lifting into the sky and sent up a howl to their north from a lone hound dog, but there was only silence coming from the farm property.

"Watch the ridgeline behind the barn," Shannon said after the silence had again settled around them. "That's the highest vantage point on the property. They'll want to see who's on the approach road. Give it ten minutes. If no one shows, I suggest we drive in."

Matthew lifted his binoculars to scan the area.

Paul took out his phone and said to Shannon, "The judge considered your handwritten statement on the graves sufficient to get us access to the property, since it led to our recovering the remains of Emily Lynn. I only needed the precise address for the farm, and GPS has given me that location. Once we enter and you've pointed out where you were held, we'll have a second warrant issued covering all the buildings."

Paul finished his call to the judge's office, then updated the sheriff. Ten minutes later, seeing no signs of life, they drove onto the property. Paul steered toward the barn while Matthew parked closer to the house. The whole place looked deserted — overgrown grass, knee-high weeds, dead flowers in the pots on the porch. A broken shutter was knocking against the side of the house in the wind gusts. They sat waiting to see if the vehicles brought any attention from inside the house. After two minutes, Paul stepped out. The rest joined him a minute later.

Shannon pointed. "The best view is from the rise behind the barn. Let me show you the farm from there."

The incline wasn't steep, but the steady climb took them four minutes to reach the crest. The panoramic view showed the main house and barn at the front end of a fan-shaped distribution of buildings. Deeper into the site were two metal grain-storage bins, then a second barn in classic red paint, its roof holding a rooster weathervane. Two outbuildings in longtime disrepair. A chicken coop. Watering troughs. Barbwire fencing marked a pasture. An oval-shaped pond. Wide gates for farm equipment. Two smaller houses. Planted fields patterned the land, the corn and beans in precise rows. Large sixty-year-old trees formed a windbreak slashing across the property. The farm was an odd mix of disrepair and neat order.

Matthew glanced over at Shannon, who stood looking around with her hands pushed into her pockets, with that enforced calm creating a mask over her features. This place represented a prison for her.

"Where did you stay when you were here?" Paul asked, watching her as well.

She pointed to the middle house. "The pale blue one, normally the second floor, east middle room." She turned to indicate the distant white house with the front porch. "The family shootout happened in that house. The lower level probably still doesn't have all the bullet holes patched."

She took a long breath. "As for the graves, that's the windmill I mentioned, and you can barely see it, but there's a bench there by the pond. The five family members" — she turned to her left — "are there, buried in a neat row to the left of that pine tree on the opposite rise. I'll walk around and flag other places I think you need to check for graves. I'd like to do that before a lot of other cops arrive."

"I'm holding off others joining us for now," Paul reassured her. "Matthew will mark locations you identify for us. For the buildings — what am I dealing with? Hard-to-find storage areas, hidden cubbyholes, loose floorboards, false walls?"

"Yes."

Paul smiled. "I should have expected that. Any buried locations of hoarded goods?"

"The only one I know of is what used to be a root cellar they covered over to look like the rest of the grounds. It's by the blue house." She scuffed her tennis shoe on the ground. "I can walk around in the buildings and point out places you'll want to check, but I don't want to talk about my history with this place. And I really don't want to be on this property for very long."

"Understandable," Paul said, his voice staying even. "How about a compromise, Shannon? Give us a quick tour through the buildings, a walk-through where you tell us only what seems relevant to you. And I won't ask you to go back into that building once you're done. I'll work with whatever you choose to give me. Flag the areas you believe we should search for graves. After that, you and Matthew can leave. You'll never have to return. If I need something specific answered, I'll bring you photos to work from. That sound workable for you?"

She hesitated, but nodded. "We'll start with the houses, see if I can get through them."

"I'm going to call the sheriff in so he can put a perimeter in place around the farm. That'll be it for officers until you've left the property. And your name isn't going to leak because of today. You have my word on that."

"Thanks."

Matthew nodded toward the blue house. "Why don't we start there?"

She didn't say anything but fell into step beside him, Theo walking a distance behind. Matthew carried a handful of metal rods with red flags attached. He'd come prepared to mark locations she identified.

"There," Shannon said, pointing out an old mailbox on a post. "It's said they buried the mailman when he got too curious, gave him a fitting marker. I think it's maybe folklore, but it was the first such story I heard. And the post does seem odd, given mail hasn't been delivered to the property in a decade. The mail is left in town in a post-office box for residents to collect."

She pointed out another location. "The root cellar is midway between that clothesline pole and the corner of the porch. It's got about a foot of dirt on top of its two heavy metal doors, but they kept waterproof crates down there that supposedly contained stolen art. I never saw one of the crates opened."

Matthew marked it, then walked up onto the porch of the blue house and held open the front door for her. She didn't want to enter the house, that was obvious, but she finally stepped through. The air felt stuffy and hot. Drapes were closed, blinds pulled.

The electricity was still on. Light switches lit the hallway and living room. The house was extremely neat — even the floor rugs were squared to the walls. Theo checked the water, found it had been shut off.

Shannon turned toward the stairs. "Let's start at the top and work our way to the basement." Matthew followed her.

She stopped in the doorway of a room. It gave no hint of being anything other than a guest room, with not a single personal item on display. The open closet stood empty. "I mostly stayed here." She crossed the room and opened the window blind, rested her hand on the sill. "That tree can be reached from here. I'd step out on that limb and climb up to be level with the roof. I could see for miles from there."

"Anything left in that tree?"

She turned her head and gave her first glimmer of a smile since they had started their quest. "Yes. I'll get it later."

She placed both hands on the windowsill, gripping the piece of wood and lifting it. "Most of the sills come off to allow access to the underlying wall. You'll want to check every window in all the buildings." Theo produced a flashlight, and she used it to search the opening. "Nothing here — I didn't think I'd left anything."

She rested her hand on the post of the bed. "Most of the furniture that's wood with an ornate post like this has been hollowed out, so that something can be rolled up and slipped inside. Documents mostly, plus new IDs, sometimes cash. They used those places for their personal items."

She walked over to the doorway and knelt down, pulled up on the threshold. When she couldn't budge it, Matthew handed her his pocketknife. Seconds later the threshold slid smoothly upward as she pried it from the corners. In the space between the floor joists lay a thin piece of canvas. She picked it up and unwrapped it. In her hand was a watch, nothing elaborate. She turned it over, held it out to Matthew, and the engraving on the back was her name and a date. "My brother gave it to me for my sixteenth birthday because I was never on time. Proof I was here." He handed the watch to Theo, as it would need to go into evidence. She took a final look around the room before walking out.

"They didn't like putting items in the attic," she said over her shoulder. "Too much heat and a chance of damage in a bad storm while they were away. The halls are another matter, though. Remove every picture and check for a piece of fishing line looped around the nail and inserted back into the wall. If there is one, you'll need to open up the wall. They have the equivalent of their own bank stored in these homes. Small objects, mostly gold coins. They sealed it up like this so that no one got tempted to lift items from the emergency fund. The fact the walls are still intact here tells me they didn't know there was trouble coming when they left. Which makes me surprised they took the dogs with them."

The tour through the blue house continued for the next thirty minutes. Matthew's gaze followed Shannon for most of the half hour. There was little emotion in her voice — factual, calm, steady, with no animation in her movements. She was doing what needed to be done. The woman he'd known since Atlanta was nowhere near the surface. She was in hiding now, just as she'd functioned on this property for most of the eleven years — merely a shadow of who she really was. It hurt him to see it.

She stepped out of the front door, and he could see her relief at the knowledge she would never have to enter the place again. She went over to the tree with its limbs reaching out toward the house and that second-floor window. "Give me a minute." She used the birdbath as an initial step and swung up to the first limb. She climbed the tree with ease, experience telling her which limb to choose next. She stopped when she was level with the roof. Paused there. She came back down carrying a camouflage pouch. "Catch."

Matthew caught the canvas bag, and she dropped the last few feet to the ground, dusted off her hands. "The last time I'll climb that one." She opened it when he handed it back to her and slid out a journal. "My diary covering the family shooting and its aftermath. I don't want Paul to read it, but I'd like you to tell him what you think he needs to know regarding the events of that day and what led up to it." She held it out to him.

He took it because it was one of the few things he could do for her here. "Are you able to enter that white house, do you think, or should we skip it?"

"We'll do it next, so I can put it behind me."

Paul was already there, talking with the sheriff. The two men headed toward the five graves she'd pointed out earlier, leaving them to do the walk-through. Matthew moved in ahead of Shannon so that the only thing the sheriff would see from his vantage point was that a woman was with Theo and him. They would finish up here, and then he'd get her away from this farm — as far away as he could take her, both physically and mentally. For her, this was like walking around once more in her own private hell.

It took five hours to finish walking the property. The day had been draining on Matthew, and he could only imagine what it had been like for Shannon. He offered her another water bottle as she perched on the gate separating the pasture from the barn. The wind had blown her hair around despite the ball cap he'd given her, and she showed signs of a light sunburn, even though she'd used the sunscreen he'd offered. She looked . . . hollowed out. She had to be feeling relief now it was all over. The memories had surrounded her, with no place to hide from them.

The cops would be out here for the next several weeks, Matthew thought. The graves, the house where the bullet holes from the shooting were still evident, the hidden locations riddling nearly every building. "You're right, they didn't leave here thinking there was trouble coming," he commented, leaning on the gate beside her.

Shannon nodded. "This is the farm as they would leave it behind every year. They liked being here, but staying in one place, even on their own property out here in the middle of mostly unoccupied countryside, left them itching to be on the move again." She shrugged. "This was their retirement nest egg. The plan was to stay here for a year or so when they retired, then sell the entire property and use the money to set up someplace where they would spend their last years. They didn't trust a bank or a mutual fund — they put their wealth into the land, into things they kept rather than sold."

She tipped the water bottle to get the final swallow. "If someone hasn't already called to tell them a sheriff's car is on their property, that word will reach them by tonight. They'll be on the run, scattering with a well-thought-out emergency plan, pulling what they can get to from storage and disappearing like ghosts. How many of them are dead by morning, deemed expendable and a liability for the future, is the question."

He knew that outcome was likely. "You can't change what they're going to do, Shannon, any more than you could change what happened before. None of this is your fault — not the killings that already occurred, not ones that might come."

"I know. It doesn't make it any easier to live with, though."

It was time to get her out of here, preferably out of Chicago too. If she didn't get a break soon, she was going to disappear inside the black emptiness surrounding her emotions, and it could be months before the woman he'd met and been getting to know since Atlanta would reappear. What to do didn't take much thought. "Come home with me to Boston for a few days. We'll fly out of Milwaukee, be on the ground in Boston in two hours. I know you don't like to fly, but you can hold my hand the entire flight. You can simply walk away from all this and catch your breath. You need that."

She turned to look at him, her expression too calm. He braced to hear her politely turn him down. She slipped off the cap, ran her hand through her hair. "Sure, why not? I don't want to be here, and Chicago is just more drama." She stepped down off the gate. "We'll need to make a stop in Indiana first. We can fly east from there."

"Something to pick up?"

"Something you should see."

They stayed the night at a hotel in Wolcott, Indiana, and the next morning Shannon directed him farther into the state toward the Tippecanoe River. When they arrived at their destination, Matthew was surprised by the setting. Crater Lake stretched a mile-plus across, its surface smooth but for the occasional protruding tree limb of a submerged fallen giant. The shoreline was made up of mostly heavy woods down to the water, and very little of the surrounding property had been developed. An old fishing boat with a trolling motor was tied up to one of the few docks they passed, suggesting the lake provided some good fishing. The cabin Shannon eventually identified for him defined isolated. He parked on a crushed gravel square, grown through with weeds. "What is this place?"

"One of Flynn's private residences. That flag is flying high above the property when he's here, letting the one neighbor nearby know to ignore the car traffic back here or the smoke coming from the chimney."

"You were thinking Flynn might be here?"

She shook her head. "I don't think he will go near anyplace I know about. But I want to check if something of mine is here." She stepped out of the car, and he joined her.

She pushed the flagpole's bracket to one side and produced a key tucked behind it. She unlocked the front door, gave a rueful smile. "The lock is more formality than substance. Someone who wanted in would just smash through a window and crawl inside. But the lock is at least a statement that it's private property."

The cabin was larger inside than it had appeared — two rooms off to the left, open doors showing a bedroom and a full bath, and on the right a larger area with a kitchen, worktable, and living room.

Shannon pulled a soldier's metal footlocker from the corner, worked the latch. "Flynn's son liked to play with all kinds of toy construction equipment, then toy soldiers, and finally it was race cars. This footlocker's spent most of its life being hauled around filled with a child's delights."

The comment caught Matthew off guard. "Flynn was married."

"Um-hmm. His wife was a nice woman. I was often assigned responsibility for his son. I made the wrong move, the boy would pay the price. I wouldn't hurt a child, and I wouldn't hurt Flynn by hurting his son. A double bind." She nodded toward the wall. "The pictures are of his wife, Karen, and their son, Taylor. There were more photos, several with Flynn in them — I snapped most of those — but he put them away after his wife and son died because the reminder hurt too much."

Matthew took a seat at the table, watched Shannon lift items from the locker, realizing an entire new fissure was opening up regarding what had happened in her life. "You were responsible for the safety of his son."

She paused to glance over at him. "The old man could spot a weakness in a heartbeat, and exploit it. Mine was Taylor. He was two when I met him for the first time. If I stepped out of line, the boy would take the punishment. Even Flynn wouldn't have been able to stop that retribution. So I lived very carefully, tried never to take a misstep."

"They died."

"One of those tragedies that seem to strike the most innocent of people. His wife and son both got food poisoning at a state fair, the doctors did what they could, but it hit them both too hard and too fast. The loss shattered Flynn. I wondered for more than a year if he'd be able to get through the grief. He would maneuver things so he was responsible for me, then leave an opening big as a truck for me to slip away — he wanted me to go so the family would kill him for his lapse. I couldn't do it. I think that's when I finally realized how much he mattered to me. I was willing to stay in that hell rather than get him killed with my escape."

"Why hadn't he taken his family and gotten out long ago?"

She rested her hands on the edge of the footlocker. "Flynn's not a Jacoby. His wife was. And she wouldn't agree to leave while her mother was alive. Flynn had begun to set up safe places like this for his family after her mother passed away, places that couldn't be traced back to him. He was looking at buying a proper home about twenty miles south of here. This cabin would have been a vacation spot for family outings." She lifted out the top tray of toys. "Ah, I wondered if they would be here." She began lifting out journals. Her diaries, he guessed. "These are most of the later years," she said, studying the covers.

"Why here?"

"Flynn was grieving. He'd come here for a few days, a week, whenever he could get away. He'd say he was going out on private business, but I knew he was coming here. I'd cover for him as best I could." She began to stack the diaries. "We'll take these with us."

"Anything else you want to look for that might be here?"

"No. I'd appreciate it if you didn't tell Paul about this place, at least not for a while."

Matthew nodded. If he broke trust with her, she'd stop showing him these locations. It was too important to know these facts. "It can wait for a couple of weeks."

She found a pen and wrote a note, *Flynn, call me. Shannon,* then included her phone number on it, and left the note on the table.

Matthew followed her outside, carrying the diaries. He was beginning to recognize the emotion in her when she spoke about Flynn. A survival kind of bond, a friendship on her side, and probably an acceptance on Flynn's side that Shannon was only going to make it out with his help. The references to Flynn in those diaries he had read, the few things she'd mentioned at the farm, had been of a man taking actions that weren't in his own interests. Now with the added knowledge there had been a wife and son in the picture, his action had definitely not been in his own interest, but he'd interceded on Shannon's behalf just the same. A man with a conscience, Matthew thought, in a family that hadn't shown much of one. Shannon had survived in large part because of Flynn. Her silence about him was beginning to make sense.

# 23

It felt good to be home. Matthew pulled into his own driveway, shut off the car, felt the strain of the recent days slide away. His own bed tonight, his own coffee mug, that same faucet drip in his bathroom. Photos of Becky, stacks of mail to sift through, the flower bed's weeds calling for attention. He'd gladly deal with all of it, for here were the memories and belongings of the last two decades of his life.

He glanced at Shannon and saw she was still asleep. She wasn't a good air traveler. She'd taken the recommended medication to prevent vertigo, clung to his hand in nervous tension through most of the flight, then promptly closed her eyes and went out like a light when finally she was safely back in a car and able to let go of the stress. It seemed like the flight had worn her out at least as much as visiting the farm.

He stepped out of the car and softly closed

the door so as not to wake her. He walked up to the house and unlocked it, walked through the rooms switching on lights, adjusting the air-conditioning to take the edge off the late afternoon's warmth. It had been some time since guests other than one of Becky's friends had visited. He hadn't exactly cleaned house before leaving for the conference. Things were neat, but the laundry wasn't done, the kitchen floor needed mopping, and fishing tackle lay spread out on the dining room table.

He checked Becky's room. She'd suggested Shannon use hers instead of the guest room, as there were locks on the inside of the door, the safety blanket of sorts his daughter had needed those first few years. He'd remade the bed when he last did laundry, so the sheets were clean. He set out fresh towels in the adjoining bathroom, turned on the bedside lamp, and changed the radio station to one with softer music than his daughter's taste. The posters on the walls and collectibles on every surface definitely said "Becky," but the room was clearly female, soft and lacy. Shannon would be comfortable here for a couple of days.

He walked back outside. Shannon was still sleeping. He eased open the passenger door, hunkered down beside her. "Can I convince you to wake up from that dream you're enjoying?" He didn't reach across to unclip the seat belt — waking her by surprise would likely get him a fist thrown or an elbow in the eye. Instead he talked, amused at her deep slumber, and waited until she began to stir. The sleepy eyes that met his were so exhausted it was like looking down a dark, bottomless well. "Hey, lady." He gently brushed her hair back from her face. "Welcome to my home."

She looked past him toward the house, sighed, and closed her eyes again. "Nice place."

He waited some more.

"I think I want to just relax here for a month or two. The travel is finally over, most of the list done," she whispered.

"Yeah. Mostly." He reached across to unfasten the seat belt. "Food, then you can sleep as long as you want."

She managed a small smile. "Heaven." Reluctantly she swung her feet around and stood. She looked at the neighborhood as they slowly walked to the front door. "Is Becky home to meet you?"

He heard the hesitation. "No, her car would have been in the drive," he replied.

"I don't want to intrude on a homecoming. I can stay at a hotel."

That idea wouldn't be going anywhere. He wanted her somewhere he knew how she was doing and what was happening. "There's no need. I'm going to enjoy introducing you to Becky, but the timing might not work out on this trip. There will be other visits." He held the front door for her.

She stepped inside, looked around the entryway, into the living room. "Has it changed much since Jessica died?"

Matthew understood the question, and the reason for it. "You're meeting Jessica in this place as well as my daughter. This has been the family home since we first married."

"She had lovely taste."

He smiled. "She did." He led her through the dining room and into the kitchen, pointed to the stool where Becky often perched to watch him work. "Sit. I'm fixing us a nice dinner. You're going to be lazy."

He saw the start of a smile. "I can do that."

He talked about Boston while he worked on a stir-fry with fixings from the freezer, got her laughing about his marathon experiences, asked her to thumb through the stack of newspapers to give him the front-page highlights while they waited for the rice to finish cooking. This city had its charms, and if she didn't want to stay in the Midwest, it would be a good place for her to settle for the summer. Florida, though, always appealed to him come mid-December.

They talked about sailing as they ate dinner — she was willing to go out should it work into the schedule — and she asked him about his work, what he did around Boston for his clients. As they talked, she ate, and he was pleased to see her appetite returning. "We're going to have our dessert out on the back deck — it's lovely weather, and the summer bugs aren't out yet in droves," he told her. "While I pick up the kitchen and figure out what we're having for that dessert, why don't you wander around, get acquainted with the house and where everything is — nothing's off-limits — and then join me on the deck. You'll rest easier knowing the layout. My daughter makes art — string-and-fabric kinds of wall hangings. She describes them better than I do, but I can tell they're pretty. Second room on the right is yours. I put your gym bag beside the bed."

"Thanks, I'll do that," Shannon said.

While she looked around the place, Matthew cleaned up the kitchen, chose a container of frozen chocolate mousse for dessert, and took a knife with him as well as plates and forks out to the deck. She wouldn't need to hurry, and it would be easier to cut if it sat out for a while.

Shannon eventually came out holding a bottle of soda, leaned against the wood railing, looked toward the sun that was beginning to disappear into the horizon. He saw she'd removed her shoes somewhere along the way. "Sunset will be about eight o'clock tonight," he told her. "There's rain in the forecast, so it may have deep-red streaks if that cloud bank cooperates."

"You talk a lot about the weather."

He smiled. "Want me to stop?"

"No. I like knowing, and I enjoy the sound of your voice. And I realize it's probably the only topic that doesn't end up somewhere you can't predict."

He raised his eyebrows. "I've noticed" was his dry comment as he cut the dessert into wedges. He passed her a plate. "It tastes better than it looks."

She grinned. "I've heard you say that before when you handed me a plate. I'm sure it tastes wonderful."

"Thank you, ma'am."

They ate the mousse in comfortable silence. He was accustomed to his daughter chattering through a meal, whatever she was thinking spilling out as she skipped from topic to topic. Even when she'd been feeling miserable in those first days, Becky had come to the dinner table dragging a box of Kleenex, talking between tears about how awful the dreams were, while she tried to do justice to the meal. His daughter had processed things by talking, only occasionally in that process requiring his input. She'd just needed someone to listen.

He would grow accustomed to Shannon's preference for silence, even while he wondered how much that silence was learned behavior over eleven years. He suspected she would become naturally more open as time went on.

A breeze kicked up, and he caught the faint scent of the ocean on the wind. "Want to watch a baseball game with me tonight?"

"Sure," she replied with a smile, "until I fall asleep out of simple boredom."

He chuckled. "Whatever works to get you some rest."

"I like your home. It's peaceful here," she noted as she stood and began collecting their dishes.

"The hedges hide the fact the neighbors are within touching distance," he said.

"I noticed. It's like that for too much of the East Coast." She turned toward the kitchen with the dishes. "I'll see if I can find a game," she offered.

"Try channel seventy-one."

When he joined her again, she was stretched out on the couch, watching a Red Sox game. He took the leather chair on the opposite side of the room — his chair, with his things piled around it and on the table beside it. The other chair near his was where his daughter liked to hang out, her legs draped over the arm, stealing his popcorn and flipping a quarter between shows to see who got to have the remote next.

The first four innings passed without either of them speaking. He got up at the bottom of the fifth and handed her the fuzzy throw his daughter used, went into the kitchen and returned with a handful of cheese cubes and crackers from the before-dinner snack tray, also carrying another soda for himself. She stirred in the seventh inning, disappeared into the kitchen, came back with an iced tea and a handful of the crackers. She settled back on the couch as the game tied up one to one. It stayed there into the bottom of the ninth and moved on to extra innings. He thought about telling her there was a TV in Becky's room if she wanted to finish the game there, but she seemed to have caught her second wind — relaxed, legs drawn up under her, eyes on the game, occasionally glancing around the room, at times lost in thought. Rarely did he catch her looking toward him. She wasn't avoiding him but wasn't paying much attention to him either.

Her phone rang, catching them both off guard. She hadn't given the number to Jeffery yet. Charlotte had the number but had called only twice. Shannon pulled it out of her pocket. "It's Becky," she said with surprise, reading the caller ID.

"I gave her your number," Matthew said. "Go ahead and answer it, say hi. She'll do the rest."

Shannon took the phone with her and stepped into the kitchen. "Hi, Becky. Yes, it's Shannon."

Matthew grinned when she said very little for a very long time.

Shannon came back into the living room, hands hugging her arms, looking rather dazed in a good way. Matthew didn't need any explanation to interpret that look. "She's twenty and you're here," he said, figuring that would explain the conversation.

"I think I got in a 'yes' twice. She asked if I liked you, and could I remember to fix your coffee with the cheap coffee beans because you didn't like the expensive coffee she'd bought you for your birthday. You don't like good coffee?"

"Blame it on all those years drinking bad coffee on the job. My daughter likes to talk."

"No. She just hides her nerves in talking. Why do I make her nervous?"

He laughed. "To repeat, she's twenty and you are here with her father. You're the first woman to ever stay in this home since her mother died."

"I really should stay at a hotel."

"No, not a good idea."

"She'll think —" Shannon stopped. "No, she won't think that. She knows you, and she certainly knows this situation. So what's she nervous about?"

"I promised I'd find a woman I could like and she could like. It was kind of our pact — she goes off to college while I deal with the empty nest syndrome. You just showed up earlier than she thought I might deliver on my part of the deal."

"What's her part of the deal?"

Matthew wasn't going to touch that question. "She can tell you one day."

Shannon curled up again on the couch. "You and your daughter are eerily alike in some ways. Listening to her was like listening to a more animated version of you."

"Thanks, I think."

"Don't worry, it's a compliment." The Red Sox second baseman managed to catch the edge of a misplaced fastball and drive it over the outfield wall for a home run, diverting their attention.

The stadium erupted in celebration and fireworks with the win. Matthew muted the volume, and they could hear the fireworks faintly outside. "A good game."

"It was." Shannon rose from the couch, stretched, gave him a little smile as she picked up her glass. "Since I now know where Becky keeps the really good bubble bath and all her nail-polish choices, I'm going to retreat and call it a night, and enjoy both."

"Do that," Matthew replied with a chuckle. "I have no plans for tomorrow, so be thinking about what you might like to do."

"I'd love to see the ocean up close. Can you find us a relatively private beach?"

"I'll show you a favorite stretch of sand," he promised.

"Thanks . . . for everything. Good night, Matthew."

"Night, Shannon." She disappeared down the hall.

Matthew waited until he heard the door close before he got up from his chair, walked into the kitchen. Having Shannon Bliss in his home was a welcome addition, if only for a few days. He dialed Becky's number. "So how are you tonight, Becky? Thanks for calling Shannon."

He listened to his daughter chat about Shannon — she seemed nice — about how classes were going, and what her roommate had planned for them for the weekend. She could change her plans to come visit. "No need, Becky. We'll be gone by the weekend. I'm thinking we'll return to Chicago either Friday afternoon or Saturday morning, depending on which day has better weather for the flight." He opened the freezer and set out steaks to thaw for tomorrow. "I'll definitely be back here the next weekend for the Fourth of July holiday, so bring your roommate this way if you like. Shannon might come back then, depending on her plans. Her next big decision is going to be where she wants to settle for a while."

Becky promptly included both her roommate and her new friend from English class for the weekend plans. "If you can man the grill, Dad, I'll fix my award-winning seafood salad."

"It's a plan," Matthew agreed easily. "Bring home whoever you like. There's plenty of room." Spectacular fireworks in

Boston Harbor could be seen within walking distance of the house. "Anything you want me to do for you while I'm home?" He made a note to find her running shoes — she wanted to try out for track this year. "I'll find them. Love you, honey. Call me tomorrow."

Content that his daughter was doing well, Matthew glanced at the time, thought about turning in himself. But while he was trying hard to give Shannon a break with this brief trip, his own to-do list was growing. His first call was to Paul. "What's the latest with the farm?"

"I'm surprised Shannon was able to walk that property and tell us what she did. So far, ground radar has indications of ten bodies: the five she was certain about, the two children she suspected, and three others she flagged for us to check. Has Shannon said anything else about their East Coast home base? I need a perimeter put in place on that property too."

"No, but it's on my urgent list. If she could put a finger down on the map, she'd already have done so. It's going to require a field trip. And walking her into another place like the farm . . . I know it has to be done, but I'm swallowing hard at the thought of it. She looks fine, she's coping, yet I'm afraid she might crack if one item too many slides into her day."

"I know that worry and share it, but time is a factor. It can't stretch out a week without damaging the credibility of the chain of custody for the evidence we might recover there."

"I hear you," Matthew agreed. "What's the tip line look like tonight?"

"Some sightings in Colorado have our attention. The names and photos went public across the country at noon. I've got cops working the names Shannon wrote on the whiteboards — those the family did business with — so they're not going to find many people out there willing to help them hide. I had Adam push the news conference up to D.C. so that he'd get better national coverage. He'll brief again tomorrow morning on the recovered kids to keep the focus on those faces."

"Good. I'll try to keep Shannon from seeing that newscast." Matthew changed the subject. "She located a batch of her journals from the later years today," he said, holding back the information about Flynn's cabin. "Seventeen diaries in all."

"That's going to be some difficult reading."

The understatement was breathtaking.

"Crushing," he admitted, remembering the entries in the two he'd read. "It needs doing, though. If she mentions a vehicle they purchased, anything concrete that might help track them down, I'll pass it on."

"Thanks. Have you spoken with Jeffery today?"

"He's my next call."

"Theo got his first question from a reporter today, left on voicemail, asking if anything new was going on with the Shannon Bliss investigation. The press has noticed that Jeffery no longer mentions his sister at his campaign appearances. He's shuffling his calendar to keep off the podium the rest of this week. The plan to make the news public on Monday is about as far as we can stretch it."

"I can work with that. Shannon knows it's coming." Matthew checked the time. "Let me give Jeffery a call now. I'll be in touch tomorrow, Paul. Call me if there's any breaking news."

"I'm hoping to have a reason to make that call," Paul replied. "Take care of her."

"My only priority," he said before ending the call and dialing Jeffery's number.

The coming days were getting blocked in. They would be back in Chicago to meet with her parents, Shannon would have one last peaceful visit with Jeffery, then it would be to tuck her somewhere private where the press couldn't find her. As it became public and Jeffery entered a firestorm of questions about his sister's return, she would need to be far away from it all.

Jeffery sounded ready for the press conference, Matthew was glad to learn, and he had a well-thought-out game plan for the evening with his parents. Matthew walked into the dining room after the call, pleased with how her brother was managing things.

The items he'd unloaded from the car had joined the fishing gear on the dining room table. Matthew sorted the journals from the footlocker by date. He picked up the oldest one and took it to the living room. He wanted a day away from this, needing the break almost as badly as Shannon did, but this case was now flowing in multiple directions. Understanding Shannon's history was the most helpful thing he could do for her, for the investigation overall. He opened the diary and started reading.

He was nearing the end of it when he stopped, shut the book, closed his eyes and physically winced. *The Fourth of July. Fireworks. Explosions. The smell of sulfur . . .* The last place Shannon should be on that weekend was in Boston, its nationally televised extravagance of fireworks over the harbor, all within walking distance of the house. Her flashbacks of that shootout in the farmhouse kitchen were going to be intense. Even if she thought she was braced for the sounds, those explosive bursts, the sulfur odor that filled the air would put her back there in hard, sharp, vivid memories.

He had known a collision would inevitably come between what was best for his daughter and what he was doing to help Shannon. Being in Boston for the upcoming holiday weekend was the last place Shannon should be. He always celebrated the holiday with his daughter, had just confirmed he would be in town — a longstanding and important family tradition. There was no uncertainty about where he had to be: in Boston with Becky. So top of the list now, with very little time to address it, were arrangements for Shannon. This coming Monday, Jeffery would tell the nation that Shannon was alive, and the following Sunday was the Fourth.

She couldn't spend that weekend with her brother — the entire national press would be camped out, watching Jeffery and her parents, hoping to capture their first glimpse of Shannon. She needed to be somewhere quiet, with safe people she trusted, where the press wasn't going to look for her. And she wasn't going to be with him. The shock he felt at that realization was eye-opening. He really didn't want her out of his sight for any length of time. She'd more than just wrapped herself around his life; he'd wrapped his own days around helping her. So their separating was going to be rather painful.

Matthew pushed aside that thought and focused on the issue at hand. Fireworks were sporadic in the neighborhood after sundown as early as July second. Where could Shannon go that was sure to be both quiet and safe? He could rule out Boston. She couldn't be in Chicago. And even his best planning couldn't guarantee a firecracker wouldn't be set off close enough to her to send her into a frightening flashback. So she needed someone with her who'd be able to manage the situation should one occur. This couldn't be just anywhere, with anyone.

*God, any ideas?*

The spontaneous prayer came as he laid aside the discord he'd been carrying with him the last few days. What had happened to Shannon . . . God hadn't intervened, at least in ways Matthew would have wished for, but she was now free, and the dark years were in the past. He didn't understand God, but he didn't want this impasse to continue. God was still God. Matthew turned back hard to the relationship he had depended on most in his life and felt the "welcome home" from his God — no rejection attached to it, just a loving acceptance.

His Father's patience with him was extraordinarily kind and long-suffering, and these recent days provided a glimpse of that mercy once more. In the coming days he'd be ready for a long conversation with God about what had happened to Shannon, and he'd be able to put the grief he felt into words without the bitter anger that had nestled itself inside. But that conversation wouldn't be tonight. There was a more pressing concern to talk with God about. *What arrangements do I make for her? I can see the crisis coming, and I've got a week to put the details of a plan in place. But where should I start? What might work?*

He ran ideas around in his mind — a place in the countryside, music turned up loud — but couldn't decide who would be with her or where that would be. He looked at his watch. It was too late to call someone. He tucked the problem into the back of his mind to mull over, picked up Shannon's diary again.

When he was finished reading, he went into the dining room and got the next one, determined to make it through at least a couple of them tonight. Shannon knew how to deal with hard days — that's what these journals told him more than anything else. A hardened, do-what-was-necessary, stubborn survivor whose true personality was still showing on these pages. He could see even in the handwriting how hard-fought it had been for her to keep her balance and not give up on that rugged optimism.

He couldn't concentrate. He looked at the time once again, computed the time zones, and made a call. "Paul, I need to talk with your wife about Shannon."

"Yeah," the man sighed, clearly having been asleep. "Hold on." The phone shifted. "Matthew, for you."

"What's going on?" Ann sounded wide awake, which she probably had been at this time of night. She'd always preferred working nights.

"A serious problem on the calendar. The Fourth of July. I'm going to be in Boston with my daughter. And Boston is the very last place Shannon should be."

Ann was quiet for a moment, then said, "Yeah, I see the problem. I'm remembering the fireworks during our one memorable date in Boston," she recalled, her smile apparent in her voice.

"A nice evening," he said with an answering smile. "The press is going to be staking out Shannon's family after the announcement. We could try to sneak her brother and his wife out somewhere, but where? It's also one of the biggest campaign weekends of the year, and Jeffery needs to spend a good part of it with the crowds. It's not like we can get him out of Chicago."

"Shannon can't spend the holiday with her brother," Ann agreed. "Her parents for the same reasons, and she can't spend it with you in Boston. Paul and I are hosting about forty of the Falcon family. She's welcome to join us, but we're downtown Chicago with fireworks going off over the lake."

"Where would you put her under ideal circumstances?"

"Canada, since they don't celebrate this holiday."

He laughed. "If I had time to get her a passport under her legal name, that might be just the ticket. Next best option?"

"Underground would deaden any chance of a surprise firecracker. I hear those tourists caves in Missouri are interesting."

"You're reaching, Ann, but then I've been too."

"Okay, more realistic. Close the windows, turn up the music — you want someone with a good home theater, preferably a soundproof room with comfortable seating. Plan a marathon of movies to get her to about four a.m. when the fireworks finally quit."

"That's actually the beginnings of an answer. Who with, and where? It's got to be someone able to handle a flashback."

"Rachel mentioned Sandy Post to you as a possible doctor?" Ann asked.

"Yes."

"I know Sandy's busiest weekend is this one, helping her patients get through the sounds and smells and crowds of the holiday, so it couldn't be her. In a pinch, I think Rachel is the one you want. Cole will be working the three-day weekend — the Fourth of July is arson duty on steroids — so give Rachel a call. She may not have anything scheduled for the weekend. She's incredibly good at dealing with traumatic memories in kids, so she could probably help Shannon. For where — give John a call. See if he and Ellie are planning to be up at Shadow Lake for the weekend or if they're going to stay in Chicago. Shadow

Lake is about a five-hour drive north. It's just enough rural it won't have a town's fireworks display nearby. There's decent surround sound and a big screen they put in when they remodeled Ellie's place, so that John could watch his ball games in comfort. Take along a lot of DVDs, and Shannon and Rachel can make a weekend of it."

Matthew was making notes. "I'll make the calls first thing in the morning. It's a workable backstop, Ann."

"Mention the matter to Charlotte as well. She's not a big fireworks fan for her own reasons. Bryce and Charlotte driving up to Shadow Lake for the weekend is a pretty common occurrence. Rachel and Shannon staying at Ellie's place, Charlotte and Bryce staying at John's — you've got a custom-made safe group to keep Shannon company."

Matthew smiled. "Not as nice as being there myself, but she would know people and be in good company."

"Problem solved," Ann agreed. There was a pause. "It's going to be hard for you to say goodbye when she doesn't need you in a month or so," she said quietly.

"I know. I realized tonight how acute it will feel. I'll be okay with it, Ann. As nice as it has been getting to know her, helping her navigate what needs to be done, I'm actually surprised we're into week two."

"She didn't want to do this alone. That's why she searched out and found you."

"And I'm more grateful for that with each passing day. It's nice to be needed." He looked at his notes. "Thanks for the ideas. I'll make some calls in the morning."

"Let me know if you need to brainstorm further. Oh, and tell Shannon if she wants to do me a serious favor, would she mind taking Black with her? My dog *hates* fireworks with a passion. Getting him out of Chicago for that weekend would be giving him a major vacation. And me a good deal of peace of mind."

Matthew laughed. "Yeah, I can see that. I'll mention it to her. Tell Paul thanks for letting me interrupt your evening."

"He likes that you call him even when you just need to pass off to me . . . just saying. It's classy of you."

"He got the ring on your finger. He's your guy. It's only right he knows when and why I'm taking up your time."

"Yeah. Like I said . . . it's nice of you. Say hi to Shannon for me."

"I will. Thanks, Ann."

He ended the call, thoughtful. He hadn't realized Ann had picked up on it, but she was right. When he could, he spoke first with Paul before he contacted Ann. They were a couple, and he'd shifted how he interacted with her to reflect that.

# 24

Shannon had asked to see the ocean. Matthew chose to take her to one of his favorite beaches. He pulled into the parking area just off a local road, which could accommodate six cars. They were the only ones there this early in the day. She pushed open the car door with a soft laugh. "It's wonderful!"

Soon she was heading down the path worn in the grass. The sand stretched almost a mile before boulders cut off the cove. He walked at a more leisurely pace down the incline. She'd stopped, hands in her pockets, about a foot from the high waterline of the breaking waves, gazing out at the expanse of ocean.

Still and quiet for a long time, a slight smile on her face, Shannon finally glanced over at him. "It's good to see the ocean again."

"I can tell you love it. I literally see you

relaxing just standing there."

"This is my idea of heaven on earth — sand, sun, and sea. There's a verse somewhere in the Bible, in Jeremiah, I think. 'Do you not fear me? says the Lord; do you not tremble before me? I placed the sand as a boundary for the sea, a perpetual barrier that it cannot pass; though the waves toss, they cannot prevail, though they roar, they cannot pass over it.' " She smiled as she finished. "Standing here is a huge reminder of the God I love. The ocean is vast. Big. Powerful. It's free. I love that. And it's contained where it belongs by God. I love the ocean for what it is, and for what it tells me about my God."

"It's big," he agreed, and she laughed. "Want to walk?"

"Sure."

She set out beside him.

Her hand slipped into his, and he glanced over, then entwined their fingers, welcoming the connection. They walked a good stretch of the beach in silence, her attention on the waves coming into the shore.

He knew it was going to disturb the moment but had no choice. He took a breath, asked as casually as he could, "Could you show me the location on the East Coast that the family used as a home base? Maybe do that tomorrow?"

Shannon gave him a sharp look. "Tomorrow?"

"The farm is known now. Chain of evidence means Paul needs to lock down the other property soon."

She weighed her answer. "Do I have to walk through the property? Can I just give you enough to direct the police with warrants to the right place?"

"I'll keep it as brief as I can for you."

She kicked up sand. "It's not far. Could we do that this morning, get it over with, then maybe come back here so I can get in a swim?"

Her suggestion surprised him. He hadn't realized it was so close by. "Sure. But as for swimming . . . the water is still awfully cool this far north. It's not like swimming in the Gulf or off the coast of Florida."

"You can act as my lifeguard. I won't go out far, only swim parallel to the shore once I'm past the breaking waves."

"If you don't mind the temperature, we can come back to this beach," he agreed.

"Then let's get that visit over with." Shannon turned so they could walk back to the car. "Has Paul said much? Has there been any activity since the photos were released?"

"A few sightings in Colorado are interesting. Nothing definite yet," Matthew replied.

She didn't ask a follow-up question, and he didn't offer more details. He knew she wouldn't rest easy until those who could cause her harm were in custody. She needed results, but hearing the play-by-play as the case unfolded wouldn't help her any. Eighteen people needed to be found and arrested in as short order as possible. Shannon had done her part. Now it was up to Paul and his team to finish the job. A week, Matthew thought, to make the arrests, maybe two. Shannon had given them such a wealth of information it was only a matter of time. He swung her hand lightly in his. "You should think about doing a charity swim later this year, one of those where you swim for distance or time and sponsors put up money for the charity based on how you do."

"Would you be one of my sponsors?"

"If you're looking for a hundred bucks per mile, I don't know if I could afford it."

She laughed. "So it's like a marathon for swimmers, with the proceeds going to a charity?"

He nodded. "They typically have a few events in August when the water temperature rises. Just something to think about."

"An interesting idea. Thanks for mentioning it."

He wanted to find a few things she'd enjoy that he could get on her calendar. Normal things she'd find fun to do.

He unlocked the car. "We're heading north?"

"Yes."

The ocean winds were carrying enough sand aloft that Matthew could hear the grit occasionally strike the car's windshield. Beaches and rocky cliffs and open ocean provided the immediate view to the east along this stretch of highway.

"You'll want to pull off the road at the next overlook," Shannon instructed. "That's their second home base ahead on the right. We'll pass it in a moment."

A hanging metal sign swinging over the entrance read in sprawling script, *Hennessey and Vine.* "There?"

"Yes, but pass by it for now. We're tourists today." A quarter mile past the sign was an official viewing spot above the expanse of water, and she directed him to turn in and park near a wooden platform. She stepped up onto it, and he joined her. The sound of the ocean surging over rocks and the whistling wind coming up the cliff face made it feel as though they were as close to the elements as they could get and still remain safe. They were high enough in elevation that they could see most of the property she had indicated.

Shannon pointed to a building in the distance. "That's the main house. There are five homes around what is basically a long circle drive. They all used to belong to one family called Hennessey; they were lobster fishermen. They made a nice living and protected this stretch of beachfront with a jealous eye for other fishermen dropping pots. The Vines were merchants. A deal between the families, a few marriages, and that sign got crafted. The two families built up this area. The way I heard it, most in the family got sick the same winter. The illness killed four of the men, left six unable to do the heavy labor of hauling lobster pots, and the remaining two couldn't keep the operation afloat. The Jacobys bought them out, homes and boats — the whole place — but never changed the sign."

"When was this?"

"Twenty years ago, I think. The Jacobys were settled here when I arrived. I spent the majority of the last eleven years around this place when I wasn't on the road. I took most of my photos down along that cove."

She pointed to the quiet waters inland from the point. "No one's on the property at the moment, based on what I can see. They've closed up this place, similar to the farm. The storm shutters are up. The break walls are closed to prevent a surge from destroying the boathouse. The cars are gone, including the three motorbikes they kept set aside for easy access just behind that second house. The property looks deserted. And no one in the family would risk coming back here once word went out to disappear."

Matthew couldn't detect any movement anywhere around the property either and concluded she was no doubt right. "Where did you stay when you were here?"

"The main house, second floor, back room. I liked that I could see the ocean."

"How many stolen goods are going to be found on this property?"

"Only a fraction of what is at the farm. They considered this site vulnerable to wind and tide, plus unwelcome neighbors coming by, trying to be helpful after a bad storm. They liked this place but didn't do much business here. I really don't want to walk the property and point things out. I'd prefer to let you call in the location of this place, and we be on our way."

"That suits me, Shannon." He made a call

to Paul with the GPS location and description of the property. "Anything of yours here you would like retrieved?"

"What's on the dresser in that back room would be some of my keepsakes — shells I gathered, figurines I won at the county fair, that kind of thing. My fingerprints will be in lipstick on the back of the bathroom mirror, and a few other similar marks. More proof I was here."

"Where did Flynn and his wife stay?"

"That first house with the swing set in the side yard. He stored most of his wife and son's things in the second-level bedroom. See the two windows close together? It would be . . . kind if the detectives would keep that room's contents together until all this is resolved. I'd hate to see her wedding dress stuffed in a box or his son's baseball glove tossed out. A few things stored there would matter to Flynn a great deal."

Matthew could understand the sentiment. He took several photos of the entrance sign and the buildings and forwarded them on to Paul, briefed him on what Shannon had shared, then listened in as Paul held a conference call with the FBI agents who would execute the warrant, and to the state cops who would secure the perimeter. Matthew put his phone away. "We're good,

Shannon. Paul has what he needs."

"I'd like to swim now, forget about this place — in fact, not think about much of anything for the rest of the day."

He placed a friendly arm across her shoulders. "A big ocean awaits you." He peered down at the waves crashing into the base of the cliff. "But let's go somewhere the ocean is in a milder mood than here," he added. "And a little warmer wouldn't hurt either."

She laughed and reached up to settle her hand over his. "The water's in a playful mood today. That stretch of your favorite beach is quieter, just whispering."

"You've spent a lot of time looking at the ocean."

"Watching it, swimming in it, trying to capture its expressions in photos — yes. The ocean was the only thing I ever saw the Jacobys fear. I found that revealing."

With the sun hot overhead, Matthew carried folding chairs down to the beach. Shannon was pulling off the shirt she'd worn over her swimsuit.

"Stay out of the water till I get back from the car with the towels and the tote bag," he told her. "I'll start a fire in the ring so we can cook a few hot dogs and you can warm up when you're done."

"Sure. I'd like that."

When he returned, she hit the water and headed out fifty yards before beginning to swim along the shore. Matthew watched the power in those strokes, the steadiness in her pacing, and understood why a small pool frustrated her so much. She'd trained herself for long-distance swims. She stayed within his sight, reversing directions when needed.

He was waiting with a thick oversized towel when she came out of the water, plus a blanket to wrap in. The fire kicked off enough heat for her chilly hands. She looked . . . happy, he thought, in a way she hadn't been since he met her. She accepted a water bottle, drank thirstily. He was remembering all the references in her diaries to having been for a swim. "How many of those eleven years did you spend in the water?"

She smiled. "I was in the water every minute I could."

She sat by the fire and hugged her knees. "That first time they pushed me overboard to drown, I decided I wasn't going to let it happen. I might drown, but it wasn't going to be from fear of the water or from not having the will to swim. I was exhausted and deeply relieved when Flynn convinced them to haul me back aboard, but from then on I went back in the water every opportunity I had. The sea and I became friends. I used to swim beside the boat for hours when we were out at sea. I wanted that endurance, knew I would need it one day. The ocean was my own world. Peaceful. I didn't have to think about anything in particular. The sea was good to me."

She pulled the blanket tighter. "When we were traveling, I'd swim whenever I could talk Flynn into driving near a beach. He accommodated me, mostly because I was a good driver, careful, and it gave him time to do more of his own business. If I was at the wheel through the night, we could make up time between expected check-in stops."

Matthew simply listened and learned. "His wife and son didn't travel with him?"

"The family controlled Flynn in their own way, just as they controlled me. His wife and son rarely traveled with him. If he'd struck out on his own, his wife would pay the price."

"Did you feel sorry for him?"

"No, not really. He came into the family because he was a thief, a very good one. He had been selling items directly to them instead of through a broker. That's how he met his wife. She'd often be the buyer, and they started secretly dating. In Flynn's defense, I don't think he understood the violence in the family until it was too late. She was pregnant, the family agreed he could marry her, join them, and only when he was already entangled and on the road with them did he realize the violence threading through their way of operating."

Matthew absorbed the information, tucking it away. For Shannon, Flynn was going to be a difficult issue. Paul would likely cut the best deal he could for Flynn in exchange for testimony against the others, but there was little doubt the man would spend the next twenty to thirty years in prison when this was over. Matthew knew he'd need to talk to Shannon about that at some point, but not today. This hour, the ocean, the swim, the calm of this place — all of it was everything he had hoped for her. A few hours of peace. She needed this day.

They ate hot dogs topped with mustard on fresh buns, stayed put until the sun began to lower in the sky, the breeze off the ocean no longer holding the warmth of the sun to push back its chill. Matthew rose, put out the fire, and gathered their things. "Why don't you take a last walk on the beach while I put this stuff in the car?"

Shannon nodded and slid into her shoes, walked down to where the waves were rolling calmly onto the sand. She turned to stroll north, her face lifted to the fading light of the day.

When she returned, she said, "Thank you," and slipped her hand into his.

He gave her a brief hug, turned her toward the car. "You're very welcome." He walked with her through the grass to the parking area. "Let's talk about tomorrow. How does being a tourist sound?"

She laughed. "Delightful."

# 25

Matthew indulged her Friday morning. They walked down to Boston Harbor, shopping for small gifts in craft booths, angled back toward the historical district. Shortly after eleven, Shannon pointed out a coffee shop. They were parked nearby, and he thought a drive down the coast for lunch would be a good plan. After he'd placed their coffee orders, she touched his arm. "Buy a third one. Black and sweet." He shot her a look but added it to the order.

"Let's take them with us," Shannon suggested when the three coffees were ready. The coffee shop provided a cardboard carrier, and Shannon took all three drinks to the car.

Matthew held the passenger door for her as she slid inside, balancing the carrier, and secured her seat belt. He didn't move from where he stood beside her open door. "Where are we heading?"

"Let's take Highway 9 north."

He studied her upturned face for a moment, but she said nothing more. He nodded and closed her door, circled the car and settled behind the wheel, checked traffic, and maneuvered into the correct lane for Highway 9. "I don't mind secrecy, Shannon, but not when it's meeting someone I don't know, in a place I don't know. Talk to me, please."

"I haven't called anyone. I'm simply hoping I might find someone where we're going."

"Who would that be?"

She avoided his question. "An open, public area. A conversation. That's all I'm hoping for. If you don't like the situation when we get there, I'll listen and back off."

Someone she knew who had worked with the family or been affiliated with the family, that much seemed certain. She hadn't deliberately caused a problem to date, but Matthew could feel her skirting around something she knew he wouldn't like. He turned on the radio, found a music station, idly wondering if the coffee would be cold by the time they arrived. Or maybe she'd taken that into account when she pointed out the coffee shop.

Fifteen minutes later, she pointed. "See

the church steeple? Aim toward the cemetery on the north side. It's extensive, almost the size of a large park. The north side has the easiest parking access."

Another cemetery. He actually wasn't surprised. It was becoming a habit with her. He found a parking place.

Shannon exited the car. "Let's walk." She handed him his coffee and carried hers and the extra coffee with her.

Many of the cemetery's headstones had flower baskets or flags, most stones in this section showing only a decade or two of being exposed to the weather. He followed her across the neatly mown grass. She eventually paused by a headstone for three plots, two names with dates chiseled into the granite: *Karen Rose Barrows* and *Taylor James Barrows.* Both had died three years ago . . . today.

"Flynn's wife and son."

He shot Shannon a sharp look.

She left the third coffee on the headstone. "There's a bench by the pond. Let's have a seat, enjoy the sun. Most times I visited here in the past were in poor weather with rain showers. I'd like to just sit for a while."

Matthew stared at the headstone, the coffee, then back at her. "Sure. We can sit for a while."

They sat and watched the five ducks on the pond, the breeze occasionally fluttering its surface. Shannon became lost in thought, and he chose not to interrupt her. The date and the purpose they were here was obvious. Shannon hoped Flynn would visit his wife and son on the anniversary of their deaths. After all, didn't he visit Jessica's grave on the anniversary of her death every year, regardless of his health or the weather or what travel arrangements he had to make to be back in town? Still, this was a very long-shot hope on Shannon's part.

Matthew took off his ball cap and put it on Shannon. She smiled and angled it best for her eyes. "Thanks."

They drank their coffee and continued watching the ducks. He figured eventually he might be able to talk her into a walk around the cemetery rather than just sitting here.

He'd put together what he hoped would be a decent Fourth of July plan, but he wanted to wait and introduce the idea over dinner tonight when he could talk some about Becky, why he would be in Boston, and why he didn't want Shannon anywhere near a fireworks display. He was anticipating some strong pushback — insisting she could handle hearing fireworks without suffering some kind of bad reaction. He could hear her arguments already. Maybe she could or maybe she couldn't, but he didn't want to take the chance.

They'd likely have their first version of a fight over the topic, and he wondered what that would look like with Shannon. He doubted it would mean tears, probably just the collision of stubborn wills. He wasn't going to give her a choice. Being out of the range of fireworks was a safety matter for her emotional health, and he'd secure cooperation from her however he needed to do so. Yet he wasn't looking forward to the disagreement he expected to arise.

Shannon reached over and put her hand on his arm, interrupting his thoughts. Matthew looked up, didn't see anything out of the ordinary around them but could feel the change in Shannon.

The man who'd stopped at the graves looked like he was in his late thirties. A good-looking man, wearing casual slacks and a golf shirt, a neat haircut and close shave. He picked up the coffee and walked straight over to them.

Shannon beside him quivered but stayed seated. Her smile literally beamed from her face. "Hello, Flynn. I'm so glad you came. It's good to see you."

"Likewise, Annie." His voice was a surprisingly mild baritone.

"Which message reached you?"

"Let's see, the one with you yelling 'Where are you?' in my voicemail was pretty loud. And you swiped my favorite baseballs. I was somewhat surprised you didn't acquire my car, just to leave me a message I couldn't miss, since you liked to drive it so much," he commented, looking amused. "Did you pick up your journals from the cabin?"

"Yes."

"Calling you back would have just . . . complicated what I needed to do. I've got company. The blue van at the east side of the lot. Leah wants to say hi."

Shannon bolted to her feet. "She's *alive*?"

"Peter's boat sank. It rather messed up his plans to dock in San Diego. I took Leah with me." He held out a fist, and she bumped hers against his.

"You didn't . . ."

He shook his head. "He didn't get what he deserved, much as I regret not delivering it. I just pumped the ballast tanks the wrong direction and crippled the boat, let the Coast Guard pay him a visit. He decided he'd rather scuttle her. He's probably still in their system, being processed through, if someone should want to find him."

"Thank you!" She headed toward the parking lot, but then paused to ask, "George?"

"Angrier than a hornet. I'd rather not let him find me at the moment. Go say hi to Leah. She's been chatting my ear off since California about your exit plans that got interrupted."

"Where did she decide she wants to go?"

"Nella's. Don't ask me why a monastery appeals, but that's her choice. We'll be there this afternoon, I'm thinking. She's expected."

"I'd hug you, but you'd get the wrong idea."

Flynn chuckled. "Then go hug her, Annie. And for pity's sake, talk her out of singing another road song. She doesn't have your voice."

Shannon ran over to the van.

Matthew studied the man, got a searching look in return. Flynn gave a sigh and took a seat on the bench. "You're Dane?"

"Yes."

"I thought she'd head to you. She always had a thing for Boston." He took a tentative sip of the coffee. "How's your daughter?"

"Doing fine. Annie?"

"Her middle name. A very old story."

Matthew nodded toward Shannon, obviously having a joyous reunion with a lady at the van. He made a strategic leap in logic. "You got Shannon out without anyone else dying."

Flynn shrugged.

"You had someone in the water to make sure she would make it."

"Turns out she didn't need help," Flynn replied. "I owed her for Karen and my son, Taylor. She wouldn't go as long as someone else would pay the price. It was necessary, the way it played out." Flynn took another sip of the coffee, grimaced. "Coffee's lukewarm. Has she recovered her photographs?"

"The ones with your baseballs."

"Tell her to look up Wilma Poet for the others. She'll recognize the name." He leaned his head back and closed his eyes against the sunlight. "Leah is not a good driver, so it's been a lot of long hours behind the wheel the last few days." He sighed. "They really were my own trophy baseballs, bought for my son for when he would be old enough to appreciate them."

"I'm not a baseball guy, but they look old and interesting."

Flynn chuckled. "You just quoted my wife, who about had a heart attack when I told her how much I'd paid for the pair of them." Flynn looked toward the parking lot when the laughter of the women drifted over to them. "I'm glad she's with you. You strike me as a man who can handle bad news and figure out what to do with it."

"Yeah. I can."

Flynn pulled an envelope out of his pocket. "Her mother arranged for her to be taken. The uncle helped. He used a lawyer named Steven Harris to make the arrangements. I'm thinking the lawyer had the initial idea. He's a divorce attorney who qualified as a snake, even in my world. The middleman in the deal on our side was a guy by the name of Lou Barks. The family would keep proof and blackmail clients years later. Shannon doesn't know, doesn't need to know, any of the envelope's contents."

"You've known all along."

"Yeah. I never could figure out how to approach the problem. Without knowing why it had originally been arranged, returning her to her parents just left her sitting vulnerable to something else happening. Not that I could have gotten her clear — it was Shannon or my son, and that made it no decision. You can decide what to do with it. Tell her. Don't tell her. Whatever seems best. I'll make sure no one in the family thinks it's in their interest to mention the information about Shannon's mom to work a better deal."

"Is there still a threat?"

"Who knows with women, and the lawyer is still around. I wouldn't leave Shannon in Chicago. But if you mean from the Jacobys — George is the only one you need to worry about in regards to Shannon. The rest might wish her out of the picture, but they won't add murder to their existing problems. The Parkview in Alabama on Sunday. Shannon knows the town. George will be there after sundown, I'll make sure of that. Tell the cops to assume he'll be heavily armed."

"Thanks."

Flynn stood, stepped over to a nearby trash bin to dispose of the cup. "Do me a favor. Don't let her come to my funeral."

"You don't need to walk into that collision, Flynn. Stay put, let it play out without you."

"George and I have some things to settle. I hope, actually intend, to walk out of it in one piece. But at this point my luck running out isn't going to bother me much. Leah has Nella. Shannon's got her brother. It's not a bad final chapter."

"Shannon doesn't need one more thing to grieve."

"Hopefully she won't have to, but she's

stronger than she looks." Flynn started toward the van.

"Flynn . . ."

He paused and looked back.

"Shannon said you used to be a thief, a good one," Matthew said.

Flynn smiled. "Art, mostly private collections, a couple of small museums. I did love the Impressionists, but I could go for a nice abstract now and again."

"The cops could use those East and West Coast ledgers."

"I imagine they could." He thought a moment, nodded. "I'll see what I can do. One last theft, and taking it from the family . . . there's poetic justice for you. And it would annoy George." He headed to the parking lot.

As Shannon and Flynn passed each other, Shannon reached out to hug him.

Matthew suspected that when he read the full course of the diaries, Flynn's early decision to keep Shannon alive would undergird most of the last eleven years. A complex man, caught in the middle of a violent family, but a good enough man that Shannon had latched on to him with an eye toward her own survival, and Flynn had kept her alive. For that reason, more than any other, Matthew let him walk away.

# 26

"Thank you for not arresting him." Shannon was on a high, joy spilling out in her expression and voice. The fact Leah was alive and Flynn still okay had lifted huge weights off her, and now she was practically floating.

"Not a cop anymore," Matthew replied with a little shrug as they walked back to the car, glad of that fact today.

Shannon impulsively hugged him. "No citizen's arrest, then, or something. It was so good to see him. What did you and Flynn talk about?"

Still enjoying the hug, Matthew chose to ignore part of her question. There was no way he was going to tell her what Flynn had said about her mother until he had a chance to review the contents of the envelope and talk to Paul, get Theo working on the names Flynn had provided. He picked an easier reply. "Flynn may be able to get his hands on the East and West Coast ledgers for Paul."

Shannon considered that, smiled. "He will probably clear out the most interesting location or two before he hands those ledgers over, but yeah, he's the one person in the family who could probably get his hands on the bulk of them."

"He also said you would know a place called The Parkview in Alabama."

"It's a motel off Highway 84 east of a small town called Juno. Why?"

"George may be there Sunday evening."

Shannon's eyes went wide, and then she looked visibly relieved. "That would be a really good arrest to get off the list."

"What did Leah have to say?" Matthew asked, hoping to divert her from further questions.

Shannon lit up with a smile. "She's doing really well. Nella's this really nice nun we both know — another story. She's got a place for Leah, along with contacts who can reach Leah's family in Brazil. I wish I'd seen that confrontation with Peter on the boat — oh, it would have been something. I almost capsized it once when I didn't move the ballast in the tanks properly. So that was an elegant choice on Flynn's part for how to cripple the boat. Leah said the farm being raided is what tipped off the family. Everyone scattered. They haven't heard from anyone out on the drive, no check-in places are active, and every contact is giving out nothing here. They've become ghosts. The thinking is that people are probably okay. If there had been some murders, the news would have filtered out."

"That's good to hear."

"If Flynn can pin down George, I'd sleep a lot easier. For all their sakes, as well as mine."

Matthew unlocked the car door for Shannon. "I need to call Paul."

She leaned on her arms across the open door, bit her lip. "If you do, Paul has to act on what you tell him. Could you live with waiting to call him until, say, around dinnertime tonight? Leah will be where she wants to go, and Flynn will have had time to at least not be sitting in the monastery parking lot. But I know that's asking a lot. Please?"

Matthew was very aware that Shannon could have figured out a way to get in touch with Flynn without him knowing about the contact. There was a balancing act going on here between what he knew — the diaries' contents, the location of Flynn's cabin, this meeting — and what he told Paul. Right now it was so strongly tipped toward Shannon, it'd become hazardous for the investigation. Matthew thought about the envelope in his pocket. He needed time to think. He had to figure out how to act on what Flynn had given him without risking Shannon's mother being arrested tomorrow. Bottom line, though, he needed to keep Shannon's trust. Her welfare remained his top priority.

"Seven tonight, six Chicago time," he said. "I'll call Paul then."

"Thank you!"

He smiled. "Let's hope I don't regret it when Paul learns the length of the delay." He started the car and considered what made sense for the next few hours. Something to eat was high on his list, something to give him time to think about the meeting that had just occurred.

Shannon clicked her seat belt in place, said quietly, "There's one thing that might be worth doing if you've got friends among the Boston police and could call in a favor."

"What's that?"

"George Jacoby knows Flynn comes here. It was a pattern, since his wife and son died, that Flynn would come here of an evening, sometimes bring a blanket and a bottle of wine, and he'd watch the sun go down. I'd pay my respects earlier in the day. If George really is that angry with Flynn, he could be here tonight, watching to see if Flynn shows up for his normal remembrance."

"That's a useful suggestion." Matthew looked around. "You sure he's not watching us right now?"

"I've been searching for even a glimpse of him, and you can bet Flynn scoped the area before he entered the cemetery. George would lie low until close to sundown, see if Flynn shows up, probably try to take him out when he leaves. George was always one for keeping family business just among family. He'd want to keep any confrontation between the two out of the public domain."

"I'll see what I can do, have some cops with photos of the man keep watch around this area tonight. Flynn won't be back?"

Shannon shook her head. "There won't be time, given where Leah's going. But he also wouldn't risk it — he knows George too well. If the farm raid convinced George I'm alive, he's likely been in Chicago looking for me. But he'd want payback with Flynn for letting me live. Or if George isn't certain about me, but the farm raid and the boat sinking convinced him that Flynn has gone rogue, George would come here hoping to catch up with him. I don't know that George risks it now that cops are looking for him, but it's possible. I'm sorry. I should have told you about this place earlier."

Matthew wasn't going to disagree with her — she should have told him — but he understood why she had not. Regardless, it was time for them to be leaving. If there was a collision with George today, he wanted Shannon far away from it. This was an easy enough place to stake out for the evening. He turned the subject away from George. "For your other photographs, Flynn said to tell you to look up Wilma Poet. Do you recognize that name?"

Shannon looked puzzled. "She was a well-known schoolteacher around the turn of the century. The public library in her hometown was named after her. I know the story because Flynn would stop and get books for me from that library. It's not far from here — due west about twenty minutes, I think. He said that's where he stored my camera memory cards?"

"All he said was to look up Wilma Poet. Why don't we go check out this library?"

"Sure. Trust Flynn to make a cryptic remark like that. I would love to recover more of my photographs, and he makes it a difficult proposition."

She sounded just enough irked at Flynn that Matthew had to chuckle. "We'll see what there is to find."

Matthew pulled the car into the Wilma Poet Public Library parking lot and chose a spot near the entrance where posted hours had the library open until seven p.m. "Any idea where he might have stored something for you?"

"None. Flynn has a sense of gamesmanship about him. He'd make it easy to find, but put it somewhere that would require me to think." She studied the library building. "I was always reading books from this library. He'd know that. So I think we need to look inside. It's going to have to do with books."

"Then inside it is." They walked into the small-town library. She scanned the shelves neatly lining the room in a sweeping U. "Maybe the category you read from the most?" he suggested.

Shannon shook her head. "I was pretty eclectic in what I read. He'd bring me a how-to guide on electrical repairs and a biography on President Truman next to the fiction titles I'd asked him to pick up. He always said I should write a book because I read so many of them. Maybe . . ." She walked over to an old-fashioned card catalog, checked the alphabet filing, pulled out a drawer for authors, looked up Shannon Bliss, and found an index card — a different typeface than the others but the same format of information, listing a book reference. She showed him the card. "I'd say that's Flynn." She wrote the number on her palm, went to the shelves, located the book, and chuckled as she pulled it off the shelf.

"What?"

She turned it so he could read the title. *Photographs of the Eastern Seaboard.* She opened the book. On the first page was an inscription: *For Shannon, from Flynn.* In pen, in the upper right corner, was a series of numbers.

Matthew's curiosity spiked. "Any idea what those numbers mean?"

"I think it's his personal safe combination. We'd need to go back to their property to check that out. I can't say that idea appeals much."

"Where's the safe exactly?"

"The room with his wife and son's things. It's not much of a safe, just a small fireproof box. I figure his marriage license is in there, negatives of their wedding photos, that kind of thing."

"We've got time today to make the drive, or I can give this information to one of the officers now at the scene."

"They would keep whatever they find in the safe as evidence."

"Probably."

"If we go check it out ourselves?"

"Paul can probably finesse things to let us take what belongs to you."

"Make a call. Let's go see if this is his safe combination."

Matthew slowed as they neared the Hennessey and Vine property. An officer was parked just inside the entrance road. Shannon tipped Matthew's ball cap down over her face. He showed his credentials to the officer, was given admittance since he'd already cleared things through Paul. He drove onto the property and stopped at the house with the swing set in the side yard. Numerous vehicles were parked in various places, from both the FBI and the state police. None were at this house. Paul had made certain the way would be cleared for them.

"Let's not linger," Shannon requested, her voice tight.

"Ten minutes," Matthew reassured. They would check the numbers and then be on their way.

Shannon retrieved a house key from behind a horseshoe nailed to a window flower box, opened the front door. She headed straight up the stairs. Matthew followed her, looking around with interest. He'd come back to this house, this property, at a later date without Shannon to get a longer look at what was here.

She disappeared into the front bedroom. Matthew stopped in the doorway. Going by the layer of dust on the furniture, the room didn't appear to have been touched in some time. A line of perfume bottles sat on the dresser. Several dresses and blouses hung in the closet; shoeboxes had been stacked haphazardly at the bottom.

Shannon knelt down on the floor and began pulling out the shoeboxes, one by one. "Here it is." The fireproof safe was almond in color, looked to be at least a decade or more in age. She slid the box over so she could read the dial for the combination. She tried the numbers starting clockwise, then counterclockwise, but the box wouldn't open.

Matthew thought about his own home safe. "For the second number, try spinning the dial all the way around, then come to stop on the number."

She tried it counterclockwise with the additional turn and the safe opened.

Shannon lifted out a manila envelope, opened it. "It's more of my camera photo cards," she confirmed, handing the envelope up to him. "What do you want me to do with the rest of the contents?" She flipped through some of the papers. "His marriage certificate, death certificates — about what I expected."

"Leave the safe open on the bed for the cops to deal with," Matthew said. He was dumping out smaller envelopes from the large one she'd handed him. "There's a note here that says, 'Shannon, also check the shoeboxes. Flynn'." Matthew handed it to her.

She looked at the note. "Huh." She began opening the shoeboxes she'd moved, glancing in each one. She went back to the closet and pulled out more shoeboxes. "More photo cards." She held the lid off to one side. "I kept more photographs than I remember."

"Check them all," Matthew suggested.

She handed him the shoebox and went back to looking through the rest. Matthew thumbed through the small manila envelopes, doing a count of the first inch and multiplying by what he could see. There were three rows, stacked two levels deep. "How many photos do you think you stashed away?"

"I had a goal to take half a million photographs, but most I deleted. I don't know how many got stored."

He let that sink in, then reached over to rest his hand on her shoulder. "I'm certain some of these are going to be worth a few dollars. The second item on your personal list could be coming true, Shannon."

"I hope so." She found one more shoebox of memory cards. She checked the last box and stood. "That's it. Those two boxes and the envelope. I didn't realize Flynn was putting all the memory cards in one spot. I thought he was storing them around in various places for me."

"That library note wasn't done recently. He had this place marked out for you after his wife's things were stored here. He probably figured the family would leave this room alone, and he was right."

She nodded. "Well, this is what I came for, Matthew. Let's head out."

"You're nervous here."

"Her things. Taylor's. There are too many reminders of the friends I lost."

Matthew would have responded, but his attention was caught by something else. "Are those your early diaries?" he asked, pointing to the lower shelf of a bookcase.

Shannon looked over, and she inhaled sharply. "Mine, some of his wife's," she whispered. "We both kept journals. I can't believe he kept them here."

He picked up a box, emptied the clothes neatly packed into it onto the bedspread, stacked the journals into the box. "He may have moved them back here recently for you to find," Matthew guessed. "Maybe retrieved and returned the bulk of the photo memory cards to the two shoeboxes as well." He picked up the box of journals, looked around the room for anything else that might have been left for her to find, saw a woman's wedding rings next to a picture of Flynn, his wife and his son, added that photo to the box and slid the rings into his pocket. "We'll give these to Flynn the next time we see him."

"Thanks, Matthew."

He glanced over at her.

"For assuming we'll see him again and be able to have that conversation." Her eyes looked wet with unshed tears.

He hoped for her sake they could have that next conversation. "Flynn strikes me as being a survivor, same as you."

"He was a pretty good survival coach, if you want the truth." She wiped her eyes, then picked up the two shoeboxes. He followed her down the stairs, stored the items in the back seat of the car, waited for her to relock the house and return the key to its place.

He tried to figure out her mood as they left the property. Clearly relieved to be away, but still caught by a raw grief this place had revived. "I'll help you start loading those memory cards onto a laptop tonight so you can get a look at your photos," he offered as a distraction.

"Sure. That would be nice."

"Shannon . . . talk to me."

"Just memories. Flynn's wife was a nice woman. I miss her."

He put a hand over hers. "She would have been happy for you, for the way this is turning out."

Shannon glanced over, tried to smile. "She would have been."

## 27

Matthew could hear Shannon singing softly along with the radio as she dealt with her windblown hair in Becky's bathroom. She had a beautiful voice, something he noticed when they'd attended church. It was nice to hear her singing again.

Shannon's biggest concern was that the investigation into what had happened to her would lead back to evidence that would put her mother in jail. Matthew was holding information in his pocket that could do just that. He went into his bedroom, pulled back one of his daughter's tapestries, opened his private safe, and put the envelope from Flynn inside it. He closed the safe door and spun the dial. If he opened that envelope, if he knew the details of what had happened, saw what proof backed up the statement Flynn had made, he would potentially trigger the one thing Shannon feared.

Shannon had to survive this. That was his

bottom line. He personally could live with her mother facing prosecution and jail time. He could live with scuttling Jeffery's campaign for governor with the timing of this. But Shannon could not.

If she took a blow so severe she couldn't recover from it, where she regretted returning to her family, where she absorbed the fallout of the truth as her responsibility, her doing, her fault — that was the line he couldn't see things cross. Shannon could only absorb so much at a time. She couldn't handle this news right now.

Three days. He was going to wait three days.

He was already withholding the Colorado address where Shannon was to have been delivered, along with the news about Flynn's cabin. He was now in possession of all Shannon's diaries and had no plans to pass them on before she determined he should do so. Delaying a decision about this latest bombshell in the envelope was an act of grace toward Shannon and one more serious infraction of his agreement to share what he knew with Paul on a timely basis.

But he had an even more serious problem. If Flynn's statement was credible, the possibility that Shannon's mother could take her own life if the news came out was a very real risk, regardless of whether the authorities became involved in the matter. He'd have to figure out some way to mitigate that peril. It was now over a week since Shannon had returned to Chicago, and so far her mother hadn't made a rash step.

Shannon had felt loved those first sixteen years of her life — that was what puzzled Matthew the most about this news. He needed to meet Shannon's mom. *Who was she? What had she done, and why?* Had it been a loving mother making an unbelievable mistake? Or a selfish, cold woman who didn't love her daughter, who had used her to address a financial problem? All Matthew knew about the woman was what others had told him, comments Jeffery had made, what Shannon had mentioned. None of it made sense; the puzzle pieces didn't fit together. For Shannon's sake he would get to the bottom of it, and as carefully as he could.

There were no good solutions in front of him, but there were several decisions that had to be made, and Matthew mentally ran down the list, settling matters in his mind as to where to start, what he would do.

The envelope was going to wait. During the next three days, Paul hopefully would arrest George Jacoby, removing the most serious threat to Shannon's security. She'd meet with her parents, and he'd get an impression of how her mother was with her. Jeffery would make the news of Shannon's return public. Three days would give him time to read the majority of the recovered diaries, and afterward he would know, and not be guessing, about Shannon's missing years.

Shannon needed her brother. She needed her father, if that relationship could be salvaged. That had to be a priority. He would make sure Shannon was never alone with her mother, that there couldn't be a whispered plea or confession that sent Shannon careening into an abyss.

When he knew Shannon's past as best he could grasp it, when he had met her mother, he would then deal with that envelope and do what could be done to check its veracity.

Then he would tell Shannon what the envelope revealed before he shared its contents with Paul. That decision surprised him, but it felt right. Her welfare would drive the decisions he made. Shannon could handle hard truths, but not all at once. No matter how else this played out, he was determined to make sure that inner core of strength of hers didn't break from stresses beyond her limit.

*God, don't let me fail Shannon now.* A

simple prayer, a simple statement, but it was the mission he was determined to accomplish. He listened to the faint sound of her singing. She was happy. He wanted . . . *needed* her to have more hours like this. They were the best gift he could give her.

He looked at the time. Dinner. Confirm his friends with the Boston PD were in place to watch the cemetery for the evening. Then call Paul and figure out how to say without sounding like an idiot, *By the way, did I mention we ran into Flynn earlier today?*

Tomorrow morning he'd convince Shannon to get on a plane with him for an hour-and-forty-minute flight back to Chicago, convince her that anything under two hours was like a bad dream that would be swiftly over. He'd read another of her diaries during the flight.

He dealt often in difficult lists, but this one was nearly crushing him with its potential for bad outcomes. He needed a couple of aspirins. The headache that had appeared wasn't easing off. The photographs could be a good distraction for Shannon. He could use that for this evening. He'd start there.

Matthew sorted through the two shoeboxes of photo memory cards. Since an important priority on Shannon's personal list was to establish a career as a photographer, reviewing the images would certainly give her a starting place. Simply sizing up the scope of the project would itself take some time, keep her occupied on a worthwhile endeavor. He found the extra laptop he kept around, set it up on the dining room table. He chose a random sample of the envelopes and began loading the memory cards to ensure the software and directories were set up properly.

Shannon joined him as the sixth card finished transferring to the hard drive. She leaned over his shoulder to look at a photo he'd clicked on to open full screen — a beautiful beach scene.

"An excellent image, Shannon. These first cards have over three hundred images each, and by my rough count there are well over a thousand cards. You could have as many as three hundred thousand images here. I've been randomly opening a variety of dates. They're reading fine."

"A lot are duplicates. Driftwood. Sunsets. Interesting waves."

He changed the screen to six similar images of the beach tiled across it. "You're going to have a difficult time choosing just one or two. They're all lovely."

She smiled at the compliment. "I think I took some good photographs," she agreed.

He got up from his seat, motioned her into it. "Spend an hour loading memory cards, sorting out images, selecting favorites. I think you've got a good basis for your dream to have a career as a photographer right here. Even if you set aside more than half of these, you'll end up with a hundred thousand images to work with. You should have someone look at these, give you a professional opinion on their value."

"I wouldn't know where to begin."

"Let's take them back to Chicago and show them to Ellie Dance."

"Doesn't she handle art, not photographs?"

"She's an expert on artistic images and their worth. You've met her and liked her. She'll be kind in what she says. And if she doesn't feel qualified to give you an opinion, she'll no doubt know someone who can." He understood her hesitation — this was a core dream for her. "Choose fifty images spread across these cards as representative of your work. When we're back in Chicago, we'll stop at that camera shop and get them printed as eight-by-tens. It's better to know, Shannon. Time isn't going to change the verdict. Being a photographer is one of your dreams, and this one strikes me as easier than getting your GED. Certainly quicker than getting married."

He got her to laugh. She looked at the images on the screen, clicked to the next ones. "You're right, Matthew, this is a big dream," she admitted softly. "Every time I clicked the shutter, I hoped I was storing away something for my future. I don't want to fail."

He put both hands on her shoulders, kneaded at the tension he could feel. "You haven't failed. I like what I see. Take a small chance, show Ellie your work, see what she has to say."

Shannon tabbed through the loaded images. "What time is our flight to Chicago?"

He gently squeezed her shoulders as she silently accepted his plan and then stepped back, letting her get to work. "Nine a.m. It will put us comfortably back at the apartment by noon. Your parents will be at Jeffery's for dinner. I told him we'd plan to come out around seven, stay an hour. If you're comfortable with how that goes, you can meet again as a family Sunday afternoon."

"When is Jeffery making the public announcement?"

"He's scheduled a press conference for

Monday at ten a.m." Matthew glanced at the time. "I'm going to go call Paul now, tell him about Flynn, get an update from him on how things have progressed. Then we'll have dinner. That work for you?"

"Yes. I'd like those steaks you set out — medium well works for me," she mentioned, "and a heaping salad. I can do the salad if you can take care of grilling the steaks."

"Perfect."

Matthew took his phone and a cold soda out to the back patio, settled in for a long conversation, called Paul.

"Good to hear from you, Matthew. Was Shannon able to locate what she thought might be there at the property?"

"She retrieved two shoeboxes' worth of camera memory cards, and I'm now in possession of all her diaries."

"That's excellent news."

"Paul, we had a face-to-face with Flynn today."

A long silence met his statement. "You did have an interesting day," Paul said slowly. "When and where?"

Matthew briefed him. "Sorry it played out this way. I was making choices as it unfolded, none of them ideal. I chose to give Shannon the delay she wanted."

"Leah got out, that's a huge win. I can see the big picture. Keeping Shannon's trust. Gaining help toward arresting the most violent man in the family. Locating those ledgers. I'm not thrilled at the time gap, but I would have made the same call."

"Not being a cop made today easier," Matthew admitted. "And I'll tell you up front, I'm sitting on other news about Flynn, nothing that I think changes your outcome but still rather big truths."

"Shannon?"

"Uh-huh. I think I've seen the full picture with her, only to discover an entire new fissure opens up. Let me get through reading the journals. When I'm done with them, hopefully I'll be past the surprises." He wasn't looking forward to those hours of reading, but it had to be done. "What's the property out here look like? I saw a lot of cops working the site."

"No graves so far. Some good leads on aliases they might be traveling under. A lot of paper to sort through. Photo albums. We'll be out there for weeks figuring it out." Paul shifted the topic. "Give me the name of the guy the Coast Guard is holding again."

"All I have is a first name, Peter. I assume it's Peter Jacoby, but who knows what alias he gave the Coast Guard. The boat was listing — Flynn's doing — and Peter deliberately scuttled the boat rather than have her boarded."

"I'll find him in the system and make sure we get custody."

"Shannon and Flynn both are focused on George as the one point of serious trouble. I've got some of Boston PD's finest watching the cemetery tonight on the slim chance George shows up. The hotel in Alabama is going to be the most likely place to arrest him. I'm sending you the photo of Flynn I snapped. My read of it, Flynn will do what he can to keep cops from getting killed making the arrest, but he's expecting George to escalate this to a gunfight. If you could not kill Flynn in the crossfire, Shannon would be enormously relieved."

"I've got some men in mind to make the arrest, the kind who can sneak up on an angry grizzly bear and walk away from the encounter without teeth or claw marks."

Matthew chuckled at the image. "Send a lot of those type guys."

"I want a smooth arrest," Paul agreed. "I'd like George in handcuffs and talking, or saying 'I want a lawyer' and not talking, rather than dead. Shannon's aware Flynn is certain to get arrested Sunday night?"

"She's aware," Matthew replied. "She's not ready for it, but she's accepted that it's going to happen. Flynn will be the one person in the family you can pretty much trust to tell it straight, Paul. There's enough in her journals to contradict him if he gives you a self-serving story. I'm not sure how many within the family he'll be willing to testify against, but it sounds like George and Peter are on the list he'd hand over on a silver platter if he can. If you can hold Flynn without charges for a while, keep him separate from the family, it'll make this easier on Shannon. Just having some time pass will help. She's going to ask you at some point if she can have a conversation with him — she hasn't said that, but I can read how she's thinking. She wants this over, but Flynn isn't someone she's seeing as only part of her past. I don't think she's put together a picture of the future, but she's made an assumption she continues to see Flynn. My best guess is writing him letters, visiting him in prison is a possibility in her mind."

"She's holding on to him," Paul remarked. "Interesting."

"How much of that is a sense of closure — she's put getting herself out and seeing him 'get out' as part of the same package to some degree — and how much of it is just their relationship flowing from the past and into the present is hard to figure. He's important to her, I know that. She doesn't move into her own future without knowing Flynn's future has settled," Matthew said.

"I'll do what I can to make this unfold so Shannon doesn't get surprised. Time is the one piece I can offer once he's in custody. There are a lot of conversations we need to have, and I'm more than willing to start with Flynn as the linchpin on the eventual trial strategy. If nothing else, that can limit how much we need Shannon." Paul shifted topics again. "Talk to me about Leah and Nella."

Matthew gave Paul what Shannon had told him, along with what he'd picked up from the diaries. He sorted through his phone images and sent the one of Leah taken at some distance. "Shannon thinks a conversation with Leah next week is the right way to proceed. Leah is taking Shannon's advice about writing a list of things to talk about with the police. Leah was mostly West Coast and on the boat with Peter, never traveled the circuit with the family. Shannon is intentionally vague about dates, but the first journal entry mentioning a Leah is four years ago. I'm guessing that's the time frame she represents."

"I'll send Rita out that way when Leah's ready to talk," Paul said. "How's Shannon doing?"

Matthew thought about the expressions he had seen on Shannon's face over the course of the day. "She's lived a lifetime today, from extreme joy to grieving tears. It was as close to a normal day in emotions as I've witnessed with her." He checked the time. He needed to get the grill started. "I'll call you tomorrow once we're back in Chicago. Would you mention to your wife I'll have a conversation with Shannon about the Fourth of July? Ann's suggestion for Shadow Lake and Rachel looks like it could work."

"I'll be sure to do that," Paul said. "And I concur with Ann — our dog would love not to be in Chicago for the Fourth if you can make that happen."

"I'm using it as a sweetener in my plan, as Shannon rather likes your dog," Matthew replied. "Talk to you later, Paul." He slid the phone into his pocket, relieved to have that call over. Paul had gone easy on him.

Dinner. A conversation about the Fourth, hopefully avoid their first serious disagreement. Matthew pushed himself out of the chair and headed into the house. "Shannon, hungry yet?"

"You were supposed to be annoyed with me for making Fourth of July plans for you without your input," Matthew noted, sitting across from her with a cold drink.

They had eaten dinner at the dining room table, and he'd told Shannon about the arrangements he had worked out. She'd nodded, said, "Sounds good," and asked him to pass the butter and basket of rolls. Now she was back to tabbing through images on the laptop while she ate the Dilly Bar he had brought from the freezer. "Becky called while you were talking to Paul," Shannon told him around a bite, and didn't elaborate.

Matthew hadn't told his daughter about his concerns, so he wasn't sure how to connect Shannon's comment to his description of the Fourth.

Shannon must have seen his confusion. She smiled and explained, "Becky gave me a list of those coming with her to make sure I was okay with so many people being around. I don't mind. She mentioned where her headphones were so I could suppress the noise from the fireworks, then came back around at the end of the conversation to warn me the cut glass vases and serving bowls in the china cupboard need to be set out on the dining room table before dark, because the percussions rattled the windows, and sometimes pictures fall off the walls and those glass items can shift to knock into each other and get chipped." Shannon paused to finish the Dilly Bar and then pointed the stick at him. "You, being the super-conscientious *you,* would not let someone who had been through a recent shooting anywhere near that close to fireworks. So I already figured you'd have something in mind." Shannon licked the stick clean. "Besides, I like Rachel and I love Black. And I enjoy Charlotte and Bryce's company. It sounds like a fun weekend. And this way you won't be hovering around me, worrying I'm getting stressed over the noise."

Matthew laughed. "Thanks, Shannon."

"For what?" she asked absently.

"Letting me plan things for you."

"It's what you do, Matthew, and do well. I kind of like it." She tapped the stick on the table. "Would there be another Dilly Bar? These are really good. I want to work on the photos for a couple more hours, make sure I get a good range of images — different subjects, different years. Not only the best ones, but a good representative sample for Ellie to look over."

"I like it. I'll find you ice cream if we're out of Dilly Bars. My daughter loves them too."

"In case I haven't mentioned it, Matthew, Becky is a delight. She sent pictures of her and her roommate all dressed up to go out tonight. Want to see them?"

"My little girl is growing up. Show me tomorrow. Otherwise I might be tempted to call her back and insist she not go out. Did she say if this is a double date?"

Shannon chuckled. "Didn't have to. Based on their dresses, I'm sure it was a real double date, not just 'hanging out.' So . . . your daughter is going out tonight. I'm working on photographs. What are you doing tonight?"

"I thought I'd read more of your journals."

Shannon's smile disappeared. "Matthew —"

"My choice, unless you have decided you don't want them read."

She thought about it and shook her head. "It's your decision. But I don't like to think about all those details running through your memories. You live with Becky's. That's enough."

He turned toward the kitchen, refusing to let this turn to serious. "I've room for your history too, Shannon. I'll step on fewer land mines if I know." He opened the freezer and called, "A Dilly Bar and a refresh on that lemonade, I think. The sweet-and-sour clash will keep you awake while you work."

"Now you're just being cruel," she called back from the dining room. "I'm drinking the pineapple-and-something-else juice, bottom shelf of the refrigerator door."

# 28

The return trip to Chicago had gone smoother than their trip out to Boston. Matthew opened the drapes in the apartment's living room to let in sunlight. "What would you like to do for the afternoon?" he asked Shannon. "Jeffery's not expecting us until seven."

"Let's go get my photographs printed, then see if Ellie is busy, get the 'What are they worth?' question answered," she suggested.

"That works for me."

She carried her gym bag down the hall to the bedroom she was using.

Out of habit, Matthew turned on the television to hear the top of the midday newscast. He watched the summary of the political and sports news, then the lead story of a shooting at a convenience store. Finding nothing that captured his attention, Matthew shut off the television as Shannon rejoined him. "How many pictures did you load onto the laptop last night?"

"Thirteen thousand. I chose thirty-five that best represented the span of what's there."

"A useful sample. We can stop for a bite to eat after we see Ellie."

It was nice to have a plan for the next forty-eight hours. They'd see Ellie this afternoon, meet up with Shannon's parents tonight, attend early church services tomorrow, spend a few hours with Jeffery and his wife Sunday afternoon, then hunker down for the press conference on Monday.

Shannon picked up her canvas bag, changed her mind, left it on the couch, pushed her phone, cash, and ATM card into her pocket. "Okay, I'm ready to go."

"Got the photos you want to print?"

She held up a flash drive. "Right here."

He picked up his keys. "Then we're off."

They went to the camera shop first. The shop owner took the flash drive of selected photos to print out. Matthew watched Shannon walk the display cases, looking at camera models and accessories. "You want to put one of these in your hands while you're here? Feel it out?" The one he had been discussing with the shop owner was center of the middle display case, bottom shelf.

She shook her head. "Cameras are something you carry around when you've got something to do with it. There's barely a tree to be seen around here. I'm not a photographer of buildings or street scenes."

"You've spent a lot of years avoiding taking photographs of people. You might enjoy it." He stopped beside her. "Indulge me." He pointed to the camera he had in mind. "Try the used one. If you're not ready to graduate to people looking back at you, why don't you practice being an animal photographer with Black? He's got personality. I think you'd enjoy trying to capture his range of expressions."

He picked up on the glimmer of interest he saw in her face. "You know you're going to end up with a camera of your own soon — it's going to be irresistible. This way you don't have to make the decision. You can photograph some dog faces while you think about what new, fully featured camera you want to carry around with you for the next five years." He smiled at her, lightly bumped her shoulder with his. "I know it's a big decision, which is probably why you haven't made it yet. So think of this one as a bridge to the one you really want."

"Yeah, okay," she said softly. The shop owner rang up the prints and got out the camera, added it to the purchase, located a box of blank memory cards for it. Shannon adjusted the fabric strap to the right length for her. The camera cradled in her hand comfortably.

Matthew signed the charge slip. "Ready?" He picked up the box of photographs and glanced at her. She had the camera aimed at his face, and he ducked away with a laugh. "I get a moratorium on my photo being taken."

"I've got to practice some people shots — might as well be on you."

She looked back at the owner before they walked out. "Thanks."

"You take nice photographs," he replied with a smile.

Shannon didn't say anything as they walked to the car, but when he unlocked the car and held her door, she gave him a hug before she slid inside.

Shannon walked into the Dance and Covey Gallery with a purposeful stride, her face calm, her nerves under that careful control Matthew had seen in Atlanta and in critical times since. She really was good at hiding what she was feeling when doing so was important to her.

A middle-aged woman with a pleasant smile came to greet them. "Good afternoon, I'm Christine. I work for the gallery. May I help you with something today or would you prefer to browse our collection?"

"I was hoping to speak with Ellie Dance if she is in today," Shannon replied.

"She is. May I have your names?"

"Shannon, and this is Matthew Dane."

"Please, look around the gallery while I let her know you're here."

The main room was filled with a stunning array of sculptures and watercolors dominating the walls. It looked as though two artists were featured this month.

"Ellie said Charlotte's work is displayed in the north gallery." Shannon spotted an archway and walked that direction. Matthew stepped with her into an adjoining, spacious room. Sketches hung at eye level in three rows circling the room — hundreds of them. "These are all Charlotte's works? Oh my," Shannon breathed. "They're exquisite."

"Bryce said she was a good sketch artist, a major understatement about his wife's talent." Matthew paused at one of a baseball game in progress, stunned by how much information was conveyed in what were only a few lines of colored pencil against a white background. It was a powerful image full of motion and humor and even pain captured on the runner's face as he attempted a slide into third base before the outfielder threw him out.

They circled the room together, Shannon pausing occasionally to point out a new favorite drawing. "Charlotte has a wonderful touch with people and places. You can see her walking through life capturing what has her attention. I so admire that."

"It's truly amazing the way she captures what she sees on the paper," Matthew agreed.

Shannon stepped into the next gallery, a long narrow room showcasing six large oil paintings on the facing wall, sweeping landscapes all signed *Marie.* "This is Wyoming," Shannon whispered, looking particularly enthralled by the one opposite the entrance. "I've been there many times. The artist is practically breathing Wyoming air, it's so vivid." She looked at the small accompanying title plate. "*Rolling Hills at Sunset.* A perfect title."

"You're looking at why you're a true artist, Shannon. Charlotte sketches, Marie paints, you photograph, but you all capture the world around you in a unique way."

Shannon glanced over with a smile.

"Thank you."

They returned to the room displaying Charlotte's sketches. "Ellie's skill is showcased too," Matthew added, "in what she's chosen to present together. This wall has a visually stunning impact all its own."

Shannon stood back to view it in its totality. "I love it."

Footsteps coming toward them had Shannon turning. "Ms. Dance."

"Ellie, please," the woman said with a smile. "Welcome to the gallery, Shannon. Hello, Matthew."

"So good to see you again, Ellie," Matthew replied.

"Charlotte's work is fascinating, don't you think?" Ellie mentioned. "She lives her life sketching things she enjoys, then hands me the sketches to decide how best to share them with the world."

"It's an impressive collection."

"I enjoy representing her talent. She's done thousands of drawings over the years, and it's always a fresh delight to see what she brings me. Have you come today to browse or can I help you with something specific?"

"I was wondering if you could look at something . . . and give me your professional opinion," Shannon said, sounding shy.

"Of course. I'd be glad to help."

Shannon held out the box of thirty-five photographs. Ellie glanced inside, smiled, and nodded to her left. "Come this way, please." Ellie led them through the gallery to an open counter behind the showrooms where items were professionally framed. She closed a laptop and moved aside business printouts, then spread the images across the long surface. "Your work, Shannon?"

"Yes."

"You're an excellent photographer."

"Thank you. I hope to be an even better one with the right direction and representation."

Ellie laughed. "I like artists who still have some humility. What are you hoping to learn today, Shannon?"

"Do you think they might be . . . well, would they sell?"

Ellie smiled. "Artists are always so uncertain about having something of worth. Yes, these will sell. Photographs have their own revenue formula. Between licensing of images and sales of the originals, there's a good living to be made by someone who has an artistic view and technical experience. You have both."

"You're not just saying that."

Ellie shook her head. "I never speak lightly on matters of business and art." She tapped the third photograph. "This one in particular is wonderfully planned. It would sell quickly as an original work of art." She slid forward another one of the photographs. "This one would be popular under a licensing arrangement. Advertising companies could put this image behind nearly any product they were marketing — use it with print ads, television, posters, you name it. Then there are postcards, greeting cards, calendars, mugs. And on the electronic side of things, computer screen savers and wallpaper, music videos, gaming apps, album covers. The list is endless for where a good image can make an impact.

"There's an entire industry built around searchable databases of images for license. Of course, it isn't the revenue stream it was before digital cameras turned everyone into a photographer, so prices have dropped. Photos that used to license for two hundred dollars might now be more like forty. But the number of businesses using photographs in their marketing is now above seventy percent, and the audience willing to pay for very good photographs is increasing in size." Ellie glanced over at Shannon. "Did I just confuse you more?"

"I think I actually understood that," Shannon replied. "A license means I'm basically renting out my photographs to someone who wants to use them as part of something else — to put some text across them as an advertisement, have one in a calendar, maybe use one as the background on a song lyric sheet."

"Exactly."

"When I want to sell a photograph, what's involved? Is that a straightforward process?"

"It's a bit more complex than people realize," Ellie said, then gestured to the seating in the office next door. "Bring your photographs, and let's have a seat while I get us something to drink. I enjoy this, Shannon, talking about the business of selling art." Ellie brought out soft drinks and bottled iced tea. They settled in comfortable chairs around a low, round table.

"To sell a photograph, you have two options," Ellie began, picking up on Shannon's question. "You can sell it as an original work of art — one print and one buyer. You agree to never print another copy of that digital file except in an official catalog of your sold works with the buyer's name and reference number listed. The buyer enjoys the print while he or she owns it, and hopes to sell that photographic print to someone else in the future for a profit."

Ellie picked up the first three of the photos Shannon had brought in. "Selling your photographs as original works of art is an option you should certainly consider. There's a 'voice,' if you will, beginning to appear in your work that makes it *look* like your work. That's a very good thing to see in an artist."

"A voice?" Shannon said.

"Yes. Did you notice with Charlotte's display, how the drawings each looked similar to the others, even though there are scores of different subjects on that wall? That's her *voice* — the way she draws curves, adds in details, shows movement. In a similar way, you've got a voice showing up in these thirty-five photographs. What's in focus and what is not, how intricate the object is that interests you." She picked up the top photograph. "You like the wood grain in the driftwood, and how this other piece of driftwood rocks back and forth, half in and half out of the ocean." She selected another. "See how these waves are propelling pieces of seaweed ashore? You liked this sand crab, and this flower growing up between the rocks. Those are the choices you bring to what you see and care about.

You didn't give me a photograph with everything in focus, but rather showed me the item you cared about — that's your developing voice, like a signature in the image."

"Oh." Shannon sounded surprised. "So that's good?"

Ellie smiled. "Your voice is unique to you. That's good. What your voice is doesn't matter nearly as much as the fact you have one. In your photos, you show what has your interest, rather than give me a scene and let me choose what might interest me. You make your photographs unique by caring about something. That's why collectors who like your works will continue to buy more of them over time. What will attract them is what *you* bring to the photograph. Someone else in the same place and time would have taken a different photo." Ellie picked up another one, a redbird on a tree limb captured in song. "I love this one."

She looked over at Shannon. "I mentioned there are two ways of selling a photograph. Your other option is to sell it as an image. In doing so you're selling not only the photograph but the digital file, releasing control of the copyright. You and the buyer agree on a price and what name will be listed as the photographer. The buyer now owns the image and may license the photograph or sell it as they wish. In an image sale, you're selling both the artistic and commercial potential of the photograph. It's more lucrative than simply selling the photograph as an original work of art. The drawback is that you lose control of what's done with the image in the future."

"I didn't realize there would be so many possibilities," Shannon said. "I was thinking I might spend some money to print the best ones, put them in a nice frame, price them for maybe fifty dollars each, and sell them at art shows and street fairs where you can rent a booth."

Ellie gave a little laugh. "Shannon, you sound very much like Charlotte. There's a reason she lets me handle the business side of her work. She has no idea how to price and sell her drawings. Charlotte wants to sketch, and the rest she leaves to me. I decide how to maximize the income from her work. Which ones to frame and sell. What price to set. When to produce a show. Charlotte has built up a strong base of loyal collectors. She still produces several hundred images a year now that she's married, and she makes a solid six-figure income from her art. I deal with the business for her, and I'm paid a percentage of her yearly income after expenses. It works for us as friends as well as business partners."

Ellie neatly squared the photographs in the stack. "Let me put your mind at ease on one point. You asked for my professional opinion. Your photographs will sell. If you want it, you have a fine career ahead of you as a photographer because you do exceptional work. You have options for how to monetize your art. The questions for you are: What do you need? What do you want? Income, cash flow, recognition as an artist, the most people possible to see your photographs? Those answers influence the direction you should go."

"I would like . . ." Shannon paused and started over. "It's important to me not to be dependent on my family financially. I may want to keep my anonymity — I haven't decided that yet. And I want the freedom to continue to take pictures that interest me."

Ellie nodded. "That's a good list, and quite doable. Charlotte signs her work 'CRM' and is rarely seen in public. Marie is never seen in public, but her latest oil painting priced at six million, so it's not hurting sales. You should choose what name you wish to have on your photographs and use that throughout your career. *Shannon Bliss* if you wish to be a public figure, something else if you want to keep your privacy. As to being financially secure, how many images do you have?"

"Conservatively, one hundred thousand. Possibly as many as triple that."

Ellie looked over, startled. "Well . . ." Then she laughed. "Mark that financial need off your list, Shannon. Unless your chosen life-style requires a fortune, you're financially secure right now. You have money today in the form of your photographs."

Matthew, watching Shannon, saw the shift in her expression as she realized what Ellie had just said. Her dream of a career involving her photography had already come true.

"Many of the images will be close duplicates," Shannon clarified, sounding cautious, "sunrises, driftwood, ocean waves. Basically more of what's here in these thirty-five."

"You'll have a useful variety even within those categories," Ellie reassured. "Every sunrise has been different since the beginning of time, and people still enjoy watching them appear. Those accumulated photographs give you the luxury of deciding what kind of life you wish to have." Ellie leaned back in her chair with a smile. "Would you like me, as an art dealer, to give you the two extremes and the middle ground?"

"I'd appreciate that, Ellie," Shannon said, still visibly stunned at what she was hearing.

"At one end of the spectrum, you could have a stress-free life selling a set number of photographs each year as original works of art. A gallery show in the spring and in the fall, some of your photographs for sale in a summer auction. The rest of your year is free of business concerns. You would need to limit how many images are sold each year, so that collectors can gauge how to invest in a living artist. Setting up an art trust means your estate continues releasing new images after you're gone, keeping your name known among the next generation of collectors. The long-term merit is a legacy you can leave to your children and grandchildren. But limiting sales to around five hundred images a year can feel restrictive over time.

"At the other end of the spectrum," Ellie continued, "you could sell your collection for a single sum and create a nest egg for yourself. You'd start your new life with money in the bank and a clean slate for whatever you want to do, whether photography or something else."

For the first time since Matthew had met her, Shannon looked truly startled. "Someone would buy the collection as it is today — unorganized digital files in stacks of memory cards?"

Ellie reached for her bottle of iced tea. "Sure. I'd be willing to buy the entire collection of images from you, Shannon. If this is a representative sample of the work and there are one hundred thousand images, possibly significantly more, I'd pay you between one and two million today depending on the actual number of images. I'd become the owner and would license them or sell them as I choose. It's a bird-in-the-hand decision for you, Shannon. If you wanted to put the entire collection up for sale with some preparation and organizing, I'm sure it could attract upwards of two and a half, maybe three million in a bidding war."

"I'm having trouble breathing," Shannon said with a strangled laugh.

Ellie leaned over and put her hand on Shannon's arm, smiled. "Art can be worth good money. It's okay to recognize that. Even if it's yours."

Matthew spoke up, breaking his silence for the first time. "Did you sell that painting by Marie you priced at six million?"

Ellie glanced over at him. "Yes. Two days after I announced it for sale."

"You think Shannon's collection of photographs is worth a million or more?"

"Even a two-million purchase price is conservatively recouped in eight years, and the images will generate income for twenty years or longer. It's a good deal for the buyer," Ellie replied.

Shannon asked carefully, "Deals like this happen, Ellie? You're not just quoting me this kind of price because I'm going to be somewhat . . . publicly known soon?"

Ellie's expression smoothed out. "No," she answered, not sounding offended and quick to assuage the worry. "There would be no marketing gimmick — *buy a photo taken during her missing eleven years.* If I buy the photographs, it would actually be easier if you chose a pseudonym. But that decision is one only you can make, Shannon.

"I'd do very well on the deal, I don't mind telling you, and it would be a pleasure to handle your photographs. If you need a clean slate — a before-and-after phase for your photography — selling the collection as a whole is an option to consider."

Ellie finished her iced tea. "The middle ground would be for you to retain ownership of the photographs, sell some as original works of art, license others, and use that to generate an income stream. It would involve more of your time, but would defer any significant decision on how to handle the body of work."

"Thanks for that, Ellie, the range of options," Shannon said. "You've given me a lot to think about. I really like the discipline of choosing the best five hundred photos to sell each year. And there's also an enormous appeal to simply putting a bow around the last eleven years and handing this entire collection over in a single sale. I know you represent Charlotte and Marie. Whichever way I go, would you be willing to take me on as a client?"

Ellie nodded. "I'd be happy to have you as a client in whatever capacity you'd like me to consider, Shannon. I know I'd enjoy working with you. Go talk about this, brainstorm, play what-if. It's been a pleasure to see these and to talk with you. My offer to buy your current set of photographs isn't about to go away." Ellie took a last look at the photos and held them out to Shannon. "I look forward to talking with you again whenever you have a question or wish to explore any of the options."

"Likewise, Ellie." Shannon stood and accepted the photos, slipped them into the box.

Minutes later, Matthew held the gallery

door open, caught Shannon's hand as he could see the tremor in it.

"She said one to two million," Shannon whispered. "I didn't hear her wrong?"

"One to two million, for those shoeboxes of memory cards and miscellaneous cards in envelopes," Matthew confirmed.

"I think I'm going to have a heart attack."

"Please, not on my watch," he teased. He put an arm around her shoulders, gave her a hug. "I admit, it was unexpected."

"She's overpaying, I'm sure of it."

Matthew had been thinking through the details. "No, I think she's being very fair to both of you. Selling five hundred photos a year for five hundred dollars apiece recoups a two-million purchase price in eight years. Ellie's calculating that she can build your images into a powerful collectors' brand. She knows her market and her business. She was being fair to both of you."

"What would you do if you were me?"

"Not my decision," he replied firmly.

"Please, I'm asking."

He drew in a long breath, let it out, decided he did want to put something on the table for her to consider. "That camera fit naturally in your hand this afternoon, Shannon. You're not done taking pictures. You could sell what you've already taken to

Ellie, get on about the business of taking more pictures. You're too close to your work to evaluate which five hundred photographs are the best ones to sell each year, and you don't need the hassle of a staff working for you. Leave the marketing of your work to an expert. That camera is your future. When you've got another twenty thousand photographs you think are excellent, sell her those images too."

Shannon's laughter bubbled. "Oh, Matthew, you make it sound so easy. Let's go get ice cream to celebrate."

Matthew loved hearing the joy in her voice. "I seem to remember I owe you an ice-cream cone," he agreed.

Shannon had to eat fast to keep ahead of the melting ice cream. They were perched on a picnic table outside the shop, so if her cone dripped it would fall on concrete rather than her outfit. "Would you like me more or less if I was wealthy?" she asked around a bite.

Matthew, startled, paused mid-bite with his more pedestrian sundae. "An interesting question. A complicated one." He sorted it out in his mind. "I would like you about the same, I think," he decided. "Wealth means you have no debt, have a steady income from your work, can choose — within reason — a lifestyle you want. If you chose an extravagant lifestyle, I probably would like you less. I'm pretty much an upper-middle-class, stay-out-of-debt kind of guy. If you're planning to be a photographer, do some traveling, buy the occasional nice pair of shoes, you're still very likable. The money is some security for you, which should make it easier to relax about the day-to-day decisions of your life, and that I would also find attractive."

"Are you wealthy?"

"I'm . . . comfortably well-off with the continuing ability to earn a good living," Matthew answered, going to the heart of the matter. "I like the level I'm at, but I've found that college is expensive," he added with a small laugh.

She smiled. "It's a nice thing you're doing — letting Becky go away to college rather than asking her to live at home, attend one locally, be safer as well as not have the extra expense."

"She needs the roommate and living away from home. She needs the confidence that she really has healed to where she can make it without me. She knows that, but she needs to experience that truth for herself. And I wanted my daughter to have something better than I had, like the freedom to focus on school without worrying about the bills, not to have to work a job while trying to study and get good grades."

"She's going to make you proud."

"She already has."

Shannon finished her cone. "I want a clean slate," she said, glancing over to meet his gaze. "I didn't realize how much I wanted that until Ellie put the option out there. What I really want to do is go get those shoeboxes and envelopes and take them back to Ellie and tell her the offer she made is fair, that she has a deal. How about you hold on to the cards in your safe while we do the paperwork?"

Matthew looked at his watch. He wasn't into impulsive decisions, particularly when it came to big ones, but sometimes one option was simply and obviously right. "Let's go do that," he said.

"Yeah?"

"You can change your mind between now and us getting back to the gallery with the photos, and I'll be okay with that. But it does mean a clean slate, it provides a career, and it gives you financial flexibility. When God hands you what you need, say yes." He passed over to her the last of his sundae. "Here, finish this while I drive. I don't want good ice cream to go to waste."

She slid off her perch. "I'm going to be a photographer and rich — this has been one very nice day."

He just laughed. He thought he was seeing one of God's gifts to her unfold. The fact she'd been able to carry a camera during those years, that her pictures had survived, had helped Shannon to endure. Now they would help her heal. God was rebuilding something very important for Shannon now by providing for her financially, but also affirming she had talent and a career she could enjoy. One of the five items on that personal list of hers was being fulfilled.

He couldn't be more pleased for her. Shannon was getting one bright spot in her life in the midst of what could be a crushing set of truths still to come. She needed this, and it couldn't have come at a better time.

# 29

Matthew pulled into the driveway of Jeffery's home just before seven that evening. Someone stood on the porch, and Shannon, undoing her seat belt to get out of the car, hesitated. Her father, Matthew realized. He reached over to squeeze her hand. "You can do this. Take a deep breath, step out of the car, give him a chance to speak first. It's going to be fine. Courage, Shannon."

She blinked hard, nodded, and pushed open the door. Matthew stepped out, watchful, knowing this was going to play out in ways he couldn't predict. Shannon and her father had to find their way back or she was going to be suffering for years to come.

The man came down the steps and toward the drive, moving slowly but purposefully.

"Shannon." Her father said her name with such longing. He stopped a few feet away, opened his arms in invitation, and she chose to step into his embrace. "I'm so glad you're home," he said, his voice low but clear, even to Matthew. "I love you, Shannon. I'm sorry for the delay in saying those words." The man leaned back to look into Shannon's face. "The light went out of my world when you disappeared. I'm truly sorry for not being there the day you came home, for causing any question in your heart about how much I love you, that I wanted to say those words to you."

"It's okay, Pop," Shannon whispered, resting her head against his shoulder, her hands coming up his back to hold him close.

"It's not okay, but thank you for being kind to your old man. I needed to talk to you before we go inside, before you see your mom. I know who your birth father is, and that's why the hesitation happened, honey — it for sure had nothing to do with you. He's a pretty good man actually, and I got fearful I'd lose you to him. I'll face the truth and deal with it; I just want you to know you're always going to be my girl, my Shannon. I want you in my life very, very much."

"You won't lose me," she said, leaning back to look into his eyes. "You and Mom . . . ?"

"We love you and Jeffery. We love our granddaughter. We've come to a peace of sorts about the rest of this. But it would have distressed her to hear what I just told you. She doesn't realize I know."

"I won't tell her," Shannon promised. "I'll know who he is one day soon — not from you or Mom. I'll get the name from someone else, because it's necessary. But you're the only father I have ever known. I don't want us to change. I need you, Dad. I love you too."

"I'm here — not going anywhere, Shannon."

She hugged him and didn't let go for a long time. "Thank you," she replied in a tear-filled whisper. She stepped back, wiped at her eyes, tried to smile. "How do you like being a grandfather?"

The man beamed. "Ashley is a treasure. Come and meet her."

Matthew gave Shannon a smile when she glanced back at him. They would smooth out the relationship with time, he thought. His next big concern now was her mother.

He followed Shannon and her father as they entered the house and turned toward the living room. Rather than be part of the introductions, Matthew chose to remain near the doorway and simply watch events unfold. Jeffery's wife joined him. "Good evening, Cindy," he said softly, and she nodded, smiled.

Shannon markedly hesitated. “Hello, Mom.”

The woman on the couch with her granddaughter on her lap had been showing the little girl the necklace she was wearing. She looked up with tears flooding her eyes, didn’t try to respond. Shannon walked over and sat beside her. “How do you like being a grandmother, Mom?”

“It’s . . . a joy.” She reached out a shaky arm to encircle Shannon’s shoulders. “Welcome home, baby.”

Shannon buried her face in her mom’s shoulder, hugged her tight.

Her mother was trying desperately not to cry. “Have you met your niece?”

“Only seen her asleep.”

Her mom struggled to find her voice. “Ashley, this is Shannon. She’s your daddy’s sister, your aunt.”

The child looked back and forth between the two women. “Hi,” she said with a question in her voice, no doubt wondering about the tears.

“Hi back,” Shannon said with a wobbly smile. She held out the picture book she’d brought with her. “I hear you love to read.”

“Kittens!” Ashley hugged the book. “I *love* kittens.”

“How many do you have?”

Ashley held up two fingers. "Two." She scrambled off her grandmother's lap, reached for Shannon's hand. "Come and see."

Shannon smiled at her mother, bent to kiss her cheek. "Back soon," she said, and let Ashley lead her toward the kitchen.

Matthew watched the exchange, as did her father and brother. The ice had been broken.

Jeffery stepped into the pause. "Anyone like a cold drink? Mom, can I get you something?"

"More tea, Jeffery."

Cindy moved to sit in the chair next to her mother-in-law, bringing a Kleenex box with her.

Jeffery paused beside Matthew before he left the room to quietly ask, "It went okay with Dad?"

"They'll be fine," Matthew replied. "But end this in an hour as planned, I think. She's hurting — they all are."

Jeffery nodded. "It's already planned that I'll take Mom home. Dad doesn't live far."

"Shannon has some news she'll probably want to share in private with you later," Matthew told him. "She's selling a large collection of photographs she took over the last eleven years."

"Thanks for that heads-up," Jeffery said,

surprised. "Sounds interesting," he added. "Ashley and the kittens worked perfectly as the first diversion, but I could use something else to get Shannon into the kitchen for a few minutes."

Shannon returned to the living room with Ashley several minutes later, the child still talking animatedly about the kittens. Shannon returned to her place on the sofa, taking a seat between her mother and father. Matthew watched as she carefully directed a question to one, then the other, occasionally touching an arm or hand on each parent. She brought up topics that would bring a smile or a chuckle, doing her best to reconnect. It looked like her parents were taking their cues from her, responding to queries about friends and family but asking none of their own. Cindy stepped in to fill any silence, mostly offering stories about Ashley for Shannon's benefit, with Ashley herself filling in most of the details to the amusement of everyone in the room.

"Is the lack of questions something I should thank you for?" Matthew asked Jeffery under his breath as the man came around with a tray of drinks. The evening was very similar to the first meeting between Shannon and Jeffery, though in this instance Shannon was asking the questions, listening to their answers, but saying very little about her years away.

Jeffery shook his head. "Not my doing. I suspect they simply don't know what to ask." He motioned with his head back to the kitchen, and the two men excused themselves.

"I've told them," Jeffery continued, putting the tray down, "that many of the people responsible for abducting Shannon are dead, that the photos the police recently released of others being sought are related to what Shannon has told authorities. I think for Shannon's sake they want her to be able to talk about it or not as she wishes."

Matthew nodded. He'd been watching Shannon's mother, overjoyed her daughter was home and wanting contact — a hand reaching out to touch her, a shared look, a smile. Her attention didn't waver from her daughter. But the woman was noticeably frail. Whatever had gone on in this family eleven years ago, Matthew knew he did not have the full truth. But the fact the woman loved her daughter was there in every bit of body language between them.

The two men returned to the living room, Jeffery continuing around with the drink tray. He must have thought it best not to get involved in the conversation this evening, to leave Shannon and her parents focused on each other, for Jeffery would step away to refill drinks, take his daughter for a snack, answer the phone when it rang. His capable wife did the smoothing out of the conversation when Shannon and her parents needed a bridge.

Matthew watched Shannon more closely when he realized her hand was trembling as she lifted her drink. "Jeffery, we need to end this early," he murmured the next time her brother returned. "That look on Shannon's face, I've seen it before — it's a practiced calm that is far from real."

Jeffery shot his sister a quick glance, gave a nod. It wasn't but a moment later before he moved into the room with a purposeful stride and a warm smile and brought the evening to a close. "Shannon, it's been a wonderful evening. I've got something for you before you leave that we all thought you might enjoy, sort of a family picture summary of the last decade. But it's rather unwieldy, so I've got it in my office. Why don't we let Ashley hug her grandparents before she's off to bed, and you and I will go figure out if you want to take the album with you tonight or pick it up another day. Mom, I'll take you home in, say, twenty minutes? I know Dad wanted a brief word with you before we all say good-night."

Shannon was turning to hug her mom, then her dad, even as Jeffery finished speaking. "I'll call you," Shannon told them both, wiping away more tears. "It was good to see you tonight." She made a point of dropping down to Ashley's level. "Can I have a hug too?"

The girl gave her a big one. "Night, Aunt Shannon." She went to her mother, who whispered something in her ear. "And thanks for the book!" she exclaimed, hurrying back to pick it up from the table.

"You're very welcome, sweetheart," Shannon replied with a smile.

"Thanks, Jeffery," Shannon murmured as she joined him. "What did you want to show me?"

Her brother slid his arm around her waist and steered her toward the office. "The family reunions you missed generated a lot of photos," Matthew heard him say as they disappeared.

It had been an exhausting night for Shannon, Matthew knew, and he didn't have to ask how she was doing. He settled on the couch beside her, took pity and leaned over to slip off the high heels she'd chosen to wear with her dress. Vanity came with a price. She quietly smiled her thanks, her eyes half closed. "It's over and done, one of the last big questions on your plate," he said, satisfied with the evening and hoping she was too.

"Dad was . . . remarkably normal, just like I remember him. Mom has aged so much I barely recognized her."

"She's lived with a lot of sorrow and questions while you were gone," he said. "How about an old movie and some popcorn to end the night?"

"I should just turn in."

"Not yet," he counseled, seeing something in her that concerned him. "Why don't you go change, get comfortable. I'll let you run the remote. I'm not tired yet, and I'd like some company," he said, making it about him rather than her so she'd be more inclined to agree.

She turned her head to study him. "You're being nice again."

"I happen to be a nice guy," he joked.

She smiled, sat forward, and picked up her shoes. "I'll go change," she agreed, reaching over to pat his arm. "Try more butter and less salt on the popcorn this time."

They spent a quiet hour sharing the popcorn and the couch, watching a movie, no conversation needed. She curled up beside him, and he found himself wishing he could move the clock forward several years when she'd likely be recovered enough that he could ask her out. He'd like more evenings like this in the future. He felt her stir.

"This is becoming a pattern," she said, not moving away.

"One I rather enjoy," he admitted.

The movie wasn't particularly sad, but Shannon was. He wasn't surprised when he saw she was silently crying. He passed her another tissue and refilled her soda from the two-liter bottle he'd brought in. "Next movie we're going to have to expand beyond popcorn," he said lightly. "There's something to be said for chips and salsa too." He wasn't ignoring the tears but choosing not to pursue the cause at the moment. Shannon's sadness wasn't something he had to rush to fix, just be present to share so she wasn't alone.

She finally wiped her eyes one last time. "I'm going to miss this place. It's a comfortable home," she said.

"Hmm." He took the tangent because it was something other than talking about her situation. "Can you imagine what the owner's job must be like, shuttling between other diplomats who have spent a lifetime cloaking their real agenda behind polite words?"

"They need him, and both sides know it. Peacemakers are a rare breed of people . . . like you, Matthew." She half smiled. "But I'm glad diplomacy doesn't happen all that quickly. His home is providing me a nice stretch of that peace."

"Your next home will be your own, and you'll turn it into something this peaceful," he predicted.

"A topic for another day," she decided. "I'm not ready to make the 'where' decision yet. But it's weird to think about choosing from virtually the entire United States. At least I've got financial flexibility now — if I want to have an apartment somewhere I can afford it." They watched the movie until the next commercial. She tilted her head to look at him. "If they arrest George on Sunday night, I'm toying with possibly standing with my brother Monday at the press conference."

He carefully set aside his glass, looked down at her. "Interesting."

"*Ah.* The diplomatic answer. You don't like the idea?"

"I think it's . . . got a certain unexpected *wow* factor to it."

"I am who I am. A survivor. If I don't

change my name, people will find me. I like my name, the family history that goes with it. So it seems better to face up to that press interest rather than try to sneak around it. Give the press what they want — photos of me — then tell them to go away until after the election. This fall I'll have an exclusive, wide-ranging interview with one network, and the others can use the film in their own formats. I can rewrite that press release to politely say, 'I'm glad to be back. I'll talk about it after the election when law enforcement is comfortable with my doing so and not before.' Jeffery and my parents can point to that press release rather than answer questions."

Matthew saw her planning skills flexing to fit new circumstances and had to smile. "You've been thinking about this."

"I have." She leaned back against the couch, finished her drink. "Besides, Charlotte pointed out this incredibly lovely dress, and I found the perfect heels. I need somewhere to wear them, and the national press would find it to be a nice visual," she stated lightly.

He laughed. When he turned serious again, he offered one observation. "Having your name and photo out there in the public domain means strangers are going to walk up to you with questions and comments and think they know you. Finding that peace you need isn't going to be as easy."

"I like people in small doses. Let's get the craziness over with so I can go on with my life." She turned to look at him. "But my going public complicates life for you. You aren't going to want that press coming anywhere close to Becky once again."

Avoiding the press was instinctive with him. But the press had its uses. "I've got forty-eight hours to think about this, so let me mull over the idea."

"This only happens if George is arrested tomorrow night."

"I'm thinking that happens. Shannon, don't worry about me and Becky. This is the kind of decision you need to make based on what's best for you. Becky and I will be fine."

Shannon nodded. "It makes sense, coming forward now. I want to keep my name. I want to walk into my brother's office when he's governor and not have people surprised to see me. I want to have a gallery show one day with the invitation saying: *Shannon Bliss, photographer.* I want to be known for who I am. Shannon Bliss. Tough survivor. Not half bad in the looks department.

Knows how to show off a great pair of high heels."

He laughed, and she joined in. He held out his hand. "Hello there, Shannon Bliss," he said, thinking she could have gone ahead and described herself as beautiful. "I'm glad you did your research and found me."

She slid her hand into his, sealing the greeting. "Thank you, Matthew. For all you've done to get me to this place."

"You're very welcome."

"This is turning out to be a nice wrap-up for the evening," she said. "I need some sleep, and since I promised no eleven p.m. moment for you to regret, I'm turning in now. I'll see you in the morning, Matthew."

"You will," he promised, understanding what she was feeling. "Good night, Shannon."

He watched her head down the hall, leaned his head against the couch. Two more days, get past the press conference, then he'd let himself think about the emotions he was feeling tonight. She was a lovely woman, brave and strong, and he was enjoying walking this journey with her. She needed him right now, and he was a better man when needed. What would come later for the two of them would have to wait for time to unfold. He wisely turned off the television and took himself off to bed.

# 30

Matthew swatted one of the few bugs that had flown by and landed on him this sunny Sunday afternoon. "Shannon's looking more relaxed," Jeffery remarked as they watched Ashley run across the backyard, showing off her skills on a Slip 'N Slide chute, screaming with delight when she landed in the water pooled at the end. Shannon was standing with Cindy in the shade of a tree, also watching the fun. Matthew was intrigued to see she had her camera out. She hadn't lifted it to take a picture yet, but she had come prepared. Ashley, along with her kittens, would be immortalized before the afternoon was over, he was sure.

Matthew didn't know how much he should say to Jeffery, but he mentally reversed their positions and thought about what he would want to know. He decided to be more expansive than he might under different circumstances. "Shannon cried last night for the good part of an hour, seemed to unwind most of her knotted emotions," he said to Jeffery. "How are your parents doing?"

"Dad called, mostly to say thanks for arranging the evening, which told me he wanted to say something else and had changed his mind. Mom didn't say much when I drove her home. She's . . . pretty subdued. I think she knows it's only a matter of time before Shannon asks who her birth father is."

"She won't ask her mother," Matthew replied. "My firm is already answering that question for her."

Jeffery shot him a quick look. "Have an answer?"

"I can tell you who is *not* her father," Matthew said. "But, yes, I think we know. DNA is running now to confirm the suspicion. Your father mentioned to Shannon last night before they went inside that he knows who her father is, thinks he's a pretty good guy. So I have a hunch the name we're looking at now is the right one."

"Are you going to tell Shannon when you know?"

"When she asks, yes. And she'll tell you if she wants you to know."

"Might be rather awkward shaking hands

with the guy, not knowing he's my sister's father."

"Nothing about this situation is particularly comfortable. Do you remember much about how things were between your mom and dad going into that Memorial Day weekend?"

"I thought Mom was going to leave my father," Jeffery replied, obviously choosing to offer an equal level of candor. "It had been a worry in the back of my mind for a couple of years. I remember that Mom had made a point of encouraging Shannon to spend the weekend with friends, confirmed with me a few times that I too had plans and would be away for the long weekend. She wanted to talk with Dad in private. Shannon probably hadn't picked up on those vibes, but I remember wondering if she was finally going to tell him she was leaving."

"She would have been okay with a divorce?"

"On her terms, yeah, Mom would have walked away. We were drifting as a family. Mom wasn't happy. It was clear even back then that they were married because they had children, not because they were close. Knowing now that Shannon wasn't his daughter, I believe Mom was simply waiting until Shannon had her driver's license, had some independence, before she announced she was done with the marriage."

"Do you think she would have gone to be with Shannon's father?"

"I don't know," Jeffery said. "What I do know is that Mom had been doing more than just a spring cleaning of the house — she had organized her world, had begun to talk about her own dreams and ideas for her future. Sometimes it would be couched in phrases like 'after you kids are grown,' and other times it would be 'I think I'll enjoy trying this over the summer.' I gradually realized Dad wasn't very prominent in her plans."

"So the divorce didn't surprise you when it came."

Jeffery shook his head. "No."

"Do you know if your parents had that conversation the weekend Shannon went missing?"

"I expect they did. But when I got home, the search for Shannon had begun. Calls to her friends. They asked me to drive the route she would have taken home in case she'd had car trouble. Whatever they talked about wasn't in the picture once it was known Shannon was missing."

"Were Shannon and your mom close?"

"Like two peas in a pod. Mom used to ask Shannon for fashion advice — and actually take it. She was dreaming of Shannon's future: a lavish wedding, a home in the area, a good husband. Mom had life for Shannon all mapped out. Not a bad dream, really, just one that seemed more Mom's desire to redo her own life. She hoped Shannon would meet her ideal guy while she was still in high school. My sister was popular — she probably would have found him if she wanted to dream that direction. But she was mostly talking about college options and becoming a chemist or maybe a pharmacist."

"Really?"

"She was taking chemistry that year and loved it."

Matthew tucked that away to think about later. "Are your parents coming over for dinner?"

"Dad said he'd pick Mom up — a first since the divorce — and that they'd be here at five. You might want to plan a call, need to leave with Shannon around quarter to six. I think less is more for all of them right now."

"I'd agree with that." Matthew shifted the subject to one he'd been pondering for several hours. "Shannon's told you she's considering coming forward at the press conference tomorrow?"

Jeffery grimaced. "Yeah, and I'll do my best to talk her out of it. One crisis in her life at a time."

Matthew drank more of his iced tea, didn't respond.

"What? You think it's a good idea?"

"It's growing on me," Matthew replied, gazing at her across the yard. "She's trying to wrestle back control of her life. Standing up to the press and saying 'I'm back' is her version of a preemptive offense. She then stays with 'No comment' until after the election. Police briefings and reporters putting together leads will wear out most of the story before she speaks about it this fall. In the meantime, people she's meeting with can get over the shock of knowing who she is. She can acknowledge the truth of her identity, but then say she can't talk about it until the investigation's complete, and the rest of their conversation will become more normal."

Jeffery gave him a long look. "You're giving me the pretty version of how this plays out. There's another not-so-pretty way. The press photographing her every step, stalking her, interviewing anyone she ever speaks with to see what she says."

Matthew could see that outcome too. "I think she wants to take the risk it doesn't go that far. If it does, she goes into hiding — which is basically what she's doing now — only with a bunch of reporters playing hide-and-seek."

"You think it's worth the gamble?"

"At your press conference tomorrow, she's there to give the press their photos. Then, over the Fourth of July weekend, you talk about how nice it is to have your sister home. The following weekend you and Cindy can host a gathering for friends and family and neighbors who want to stop by, so that Shannon can meet people in your personal circle. She announces which reporter she will sit down with for an interview after the election. The worst is over in a couple of weeks. You avoid the charge you're using the publicity of her return to benefit your own political chances, as well as any charge you hid something from the public."

Jeffery thought about it. "I don't know, Matthew. If we stay with the plan that I announce her return and state she's not in Illinois, the press can follow me but they can't get to her for the rest of the summer. She needs those months without any added stress. This puts her immediately into the thick of things without a break."

Matthew understood his concern, yet he also saw Shannon's point of view. "If we wait, going public is something else to have to deal with in her future. She wants to get the problem over with, not have it hanging over her."

"You think she'd be okay?"

"If George is arrested tonight, Shannon wants to do this. I'm inclined to say okay, try to move aside any obstacles rather than try to talk her out of it. It's a big decision, and I believe she's made it. So I say we stand with her and let her do it."

Jeffery took a while to respond. "If we go this route, I need to make around, oh, thirty calls tonight to get people organized. Everything from security for Mom and Dad, so reporters aren't ringing their doorbells every few minutes, to some additional security for Ashley at day care. Reporters will interview even a two-year-old if given the opportunity."

"If you think of the relief you'll feel when you're past all this, the idea's not so bad," Matthew commented.

Jeffery smiled. "You're talking me into it. There are family members I was going to call before the press conference — Mom's got a sister out in Colorado, who will want to travel back to see Shannon, and there are cousins in Texas. I'll start making those calls tonight. We do this, Matthew, you'll be able to keep her safe?"

"John's convinced me he can get Shannon out of the building where the press conference is being held and back to the apartment without the press trailing us. Since he's done a lot of this kind of thing, I'll take his word for it. It's already arranged for Shannon and Rachel to go up to Shadow Lake for the following weekend. Shannon will be fine; no one will be able to locate her there. You and Cindy, your parents, aren't going to be so tucked away, but it's not going to last more than a few weeks."

"I'll talk to Cindy tonight, let her know. When will you know about this George guy?"

"By ten tonight is my guess."

Jeffery nodded. "We announce her return two weeks after she's reappeared. I suppose there's a symmetry to the way it's playing out. The election is certainly going to decrease in importance. To be fair, I should call my opponents about an hour before the press conference, so they hear this from me before it's on the airwaves."

"Make it half an hour. It's the gentlemanly thing to do, but I want Shannon in the building first, not on the way."

Jeffery chuckled. "Deal."

Matthew crouched down beside the patio chair, where Shannon was sitting between her parents, sharing coffee with them. "Shannon, we need to go," he said quietly. She turned to look at him. He added before she could ask, "It's early, and there isn't news yet. But if you plan to attend the press conference tomorrow, there are some logistics to deal with still this evening."

She nodded, excused herself from her parents with warm hugs for each, gathered up her camera and canvas bag. She went over to say goodbye to Ashley, thanked Jeffery and Cindy for the evening.

"Their backyard neighbor has realized who I am," she told him as they walked to the car, "either on his own, or maybe Ashley said my name this morning when she took over her new favorite picture book to show him. He didn't come over, but he gave me a smile and a little wave as he was watering his roses."

"We knew this was likely, one way or another. In a day the news goes public. He'll be able to say he knew a day before everyone else."

"What kind of arrangements for tomorrow?" she asked as he backed out of the driveway.

"John has some instructions to go over with you. And Paul called."

"What's going on?"

"They arrested six people in New Mexico without incident about an hour ago." He pulled out his phone, offered it to her so she could read the names.

He glanced over. She'd gone very still. Stress had rolled back in on her. "How'd it feel being around your parents today?" he asked to pull her out of the memory.

She handed him back his phone. "Okay. It's hard for me to get over how much they have changed in eleven years, especially my mother. On the whole it's easier to talk with Dad than Mom. She seems . . . more worried about what this has done to our relationship than when we first saw each other. She didn't comment on my dress, my hairstyle, the makeup. In the past I would have expected something personal. She asked about you, what I thought about Jeffery and Cindy, how I liked being an aunt. On the bright side, my parents do seem cordial with each other."

Matthew was pleased she was saying "my parents" without any hesitation. "I'm glad it's not turning out to be as awkward as you had feared."

"We'll get through this." She looked over at him. "Do you know who my real father is?"

He glanced at her, then back at the road. "Are you ready to hear that?"

"Dad sat there at the table knowing the answer, and Mom of course knows. I didn't. It felt like an elephant was sitting there with us."

"We've narrowed it down to a likely name. I might have something confirmed to tell you later tomorrow."

"Tell me, please, when you know. I want all these shocks to be over as soon as possible. I want the truth about my birth father. I want the cops to make the arrests, get the evidence sorted out. I want the press to know who I am, for them to get beyond their interest in me."

Matthew reached over for her hand. "Crashing through walls works so long as you don't break something in the process."

"I know it's not logical and it sounds nearly manic, this all-out push forward, but I feel such an incredible internal pressure now to get this done, whatever the price. Let the chips fall. Let me deal with it. It's got to be less stressful than this daily drip-drip of something else landing on me."

He could see the struggle in her expression, but he also saw signs of something really positive happening. Her emotions were unlocking and she was feeling again, when in the past she'd had everything so tightly controlled she turned numb. He would have to help her gauge where the guardrails were so she didn't end up in a downward spiral during the process, though that was a minor concern. She was alive again.

"We'll let matters play out," he agreed, "but you'll take advice from the people who care about you — Jeffery, John, me? Let us buffer those shocks so that you get through them in an orderly fashion."

She nodded. "Can you just get me to the end of this?" Her voice had turned almost to pleading. "That's what I want. That's what I *need.*"

He tightened his hand on hers. "I'll get you there, Shannon."

She'd gone from the tight control of a survivor, thinking once she got to freedom, the most intense moments would be over, to the reality that freedom only brought more layers of those moving pieces — law enforcement and family, along with decisions to make on her own future. He was hearing her need to be through this for what it was — the deep desire to have her world stop rocking and simply be the same from one day to the next. A few more hard days, and then he could get her to that place where the world stopped shifting on her.

# 31

His phone rang just after nine p.m. "Yes, Paul." Matthew moved his arm from around Shannon and got up from the couch, walked into the office. She muted the television when he returned.

"They arrested George Jacoby," he told her. "Two cops were slightly hurt, and there was some damage to the motel room. But otherwise all went smoothly. Flynn had set himself up in the café across the street. He made a call, got George distracted for an instant so the cops could get in and surround him. Flynn's on his way to Chicago. They'll keep George in Alabama for now."

"How many years in jail is Flynn facing?"

Matthew shook his head. "That's yet to be determined, but the conversations starting tonight will influence that decision. Paul said to pass the word that Flynn seemed in good spirits, was mostly relieved this was concluding. Another week or so, Paul will see about arranging a conversation for you with Flynn, if you'd like that."

"His birthday is at the end of July. I'd like to take him a cupcake or something."

"That would be a nice gesture." Matthew thought about how to end the day, walked over and took a seat beside Shannon on the couch.

"You're still looking pensive," she said, watching him warily.

"I need to tell you something about your mom before the press conference tomorrow."

"Okay."

"Something hard to hear."

"It's going to be easier to hear than all this buildup."

Matthew was careful to keep his voice level as he said, "Flynn told me your mom was behind your abduction. He provided an envelope that he said held proof of it."

Her eyes went glassy.

He took her hand, squeezed it. "Take a breath," he said firmly, and waited until she'd done so. "Another one, please."

Her face was a mask, wiped of all expression. "Why did you tell me?" she whispered.

"The final shocks are coming, and this is the biggest one. I'm going to ask Jeffery to arrange for someone who has medical training to be with her . . . in case she can't absorb another wave of guilt."

"Oh. Oh, Matthew, I can't . . . I don't . . ."

He eased her over against his shoulder. "That's better," he murmured. "When I get back to Boston, I think I should burn that envelope."

Her tears drenched his shirt.

It took a long time before she spoke again. "Tell me what you know."

"Jeffery has been calling your family to alert them to what's coming at the press conference in the morning. Your mom's sister lives in Colorado, not that far from the address you gave me for Sanford Bliss. Now that she knows about your return, I called her. I asked your aunt some rather direct questions about what was happening eleven years ago.

"I found out your mother was talking about going out to Colorado to live. She wanted you to go to the high school for gifted students that's nearby. Her sister didn't have room at her condo, but Sanford had said the two of you could come stay with him. It was all very tentative, and your aunt was trying to talk your mom out of the idea. But she seemed determined.

"It sounds like your mother was going to talk with your father that weekend about ending the marriage, and she worried that the truth of the affair and that you aren't his daughter would come out. She wanted you to be with your friends, and Jeffery being away that weekend would avoid either of you overhearing any confrontation.

"I believe your mom talked not only to your aunt but also to your uncle about her plans," Matthew continued, focusing on how he thought this had gone wrong. "But your uncle saw the coming divorce as inevitably exposing what he'd been doing with company funds. He panicked. I think the truth is your uncle was behind what happened to you. He wanted your parents to both realize how much they loved you and that they needed to stay together for your sake. Failing that, he'd use the ransom money to cover up his theft of company funds.

"I believe your uncle arranged for you to be taken out to Sanford's place, trusting that Sanford would get you safely back home. Only it turned out that what was to be a three-day abduction, ransom, and you're back home, turned into a tragedy. Sanford was innocent in this, and your mother's only part was to speak to someone she trusted before she took the steps to leave her marriage."

Shannon's hand tightened on his. "You think your original idea of what happened is the right one. You're back to thinking my uncle was behind it all."

"Your mother loves you. I cannot put together under any scenario your mom arranging to send you out to Sanford with strangers. That simply doesn't fit with your mother then or now, Shannon. Whatever Flynn has, it's evidence that comes from what the smuggling family was told about you, the photo they had, the place to drop you off. Flynn gave me the lawyer's name who made the arrangements. I think I could prove it was your uncle and not your mother who was using that lawyer to arrange what happened, that it was your uncle at the heart of it." He stopped and gently turned her face toward his. "But I'd rather not even try. I'd rather trust what I see.

"Once your uncle committed suicide, I imagine your mother has always wondered what she might have set into motion, what part she might have played in what happened. I don't want her to learn you were to be left at the home of Sanford Bliss. I think that confirms her terrible fears, maybe shocks her into a heart attack. I think we never tell Paul that address. We never give him the first diary. And I burn that envelope

Flynn gave me."

Shannon shuddered as he finished speaking, a sob shaking her frame.

"Keep the envelope, but unopened," she finally whispered. "Someone makes an accusation against Mom, we might need to use it to unravel matters to prove what you suspect."

Silence stretched and she offered nothing else.

"Talk to me, Shannon."

"Whatever happened, to punish my mother now would be to punish me even more. My choice. Leave it in the past. Whatever happened eleven years ago, I don't want it robbing me of anything else I value. I need my mother," she choked out.

He wrapped his arms around her, let her rest against him as the tears fell. "I can live with that too," he said softly.

Shannon worked her fingers between his, gripping his hand. Matthew liked the interlocking image. "Tomorrow at the press conference," Shannon said, "would you be there, behind the scenes? We're friends. I don't want to box you into something that might seem like it's more than that. John's going to stand up with me, the visible security presence. For Becky's sake, it would be better if you're simply someone I arranged to help me through my return, all the legal stuff, and so forth."

"I don't mind if the press sees us together, even if they wonder about us." Matthew had talked matters over with Becky, thought they had a plan in place that would work for her too. "And who knows," he finished lightly, "you and I might be a couple one day . . . maybe five years from now."

She leaned back to study his face. "Do I have to go out with half a dozen guys before I can come back and say you're still my choice? Or can it be, like, maybe one or two? I like you, Matthew. And I know you like me."

"I'm not the best guy for you," he replied gently. "For one thing, I'm too old."

She made a face at him. "You've got the experience with Becky that helps you understand where I've been, what I've faced. If you were younger, you wouldn't have that. And your daughter I already love."

He smiled. "You make it all sound very appealing, Shannon. And I can already tell Becky would adore having you around."

"Let me hope, Matthew, that one day you and I could be a couple. It makes the full recovery seem like a stepping-stone to something good. Maybe even something wonderful."

He ran a hand down her hair. "I'll give you reality instead. I like you, Shannon. I plan to walk these next months and years with you. If we turn that friendship into something more one day, that would be fine with me."

"Thanks."

"For what?"

"Being willing to see past my present mess."

"You'll heal. And you will have completed those five items one day."

"One day," she responded, sounding reflective. "But I didn't realize to get my high school diploma I'm going to have to pass American history."

Matthew laughed. "Becky found that one challenging too. By the way, what's number five on your list? Every Christmas Eve and New Year's Eve . . . you marked over it."

"It's private, and it's the last one for a reason. I pretty much need the first four to come true before I can have number five."

He thought about that, grinned. "Okay."

She turned her head to look up at him. "What do you think it is?"

"I think I'll keep my idea to myself."

She smiled and moved to stand. "It's late. I'm turning in. I need a couple of hours in the morning to get ready for that press conference. And breakfast had better be very bland so I don't get sick from stage fright."

"A banana and a glazed donut, I think."

"I like you."

"I'll try to get you to eat healthy when it's a low-stress season in life." He held out the pillow she'd brought in to take back with her. "Sleep well, Shannon."

Her eyes were puffy, she clearly had a headache, she looked tired, but her smile was real. "Good night, Matthew."

He watched her disappear down the hall. She was feeling again — everything that had happened, the good and the bad. "Thanks, God," he whispered. He shut off the lights and took himself across the hall.

# 32

Matthew settled in the green room just off the stage. The press room held sixty chairs, and it appeared most of them were occupied. Television cameras from two national news-affiliated channels were set up and ready to go, their images key to how the event would unfold across Chicago and the nation in the next hour. Matthew chose to watch the large-screen television rather than view it live; he'd be able to give Shannon better feedback on how it went if he'd viewed it like the TV audience would be seeing it. Charlotte and Ann were assisting Shannon with last-minute hair and makeup checks, and he couldn't help there.

Jeffery stepped to the podium, and instantly the room quieted. Matthew found himself holding his breath.

"Ladies and gentlemen, welcome to the press conference I've hoped to hold for the last eleven years," Jeffery began, looking out at the reporters relaxed, confident, a man with good news to share. "I would like to thank the thousands of individuals who have helped search for my sister over the years, and also the numerous organizations and businesses that went out of their way to assist in this effort.

"My sister, Shannon Bliss, escaped from her captors and was able to make contact with a retired member of law enforcement. She returned to Chicago on the night of June fourteen. She is in good health and good spirits." There was an immediate stir among the newspeople. A hand or two shot up, but Jeffery gave a short shake of his head.

"The FBI and Chicago Police Department," he continued, "assisted by numerous law-enforcement agencies around the country, are now in the process of arresting eighteen individuals associated with the abduction of my sister, as well as several other children. They will be releasing information regarding her case when it's appropriate and when it will not compromise the investigation.

"My sister has chosen not to speak about any details of this matter until after the election, and I will respect her wishes. I will be taking no questions at this time. All inquiries to me and the Bliss family will be directed back to this press conference and accompanying press statement. After the election, Shannon will sit down for one comprehensive interview with a television and print journalist of her choosing, and she will endeavor to answer all pertinent questions covering the last eleven years.

"Again, I wish to say thank you on behalf of myself and the Bliss family for the work done by so many to locate and bring my sister home. This is a day full of joy for so many.

"Ladies and gentlemen, my sister, Shannon Bliss."

Shannon walked onstage wearing her drop-dead-gorgeous dress — looking poised, confident, comfortable in the high heels, a natural smile on her face. A couple of shouted questions emerged over the applause. She paused in front of the microphone. "Thank you, Chicago. It's nice to be home." Her brother wrapped his arm around her waist, and they weathered the flashbulbs going off like strobe lights, illuminating their faces.

Shannon gave the photographers two minutes, then stepped briefly to the microphone once more. "I won't be talking about matters until law enforcement has completed their work and the election is past — that seems only common sense at this time. But I look forward to answering your questions in the fall. I plan to be around some during the next few months, but on the advice of doctors, I'll mostly be resting. You'll forgive me if I prefer to do that on a beach somewhere." Spontaneous laughter met her remark. "Please," she said when it was quiet again, "don't take my absence as a lack of interest in my brother's campaign. I'd be a distraction, and I'd rather like him to win, so I'll see you again in mid-November." She reached up and kissed her brother's cheek, turned and walked back offstage.

"How did I do?"

Shannon was trembling so hard, Matthew closed his hand around hers to hold her glass of water. "You were fabulous. Drink some more. It's a good thing you only get the shakes *after* the moment's over."

"I was pretending to be someone else. Imagining Jeffery standing up several times a week to give a speech — and doing it voluntarily — is enough to make me question his sanity." She tried to laugh.

Her brother behind her picked up the last of her words, and he laughed as he took her arm. "It's only fearful if you think you're supposed to make them like you. You did great, Shannon. Where's John?"

"Here," John said from near the door.

"It's time to get you out of here, Shannon, before they come clambering through the doors and track you down. I'm old news today," Jeffery admitted with a grin.

Shannon pointed toward a nice-looking lady dressed as her twin. "My decoy is ready. Let me go get changed. Five minutes, Jeffery, I'll be safely out of here. If I don't see you in the next few days, have a wonderful Fourth."

"I'm so proud of you. I'll go buy a few more minutes of distraction for you — let the press ask something pedestrian, like what your return is going to mean for the campaign." He smiled and headed back toward the podium.

"He actually loves this," Shannon said, shaking her head.

Matthew laughed. "He does. Go change. He's right about the time."

Shannon grabbed her gym bag and rushed across the hall to the restroom. Soon she came back dressed in jeans and her favorite Tex-Mex T-shirt, her feet pushed into the old blue tennis shoes. "I left my dress in its garment bag. Jeffery promised that his assistant would see it safely home."

John signaled it was time, and the lady dressed as Shannon had been, along with two security officers, headed down the private elevator to the basement parking garage, the route often used by VIPs. Reporters would be watching for her to leave the building, expecting that to be the route, and the decoy would hopefully draw at least a few of them away.

Matthew took Shannon's hand and followed John down to the lower level of the building, through the maintenance department to the loading dock, where a semi with trailer had backed up to unload cases of paper goods. They stepped down beside the truck to the waiting car wedged in behind the angled semi's cab. John had the car running with the air-conditioning on while he made a few calls, then gave a thumbs-up to the truck driver. The semi pulled forward, clearing their path. They pulled out of the parking lot, into the street heading north, no one the wiser. Five minutes later, John had confirmed they weren't being followed, and he turned east in the direction of the apartment.

# 33

"How are you doing?" Matthew asked quietly, hunkering down beside the bed.

Shannon opened drowsy eyes. "Wonderful. Go away." Her eyes closed again.

"You've been asleep since six p.m. yesterday," he told her, amused. "It's going to be night again soon; you slept away a full day. Your brother's getting worried about you. So am I. You've barely moved. Sometimes I've wondered if you were even breathing." She was lying facedown, blankets pulled up past her chin, one of her arms thrown across a pillow — she had squeezed the life out of the feathers inside that pillow. The most he could see was ruffled hair, pretty eyes, and part of a sleepy face.

She opened her eyes again and briefly considered him. "I woke up occasionally, thought some about life, decided I'd like to sleep instead."

He wanted to lean forward and kiss that

delightful face, but he didn't let himself move. "What's the problem?"

"This is goodbye, isn't it? You're going to Boston for the Fourth and not coming back to Chicago."

He would have preferred to have this conversation over dinner, but accepted reality. He sat down on the floor beside the bed, rested an arm across his bent knee. "Yes."

She blinked at the admission, nodded. "I worked it out finally, what had to be next on your list. So what do you have planned for me?"

"You'll meet Sandy Post for a walk tomorrow morning, see if you think you might want her to be your counselor. You need a good driver who knows Chicago's streets — John's got a guy who can be that for you, as well as two others who are going to be a buffer with the press. On Thursday, you'll head to Shadow Lake for the weekend, and I'll leave for Boston. The next weekend, Jeffery hosts an open house for family and friends to meet you. You'll want to be in Chicago for Flynn's birthday later this month. You'll stay with Jeffery and Cindy while you look around at options for your own place. Cindy, Charlotte, Ann — are all volunteering to go apartment and condo hunting with you. John's got several places in mind with good security he thinks you might like. I'll be back in Chicago at the end of the month to see how you're doing. If you want to come out to Boston then, you can drive back with me. If you decide to stay out East for a while, I'll help you find an apartment there you like."

She leaned up on her elbow. "I didn't want it to end like this."

"It was always going to end, Shannon, we both knew that. You can't live in my pocket, and I can't live in yours, not while you work on what's next in your recovery. We'll transition this to a friendship that might one day be something more. I'm going to be just a phone call away. I'm not abandoning you. I've got your journals to finish reading, while Paul wants some help identifying ownership of the recovered items. Trust me — you'll be on my mind constantly. But this is the next step you need me to take."

"I'll get better faster if you're around."

He shook his head. "You're ready to fly without me. The best thing I can do is let you go enjoy that freedom. You're up for it, Shannon."

"And if I'm not?"

He smiled. "The woman who walked out in front of the press yesterday morning is ready to face anything, even if she might quiver for a while afterwards."

"Would you do me a favor?"

"If I can."

"Find me an apartment in Boston you know I would like, so that if I need to bolt out of here or just want to visit, I'll have somewhere to stay. If the pressure gets intense and I need to get away, at least I can run to you."

"Still have my number memorized?"

"Yes."

"I'll do that, Shannon." He leaned forward and placed a gentle kiss on her forehead. "Come join me for dinner and then a game of Scrabble. Paul's been calling with regular updates today. The arrests are now at thirteen."

Her face disappeared under the pillow. "Give me an hour. And I don't want to hear the updates. I'm done."

"Jeffery says you've had two hundred eighteen press calls."

She groaned.

He got to his feet, tousled the hair he could see. "Face it, you're famous. Want me to show you the newspapers? You make a nice photo standing with your brother."

"Go away. Now you're just making this even more difficult."

"Half an hour or dinner will start getting cold."

"What are we having?"

"Pot roast, potatoes, carrots."

Her face reappeared. "I think I'm hungry."

"Good." He smiled at her expression. The face he was seeing now, the look in her eyes, was that of a woman ready to start living again. "Your phone is filled with messages too. You should call your aunt. She seems like a very nice woman."

"Did Mom or Dad call?"

"Occasionally yesterday, only every hour since about noon today. I had to promise your mom I'd call her myself when you opened your eyes, which I shall now go do to stay in her good graces."

"She's doing okay?"

"She said you looked lovely at the press conference — she thought the dress and the jewelry and the hairstyle were perfect, and she was proud of you."

Shannon's smile softened. "That's more the mom I remember."

"I think she'll be fine. Okay, it's twenty-five minutes now. I'm going to set the table." He left her to get ready, returned to the kitchen, made the promised call to Shannon's mother, then set the table. He was acutely aware he was turning a page with Shannon, starting a new chapter. Distance was going to either loosen the bond between them or make the heart grow fonder. He had an idea as to which way his was going to go.

He had one last piece of information to give Shannon in the next day: the name of her birth father. But he thought she could weather that knowledge okay. Her mom had dated the man in high school, seen him again at a high school reunion at a particularly low point in her marriage, and Shannon had been born nine months later. Everything Matthew had found out to date indicated he was a decent guy. He had never married, so there wasn't a family on his side to be hurt if Shannon decided to make a connection as his daughter. Matthew thought it was a fifty-fifty proposition whether Shannon would choose to have that conversation one day.

His phone rang, and he saw it was Becky. "Hi, honey." He talked with her while he waited for Shannon. He finished the call and checked on dessert. The phone rang again, Jeffery this time. Shannon appeared forty minutes later, hair still damp, while he was on the phone with her brother. He had to smile. She was in comfortable jeans and a shirt, but she'd found fuzzy slippers from somewhere. "Hold on, Jeffery. You can ask her yourself."

He handed over the phone and moved to check on the dinner rolls he'd slid into the oven.

"Do I want to do a public sit-down lunch with Jeffery tomorrow to give reporters more casual photos?" Shannon asked, holding the phone against her shoulder.

"Yes. Tell him to make reservations at Falcons for one o'clock, a window table. You might as well give Paul's sister's restaurant the publicity."

"The premise being the more photos reporters have, the less they will badger me for more."

"That's the idea, yes."

Shannon made the arrangements with Jeffery, handed back the phone. "He sounds like he's in a good mood."

"There's nothing a politician likes better than good news and lots of press interested in that good news. He comes across as what he is, a protective, loving brother. You've helped him make an overnight bump in the tracking polls. Even people who don't care about voting now remember his name and like him."

He brought over a platter with their meal, pulled the rolls from the oven and dropped them into a basket. "I'm saying a very short grace, if you don't mind, because this food needs blessing."

She grinned. "You're not that bad a cook."

"Years of failures have taught me a few things." He reached across for her hand. "Jesus, I'm taking advantage of the fact I like to pray before a meal to hold her hand — I'm just saying what you already know. I appreciate this place we've been able to stay, and our absent host who's been so accommodating with his home. I thank you that Shannon has gotten some much-needed sleep and looks rested, was able to find fuzzy slippers to keep her toes warm and me amused. She needs the rest of the week to be safe — from the press and the questions, and we would both like your help sorting out the coming summer. Amen."

Matthew wasn't surprised when her hand tightened around his and didn't release for a long moment, but also wasn't surprised when she wouldn't meet his gaze. He didn't fluster her often, but he'd been aware he could.

He buttered a roll while she fixed her plate, then passed him the serving fork. He filled his plate.

"You're good at that," she mentioned.

"What?"

"Speaking your mind to God."

"I imagine you are too."

"Not out loud."

"You can learn. Because if you want to share a prayer with me, you'll either need to say it out loud or write it down and let me read it."

"Do you want me to share my prayers?"

"Yes. Or at least tell me what you're talking about with God. He's your best friend, Shannon. It's kind of hard to really know you if I don't know what you and God are talking about."

"Oh. I see your point." She thought about that, and her smile widened. She nodded. "Okay."

"Now eat. My cooking is definitely not going to be good cold."

She picked up her fork, and they ate in comfortable silence.

A few moments later, as she buttered a roll, Shannon asked, "How much do reporters know about me and the case?"

"Sure you wouldn't just like to read the newspapers?"

"Just give me the highlights."

Matthew nodded, cleared his throat. "They have what the FBI has made public: the abducted children, the farm, the eighteen names being searched for, the arrests so far. They picked up on the East Coast location this morning, and the noon news report had some information about stolen artworks being recovered. The news cycles have been full enough that there hasn't been much speculation about your last eleven years, but that will come when the other facts start to slow down."

"People will begin to pity me."

"Only until they meet you. You're a survivor, not a victim. It's clearly evident."

"Thanks."

He smiled. "You're welcome."

"What's for dessert?"

"Brownies."

"Not a bad meal."

"I spent most of the day waiting for you to wake up — I had to fill the time somehow."

She broke open another dinner roll. "Ideally, what would you like this summer to be?"

He thought about it. "You hanging out with Cindy, Charlotte, Ellie, Ann, babysitting Ashley, taking a few thousand photographs. Laughter becoming a regular part of your day."

"That's . . . I was going to say 'sweet,' but it's more like a practical 'nice.' "

"I want you to find a place you like,

decorate it, and enjoy the summer. You need months spent without a list to accomplish."

"And for yourself?"

"I'm going to enjoy hearing about what you're doing. And the business needs me back in the office."

Shannon went to fetch the brownies. "I suppose I can do that this summer. It sounds nice. I bought the fuzzy slippers when I went shoe shopping, because I knew they would get a comment from you."

He studied her over his fork. "Are they warm?"

"Very comfortable."

"They are cute," he agreed, amused with her. "Are we playing Scrabble tonight?"

"That, or we're watching a really lame movie. I'd hate for us to break tradition."

Matthew got up to find the Scrabble board. "I enjoy doing both with you."

"I know." She began flipping tiles face-down.

"You're going to do okay this summer," he felt compelled to mention.

"If not, I'll be calling you, so I'll agree with that," she replied and played the first word on the board.

He picked up his next tile, then played the word *brownie.*

Shannon laughed. "You and Becky play

this game a lot."

"We have a lot of conversations," Matthew replied. "A board game tends to be part of that process."

"I was thinking I would buy Jeffery a Scrabble board so I could talk with him at a measured pace this summer."

He looked carefully over at her. "I think that's a wise idea."

"He needs to know."

Matthew hesitated. "He's your brother. He needs to know the big picture, not necessarily all the details. Tell him to call me if he has a specific question."

"Thank you."

"Hmm." He played *time* and wished they had more of it. He'd let her go with grace because it was the right thing to do. It was time for her to spread her wings without him. But nothing said it was going to be easy for him to walk away.

# 34

Matthew had left something precious behind in Chicago. He knew their goodbye would be painful. Even being prepared for it, the reality was worse than he'd expected.

His kitchen was quiet again, the windows no longer rattling from the large fireworks going off, no more of Becky's college friends raiding the refrigerator. She had managed to talk four of them into coming for the weekend. At least having guests had saved him from having too much time in which to think. Matthew found the mug he was after, poured himself more decaf, and took it with him out to the back deck. The drifting odor of sulfur was still heavy in the air, and it made his eyes water.

He leaned against the patio railing, studied the moon, listened to random firecrackers still exploding around the neighborhood, wondered idly if Shannon had also stepped outside tonight to take in the full moon. It had been three days since he'd seen her, and he thought he was actually moping. *At my age, even with her a phone call away, I'm dragging around like a lost puppy.*

"You miss her."

He glanced over, realized his daughter had joined him. He draped his arm around her shoulders. "When did you get to be so smart?"

"Why don't you call her?"

"It's late."

"But it's an hour earlier there." When he simply shook his head at her, she asked, "Is she coming out to Boston?"

"If she doesn't, we'll visit her together in Chicago," he replied, brushing back a lock of her hair, wondering when this daughter of his had turned into a spitting image of her mom. "I'm glad you're enjoying college."

"I think it's a rite of passage to be homesick. I miss home, but *mostly* I'm enjoying being there."

He smiled, knowing what she meant. "Home is now for visiting, not staying."

"You should call her."

He shook his head. "She's sad I'm not going back to Chicago."

"Why aren't you?"

"She needs to know she's strong enough

to stand without me. If I'm there, she won't know that. She's also got family and friends to help her."

"She'll think you don't want her."

"Maybe. Or maybe she'll accept that I can't with a clear conscience let her fall for the first safe guy she finds after she returned."

Becky took his coffee mug and sipped at it. "You had a really interesting last three weeks."

The understatement of the decade, Matthew thought. "I did."

"Do you mind that she looked you up, found you?"

"No, I like that she did. I enjoy being useful."

"Is that the only reason you like her?"

He thought of the wealth of feelings he had for Shannon and wisely only said, "No. And it's not a conversation for you and me to have tonight."

"Okay." She handed him back his coffee. "I prefer it with some cream." She pulled her phone out of her pocket. "Oops. I forgot to hang it up. I was talking to Shannon." She held out her phone. "She probably heard what we said, if you want to clarify any of your remarks."

He chuckled as he reached for her phone.

"Way too sneaky. What are they teaching you at that college?"

"One does what one has to," she said with a smile and a shrug, then leaned in to give him a hug. "I love you, Dad."

"It's mutual, kiddo. Now scat."

He held the phone as if it were a live explosive and risked asking Shannon, "First, how badly did she just embarrass you with this stunt?"

"I can deal with Becky's idea of patching up a problem. How are you, Matthew?"

"Missing you, as you no doubt heard. How's your weekend going?"

"I'm playing cards with Rachel, Charlotte, and Bryce. I think Rachel and I are winning, but bridge isn't my game. Black is presently sprawled across my feet."

"Wish you were here." They both spoke the same thought at the same time and shared a laugh.

"You actually wouldn't have enjoyed Boston with the sights and smells tonight," Matthew added, "but the sentiment is real."

"I'm coming east to see you on the seventeenth, Matthew. The driver John arranged for me is going to fly with me and make sure I survive the flight. Can you meet me at the airport?"

"Sure."

"Find me a nice place to rent out there. I'm going to sign the lease on one in a suburb of Chicago this next week. I decided I've probably got enough income to have two homes."

"You do."

"I'm packing my pink dress and those high heels. I want to go dancing."

He rested against the railing and smiled. "Do you?"

"I've also decided that dating a bunch of guys just to discover I still like you more is only accommodating your worry versus acting in my best interests. I'm not dating for a year — I agreed with my counselor on that, so don't go all honorable on me and say no. You can just take me to dinner and dancing when I visit, the courteous thing to do with an old friend." Neither of them could resist laughing at her description. "If in a year I don't like you as much as I thought," she continued, "I'll ask to meet some of the guys you think might be a good fit."

That list would probably have zero names on it, since he wasn't inclined toward her finding someone else. "I'll enjoy taking you dancing," he replied, bypassing the rest of what she'd said.

She laughed again. "Becky said you would be reluctantly accommodating. Is this you being reluctantly accommodating?"

"This is me being aware you're very amused right now."

"I like you, Matthew."

"It's mutual," he admitted. "Enjoy your evening, Shannon. I'll call you tomorrow."

"Not too early."

"Not too early," he promised.

He hung up and held out the phone toward Becky, aware all along of her watching from inside the patio door.

She rejoined him on the deck. "Mad?"

"No. Hearing her voice made me feel better."

His daughter hugged him. "I like her."

"I do too."

Becky said good-night and headed back inside, looking just a bit triumphant.

Getting married again wouldn't be such a bad next chapter in his life, Matthew decided. Give Shannon a few years, see if she still thought he was at the top of her list, then ask her the question. When he was young, any number of years would have sounded like an eternity. Now that he was older, the years seemed to be passing by in the blink of an eye.

He understood her problems better than she did, he thought. He'd read most of the journals, would have all of them read soon, and had walked a similar road with Becky. They could make it work, he knew. It wouldn't be an easy next year or two for Shannon, but she was further along the road to recovery than he'd expected, and it wasn't such an impossibly hard climb that he wasn't willing to make it with someone again.

Tomorrow he'd start looking for that apartment. He didn't have to ask to realize her intentions. She'd be living out here to avoid the press around her brother, to take advantage of being near the ocean so she could swim often. She'd start using her camera in a serious way again, and she'd invade his life however he let her. Matthew smiled. She needed this summer to be light and fun and filled with occasions to show off those high heels. He'd accommodate her. It would be a good summer for him too.

# 35

Matthew pulled out a chair beside Paul at the patio table, leaned back to watch Charlotte and Bryce, Shannon and Ann play croquet in the Bishops' backyard. The two Irish Setters and Ann's dog Black lay sprawled as a group in the shade, content to watch the game rather than chase the croquet balls.

"Glad to have this summer about over?" Paul asked.

Matthew smiled. "Hmm." This was the first trip back to Chicago with nothing on the schedule but a chance for Shannon to visit family and friends. The next major event on the calendar would be November fourth and the vote to see if Jeffery became the next governor of Illinois. The polling data was still looking promising. The case that had begun with Shannon's reappearance was in its final stages, the last of the arrests had been made, with answers for the final questions being slowly teased out of the evidence. The retired cop in him was pleased to see the truth sorting itself out.

"You figured out who was behind her abduction. You know why it happened," Paul said, sounding pretty sure of himself.

Matthew considered the ice in his glass, not surprised by the question, and finally glanced over at Paul. "Yes." He figured Paul had mostly sorted out that same answer too, knew the question wouldn't have come unless Paul was leading somewhere.

Paul idly swatted a fly. "Can we do anything about it?"

"No."

Paul mulled that over, leaned across the table to nudge the lid off the relish tray. "So we could do something about it, but Shannon doesn't want us to? Or we couldn't do anything about it even if we wanted to?"

Matthew chose to answer by simply tipping his glass toward Shannon.

"You okay with that?"

Matthew shrugged. "It is what it is."

"The address where she was to be dropped off is a rather glaring hole in the evidence record."

"I can imagine," Matthew agreed.

Paul ate another olive off the tray. "Any problem if I go arrest a couple of lawyers?

I've been gleaning some interesting facts from hither and yon."

Matthew smiled at the way Paul said it. He calculated the odds that one lawyer in particular would try to bring Shannon's mom into matters, be believed, and think it in his own best interest to be associated with one of the most well-publicized abduction cases in the last decade. "Have at it."

Paul nodded. "Adam likes arresting lawyers. Theo thinks we should give him the honor."

"Works for me," Matthew said. "Adam also likes working the press, and he's good at it. The publicity won't hurt his career either."

"Our thoughts exactly. Theo and I are both ready for reporters to lose track of our phone numbers."

Matthew reached over and picked up a slice of green pepper. "Shannon asked me to bring out the journals for you to put into evidence, all but the first month. She doesn't want any of the diaries to see the light of day if you can avoid it, but she won't risk the first one."

Paul lifted an eyebrow but didn't say anything.

"I've read them all," Matthew confirmed. He never wanted to have to discuss what he'd read, but when Shannon occasionally shared a look with him that showed him another slice of pain, he had a sense of what memory had just flared up. They replayed in vivid colors at times, and the number of hours she spent swimming, letting go of those memories, were steadily climbing. Her counselor was swimming with her some days, training for a long-distance charity swim they planned to do together next year.

"I'm hoping the journals aren't necessary," Paul said. "I think it'll work itself down to three trials, and the rest as plea deals. Flynn testifying is really hurting the family."

"His plea worked out yet?"

"We'll sort it out after the trials are done. I'm guessing he gets twenty-five years, serves fifteen of it."

"I think Shannon could live with that."

"She hasn't been back to see him since that first time."

"Flynn told her to visit him on birthdays and anniversaries, and to write occasionally. She's honoring that. She doesn't talk about him much these days. How's the collection of stolen goods coming along?"

"We've accumulated a small warehouse of items to sift through," Paul replied with some humor. "The paperwork involved is drowning my clerical staff."

Matthew remembered all the paperwork involved in robbery cases. "And is the rest of your life settling down now?"

Paul shrugged. "Someone tried to put a bomb in the mayor's car last week. That rather got our attention."

"One major crisis solved, the next one takes its place."

"Yeah. It's good being a cop. It has a nice permanence to it. Will you go back to being a Boston cop?" Paul asked, curious.

"Don't quite know yet. Nor have Shannon and I sorted things out."

Paul grinned. "She's sorted *you* out. I notice every time I talk to her, it's Matthew this, and Matthew that. She's not looking anywhere else."

"Shannon and Becky have decided between them that since Shannon isn't going to date this year, she will instead just hang out with me."

Paul laughed.

"I'm not minding it," Matthew admitted.

Shannon joined them. "Not minding what?"

"Having a camera in my face every time I turn around," Matthew replied smoothly.

"Photos from one sailing trip," she countered. "Which turned out to be mostly your sunglasses and your hat when you look at the photos, so don't think I'm not going to try again one day. I promised Becky an interesting photo of you before the summer's over."

Black wandered over to lean into Shannon's knee. She bent down to pet him.

"I saw Ellie's invitation for the gallery show," Paul mentioned. "Congratulations on that, Shannon."

"Thanks. It's pretty satisfying, seeing my name on the formal invitation. Ellie's putting on sale five hundred photos from the ones she bought from me. I hope they sell for her or I'm going to feel awful for taking her money."

"Ellie rarely makes a mistake pricing art," Paul reassured.

"I saw some of the paintings around your place," Shannon said. "You've been seriously collecting for years."

"I have. And I'll be at the show with an eye to buy," Paul added.

Shannon grinned. "You can say you knew me when . . ."

Paul laughed and made room for Ann. His wife acquired his glass to eat some of the ice. "We women are picking up Cindy and Ashley in about an hour and going shopping," Ann announced, "so if you guys have any plans for today, you'll have a few hours without us."

Matthew looked over at Bryce, who had joined them. "Darts and lasagna?"

"Sure beats running five miles."

"You could do both," Shannon suggested. "Matthew needs to get back to training," she told Paul. "I want him to run his tenth Boston Marathon so I can get some good photos."

"You do?" Matthew said. This was the first he was hearing about it.

Shannon gave him a nod. "If asked next year why you aren't running, is your answer going to be that you're too old?"

"A person can use that argument only a few times and have it still be effective," he said, not rising to the bait. She'd been tackling their age difference with good humor and routinely giving him back that answer. Bottom line, he wasn't going to get away with not asking her out on an official date next year because he was "too old" for her.

"I suppose you could switch over and take up swimming," she suggested, "because I'm never going to be much of a runner."

Three phones chimed at nearly the same instant, and Charlotte got hers out first. "Ellie's found her wedding dress!" she called out, excited. "Come on, Ann, Shannon. This we have got to see." Charlotte paused to kiss her husband. "We'll probably be late," she said, and headed into the house, telling Ellie at the other end of the line, "Stay where you are — we're coming to see it." John trailed behind the women with a nod to Bryce. John would make sure security was with the group.

Matthew looked around the table at Bryce and Paul. "Why do I get the feeling the best part of our lives just disappeared together?"

Bryce chuckled. "You do get used to them being around. So . . . how many miles do you need to run to train for a marathon?"

Matthew felt the blisters already forming. "Start at a hundred miles a week if you don't want to be gasping for air like a fish out of water around mile seventeen. I'm going to end up running this marathon just so Shannon can cheer me on and take pictures."

Paul pushed the relish tray back over to him. "Yep."

"Sounds about right," Bryce agreed. "So, darts and lasagna, and we say we discussed his training schedule? Or do we actually go find the appropriate shoes and run?"

"We're not *that* old yet," Paul said. "Five miles?"

"What was your best marathon time?" Bryce asked.

Matthew could see where this was heading. "I'm not answering that, and five miles sounds fine to me — if you two can do it without puffing."

Bryce shared a look with Paul. "He's the one who'll be puffing before we let him off the track today."

"I do believe he will," Paul said. "We're both runners, Matthew. Bryce because Charlotte likes to run with him, and I've got a reputation at the office to maintain." He pushed back his chair. "Shall we meet at the track in about forty minutes?"

Matthew got up with them, good-natured about what was coming. "You two do realize that I've done nine marathons and more than ten thousand miles of training runs over the last decade? We could call it a warm-up run and save ourselves some aching muscles."

"What would be the fun in that?" Paul said. "Come on, old man."

Matthew sighed and let himself settle to the fact he would be running his tenth Boston Marathon in the spring. He'd run it for Shannon. Becky could get him a shirt made with *Boston Marathon #10* printed on it. Maybe when the marathon was over he'd

The employees of Thorndike Press hope you have enjoyed this Large Print book. All our Thorndike, Wheeler, and Kennebec Large Print titles are designed for easy reading, and all our books are made to last. Other Thorndike Press Large Print books are available at your library, through selected bookstores, or directly from us.

For information about titles, please call:
(800) 223-1244

or visit our Web site at:
http://gale.cengage.com/thorndike

To share your comments, please write:
Publisher
Thorndike Press
10 Water St., Suite 310
Waterville, ME 04901